THE
WEDDING

Cathy Cole is a novelist, prize-winning short-story writer and Pushcart-nominated poet who lives in a small, picturesque town that straddles the border between Northern and Southern Ireland. You can find out more about her, and her work, on her website: **cathycoleauthor.com**

THE WEDDING

CATHY COLE

ORION

First published in Great Britain in 2026 by Orion Fiction,
an imprint of The Orion Publishing Group Ltd.
Carmelite House, 50 Victoria Embankment
London EC4Y 0DZ

An Hachette UK Company

The authorised representative in the EEA is Hachette Ireland, 8 Castlecourt Centre, Castleknock Road, Castleknock, Dublin 15, D15 XTP3, Republic of Ireland (email: info@hbgi.ie)

1 3 5 7 9 10 8 6 4 2

Copyright © Catherine Cole 2026

The moral right of Catherine Cole to be identified as
the author of this work has been asserted in accordance
with the Copyright, Designs and Patents Act of 1988.

All rights reserved. No part of this publication may be
reproduced, stored in a retrieval system, or transmitted
in any form or by any means, electronic, mechanical,
photocopying, recording or otherwise, without the
prior permission of both the copyright owner and the
above publisher of this book.

All the characters in this book are fictitious, and any resemblance
to actual persons, living or dead, is purely coincidental.

A CIP catalogue record for this book is
available from the British Library.

ISBN (Mass Market Paperback) 978 1 3987 2553 9
ISBN (eBook) 978 1 3987 2554 6
ISBN (Audio) 978 1 3987 2555 3

Typeset by Born Group
Printed and bound in Great Britain by Clays Ltd, Elcograf S.p.A.

For Paul. I love you because *you* think I think the ice cubes keep the freezer cold.
(If you know, you know.)
So glad you're by my side, keeping me sane in this crazy, crazy world.

Love you always.

Author Note

I have always loved lighthouses, probably because my father was a lighthouse keeper and our family – until my siblings and I came of school age - followed Dad to wherever he was stationed. Sometimes that was next to the lighthouse in the lighthouse keeper's dwellings. Other times we were across the water from him, looking over at those lonely spires of the sea. While lighthouses are fully automated now, I tip my hat to all those hardy people who spent months at a time away from their families and loved ones.

Chapter One

There wasn't really a good time to discover a body, but slap bang in the middle of your wedding day had to be the absolute worst time ever.

Was it an omen? Jenny, the new Mrs Richard Durkin, wondered, trying to swallow back a scream of hysteria. She was a grown-ass woman – a *married* grown-ass woman – and midwife to boot. She didn't do hysteria. Especially not today.

The strange thing was that for a hastily arranged, last-minute wedding, everything had gone surprisingly to plan. She hadn't even baulked at Richard insisting they return to her hometown of Innisard to tie the knot. An orphan like her, Richard figured one of them should have family present, and seeing as she was the only one with any extended family, whom, he pointed out, she'd never introduced him to, he'd decided now was as good a time as ever to remedy that.

Part of her was happy to go back, especially when she'd heard from Aunt Gert that Maggie's Point – the old lighthouse she'd spent many a happy day playing in and around – had been newly restored and was available to rent as an upmarket B&B. What better place for a wedding reception than her childhood tower of solace?

And the lighthouse hadn't disappointed. Fresh white paint coated the exterior, a stunning contrast to the post-box red railing circling the top deck, which had once housed the immense light that had steered innumerable ships to safety. Inside, Jenny was delighted to find the lighthouse held true to its original shape, with deeply recessed windows – so wide and thick you could put a cushion in them and sit and stare out to sea in comfort for as long as you wanted – and a black iron spiral staircase that wound upward to the bedroom and top deck above.

It was so much more than she remembered; light and airy inside, with its fresh, bleached-wood furniture and blue/white decor, very shakerish in appearance. A palate that was immediately soothing and calming. *Like coming home.*

Unlike the response when she told the aunts that she and Richard intended to stay there together the night *before* the wedding.

'Scandalous!' Aunt Evil had told Jenny in a phone call the day before, the word ending in a sound only audible to cats or dogs.

Evil wasn't her real name, of course. It was Evie. Jenny and her cousins had named her that when they were little. Evie becoming Evil – changing that one letter – made the name feel much more fitting, because the woman was a total harridan. The bane of their childhood.

'The groom shouldn't see the bride before the wedding,' Evil had continued. 'It's bad luck.'

'I'll make sure to blindfold him before he goes to sleep,' Jenny had joked, but Evil wasn't appeased.

'You'd think with your history you'd give more credence to tradition, missy.'

A sharp, painful flashback to a dark night, eighteen years ago. 'You say tradition, I say superstition,' Jenny had countered, trying to quash the memory.

'Be that as it may, but we all know what happens when we think we're above such things, don't we?'

Jenny had refused to rise to the bait, or give in to the narrow-minded opinions of the village she had grown up in and left at the first chance she got. It was Richard who had convinced her that spending the night before the wedding apart was a good idea. 'Surely it's a small price to pay,' he'd told her. 'They're hosting our wedding, and if it makes them happy . . .? Plus,' his eyes had twinkled, 'we will have the rest of our lives to spend together, what's a couple of days?'

Jenny could refuse him nothing when he smiled at her like that, blue eyes sparkling, sexy dimple dimpling. Which was why her groom had spent the night before their wedding in a B&B with his best man Sean, and she had spent hers attempting to stop her best friend Ita from trying to get them both wasted. Jenny wanted to be fresh for her wedding day. In the end, Ita was content to drink alone. She remembered Ita's hungover expression when she'd called her that morning for breakfast, the elegant dark brows pulled together, a fragile frown on her smooth brown skin.

The aunts had pulled out all the stops – hairdressers, beauticians, cars. They'd even laid on a bus to take the guests to and from the reception at Maggie's Point. Aunt Gert had been exceptionally clever in assigning roles so no one was left out. Jenny had felt slightly overwhelmed by the volume of cousins, cousins' children and all the other sundry relatives who had appeared from the woodwork. Luckily, apart from Ita and Richard's best man Sean, there had been no other outsiders at the wedding ceremony itself, with Jenny's sickly pale cousin Dermot the main usher, directing proceedings with his usual cavalier attitude of 'sit wherever you want, man'.

It had been pitiful to see so few people stand behind Richard in the groom's pews, but she'd loved him even more as he'd squared his shoulders, turned to embrace her as she walked up the aisle, and in doing so embraced her whole wonky family at the same time. It was only standing in that packed chapel that Jenny truly realised how alone Richard must feel, having no other family at all. And a wave of love for him had flowed over her. How was it even possible to love him even more than she did already?

They had said their vows without a hint of hesitation, their voices ringing to the rafters in her old childhood church. They'd left the chapel amid applause, grinning, smiling faces lining their departure.

Perfect. Everything, and more importantly everyone, in their place.

Except for the dead body.

Chapter Two

AN HOUR EARLIER:

The wedding car, driven by one of Jenny's uncles, took them the short distance to the graveyard nestled on a small hill close to the seafront. It wasn't a huge graveyard, but it was meticulously tended. Innisarders took excellent care of their dead. On a good day, like today, you could sit on one of the benches dotted around the area and bask in the warmth of the sun while enjoying the stunning vista of sea and sand. A beautiful spot to rest for all eternity. A strange place to visit on your wedding day, some might think, but Jenny wanted to share the happiest day of her life with the two people she wished with all her heart could have been there to share it with her. Her parents. She approached the grave with an odd mixture of guilt and trepidation.

'Thanks for doing this,' she told Richard. 'I know it's silly, but . . .'

'It's not silly at all.' Richard took her hand.

'I just want to lay my bouquet here so they can be . . . I don't know, involved somehow.'

'It's a beautiful thought. I really wish I could have met them.'

'Me, too.' Jenny looked at the simple headstone inscribed with her parents' names and date of death. Eighteen long years ago. Guilt was an aged, yet still ravenous beast that she'd spent far too long feeding.

If only I hadn't gone out that night, did what I did, they'd still be here. They'd still be alive.

It was hard to believe she was now the same age her mother was when she died. Thirty-two. No age at all, and yet she'd been parent to a stroppy, out-of-control fourteen-year-old at that point. Teenage years. Not a good time to lose your parents, but then again, was any time good?

'We know they're with us today. Maybe our parents are having a right old party in heaven, just for us.' Richard smiled, and she squeezed his hand, feeling her new wedding band pinch as it met her engagement ring and fought for its place.

That's what Jenny loved about Richard – or one of the many things she loved about him. He understood. He knew what it felt like to be alone in the world.

But they were no longer alone. They had each other. Love swelled in her heart, filling her with warmth.

'You ready?' Richard asked.

Jenny nodded. 'Yes.' She took one last look at the grave. 'Let's not take the car,' she said, a spur-of-the-moment decision as they left the graveyard. 'We can go back to the lighthouse that way.' She pointed to the beach.

'Are you mad?' Richard looked nervously at the thundering sea.

'The tide will be in soon, never mind all those steps. You remember the steps? All one hundred and five tiny, cracked and broken steps. They suit their name: the Devil's Teeth.' He shuddered. 'I swear you're out to torment me, making me, an acrophobic, honeymoon in a lighthouse on top of a cliff.'

Jenny laughed, knowing he didn't mean it. Richard's fear of heights was legendary – even going up a flight of stairs could trigger it – but, being a psychiatrist, he refused to give into it, constantly pushing himself to overcome what he saw as a weakness. 'Just think of it as extra exposure therapy,' she told him. 'Now, come on, don't be a wuss. If we hurry, we can make Smugglers Cove before it floods.'

Smugglers Cove lay just beyond the beach, gained by a narrow strip of sand that was only accessible at low tide.

When Richard hesitated, Jenny grabbed his hand. 'I promise if we reach the cliff base and the tide is too far in, we'll come right back.'

'But the car will be gone by then, and—'

'I'll make it worth your while.' Jenny wriggled her eyebrows suggestively.

'Witch.' Richard brushed a strand of fiery red hair out of her eyes. 'How can I say no to that? To you?'

'You can't.'

'No,' he said softly, 'I can't. Not even when I should.'

'We're going to walk to the reception, Cap,' Jenny shouted to her uncle, waving for him to go ahead without them.

'Cap?' Richard asked. 'I thought his name was Mick?'

'It is. Cap is a nickname – Captain Mick – he sails a lot,' she said as if it should be obvious.

'Oh.'

'We call his wife, my aunt Sheila, Scuttlebutt.'

'Scuttlebutt?'

Jenny giggled. 'You'll understand when you meet her.'

Cap, huge belly straining in his too-tight suit, wasn't laughing. He appeared flustered that they weren't returning in his beautiful car, angry even. He muttered something they couldn't hear.

'I fear we may have upset him?' Richard said.

'He'll get over it.'

'Then let's go, wife.'

Wife. Jenny liked the sound of that.

She used Richard's shoulder to steady herself as she took off her high heels and laced the straps through her fingers, before linking arms with her new husband.

The beach was deserted. Understandable. When the tide was on the turn, it could be dangerous, sweeping in so fast it was easy to get cut off. Many an unwary tourist had met a watery end, so much so that huge signs now dotted the shoreline warning of the danger. Plus, given the chill September day and forecasted storm for Sunday – reported as going to be the worst storm Ireland had seen in over forty years – it was no wonder they had the beach to themselves. Jenny was half disappointed that they were going to miss it. Riding out a storm in Maggie's Point sounded right up her street – the angry sea, the howling wind and driving rain . . . all experienced from the safety of the lighthouse atop the high cliff. Bliss.

But Richard had been adamant they weren't going to delay their honeymoon, scheduling their flight for early tomorrow afternoon, well before the storm was due to strike.

'Come on.' Richard tugged her hand.

'There's no hurry.' Jenny was enjoying the feeling of cold sand between her toes and the sound of the waves as they thundered to shore; being, just for a moment, alone and accountable to no one. The second they hit the reception they would be on call to numerous aunts, uncles, cousins, old friends – people she hadn't seen in an eternity. She wanted to hold on to these few minutes, just her and Richard, for as long as she could. 'No hurry,' she said again.

'Oh, I think there is.' Richard swung her around and pulled her tight to his chest. 'The sooner I get you there, the sooner we get this over and done with and I finally get you alone.'

'"Get *this* over and done with?" You mean our wedding reception?' Jenny tried to sound angry, but she was too happy, and it showed.

'Exactly, Mrs Durkin.' Richard lifted a curl of red hair from her face, wound it around his finger. 'As gorgeous as that dress is – and it *is* gorgeous – I'd sooner see you out of it.'

Jenny's knees weakened at the sight of his sexy dimple. He'd only one, at the right-hand side of his mouth, but it was enough. She touched it now, trailed a finger over his lips, before tugging his shirt free from his trousers, slipping her hands inside, running them up and down his back, fingers finding the scar in the dip of his spine, tickling, teasing.

'Good, because there's method in my madness.' She nodded to the beach. 'This way gets us there ten minutes sooner than if we'd taken the car back. Ten minutes when no one is expecting us. And,' she said with a flutter of eyelashes, 'we have to pass Maggie's Point to get to the reception. No one will know if we duck inside the lighthouse and put those ten minutes to good use.'

Richard threw back his head, laughed. 'I like your thinking, although I must admit to a slight outrage that you think ten minutes will be enough. It takes at least five minutes to get up that bloody spiral staircase.'

'That's because you do it almost on your hands and knees – with your eyes closed – but who said I was talking about the bedroom?' Jenny grinned impishly. 'Come on. Let's go.'

Hand in hand, they raced up the beach, around the small sliver of sand that was still visible at the cliff edge, and were soon out of sight of the village and alone in the small, pretty inlet of Smugglers Cove. It was a lovers' paradise, pure white sand, towering cliffs either side, stunning blue waves with white-tipped peaks as far as the eye could see.

'Much too cold,' Jenny said, catching the lustful glint in Richard's eyes and feeling an answering echo. She kissed him roughly, grabbing his bottom lip with her teeth. 'And no time before the tide comes in.'

She was right. Already the tide was racing towards them, beginning to fill the small sandy beach.

'Hurry.' Jenny scrambled up the first of the Devil's Teeth – the flight of uneven stone steps cut into the cliff side that led to the lighthouse – Richard right behind her. Waves thundered after them. Jenny grabbed Richard's hand, dragging him with her up the next few steps and around a tight bend to the next one. They were out of breath by this time. Jenny panting through her smile. 'I told you we would make i—' Her voice broke off. 'What's that?' She pointed ahead to something on the third step of the Devil's Teeth. 'Oh my God, it's . . . it's—'

Richard leaned past her, saw the prone figure and immediately tried to shield her.

Jenny didn't need shielding. As a nurse, she'd seen her fair share of dead bodies and she knew immediately that's what this was.

The bloodied, jeans-clad body lay face down, immobile, the amount of congealed blood pooled around it enough to tell anyone with half a brain, never mind someone with a nursing degree, that there was nothing to be done. Still, Jenny bent and checked for a pulse. Nothing. It looked like the man – and she was sure it was a man by the build and clothes – had been beaten and stabbed multiple times, judging by the jagged slashes in his clothing. Only then did she wonder who the body might be. Her thoughts immediately shot to her male cousins. Could it be one of them?

Richard was obviously thinking along the same lines; his first thought for his friend and best man. 'Is it . . . is it Sean?'

Sean, slightly shorter than Richard, stood about 5'10". 'Body's too tall,' Jenny said. 'I don't think it's Sean.'

'Thank God.'

No relief for Jenny as she still didn't know whether it was someone she knew. Forgetting her training, she reached out to turn the body to make sure.

'Don't!' Richard grabbed her hand. 'We shouldn't touch him until the gardaí get here. They'll ID him.'

'You're right. Of course, you're right, but what if it's someone we—'

'Don't torture yourself.' Richard pulled her to him, held her tight. 'It's going to be OK. I promise it's going to be OK,' he breathed into her hair.

Jenny loved him for trying, but it wasn't going to be OK. This was their wedding day and a dead body wasn't exactly top of her wedding gift list.

Chapter Three

In the end, they had to move the body.

'We have to,' Jenny told Richard.

'We shouldn't touch anything; we could be destroying evidence.' As a psychiatrist, Richard might have left the blood and guts of the ER a long time ago, but he obviously remembered protocol.

'There won't be any evidence to destroy in a few minutes.' Jenny pointed to where waves were quickly rising towards the step they were standing on. Finding a dead body was bad enough but the thought of it being carried off was too horrific to contemplate. 'We have to move the body before it's washed out to sea.'

'Damn it. OK, I'll do it, but first we need to phone the gardaí.'

'Agreed. Give me your phone.' Jenny held out her hand.

'Damn it,' Richard said again.

'What's wrong?'

'Sean has my phone. We didn't want it going off during the ceremony. He was going to give it back to me at the reception. I don't suppose you—'

'Seriously?' Jenny gestured to her slim-fitting wedding dress. 'Where would I put it?'

'OK. You go, find someone. There's bound to be plenty of people milling around, ask one of them to phone.'

Jenny stared up the narrow steps, not liking the idea

of going up the rest of the Devil's Teeth alone. What if whoever had killed this person was waiting up there for her? What if—?

Richard seemed to sense her fear. 'I know, love. I don't want you going up there alone either, but I'm sure whoever did this is long gone. The blood has been dried for hours.'

Of course! Jenny felt silly. The blood on the steps wasn't fresh. It was caked, hardened. Still . . .

'This has nothing to do with any of that other nonsense, Jenny. That's all over and done with.'

He knew her so well; knew her mind would automatically go there. 'You sure?' Jenny hated to think their troubles had followed them from Dublin.

Richard's face softened. 'As sure as I can be. What I *am* sure about,' he told her, 'is that our reception is up there.' He nodded to the steps. 'People. Lots and lots of people. You'll be safe. The marquee is close to the lighthouse. Go there first, find someone to call this in.'

Still Jenny hesitated, strangely reluctant to leave him.

'One of us has to stay here and move the body, and one of us has to contact the gardaí. I'm stronger, so it stands to reason I should be the one to drag the body up these blasted steps, but I'm happy for you to disagree?' he added, almost hopefully.

Jenny smiled sadly, cupping his face with her hand. 'You're right, I know you are, but I don't have to like it.'

'You and me both, love.'

'I'll be back as quickly as I can,' she promised.

'I'll hold you to that.' Richard kissed her, hard, deep. 'Now, go.'

Jenny turned and, hitching her long dress to her knees, raced up the wickedly sharp steps in her bare feet, uncaring of how they cut into her skin.

Usually, she counted the steps as she went, made a game of it, but she was too focused on finding help and getting back to Richard to do so this time. She had to hurry. She had to—

Jenny almost screamed as a figure appeared. She spied the long legs first in the too-short dress trousers, the thin, sloping shoulders and long greasy hair. Dermot, who she'd last seen ushering their guests into their seats. One cousin accounted for. Only then did Jenny realise that panic had stolen her senses. No way Dermot could have been the body on the steps, he was much too thin. And tall.

'Hey, Cuz.' Dermot stared down at her.

Jenny was still getting used to this new Dermot. He was only two years older than her, but looked a lot more. Once tubby, he now appeared emaciated, the bones on his face and wrists sharp and obvious. Dark shadows lined his eyes and not even his goatee and adolescent-looking moustache could hide the shrunken shape of his face. She could hazard a guess as to what ailed him, but hadn't had the courage to ask him about it.

'Dermot. I'm . . . so happy to see you,' she panted.

'Not your usual greeting, Cuz,' Dermot drawled. 'Not anyone's usual greeting lately,' he added softly. 'What's up?' he asked casually, as if the fact that his cousin was racing up the Devil's Teeth, in her wedding dress, barefoot and clearly distraught were an everyday occurrence.

'I need . . . help. Phone . . . gardaí,' Jenny said, trying to catch her breath.

'The garda?' At that, Dermot seemed to perk up, looking strangely anxious. 'You want me to call the garda?'

'Yes. Hurry, there's a body down there.' She pointed back the way she'd come.

'A . . . body?' Dermot peered past her. 'I don't see no body.'

God give me strength. Luckily, before Jenny could strangle her cousin, another figure emerged; Dermot's sister Dana. Heavily pregnant, she lumbered into view in her diamanté-strewn ice-blue smock and sensible heels. 'Dana, thank God. I need you to phone the gardaí.' Jenny was getting her breath back and with it her urgency to get back to Richard.

'The gardaí?' Dana shot a look at her brother. 'Whatever for?'

'There's a body, down the steps.'

'A body?' Dana held one hand to her mouth, the other to the swollen mound of her stomach. 'Who?' Her gaze turned to Dermot again and there was something in the look that caught Jenny's attention.

'Are you OK, Dana?' Her cousin looked like she'd been crying and Jenny recalled someone telling her that Dana had fainted in the chapel earlier, before she had arrived to get married. 'Is it the baby? Do you have any pain, tightness in your abdomen?'

'I'm fine.' The words were brusque. 'I'm just . . . shocked, that's all.'

'You sure?'

'I'm sure.' Dana smiled, but her pale eyes remained hard, cold. 'Don't be listening to Aunt Gert. I'm no weeping widow; I'm a lot stronger than I look.'

'I know you are.' Jenny moved up a step, took Dana's hand, knowing now wasn't the time to commiserate on the loss of her husband, but wanting to say something. 'But if you ever—'

'I said I'm fine.' Dana pulled her hand free.

She didn't look it. She looked upset, angry. 'Dana, if you—'

'You don't know who . . .?' Dana stepped back, nodding down the Devil's Teeth.

Jenny got the message, allowing her cousin to change the subject. 'No. Richard is with the body, but I need to get back to him. Will you—?'

'Of course.' Dana seemed to pull herself together. 'You go back to your . . . husband. Dermot and I will inform the authorities.'

'Yeah, Cuz, you can count on us.' Dermot winked, but Jenny ignored him, racing back down the way she'd come.

She found Richard not far from where she'd left him. He was panting, leaning over the corpse. Dragging a dead body uphill, over sharp steps, was obviously as hard as it looked.

'Jenny.' Richard seemed surprised to see her back so quickly. 'What are you . . .? Did you call the gardaí?'

'The double Ds are doing that.'

'The double . . . Ah, your cousins Dermot and Dana?' He pawed the air. 'The usher and . . . really pregnant reader at our wedding? Yes?'

'Yes. I met them on the way up – lucky, huh?'

'More like odd. What were they doing there?'

'Don't know.' Jenny shrugged, trying not to think of the anxious look on Dermot's face when she'd first seen him. He may have changed from the cousin she knew, but no way was he involved in this. Was he? 'Dermot was there first. I got the impression Dana was following him, for whatever reason. I don't really care, I'm just glad to be here with you.'

'Me, too.' Richard stood, wrapping his arm around Jenny, breathing into her neck. 'What do we do now?'

'We wait,' Jenny said, snuggling into his side, staring at the body. 'We wait.'

★

'Oh, man. Oh, man.'

Dermot Gibson was freaking out. He'd been hoping to have a little 'me' time on the Devil's Teeth, but his blasted sister had followed him and, if that wasn't bad enough, their estranged cousin Jenny had also appeared – with a dead body in tow!

What the absolute fuck!

'This day is just full of fucking surprises – and none of them good,' he told his sister as they manoeuvred their way back up the Devil's Teeth. 'We're in so much shit. We call the garda and they're gonna—'

'Calm down, Dermot. We're fine. No one knows anything. And they won't, if you keep your big mouth shut. We do as Jenny has asked, call the garda, civic duty done.'

'But Big Benny will—'

Dana stopped, grabbed her brother around the throat, her face twisted with anger and paled by fear. 'Do *not* mention that name again. You hear me?'

'I hear you. I hear you.' Dermot prised her hands off his throat. For such a tiny person, she was incredibly strong.

'Good. Then let's get this done.' She waddled off, her gait changed by her pregnancy.

Dermot had always had a healthy respect for his sister, but now it morphed into uneasiness. How could she be so calm, especially now. They were so linked to this shit. He just knew it. This had Big Benny's pawprints all over it.

Which meant they were beyond fucked.

Chapter Four

'Mrs Durkin?'

'Huh?' It took Jenny a moment for her new name to register. When it did, she dragged her eyes from the mangled body to see a garda pulling a white protective suit over his An Garda Síochána uniform of pale blue polo shirt and two-tone softshell jacket and trousers, fixing the hood carefully over his peaked cap. He'd arrived a few minutes earlier, immediately radioing in for back-up and ordering someone to stand guard at the gate leading to Maggie's Point to stop looky-loos getting in. Or maybe it was to stop her guests from getting out? She could hear another garda further up the steps following his orders to secure the scene.

'Garda Fern has arranged a path for us. So, if we could move up the steps and away from the crime scene that would be grea—'

'What we got, Tom?' A figure descended the steps also dressed in a white protective jumpsuit. The only part of him to be seen was an ebony face, with dark, clever eyes.

'Winston, you got here quickly.'

'Was in the neighbourhood.' The pathologist squeezed past the garda and knelt next to the body.

There wasn't much room on the steps, so the garda motioned again to Jenny and Richard. 'We should move up, out of the way. I'll need to take your fingerprints – for exclusion purposes only,' he said when Richard shook his head.

'It's not that I won't give them to you, Garda . . .?'

'Carr,' the garda offered. 'Sergeant Tom Carr.'

'Sorry, yes – it's not that I won't give them to you, Sergeant Carr, it's that I can't.' Richard held out his hands, the tips of which were unnaturally smooth. 'Adermatoglyphia,' he said, before the garda could ask. 'It runs in my family and is very rare.'

The garda shot a look to the pathologist, who nodded gravely. 'I've heard of it, but that's about it. It is, indeed, extremely rare.'

'Hmm.' Sergeant Carr scribbled something in his notebook. 'Would you mind if I asked you a couple of quick questions?'

Would it matter if we did? Jenny thought grimly, but the garda, for all his stern appearance, had kind eyes so she nodded. 'Go ahead.'

She grabbed Richard's hand; glad to have his steadying presence beside her. Time had lost all meaning. Jenny didn't know how long it had been since she'd run up the steps and encountered Dermot and Dana. She didn't know how long she and Richard had held each other, watching the body, checking the tide that was even now beginning to lap at the nearest step to them. She wondered what their guests were thinking above at the reception. Did they know what was going on? Then she berated herself for such mundane thoughts. A man had lost his life, they needed to do everything they could to help the gardaí find out why, and who had killed him.

'I'm sorry, I've forgotten your name,' she said to the garda – a short, stocky man with thick black hair and a neatly trimmed beard showing the first signs of grey. It suited him. Gave him an air of gravitas that his job probably needed, and helped offset the curse of those kind brown eyes.

'No need to apologise. Shock does strange things to the mind, Mrs Durkin. My name is Sergeant Tom Carr. And you are Jenny and Richard Durkin, newly married.' His face softened. 'I'm sorry this has happened to you, today of all days.'

'Thank you,' Richard said stiffly. 'But if we could get on with this. We have guests we need to attend to.'

'Richard,' Jenny admonished, surprised at his abruptness.

'Your husband is right: the sooner we get this done, the sooner you can get back to your guests. Now,' Sergeant Carr said, 'if you can walk me through what happened, and take it from the start, from your wedding onwards.'

So, they did, both of them filling in whatever the other may have left out. From the wedding, to the graveyard, the beach and on to Smugglers Cove before finding the body on the Devil's Teeth.

'You moved the body?' Sergeant Carr's eyes were no longer smiling.

'We had to. The tide was coming in, it would have been washed away,' Jenny said, 'and with it all your forensics.'

'And what do you know about forensics?' he asked bluntly.

'After working in an ER, I know enough,' Jenny snapped, annoyed by his tone. 'Better our DNA on the body, than to lose everything, including the corpse.'

'So, you're a nurse?'

'Midwife. But I have a nursing degree, did a rotation through ER.'

'And I am a medical doctor, a psychiatrist,' Richard said. 'So, we both know our way around the protocols of dead bodies, but we can debate the rights or wrongs of our actions later, Sergeant. For now, can we get on with this? I'd like to enjoy at least some of our reception.'

'Enjoy some . . .?' The garda's dark eyebrows rose.

'I didn't mean that the way it sounded,' Richard added hurriedly.

'Of course you didn't.' Sergeant Carr scribbled again in his notebook. 'As I said before, shock can do strange things to the mind. So, did either of you see anyone on the beach as you approached Smugglers Cove? Were there any boats in the vicinity? Anyone on the steps?'

'No, no and no,' Richard said, answering for both of them.

'Did you hear anything, notice anything?'

'No,' Richard said again.

Jenny shook her head when Sergeant Carr looked at her for confirmation.

'So, you didn't see Dermot Gibson or his sister Dana Gibson-Mayfield?'

'That was later,' Jenny said, 'when I ran up the steps for help. They were coming down and I—'

'Coming down or going up?' Sergeant Carr wrote in his book again.

'Coming down,' Jenny said.

'You sure?'

Was she? Jenny reran the scene in her mind: seeing Dermot's legs, those long skinny legs in the too-short trousers. Were they moving up the steps, or down? She couldn't be sure. But there was one thing she *was* sure about. 'The body had been dead for hours at that point, which makes my cousins being there immaterial, surely?' She didn't mention Dermot's guilty, anxious demeanour. Her cousin was obviously dealing with his own demons. Jenny had seen enough junkies in the hospital she worked at to be only too aware of the signs. But that didn't make him a killer. He was family. And family had to be protected.

One would think.

Jenny had gone from liking the garda to actively disliking him.

Richard obviously felt the same way. 'Can we go now, Sergeant? My wife has had an awful shock.'

'Of course, we can finish this topside. Just one more question. I promise I'll be quick. Does either of you know the deceased?'

Jenny forced her eyes past him to the corpse lying face down on the Devil's Teeth, dressed in generic blue jeans and a ripped and bloodied T-shirt. 'I don't think so. Richard?' She turned to her new husband.

Richard's face was set and hard. As if unable to stay still, he dropped Jenny's hand and moved down a step until he was standing next to the garda. 'How can I possibly say. All we can see is the back of his head. It could be anyone.'

'Winston?' Sergeant Carr barked to the man kneeling by the corpse on the step below them. 'You finished with that side?'

The other man nodded and Carr made a rolling gesture. 'Turn him over then. Let's take a look.'

Winston did as he was ordered and Jenny heard Richard gasp, saw his tanned skin pale.

'Richard?' But her husband wasn't listening. He dropped to his knees beside the bloodied body. 'Richard?'

Tentatively, Jenny went to follow him.

The back of the corpse's head might have been destroyed, but the face was intact; swollen, turning mottled red with lividity, but totally recognisable.

'Oh my God!' Her hand flew to her mouth, and she stumbled backwards.

Sergeant Carr caught her before she could fall, his eyes sharp. 'You could have informed us that the gentleman was part of your wedding party, Mrs Durkin.'

'But . . . he . . . wasn't . . . Richard?' Disbelieving, Jenny watched her husband reach out a hand to the limp body – a hand that was unceremoniously stopped by the pathologist.

'This is a crime scene, sir. I'm sorry, but I can't let you touch the body.'

'Are you telling me this . . . man,' Sergeant Carr pointed to the corpse, 'wasn't invited to your wedding?'

Jenny could only shake her head, bewildered. 'No, I—'

'I find that hard to believe.'

So did Jenny.

She stared at her husband, who was staring at the corpse's face. A face that was a mirror image of his own, except for the blood, of course.

'Then you could have told us your husband had a twin.'

'I would have,' Jenny said when she could finally speak, 'if I had known myself.'

Chapter Five

'Maybe it is a doppelganger?' Winston, the pathologist, offered. 'They say everyone has one.'

Jenny wasn't sure she appreciated his attempt at levity, although maybe she was doing him a disservice as his smooth face showed only concern and a deep, sincere sympathy. She didn't want sympathy. She wanted answers.

'Richard?' She stared at her new husband on his knees next to the body, unmoving. 'Richard?' she said, her voice begging him to answer, to tell her something that would make sense.

'Jenny I—' Richard looked at the body, stifling a sob. 'John. Oh, God, John.'

'So, this *is* your brother?' Sergeant Carr said, writing in his notebook before putting his pen away. 'Maybe we should take this topside, where there's more room?' he suggested.

Jenny realised he didn't really mean they needed more room, but some distance between Richard and the body of his twin. His twin! Jenny was still having trouble with that idea.

Numb, Jenny allowed Sergeant Carr to escort her up the Devil's Teeth, knew Winston was doing the same for Richard. Her mind bubbled, churned: *In sickness and health. For better or worse.* The vows she'd uttered so recently taunted her. Neither she nor Richard was sick, but they were definitely in the *better or worse* stage already. Richard had lied to her. And not a little lie. This was a humongous one. They had bonded over being alone in the world. It was what had brought them together.

But not what kept us together, Jenny reminded herself. She had fallen in love with the man, not his lack of family – or not, as it turned out.

Richard lied to me!

Pain descended like an anvil in her chest, crushing her. She wasn't sure she could ever forgive him. The lie was so huge, so . . . personal. He had to have a reason. Didn't he? Right at the moment, Jenny couldn't imagine one that would explain why Richard had betrayed her trust this way.

When they reached the top step of the Devil's Teeth, Sergeant Carr motioned to a female garda. 'Devlin, can you look after Mrs Durkin?'

He steered the couple away from the edge of the cliff, deftly separating them in the process, leaving Jenny with the new garda.

'Anne Devlin,' the garda said, introducing herself to Jenny. 'I'll only keep you a minute.'

'Can't I stay with my husband?' Jenny looked over to where Sergeant Carr was talking earnestly to Richard.

'You'll be with him soon. I just have a few questions I need to ask, if you don't mind?'

It was couched as a question, but Jenny had no doubt she required to answer. The garda didn't so much as pause before she began.

'When did you arrive in Innisard?' Garda Devlin opened her notebook.

'Yesterday, late evening.'

'And you stayed where?'

'At Maggie's Point with my best friend Ita.' Jenny gestured to the lighthouse.

'And she was with you all night?'
'Yes.'
'Did you leave the lighthouse at any point?'
'No. Not until I left to get married this morning,' Jenny answered on autopilot.

The garda's face, with its sprinkle of freckles, creased with sympathy. 'I know this must be so awful for you,' she said softly. 'I promise I won't keep you a second longer than necessary.'

Jenny was grateful for her understanding.

'So, your friend Ita . . .?'

'Sharma.'

'Ita Sharma can vouch for your whereabouts last night and this morning?'

'Yes.'

'How did you travel to Innisard?'

'To Innisard?' Jenny asked, puzzled. 'By car. Richard and I travelled here together, but what has that to do with—'

'Did you stop anywhere?'

'Is that really relevant?'

The garda's grey eyes didn't waver from Jenny's face. 'For now, everything is relevant.'

'No, we didn't stop anywhere. We drove straight here from Dublin.'

'So what did you do for food? You must have been hungry.'

'My aunts had left something for us at the lighthouse. We ate there – Ita, me, Richard and his best man, Sean O'Hare.'

Garda Devlin scribbled the name down. 'Did you all stay there or—?'

'Richard and Sean left around 10 p.m. for the B&B in town.'

'And your aunts didn't visit?'

'No.'

'Did you see them at all? Anyone other than your immediate wedding party?'

Jenny could understand the garda's surprise, but she was in no mood to explain her family's complicated history. 'No. Not until today, at the wedding.'

'So you didn't talk to anyone else? Go anywhere?'

'No, and no.'

As if sensing Jenny had had enough, Garda Devlin looked over to Sergeant Carr, who nodded and approached with Richard in tow.

'I can only give you a few minutes,' he told the couple. 'To inform your guests,' he added at their questioning look. 'After that, my officers will be in to interview everyone, and I will need you two to sit down with me and go over the events of the day one more time.' He took a toothpick from his pocket and placed it in his mouth. 'I've already stationed a car at the exit to Wishers Woods and have left men on the clifftop guarding the Devil's Teeth, so no one can leave.'

'Great. So, we, and our guests, are now essentially prisoners?' Richard stood next to Jenny. His earlier shock seeming to have been replaced by irritation.

'I'm sorry, but it's important to question witnesses as early as possible, while their memories are fresh.'

'Of course it is.' Jenny took Richard's hand.

At her touch, Richard seemed to realise he was out of order. 'I'm sorry, Sergeant. Shock has obviously addled my brains. We appreciate your thoughtfulness.'

'Yes, thank you, Sergeant.'

Sergeant Carr gave an abrupt nod before leaving with Garda Devlin to begin doing whatever it was that the gardaí actually did at scenes like this.

'I wouldn't go as far as thanking him,' Richard said when the two gardaí were out of earshot. 'He's totally ruined our wedding reception.'

'I'm thanking him because he didn't have to extend us the courtesy of being the ones to inform our guests. As for ruining our wedding . . .' Jenny let go of his hand. 'I think you have more to answer for that than he does, don't you?'

Richard squirmed. 'Jenny, I—'

'You should have told him about the other things that happened before we came here. Maybe they're connected to—'

'They're not!'

'You can't know that. You should have told him about—'

'I told you, it's not him,' Richard said, sounding exasperated. 'That was nothing. It's over.'

'Is it?' Jenny stood her ground. 'I really think we—'

'About time you two appeared. What's this I hear about a body?' Jenny's aunt Gert, a force of nature on a good day, was in full tornado mode, blasting towards them. In honour of the wedding, she'd forgone her usual black mourning attire for a deep maroon outfit – long skirt, long-sleeved jacket, sensible shoes. A feathered fascinator bobbed awkwardly over her left ear. 'Do you know who—?'

Jenny looked quickly at Richard, then back at her aunt Gert, shaking her head. 'Nothing confirmed yet.'

She saw that Gert had noted the 'nothing confirmed'. The green eyes, so similar to her own, held hers for a moment, then her aunt nodded. 'God's will be done,' she intoned, blessing herself. 'Are you OK?' She eyed Jenny through her thick-rimmed glasses, taking in the dirty bare feet, the grubby rim of her wedding dress, red tresses in disarray. One hand rose, as if to brush back a curl, then seemed to think better of it, dropping to her side.

'I'm— We're fine, Aunt Gert,' Jenny said, reaching out to do what she knew her aunt couldn't. She wrapped her arms around the stick-like figure, pressed her chin to her aunt's head. There was a moment of rigidity, then the old bones softened, leaned into hers.

'You sure?' Gert whispered.

'I'm sure.' With the lost years that stood between them, the embrace should have been awkward, but it wasn't. It was like Maggie's Point; it felt like home, albeit an odd, strangely familiar and bony home.

Gert had never been a demonstrative person; not in all the time Jenny had known her. She knew Gert had been married once, but her husband had died early in their marriage. There were whispers that Gert had murdered him, or just plain froze him to death with her icy manner. But Jenny knew Gert had loved her husband, loved him so deeply that she'd never so much as looked at another man after he'd gone – hence the widow's black she always wore, except on special occasions, like today. Gert had channelled all that repressed love into nurturing her four siblings, rigidly bullying them not-so-gently into adulthood.

Jenny's mum had been the youngest of those siblings and had been more like Gert's own child than a sister. When Jenny's parents had died, Gert had quickly stepped in to become Jenny's guardian.

Not one to wear her heart on her sleeve, Gert had done her best with the bereaved fourteen-year-old. Through many trials and tribulations, the pair had ended up forming a grudging respect for one another. It just hadn't been enough to keep Jenny in Innisard. Her need to escape the accusing eyes and wagging tongues stronger than her love for her aunt.

'You're supposed to be looking after my niece,' Gert scolded Richard. 'Yet here we are, mere hours after I left her in your protection, with the gardaí at our door.'

Richard hung his head. 'I'm sorry, Gert. I—'

'Explanations later. You look like you've been hit by a steamroller. You bearing up?' Keen eyes studied him.

'We'll be fine,' Jenny said quickly. 'We just need a moment to . . . talk.' She didn't look at Richard. Sergeant Carr might have given them time to inform their guests, but the only person she wanted to talk to, the only story she wanted to hear, was from her husband.

'Right.' Gert glanced between them, seeming to sense the tension. 'I'll see what I can do. After that,' she impaled Richard with a gimlet eye, 'I want to talk to you myself.' Before either Richard or Jenny could ask why, Gert forged on. 'I'll assemble everyone in the main tent, tell DJ Joe to play his best music, keep your guests occupied until you get there. Don't worry,' she held up a hand, 'no one knows anything. I warned Dana and Dermot to keep quiet, and believe me, they will, until I give the go-ahead.' Her grin was pure Machiavellian. She pressed a hand to Jenny's shoulder, squeezed gently, before marching off, feather fascinator bobbing, to put her plan in action.

'She's some woman, your aunt Gert,' Richard said, watching the old woman striding away.

'Yes, she is. But why does she want to talk to you?'

'No idea. I'm guessing she's not best pleased at the gardaí being here, upsetting her precious wedding and her precious niece.' He reached out a hand to brush a lock of hair from her face.

Jenny stepped back. 'Whatever the reason, she's given us a few minutes to ourselves. What say we use them?'

Richard dropped his hand and glanced at the huge marquee, then back at the lighthouse. 'We can talk in there.'

Jenny nodded. From childhood, Maggie's Point had been her tower of solace. It was where she ran the night her parents died; the place she'd left with such excitement and expectation this morning to get married. Now she wondered if it could work its magic, save her marriage, her trust in her new husband. But before they got there, the quiet was broken by a voice.

'Ricky! Jenny!' The cry was repeated. 'Ricky. Jenny. Over here.' Sean O'Hare, Richard's best man, and the only person to ever call him Ricky, appeared from the marquee, waving frantically. 'Come on, guys, everyone is waiting.' His handsome face showed the strain of a man who had been fielding questions for far too long.

'I have to tell him, Jenny,' Richard said. 'It's only fair, he's my best mate.'

'And I'm your wife. I think I deserve to know first why you didn't tell me you had a twin brother.'

'You do, and I will, but Sean needs to know what's going on. All our guests do before those damn gardaí appear to question them. You and I . . . we can talk later, when we're alone?'

Jenny wanted to scream at Richard that no, they couldn't talk later, she wanted to talk now. But she could see other figures behind Sean; their guests were getting antsy, Aunt Gert's fearsome persona and DJ Joe's musical moves obviously not enough to hold them.

'Please, Jenny. Let's see to our guests, then, I promise, we'll talk.'

Jenny hated that he made her feel guilty for wanting her answers first, then hated that she thought that way. Richard was right. They could talk better later, without the gardaí, expectant wedding guests and family waiting on them. When they were alone, she'd finally get the truth and Richard wouldn't feel like a stranger. This whole day would no longer be a nightmare when she was in her husband's arms, together in Maggie's Point. At least that's what she hoped.

'Damn it! I look like shit.' She shook out her dress, tried to tame her mane of red hair, knew it was a losing battle. She had no idea where her shoes were, and her dress was ripped and caked in dirt.

'Hush.' Richard turned her until she was facing him and dropped a kiss on her lips. 'You, Mrs Durkin, are the most beautiful woman in the world.' He pulled her close and she could feel his heart beating frantically next to hers. 'Trust in us,' he whispered in her ear. 'We *will* get through this.'

'Of course we will.' But Jenny wasn't as sure as she sounded.

Chapter Six

Sergeant Tom Carr and Winston, the pathologist, stood on the cliff at the top of the Devil's Teeth in their protective gear. To the left of them, there was only a few inches of ground before the cliff was swallowed by the thick trees of Wishers Woods.

'One of these days, those trees will start falling into the sea. And I don't think it's the too distant future,' Winston told Tom.

'Well, let's hope today isn't the day,' Tom said, but he took a step to his right, where the ground was firmer.

They both looked towards the huge white marquee, where the dishevelled bride and groom were being led inside by a handsome man dressed in the same fitted navy suit and daffodil-yellow tie and pocket square as the groom. The best man, Tom guessed.

Remembering his own wedding day – a mere eight months ago – he felt a modicum of pity for the couple: no chance to talk before being accosted first by Gert Foley, then their best man. He didn't envy them having to give their guests the bad news. His eyes followed the figures until they disappeared from sight.

'What are the odds, do you think, Winston, that our groom didn't know his brother was in town?'

''Bout the same as him having adermatoglyphia – which is about one in a few million.'

'So you're going with pretty slim?'

Winston laughed. 'It's a small town, not many places to hide. And it is his wedding after all.'

'True. Even odder that he hadn't invited him to the wedding, don't you think?'

'Families can be tough, you know that, Tom. Got to say, the bride did seem surprised to find out her husband had a twin brother.'

Tom considered that. 'Maybe. Right, what you got for me?'

'No surprises here, Tom. Body has a large contusion on the head, probably enough to incapacitate, then, once he was prone, he was stabbed multiple times in the back – I lost count at twenty. I'll know more when I get him cleaned up for the post, but you have to figure he didn't do any of them to himself.'

'Damn it.' Tom reached for his cigarettes, stopped.

'How long now?' Winston asked sympathetically, having gone through the same torture himself a few years previously.

'Two weeks.' Tom took the toothpick from his mouth, looked at it sadly, before popping it back in, chewing angrily.

'It gets easier.'

'It damn well better.' Tom bit down so hard he broke the toothpick. 'Shit!' He pulled another from his pocket, dropping the splintered one into his other pocket, careful not to contaminate the scene. 'So we're looking at a frenzied attack, a crime of passion, which usually suggests the killer knew the victim.' He looked over at the wedding marquee again. 'What else?'

'It looks like our victim was killed here at the top of the steps and dragged down to where we found him. Guessing our perpetrator was hoping the tide would come in and get rid of the body before anyone spotted it. You ought to thank our bride and groom.'

That wasn't exactly number one on Tom's to-do list. 'Anything else you can give me?'

'You know better than that, Tom.' Winston's teeth gleamed white against his dark skin. 'Talk to me after the post.' A hairless brow lifted. 'What I can give you is advice – nicotine patches. Seriously, mate. So much better than those wooden stakes.'

'I'm going cold turkey.'

'Random fact: they say never to look a wild turkey in the eye. And I can see why,' Winston added quickly when Tom glared at him. 'But back to the task in hand . . . We've gathered what we can from the scene. It's down to you now. Or, rather, your plain-clothed counterparts.'

'Don't remind me,' Tom groaned. 'I phoned the superintendent. He'll assign an SIO. Thanks, Winston. I'll catch up with you later. Fern?' Tom called his newest garda constable over. Fern had only been with them for two weeks, but he was shaping up to be a good officer. At the moment, he was too green to do more than scut work, which was exactly what Tom wanted him for.

'Yes, sir— Sorry, Sergeant Carr,' Fern took off his cap, wiped his brow, put his cap on again and stood to attention. 'What do you need me to do?'

'Get on the radio. Check out the names Richard and John Durkin. Also, Jenny Durkin, nee Hislop.'

'Yes, si— Sarge. Anything in particular I'm looking for?'

'Just prelim for now. Might go deeper later. Bear that in mind.'

'Yes, Sarge.' Fern obviously caught the warning, scribbling furiously in his notebook.

'And, Fern . . .'

'Yes, Sarge?'

'Make it snappy, there's a good man, and when you've done that, I want you to start questioning the guests.'

'On my own, Sarge?'

'You want me to hold your hand, Garda Fern? Or maybe I should ask Winston here? I'm sure he won't mind postponing his return to Saint Mary Margaret's in order to keep you company.'

Winston, who had lifted his head on hearing his name, smiled and waved his hand at Tom, saying, 'Alas, like bodies, the hospital waits for no man.'

'You're a pathologist, Winston, your patients aren't going anywhere – hopefully.' Tom grinned. ''Cause that would be kinda hard to explain.'

'And yet, explain it I could,' Winston said with a smile that reminded Tom that this was a man who knew how to kill a person ten ways to hell – and all without getting caught.

'You hear that, Fern?'

'No, Sarge. I mean . . . yes, Sarge. I can do it. I was just . . . er . . .'

Tom took pity on him. 'The others are already in the marquee. Hurry it up, there's a good man.'

'Right. Right. I'll just go and . . . get that background info for you . . . er, first.'

'You just do that.' Tom watched the now beetroot-red Fern hurry off, almost tripping over his size thirteen boots in his haste. Man, the guy had big feet. He wondered if he'd ever been that naïve, that eager. Knew he had been, once upon a time. Now all he wanted was for this to be an easy solve, especially before the scene investigative officer got there.

'You finished getting your jollies?' Winston asked, clicking the lid of his field case closed, checking around to make sure he hadn't forgotten anything.

'Hey, scaring the help is the only joy in this godforsaken job.'

'Uh-huh. You know you love it.'

Tom had. Once. Now, he just wanted to be home with his wife, waiting with her for their new life to begin. Every day as her stomach expanded, so did his joy and fear. A murderer on the loose in Innisard wasn't good – for anyone.

He took another toothpick from his pocket, popped it in his mouth and began divesting himself of his protective gear. He figured he'd given the newly-weds enough time to inform their guests. Now it was his turn to get some answers.

Chapter Seven

Jenny Hislop is back in Innisard.
 A leap of joy in a heart that has grown weary waiting.
 She is back where she belongs, in the bosom of her family.
 But, most importantly, back within my reach.
 I'm not about to waste the opportunity.
 Not this time.

Chapter Eight

'Hey.' Jenny's best friend, Ita Sharma, stood, hands on hips, glaring at Jenny the second she and Richard entered the marquee with Sean. 'I know you didn't drag me halfway across the country to abandon me in this seventh circle of hell,' she said, dark eyes flashing, full lips pouting. 'What gives?'

'I won't be long.' Richard gave Jenny a quick peck on the cheek, before slipping away with Sean to the bar to talk.

'And why do you look like you've been dragged through a hedge backwards?' Ita continued. 'No, don't answer that. You promised me a quiet, sedate ceremony: free drinks, a bit of a singsong and maybe a tasty man, or two.' She looked around the packed tent. 'What the hell?'

As dire as the circumstances were, Jenny had to smile at Ita's ferocious expression. Her friend stood barely 5' 3" in heels, but she was a demon when riled. And she was totally riled. Rightly so. The wedding was supposed to be small, just Jenny, Richard and their two best friends, Sean and Ita. Then Richard had laid out the whole 'I have no family, but you have. Let them celebrate with us' thing. And oh, boy, had they. Three bridesmaids, two flower girls, one ringbearer, an usher, a DJ and an enormous marquee – filled with half the town – later, here they were at their not-so-small wedding. And now there was a dead body to add to the equation.

Ita didn't stop to draw breath. 'All I can say is thank Christ I'm not a bridesmaid.' She held her hands up as if stopping traffic. 'One word, two very long syllables. Shock-ing.'

Jenny had to agree. Her poor bridesmaids looked like they were wrapped in a mountain of garish yellow flocked wallpaper and iridescent gauze. Aunt Evil's doing, she guessed, the doyenne of bad taste and whose daughter Dana was fortunate enough not to be a bridesmaid owing to her advanced pregnancy.

Almost as if the thought conjured her, Aunt Evil appeared at Jenny's side. 'Well, missy.' Wrinkled lips pursed. 'This is a right to-do and no mistake. What do you have to say for yourself, keeping your guests waiting all this time? So rude.'

Jenny was relieved that Evil seemed oblivious to what had happened on the Devil's Teeth. 'I . . . Er—

'Give it a break, Evie. None of this is our niece's doing.' Hugh, Evil's brother, approached. Well over six foot, with muscles a wrestler would be proud of and completely covered in tattoos – leftovers from his bad-boy past that no one ever talked about – Hugh had to stoop to hug Jenny.

'You never told me your uncle was He-Man,' Ita whispered out of the side of her mouth.

Jenny hid a smile. He-Man was an apt description for her uncle, but while Hugh might appear formidable, he was one of the gentlest men she knew.

'I'm so sorry this has happened to you, especially today,' Hugh said, giving Jenny an extra squeeze.

Damnit. News travelled fast. If her uncle Hugh had heard then it wouldn't be long before everyone else did, too. Jenny wanted to be away from here before that happened. She didn't dare look at Ita, the questioning expression she knew would be on her friend's face.

'This is all happening because the Arras coin wasn't given.'

Evil was still talking about Jenny's tardiness. Nose wrinkling, she shifted up a gear. 'Bucking tradition has consequences, as you should know only too well, missy.' Cold eyes held Jenny's. 'Seems you've learned nothing in your time away.'

Ita now looked doubly confused. 'Arras coin?' she asked Jenny. 'What the frig?'

Jenny shrugged. 'No idea. Never been married before so . . .?' She paused. 'Although . . . I vaguely recall Mum and Dad saying something about a coin at their wedding. Something silly like a five or ten pence piece?'

'It was ten pence,' Hugh said gruffly. 'Your dad said he couldn't afford gold, so he gave your mum silver and promised that she would have all the silver he had to give for the rest of his life.'

'Oh, how sweet.' The story made Jenny feel connected to her parents in a way she never had before. She could imagine them feeling the same way she did at this exact moment in time. Their wedding day. The love, the excitement, all of it . . . Well, perhaps not the dead secret twin.

'But why give a coin? Apart from Jenny's dad obviously being the last of the big spenders with his ten pence.' Ita sniggered. 'At least in a Nepali ceremony, the coins are gold and made into jewellery – pretty and practical.'

'In olden days,' Hugh told her, 'the Arras coin – usually gold or silver – was given by the groom to his bride, a symbolic gesture of all he possessed.'

'And the bride?' Ita arched a brow. 'Did she give this Arras coin, too?'

'Not usually.' Hugh grinned good-naturedly. 'Women back then didn't own much coin, at least not in their own name. As I said, it's an old, very outdated custom.'

'That's probably why Jenny and Richard didn't include it. They're a very modern couple.' She pinned him with a steady gaze. 'There's a reason some customs die out, you know.'

'Exactly.' Hugh's laughter rumbled from deep in his chest. 'I like your friend,' he told Jenny.

'I like her, too, but let's not tell her.' Jenny winked at her uncle. 'She's inclined to get above herself sometimes.'

Ita stuck her tongue out at them.

'See what I have to work with?'

Their laughter was cut off by a voice, saying, 'I don't know whether to hug you or punch you, Cuz.' Tina, Hugh's daughter and one of Jenny's unfortunate bridesmaids, approached. 'I mean, how could you?' Tina gestured to her dress, not looking at Aunt Evil, who was glaring at her.

'I think you look beautiful.' Hugh grinned at his daughter.

'Not helping, Dad.' Tina shook her dress. 'It's like hoops and tulle had a baby – an explosion of babies; very big, very ugly babies,' she added deadpan as she tried to squeeze through the tightly packed chairs. 'Bloody thing should be registered as a lethal weapon.'

Jenny tried not to smile as Tina's skirt flipped right, then left as the rigid underskirt hit the chairs either side, making Tina wobble like an overgrown lemon blancmange.

Tina leaned in to hug Jenny. 'I'm here if you need me, OK?' she said softly.

Jenny nodded. Tina, a lawyer, had also obviously heard something. Time to put the rumour mill to rest.

She looked over at Richard again, huddled next to Sean, hoping to get his attention.

Tina followed her gaze. 'That is one fine-looking man.'

'Richard?'

'Oh, no. God!' Tina laughed, full-bodied and contagious.

Ita joined in. 'Love is so blind,' she told Jenny, shaking her head sadly.

'Only reason I'm not killing you for making me wear this dress,' Tina informed Jenny, 'is the man standing next to your new husband. Although having that damn fine man seeing me in this monstrosity at the chapel this morning is making me a little crazy.'

'Crazy I can deal with,' Ita told Tina. 'And Sean and I are good friends. What say I help break the ice?'

Tina grinned. 'I say break away.'

It pleased Jenny to see her best friend and closest cousin getting on. Maybe now she wouldn't feel so guilty for leaving Ita on her own in a room full of strangers.

'I get to play matchmaker. Delicious. This debacle is finally looking up,' Ita told Jenny. 'Not that I'm forgiving you just yet.'

'Me neither,' Tina said.

Ita linked arms with Tina, 'With me.'

Jenny smiled at Tina's slightly stunned, yet eager expression as she was dragged off. Ita might be tiny, but she was mighty. No better person to have in your corner.

For a second, she wanted her best friend back with her. She wanted to ask Ita what she should do, but she knew exactly what Ita would say, and just how she'd say it. 'It's not complicated, girl. Talk to your husband.'

Which was exactly what she was about to do.

No sooner had the thought sparked, than Gert appeared.

'Here.' Gert held out a pair of flip-flops.

'Oh, you're a lifesaver.' Jenny grabbed the shoes, hugging them to her chest, before bending to slip the flip-flops on her aching feet. She wondered fleetingly whether her gorgeous wedding shoes were now bagged and tagged somewhere as evidence. Would she ever see them again? Did she really want to?

'I've told DJ Joe what's going on,' Gert continued. 'He'll announce that a body has been found and that the gardaí will want to talk to everyone.'

'Probably one of those cliff walker people,' Aunt Evil, who had edged closer, said. 'They never read the signs; think they know better than the locals.'

'The gardaí haven't confirmed any ID yet,' Jenny said, unable to meet her aunt's eyes.

Gert waved her sister away. 'I've arranged with the waiters to keep glasses topped up, and to serve the buffet in roughly ten minutes – full bellies should stop at least half of your guests from stampeding,' she told Jenny. 'The second you and Richard are out of here, I'll give DJ Joe the nod.'

Jenny had never loved her aunt more. 'Thanks, Gert.'

Gert touched her arm. 'You take care now, you hear?'

There was something in her voice that made Jenny pause. 'I'll be fine. I'll be with Richard.'

A harrumph was her only answer.

'Which reminds me, why did you want to talk to him?' Jenny asked Gert.

'That's between me and your new husband.'

Jenny knew that look well. Gert would say nothing until she was good and ready. 'Fair enough.' She turned to go.

'How long have you known him? A few weeks?'

Not this. And just when the day was going so super-duper well too. 'Fourteen months.'

'That's no time at all.'

'How long does it take to fall in love?'

'Piffle.' Gert waved her hand. 'That's nonsense talk. Attraction is fast. Love takes time.'

'And how long did it take you to fall in love?' Jenny retorted, stung, but immediately felt sorry when she saw the wizened face fall at the mention of her dead husband.

'No time at all. But I knew my husband all my life. And I loved him every single second of it.'

Shame covered Jenny. 'I'm sorry, Aunt Gert, I—'

'It's fine. You're a grown woman, and you're married now. All I'm saying is . . . be careful.'

'I am. I will.'

Gert stared at her for the longest time. 'Then God's will be done.'

Gert's pious answer to everything.

I'm bloody putting that on her gravestone.

But Gert had spoken from the heart and Jenny felt the urge to do the same. She was no longer a scared, guilt-ridden, newly orphaned teenager. She was a woman grown. Gert had given her a home when she had needed it, and wise counsel even when she hadn't wanted it. She'd put up with her shit, all her teenage angsts and asked nothing in return. 'It's not fine, Gert. I shouldn't have said that to you. I also should have told you how grateful I am that you took me in when—'

'Took you in?' The maroon-clad shoulders stiffened. 'You're family, part of me . . . us. My sister would have done the same for me if the roles had been reversed. We made a promise to always be there for one another. It's what families do.'

'Still, I was an ungrateful bitc— handful,' Jenny amended quickly at Gert's frown. Her aunt hated profanity of any sort, something the teenage Jenny had taken delight in exploiting. Probably another reason why she and the foul-mouthed Ita were such good friends?

'After my husband, you were the best thing that ever happened to me,' Gert said softly, then she poked Jenny in the shoulder with a bony finger. 'Now, go, find Richard and sort this out so we can all enjoy this wedding we worked incredibly hard to put together.'

'About that, I never thanked—'

'Piffle,' Gert said again. 'Go, get.' But she was smiling.

For once, the ravenous beast of guilt living within Jenny was quiet. Sated, or just waiting to pounce? Jenny didn't know, but she welcomed the reprieve, for however long it lasted. And, even with what was happening, she had to admit that being back home with her family wasn't the horrible chore she thought it would be. Something she'd thank Richard for later – much later. After they had a chance to talk and she grilled him about why he hadn't told her he had a brother, and a twin at that. Which reminded her . . .

Jenny hurried over to where Richard stood alone, Sean having been hijacked by Ita and what looked like a truly smitten Tina. 'It's time we talked.'

'Agreed.' Richard took her arm. 'Let's go.'

Even as close as they were to the exit to the marquee, it still took them long minutes to work their way outside. Jenny couldn't remember who she talked to, what she said. It had to be worse for Richard; these were all strangers to him.

Like he is to you now. The thought was there before she could stop it.

Chapter Nine

There is a certain kind of . . . enjoyment. No, not enjoyment, more . . . anticipation, in watching the results of my labours unfold.

Wedding guests, gardaí, all scurrying for answers, but none more so than my beautiful Jenny.

She will need me more than ever now.

Excitement nibbles. I've watched her for so long. Now it's almost time to make myself known. I shiver with anticipation.

Other girls are nothing compared to my beautiful Jenny – less than nothing. She leaves every other woman in the dust with her beauty, her grace, her goodness.

Richard isn't the man for her, and she will soon come to understand that.

Understand that she is mine.

Chapter Ten

'Thank goodness we're finally alone.' Jenny slumped against the door of the lighthouse. But if she had hoped to find refuge within the curved walls of Maggie's Point, she was to be disappointed.

'Speaking of being alone . . .' Richard rounded on her. 'I can't believe how many people are in that damn marquee. I thought you weren't close to your family.'

Jenny couldn't believe he was questioning her. 'I'm not, I—'

'Really? Did you see that crowd?' Richard paced furiously. 'You have an entire village out there.' His voice suddenly lost its fire, turning sad, reflective. 'A village of people who care about you. A family. And yet you said you were like me – alone in the world.'

'I was.' She bit the words out, involuntarily thinking of her parents. 'I am.'

'Not like me.'

'No, not like you,' Jenny acknowledged, shock giving way to anger. 'But you weren't alone either, were you?'

Richard paused in his pacing. 'No, I wasn't, but I am now. Totally, totally alone.'

Jenny may be reeling from his betrayal, but Richard was attempting to come to terms with the grief of his brother's death. His twin. An attempt that was bound to fail.

And it did.

'John is gone.' Richard said the words as if they'd just occurred to him. 'John is . . . gone.' He staggered as if he'd been punched, then collapsed to his knees, dropping his head into his hands. 'Jesus! He's gone.'

Jenny immediately knelt by his side, putting her arms around her husband's trembling shoulders. 'I'm so sorry, Richard. I'm so very sorry.'

No matter why Richard had lied to her, he had just lost his brother. Jenny knew what it felt like to lose someone you loved. He had to be hurting, and she needed to be there for him.

Richard grabbed her hands, squeezed, and then he cried, sobbed as if his heart were breaking. They stayed that way for a long time, Jenny hunched over, awkwardly cradling him.

When Richard finally composed himself, they moved into the lighthouse kitchen. Without asking, Jenny switched on the coffee machine she'd left ready that morning. 'Did you move the cups?' she asked Richard, looking around the empty counter. She was sure she'd left everything ready for them.

'Cups? What?'

'Don't worry about it.' Jenny figured she was mistaken. A little confusion was understandable given the circumstances. She opened the cupboard and took down two cups.

When the coffee was ready, they settled into the sofa in the glass-fronted living area, looking out at the ocean far below; the heavy thrum of the waves steady and comforting. Jenny kicked off her borrowed flip-flops, wished she could divest herself of her grubby wedding dress as easily, but she said nothing, settling next to Richard. They sipped their coffee and she waited until finally Richard laid down his cup and said, 'I should have told you about John.'

'Yes, you should have. But I'm guessing you had your reasons?'

'Yes, the best – or should I say worst.' Richard picked up his cup again, as if he needed to have something in his hands. 'Oh, God, this isn't easy.'

'Take your time,' Jenny said, but inside she was urging him to hurry up. Sergeant Carr would be here any minute and she wanted to be armed with all the facts before he questioned them.

'I didn't really lie to you. I was alone, have been for a very long time.'

'Your parents?' Jenny asked.

'Dead.' The word was ground out. 'My sister, too.'

'Sister?' The hits just kept coming.

'Sarah.' Richard's voice softened on the name. 'She'd just turned fifteen, was all sass and attitude, you know?'

Jenny did. Having once been a spirited fifteen-year-old girl herself, she knew exactly what he meant. 'Was she older or younger than you?'

'What? Jesus . . .' Richard ran his hands through his short blond hair, making it stand to attention. 'I'm sorry you even have to ask that question. I was seventeen when Sarah died. She was my baby sister.' He paused, seeming to stare into the air, or maybe it was the past, blue eyes darkening.

Jenny waited, sipped her coffee even though it made her stomach churn. When Richard remained quiet, she said softly, 'So there were three of you, close enough in age, you must have got on?'

'Huh?' Richard jumped, as if called back across the years. 'Sarah and I did. John was . . . different. Quiet. Into himself, you know?'

Jenny nodded, even though she didn't.

'John, he . . .' Richard stopped, shuddered.

'What is it?' Jenny asked softly. 'You can tell me.' She set her cup on the table, taking both Richard's hands in hers. 'You can tell me anything. I'm here, for better – or worse,' she added, gesturing to her wedding dress, which raised a weak smile.

'I know you are, and I've never been more grateful for anything in my life. Having you by my side . . .' Richard dragged Jenny into his arms, holding her so tight she found it hard to breathe. 'But it's finally time I told you the truth,' he said into her hair. 'And I can't look at you when I do.' He rose, striding to the window to stare out over the sea.

Jenny tried not to let the coldness she felt at his leaving affect her, or the fact that he would rather fight his acrophobia than face her when he told her whatever it was he had to say. She rubbed her chilled arms, wishing she had a jacket or cardigan, something more than her flimsy wedding dress because, somehow, she knew what Richard was going to tell her was going to change their lives forever.

'Sharon Sumner was the prettiest girl I'd ever seen,' Richard began. 'She had this . . . fire inside her; jumped headfirst into everything. I admired that in her so much,' he admitted in a soft voice, not looking at Jenny. 'People thought I was so confident, John the quieter brother, but it wasn't that way at all. John was easy in his own skin, knew exactly who he was from an early age. He never seemed to feel the need to try to fit in. I envied that in him. He and Sharon were very alike in that respect. Anyway, first love. They say it hits hard, and boy, they were right. I was totally floored.'

He turned to face Jenny, the dimple at the side of his mouth lifting slightly. 'Nothing compared to what we have, my love, but to a horny teenager . . . Sharon Sumner was *the* dream girl.' He smiled in memory. 'When she asked to meet me at Oliver Stanton's party, I knew I'd be there, no matter what. The problem was our parents were very strait-laced, and more than just early curfews and homework before TV. They played us off one another – John and I more than Sarah. If I got a ninety-eight per cent in my test and John a ninety-seven per cent, he'd be grounded for a week. Ditto if I came second. We thought if we gained the same result, things would be better. They weren't.

'When we came home with a joint ninety-nine per cent, Mum and Dad said we must have cheated and they grounded us both for two whole months, no mobile or laptop privileges. It was like they could only be happy if one of us was winning. Plus, they had a zero-tolerance policy for parties.' His dimple trembled. 'John and I had a system for that, for when we wanted to slip out, to catch up with the guys, meet a girl, that kind of thing, except . . . This time I couldn't ask him to cover for me. You see, he liked Sharon. We both did. But Sharon made it clear she fancied me. Me!'

He stopped, his mind obviously moving back in time. Jenny wanted to be jealous, but it was clear this love story didn't have a happy ending. She ached to hold Richard, but knew by his stiff posture that he needed to get this out first.

'So, Sharon saw *you*. The real you?' Jenny prompted.

'Yes. You know that scar I have on my back?' he asked. When Jenny nodded, he said, 'I got it that night. Sharon and I were sitting on this old, rickety fence. It wasn't that high, but you know me,' he said ruefully. 'Plus, we'd both had a little too much to drink and she lost her balance, toppled over. I managed to land first, so she didn't hurt herself, but there was this huge, sharp boulder on the ground. Stung like the very devil.'

'My hero.' Jenny tried to inject some levity, but it fell flat.

'Some hero.' The words were ground out. 'For the first time in my life, I lied to my brother, didn't tell him I was going out. I waited until he was asleep and then I slipped away.'

'Hey, we've all done crazy things when we were teens.' Jenny tried not to think of the awful thing she had done, the stupid mistake that had destroyed her life; her parents . . . 'Lying to your brother, slipping out of the house, that's not so ba—'

'You don't understand,' he said flatly.

'Then help me understand, Richard. What happened that was so bad?'

'My family . . . I left them.'

'Surely that's n—'

'I left them, and while I was out, they were . . .' His voice trembled. 'They were murdered.'

'What? Jesus, Richard. How could you know? This is *not* on you.' She gave into instinct and went to her husband, wrapping her arms around him. 'This is *not* on you,' she said again, trying to absorb the enormity of his words. His family had been murdered! This was a surreal conversation to be having on their wedding day. On any day.

'But it is,' Richard told her, standing rigid in her arms. 'It is. I knew it was going to happen. Oh, not that night,' he said, when Jenny stiffened, 'but at some point. It was always going to happen.'

'I don't understand.' Jenny leaned back, staring into Richard's face. 'How could you know your family would be murdered?'

'Because he told me. He told me he was going to kill them. Kill me.'

Jenny tightened her arms around Richard's waist. Trying to make sense of what he was saying. 'Who? Who told you that?'

But she wasn't prepared for the answer.

'John. My brother told me. But I swear I didn't think he meant it. I didn't,' Richard said again.

'Of course you didn't. How could you?' Jenny soothed, even as she grappled with the knowledge that Richard's brother had murdered his family. Why would a child do something so horrific? And suddenly she knew why her brilliant husband had turned his back on the more lucrative career paths he could have taken, and chosen the profession he had. Psychiatrist; caring for people like his brother with broken, fractured minds. Looking for answers. Answers he'd probably never find.

'He even told me how he was going to do it,' Richard continued, his voice a monotone. 'A hammer. He used a hammer, bludgeoned them to death. I've always wondered how many swings it took for each of them? Did Mum and Dad take more than Sarah? Dad was so big, Sarah . . . she was tiny, fine-boned. Maybe that meant she died quicker? Easier?' he said, almost eagerly.

At Jenny's shocked expression, he added, 'I know that must sound callous, but Mum and Dad would have wanted that. I want that. To think of her, of them, in pain, the fear they must have felt . . .' He closed his eyes, as if the thought was more than he could bear.

'Oh, my love.' Jenny rocked him, like she would a child, even as her stomach rolled with the horror of what she was hearing. What a thing to live with. How had her sweet, sweet Richard ever come through something like that intact?

'I got there too late. Too late to save them. John was waiting for me. We fought. To this day, I don't know how I got away, but I did. And I ran. I ran so fast. So far, Jenny. I had to escape. But I left them. I left my family behind.'

Jenny held her husband tighter. 'I'm so sorry, Richard. So very, very sorry.' She let go of her ego; it had no place here. Yes, Richard should have told her about his family before they married, just like she should have told him about her complicated relationship with her Innisard relatives. But what he'd gone through . . . his story crushed every argument she may have had into insignificance. And while she had questions – many, many questions – now wasn't the time to get into them.

The truth was finally out. They would move forward with no secrets between them; start anew and be stronger for it. She wasn't naïve. She knew it wouldn't be easy, but they would do it. Together.

Richard buried his head in her neck, held her tightly. 'On a professional level, I now know why my brother did what he did – or, at least, I can make an educated guess. On an emotional level . . . I'm still grappling with his actions, the visceral reality of it. I've lived with this for so long. Time anaesthetises even the deepest wound, but you, my darling Jenny, give me hope, a belief that life can get better. I need you, Jenny.' Richard tightened his hold on her, breathing heavy, voice thickening with passion. 'I need you now, want you more than I ever have before.'

Jenny wanted him, too; to lose herself in his arms. Comfort could be found in the strangest ways. And it *was* their wedding day . . .

'Come on, husband.' She held out her hand. 'Let's go christen this marital bed of ours.'

Together, they moved towards the spiral staircase, only to be stopped by a firm knock on the door, followed by an equally firm voice.

'Gardaí. Open up.'

'What should we do?' Richard froze.

'We tell the truth.' Jenny took his face in her hands, stared deeply into his eyes. 'If there's one thing we've both learned from this, it's that we need to tell the truth, face things head-on. Together.' Her hands held his face gently, as did her eyes. 'But I'm with you, whatever you decide.'

'I do love you, Mrs Durkin,' Richard said, laying his head against hers. He heaved a sigh. 'We go with truth all the way.'

'Then let's do this.' Jenny took Richard's hand and together they moved towards the door.

Chapter Eleven

'Well, this is a right pickle, and no mistake,' Evie said after DJ Joe, per Gert's instructions, delivered the bad news to the reception guests. Stunned silence swiftly turned into hushed whispers and sly looks. 'We're now the talk of the town.' She glared around the tent.

Gert quickly motioned DJ Joe to start the music up again before saying, 'Yes, because today is all about you.'

'You know what I mean.' Evie flicked her hand, irritated. 'This is just so Jenny; bucking tradition, mocking superstition. Never thinks before she acts. You'd figure she would have learned after what happened to her parents, but oh, no. She's a walking disaster and she brings it on herself.'

'What? Being a typical teenager back then or finding a dead body on her wedding day?' Hugh glared at his sister. 'I suppose you're going to tell us that she's responsible for this huge storm that's supposed to hit us this weekend, too? Seriously, Evie.' His voice rumbled angrily from deep in his barrel chest. 'Do you even think before you speak?'

'You shouldn't mock, Hugh. They say this storm is going to be as bad as *Oíche na Gaoithe Móire*, and you know how bad that was.'

'The night of the big storm was back in 1839, Evie, so no, I don't know how bad it was. I wasn't born then, and neither were you. Although, it would explain a lot if you were,' he muttered.

'Enough!' Gert admonished her siblings. 'This isn't getting us anywhere. We need Tina.' She looked pointedly at Hugh. 'Being a lawyer, Tina can help. She knows the local gardaí. Maybe she's heard something?'

Hugh nodded. 'I'll get her.'

'She'll hardly know more than my two,' Evie said with another sniff. 'After all, Dermot and Dana were right there, on scene, as they say.'

'And exactly what were they doing there?' Hugh asked. 'Up to no good, no doubt.'

'Just what do you mean by that?' Evie snapped.

'Exactly what I said.' Hugh wasn't backing down. 'People talk. And it's not like Dermot doesn't have a record, is it? Dana is always dragging him out of trouble. I'm not surprised her accountancy firm closed down. Looking after Dermot is a full-time job for her. One of these days Dermot is going to drag her in so far, neither one of them will be able to get out.'

'You should know,' Evie said, her voice full of venom. 'It's not like you have a spotless record either.'

Hugh's face flushed with anger, tattooed fists clenching.

'Enough,' Gert said again. 'We should be pulling together, not fighting with each other.'

'You're right.' Hugh shook his head. 'Sorry. I'll go and get Tina.' He strode off.

While Evie sulked, Gert sat quietly, waiting for Hugh to reappear with his daughter. In those few moments of peaceful contemplation, Gert pondered on what had been niggling at her all day. It was such a small thing in the grand scheme of things, and she doubted it had anything to do with the body on the Devil's Teeth, but it was an inconsistency that grated; an anomaly in a day where there shouldn't have been any.

Her mantra might be God's will be done, but in this case, Gert's will was stronger. Where her niece Jenny was concerned, Gert wasn't about to take any chances.

And what harm would it do to ask a few questions?

Chapter Twelve

Richard's best man, Sean O'Hare, was finding it hard to keep his eyes off Jenny's cousin, Tina Connors. Even in her dreadful yellow bridesmaid dress, she was the most beautiful woman in the room, with her long auburn hair and mesmerising blue eyes that held his with an intensity that was almost painful.

'Earth to Sean.' A voice interrupted his thoughts.

'Sorry?'

Ita was laughing, enjoying his discomfort. 'You were telling Tina about your job. You know, the one that's so' – she covered her mouth with her hand, yawning – 'interesting. And you suddenly went silent. What's up, big man, cat got your tongue?'

'I . . . er . . .'

'Being a hedge fund manager sounds interesting,' Tina said, obviously taking pity on him. 'But it must be incredibly stressful, being responsible for such huge sums of money.'

'It can be,' Sean admitted. 'But it can also be very rewarding.'

'You're not just talking about the money, are you?' Tina said.

'No.' Sean looked at her. Most people didn't get that. They thought making huge amounts of money was the goal – and it was, for the client. And yes, for him, too. He was no fool. He liked money, liked what it could buy and his job bought him a lot; the freedom to do what he wanted, when he wanted. But that wasn't what drove him. He could retire right this second and never want for money for the rest of his life.

'It's the thrill, isn't it?'

Tina Connors went further up in his estimation. 'Yes. But more than that, it's the satisfaction of playing the odds and playing them right. Of being damn good at what I do,' he said, smiling. He could tell Tina felt the same; saw the spark in her eyes, the hitch of her breath at a remembered thrill of her own. The law obviously contained the same stimulating qualities equities had for him. This gorgeous woman was a kindred spirit. The thought was incredibly sexy.

'Would either of you like to share some of that "joy" with the rest of us paupers, buy a poor, impoverished and starving nurse a drink, would ya?' Ita begged à la Oliver Twist.

Sean laughed. 'It's a free bar, Ita.'

'Free bar? Why didn't you say so? Those are my two absolute fave words.' Ita waved to the bartender. 'Tina, you want anything?'

'I'm OK for now.' Tina dragged her gaze from Sean, looking back to where Jenny and Richard had just left the marquee. 'I have a feeling I may need to keep a clear head.'

Emboldened, Sean stepped closer, lowering his voice. 'Ricky told you?'

Tina shook her head. 'No, but being the local lawyer – the one and only in Innisard, I might add – I hear a lot of things.'

'What kind of things?' Ita asked, slurping the glowing orange cocktail she'd been handed. 'What?' Her eyes slid between Tina and Sean, sensing something. 'What have I missed? This is more than that Arras coin thingy, isn't it?'

'Arras coin?' Sean asked, confused.

Tina quickly explained the old custom of coin giving at a wedding, before saying, 'I'm not sure what's going on, Ita, but I have a feeling Sean does.'

Two sets of eyes fixed on him, and neither was easy to avoid – for very different reasons. Sean squirmed as Tina's perfume settled around him, subtle, memorable, like the woman herself. 'OK.' He held up his hands. 'Not giving away any secrets here because everyone will know soon enough, but Ricky told me—' He stopped as the music died away and the DJ spoke into his mic, telling the wedding guests that a body had been found and that the gardaí would be in to talk to everyone in due course. 'Talk about being pre-empted.'

'Oh, no, you don't get off that easily,' Tina told him. 'Tell me *exactly* what Richard said.'

'Not much more than you've just heard. Ricky told me he and Jenny found a body on the Devil's Teeth on their way back from laying flowers at Jenny's parents' grave.'

'The Devil's Teeth?' Ita asked, sounding horrified as she sucked on her cocktail.

'The steps leading from the lighthouse down to the beach,' Tina told her, before asking Sean. 'I'm guessing it wasn't a natural death?'

'No.'

'Damn.'

'Yeah.'

Just then, someone banged into Tina; a drunken reveller, knocking her off balance. Sean reached out to grab her before she could fall.

'Thanks,' Tina said, huskily, placing her hand on his chest. Then, as if realising where she was, and what she was doing, she went to pull her hand away. 'I really should find Jenny, see if . . .'

Sean covered her hand with his own, warmth filling him. 'And I should find Ricky.' But neither of them moved. Sean dipped his head, lost in Tina's amazing blue eyes, their lips so close he could almost taste her breath: fresh mints and salty air. He wanted to kiss her so badly, had never wanted anything more in his life. It was like he was hypnotised, drunk. His other hand rose to trace the curve of her cheekbone and she tilted her head towards his.

'Tina.' A mountain of a man with faded auburn hair and a swathe of tattoos strode towards them. 'We need you.'

Sean cursed inwardly. He needed her, too; needed to finish this kiss, see if it meant anything, because he had a feeling that it did, that this moment was pivotal for him. Maybe for Tina, too. But he was a stranger, and this person obviously wasn't. A fact borne out when Tina slipped from his grasp, dress swaying as she moved towards the man mountain.

'What's up, Dad?'

But Sean knew, they all knew. Ricky and Jenny needed them. So Sean controlled his frustration as Ita lifted her glass, waving a quick goodbye to the barman. Then they all followed the huge figure of Tina's dad back to the table where the rest of Jenny's family waited.

63

Chapter Thirteen

'Do we know who the body is yet?' Tina approached the table, her dad, Hugh, towering by her side, Ita and best man Sean following closely behind. She noted her aunt Scuttlebutt and husband Cap were now sitting with the rest of the family, and wondered where they'd been.

It was Scuttlebutt who spoke first. 'Why are you looking at me?' she asked Tina.

'Well, you're usually the one who . . . you know . . .' Tina looked around the table for help.

'What she means is you're a gossip. There's a reason we call you "Scuttlebutt", you know, Sheila,' Evil shot in snidely. 'If there's something to be known in Innisard, sister dearest, you're bound to hear it.'

'Well, I don't this time. And you know I hate that nickname, *Evil*.' Scuttlebutt turned to the group. 'I'm NOT a gossip. I just like to be involved in our village life. Is that so terrible?'

'No, it's not,' Gert soothed. 'We've heard nothing definite,' she told Tina. 'We were hoping you'd know more.'

'Damn. I should talk to Jenny—'

'You give that girl a moment's peace, you hear?' Gert's voice turned fierce.

'Of course, Aunt Gert. I would never . . .' But everyone in the room knew she would. Single-minded from an early age, Tina Connors had been born with an analytical mind, coupled with an inquisitiveness that she'd never been able to control. She made no bones about her aspirations to become the best in her field, a top lawyer in the most prestigious firm in the city, the world . . . Tina's ambition had no limits, and she had the ability and talent to do it.

'I'll give them a moment, Aunt Gert, but no more than that. They're going to need me,' she said when Gert went to protest. 'Jenny and Richard found the body. They're renting Maggie's Point, which is next to the crime scene. The gardaí are going to have questions and I want to be there to steer them through those questions. Trust me, you want me to be there too.'

Gert bristled, but all she said was, 'God's will be done.'

Tina hid a smile. That was as good a go-ahead as she was going to get.

'So, the body is probably an out-of-towner, a stranger?' Scuttlebutt looked relieved. 'Or we would surely have heard something by now.'

'We can only hope,' Tina said, explaining. 'If we have no relationship to whomever died on the Devil's Teeth, then it stands to reason we have no reason to murder them.'

'Murder?' Cap exclaimed. 'Nobody said nothing about murder. I thought—'

'I'm saying it,' Tina told him firmly. 'If this were a case of natural death, I'd know. The gardaí are being tight-lipped. We need to be prepared for—'

'Speaking of strangers,' Evil interrupted, glaring at Sean and Ita, the whole murder revelation seeming to have gone right over her head. 'What do we know about these . . . people? Who's to say they're not involved?'

'For starters, Aunt Evi-e,' Tina said calmly, not daring to look at Sean, still shaken by the moment they'd just shared at the bar. 'They may be strangers to you, but to

Jenny and Richard they're family – their city family. The ones they've invited here expecting us to welcome them – *with open arms*,' she added pointedly.

Gert wasn't as diplomatic. 'Evie!' she said in a tone of voice that had everyone at the table sitting up straight, even Ita and Sean. 'Apologise at once.'

Evil's mouth worked, lips doing their usual twisted dance before she finally gave in. 'I mean no disrespect,' she told Ita and Sean. 'This is a . . . delicate time for us as a family. You can't blame me for being emotional. I'm only looking out for Jenny,' she finished with ill grace.

'Me, too,' Ita said. 'That girl is my sister from another mister. You get what that means, right?' When Evil looked blank, Ita took a sip of her drink, then leaned her arms on the table, impaling Evil with a glare. 'It means if anyone hurts my Boo, I'll hurt them back. I'll hurt them so badly, they'll scream for death. You get *that*?' she asked Evil again.

Evil stared at Ita with equal fierceness, before nodding curtly.

'Good.' Ita's lips parted in a feral smile. 'As long as we're all on the same page, we'll be just fine.'

Tina wanted to laugh at the look of horror on Evil's face. Tiny Ita was one formidable lady, but she was only echoing what most of them felt – you hurt one member of the family, you hurt all. Rows, feuds would be forgotten. They'd come together to protect Jenny, because even though she'd left them, left Innisard, she was still one of them. And no one – *no one* – would be allowed to hurt her.

Not on their watch.

No way.

Chapter Fourteen

'Sergeant Carr.' Jenny Durkin opened the door of the lighthouse, seeming surprised to find him alone. 'Come in.' She ushered him inside.

'Small Garda force,' Tom said, answering her unasked question as he took a moment to survey his surroundings. A black iron spiral staircase stood directly to his left, while, ahead, the circular room combined a stylish sitting and kitchen area with deeply recessed windows that flooded the area with light. He'd thought the renovated lighthouse would have been dark, cramped. It was anything but. 'The big guns from the city will be here soon,' he continued. 'For now, my other officers are at the reception, questioning your guests. I'll join them later.' He saw Jenny wince at the thought of her guests being questioned. No such response from the husband, who seemed to have gone from vocal to a dazed silence. *Poor bastard.* 'Shall we sit down?'

'Of course.' Richard Durkin finally seemed to come to life, ushering Tom to a chair. Tom ignored the suggestion, taking the plump couch, forcing the couple to sit apart on equally plump, but separate chairs. He watched Jenny reach out to take her husband's hand as they sat. Obviously, they'd made up. Thirty minutes, give or take. Pretty quick for such a huge oversight as failing to inform a spouse of a twin brother. Made him even more intrigued to hear the story. But first he had to cover all his bases. 'Mr Durkin, I have to ask, did you know . . . were you adopted?'

'Adopted?' Richard shook his head. 'No. I wasn't adopted, Sergeant. And it's actually Doctor Durkin.'

Well, OK then. 'In that case, *Doctor* Durkin, I would like to offer my condolences for your loss. Both your loss,' he nodded to Jenny.

'Thank you.' Richard tipped his head. Jenny said nothing.

'Right.' Niceties over, Tom cut straight to the questions he wanted to ask. 'You said you didn't know your brother John was in town?'

'No, I didn't.'

'And you, Mrs Durkin? Did you know John was in Innisard?'

'No, I— No,' Jenny said again, not looking at Richard.

'OK. So, I have to ask' – Tom looked between the couple – 'why wasn't John invited to the wedding? Were you estranged?' he asked Richard.

'You could say that.'

Tom saw Jenny squeeze her husband's hand; her face wreathed in sympathy. *Sympathy?* He settled back in the couch. *Oh, this was going to be good.* He took out his notebook and pen, waited.

Richard, handsome face twisted with grief, said, 'My brother and I may have been twins, but in one respect we were very, very different. John was sick, mentally. A lot sicker than any of us realised. He's the reason I chose my profession. I'm a psychiatrist,' he told Tom. 'I work with young people, teens, children, helping them in a way no one ever helped John. Maybe if he'd been given the support he needed, he never would have—'

'I don't mean to be insensitive,' Tom said, 'but if you could get to the point?'

'Sorry, Sergeant.' In a calm, controlled manner, Richard proceeded to recount his family's history.

Tom jotted down the details, his mind in a whirl. Yeah, he could understand not inviting a psycho to your wedding. And yet it niggled that Richard hadn't told his wife about his brother. Why? Did he think so little of her that he thought she wouldn't understand? Starting off married life with a lie didn't augur well for a long and happy relationship. And if Richard had lied about that, what else had he lied about? 'I take it you knew none of this?' he asked Jenny.

'No. Richard only told me about his brother and his family, how they . . . died, just before you got here, Sergeant. But I totally understand why he kept it from me,' she added, as if sensing his censure.

'So, you moving the body had nothing to do with you knowing the victim?'

'No!' Jenny sounded genuinely shocked. 'Of course it didn't.'

'Ah, yes . . .' Tom pretended to check his notebook. 'You moved the body to preserve evidence. Quick thinking.'

'As I told you, Sergeant, I'm a certified nurse midwife. During my training, I worked in A & E, I'm up-to-date on evidence preservation, as is my husband.'

Thinking of his wife, of their lovely midwife, Tom found it hard to push the point, but he did. 'A good skill for a criminal to have, don't you think?'

'I . . .' Jenny looked at her husband, who jumped to his feet.

'I don't like your inference, Sergeant.'

Tough. But all Tom said was, 'Does either of you know why Dermot Gibson and Dana Gibson-Mayfield were at the Devil's Teeth?'

'What?' Richard seemed thrown by the question, just as Tom had hoped. 'Why on earth would we know why they were there?' he asked, sitting back down.

'Mrs Durkin?'

Before Jenny could answer, there was a quick knock on the lighthouse door and an avalanche of tulle, frills and flounces appeared.

'Damn and blast!' Richer curses followed as the figure attempted to manoeuvre the huge yellow skirt through the narrow frame.

'Let me.' The man behind her scooped the huge hoop, bending it to allow her to slip through the doorway.

Tina Connors. Tom sighed as he spied the attractive auburn-haired lawyer. He was hoping to avoid her for a little longer. He pulled a toothpick from his pocket, shoved it in his mouth, chewing angrily. The woman was the scourge of his life, as tenacious as a bloodhound. The man helping her was the one Tom had seen earlier, leading Jenny and Richard into the marquee. The best man, he'd guessed then – a guess that was proven right when the man held out his hand.

'Sean O'Hare, Ricky's best man.'

Tom bit down on the toothpick, shaking hands, then turned to the woman accompanying him. 'Tina, you know better than to bring a civilian into this.'

'It's Ms Connors, Sergeant Carr,' Tina said primly, 'I am now in my lawyer guise, can't you tell?' She gestured to her dress. 'And Sean is here as my aide.'

'Aide?'

Tina shook her dress, hoop swirling in all directions. 'For this fricking monstrosity. Anyway . . .' her voice calmed, 'I'm here to represent my cousin, Jenny Hislop— Durkin,' she amended quickly, 'and her husband Richard.'

'I'm only asking questions for now, Tina— Ms Connors. Mr— Doctor and Mrs Durkin aren't under arrest; they're just helping me with my enquiries.'

'Yeah, tell that to all the dumb bastards languishing in prison right this very minute. You know, the ones who were only "helping you with your enquiries".' She made air quotes with her fingers. 'I also didn't realise you were SIO on the case?'

Tom grimaced. Tina bloody Connors knew full well the scene investigative officer would be here soon enough to take over. His reach was limited, and they both knew it. They also both knew it was in their best interest for the local gardaí to resolve the matter before the plainclothes got there. Outsiders – even experts like the plainclothes – didn't have the local knowledge his gardaí did. The second the SIO and his team rolled up, the people of Innisard would clam up, and that didn't help anyone. 'Just garnering as much information as I can while it's still fresh.'

'Uh-huh. Well, here's some information for you: either arrest my clients or get lost,' said with a smile straight out of a Stephen King novel.

'Always a pleasure to do business with you, Ms Connors.' Tom snapped his notebook closed, before slipping it into his pocket. 'But this isn't over,' he warned Richard and Jenny. 'I'm sure you want to know who killed John as much as I do?'

'And, goodbye, Sergeant.' Tina winked as she escorted him to the door.

'Wish I had a camera.' Tom made a frame with his fingers. 'You in that thing . . .' He laughed around the toothpick. 'Magda would love it. Guessing you're going to miss her book club this evening?'

''Fraid so. You let her know for me?'

'You know I will.' Tom left, wishing, not for the first time, that his wife wasn't best friends with the local cut-throat lawyer.

Chapter Fifteen

'I know Tom Carr,' Tina said, the second the door to the lighthouse closed behind the garda. 'The man was on to something, something I interrupted. What was he asking you about?'

'Dana and Dermot,' Jenny said. 'He wanted to know whether we knew why they were at the Devil's Teeth.'

'And did you? Know, that is?'

Both Richard and Jenny shook their heads. 'How on earth would we know?' Jenny grumbled. 'Which is exactly what I told him. I'm guessing it has something to do with Dermot's drastic weight loss and all-over skeevy demeanour.' Jenny looked to Tina, who knew most everything that went on in Innisard, especially when it involved family. 'Drugs?' When Tina nodded, Jenny frowned. 'How bad?'

'Bad.'

The cousins were quiet for a moment. Tina guessed Jenny was remembering the tubby, shy cousin of their youth and trying to reconcile it with the emaciated person she'd met today.

'Did Sergeant Carr mention drugs directly?'

'No.' This from Richard.

'Just fishing for the moment then. Did he say anything else?'

'He asked me something similar when we first found the body,' Jenny told her cousin. 'Only then he wanted to know whether Dana and Dermot were going down the Devil's Teeth or going up when I encountered them.'

'And?'

'I honestly don't know. Could be either. I was kinda focused on something else at the time. Just like I am now.'

Tina had clocked the atmosphere when she and Sean had entered the lighthouse. She looked at the couple. 'The "John" Sergeant Carr mentioned when he was leaving. You want to tell me about him?'

'Not really, but we have to.' Richard explained his relationship to the deceased John.

'Brother? The DB— sorry, the victim, John, is your twin brother?'

'Yes.'

'Oh, for Pete's sake!' Tina muttered as she wrestled with her dress, trying to sit down. 'I hope whoever invented this method of torture died a horrible, painful death. Have you any idea how hard it is to go to the toilet in this blasted thing?' she asked no one in particular, cursing loudly.

'Here, let me . . .' Sean swooped in to settle Tina in her chair. 'Better?'

'I will be, when I get out of this hideous thing.'

'Now there's something I'd like to see.' Sean's brown eyes gleamed suggestively.

'Ahem.' Richard cleared his throat loudly.

'Sorry.' Tina tried to ignore the tingle running down her spine. Dear Lord. Where had that come from? There was too much at stake for her to be distracted now. She had a very strict Heat-O-Meter and it didn't ding for just anyone, and it most certainly didn't ding when she was working. She ignored the memory of their almost kiss back at the bar, focusing on her cousin and new husband. 'This is not good, Jenny.'

'I know, but Richard is innocent. I am innocent. We have nothing to do with this.'

'Hey, I believe you. I'm on your side,' she said, holding Jenny's eyes. '*We're* on your side.' She gestured to Sean, who quickly nodded in agreement, slapping a hand on Richard's back. 'But I need you to answer my questions. Both of you. And I need you to answer me honestly.'

'Of course we'll do that. Won't we, Richard?'

'Yes, and we can't thank you enough for your help, Tina. This whole thing . . . it's a total nightmare.'

'And when Richard says nightmare, he means exactly that,' Jenny said softly.

Something in her cousin's voice brought Tina to attention. 'I need to know everything, guys.'

'You want to tell her, Richard, or do you want me . . .?'

'I . . . can't go through it again.' Richard shook his head, looking older than any thirty-four-year-old should ever look. 'I need a moment to process. Why don't I make us . . . coffee?'

'Think we probably need something stronger, mate.' Sean slung an arm around Richard's shoulder. 'C'mon, Ricky, let's pop open the drinks cabinet and hope Jenny and Ita didn't scarf it all down last night.'

They moved into the kitchen, close enough to be part of the conversation, Tina noted, but far enough away to give Richard space if *he* needed it, which he clearly did. 'OK,' she told her cousin when they were alone. 'Fill me in.'

Jenny did, and when she was finished, Tina sank back in her seat.

'OK, wasn't expecting that.' Her blue eyes narrowed. 'And this is the first you're hearing of it? Today?'

'Yes, Richard told me he's been running all these years, hiding. He couldn't let word get back to John, it was too dangerous. He had to go it alone, make a whole new life for himself.'

'I still should have told you,' Richard said, coming back to sit beside Jenny. 'But I figured after all these years with no word and no contact that I'd escaped. I finally felt safe to live again.' He took Jenny's hand. 'To fall in love, get married.'

'So why didn't you tell her then? When you felt *so* safe?' Tina asked tartly.

'Tina!' Jenny admonished.

'No, your cousin is right. I should have, I would have, except lately I had a feeling . . .'

'The stalker?' Jenny's face blanched. 'I told you we should have—'

'Stalker?' Tina asked quickly. 'What stalker?'

'We've had a few . . . things happen to us, back in Dublin; silent phone calls, unwanted gifts, that kind of thing. Richard even thought someone was watching us,' Jenny said. 'He became a little' – she shot her husband an apologetic look – 'paranoid about it.'

'I did. I'm sorry about that,' Richard said. 'But I was wrong. It was just me being—'

'Did you tell the gardaí?' Tina asked Richard.

'No . . . I'd forgotten about it until today.'

'You forgot about someone stalking you?' Tina's tone left no one in any doubt that she wasn't buying it.

'No, sorry.' Richard rubbed his goatee, looking embarrassed. 'It wasn't so much that I forgot, more I thought it was a kind of reverse psychology thing. It's hard to explain, but basically, because for the first time in a very long while, I felt safe, happy, I figured – hoped – it was just my brain trying to scupper things; inventing a stalker, a threat to our happiness. I know, doctor heal thyself,' he added self-deprecatingly. 'I made a piss-poor job of that, didn't I? But that's why I didn't go to the gardaí. It would have made it all too real. I guess that's also why I didn't tell Jenny about John. But I should have. I'm sorry.'

'You've told me now. That's all that matters.'

'Jesus, Ricky. If Ita hadn't drunk all the blasted whiskey, I'd be offering doubles all round. As it is . . .' Sean shook the almost empty bottle, 'I think you need it more than any of us.' He filled Richard's glass, leaving only a small dram for himself, then he paused. 'Do you think that guy giving you grief when we first arrived could be your stalker?'

'What guy?' Richard asked.

'You know the one: long drip of water, glasses, floppy hair. You can't have forgotten. The man was in your face saying how much of a bastard you were.'

'Oh, him. Yeah. I told you about him, Jenny, didn't I? The crazy drunk guy?' Jenny nodded. 'He's nothing to worry about. I could have taken him.'

'A strong gust of wind could have taken him, mate.' Sean huffed a laugh.

'True, but no glory in beating up a drunk man.'

'You're too good for this world, you know that.' Sean raised his drink. 'To you and Jenny. The kindest and strongest couple I know. You two can handle anything, and we' – he gestured to Tina – 'are right here with you. *Sláinte.*'

'*Sláinte,*' Richard echoed, draining his glass.

Tina eyed her cousin. Jenny still looked uneasy. Rightly so, in Tina's opinion, but the stalker – or not – was a problem for another time. She waited until the men finished their toast. 'And being with you means I'm here to ask the hard questions. You OK with that?' she asked the couple, but really speaking to Jenny, who would know her well enough to know what that meant.

'Yes. We're OK with that. Do your worst, Cuz.'

Jenny's smile wasn't a patch on her normal one, but still good to see. Pity Tina was going to kill it. Stone dead.

'So, up until Richard told you his story, you knew nothing about his background?'

'That's the second time you've asked me that,' Jenny said, her voice tight. 'And the answer is still the same. No. I had no idea about John until Richard told me a few minutes ago.'

'Good.' When Jenny glared at her, Tina added quickly, 'Not good good, but good that you had no prior knowledge. Helps with a defence.'

'I don't need a defence.' Jenny stood, began to pace. 'Neither does Richard. This is our wedding day, for pity's sake. How could anyone think either of us would take time out to kill someone. Sorry,' she turned to Richard in apology. 'John wasn't just someone. But, honestly, how could anyone believe we'd do something so heinous as killing your brother on our wedding day?'

'The gardaí would,' Tina said flatly. 'I feel for you and Richard,' she added, 'I really do. But until the gardaí can corroborate your story, you two' – she pointed at them both – 'are now the main suspects.'

Chapter Sixteen

'Sarge. Sarge.' Garda Fern ran towards Tom Carr when he entered the marquee, stumbling in his eagerness. 'Sorry, Sarge.' He righted himself before he face-planted at Tom's feet.

'Excited to see you, too, Fern,' Tom joked, but he automatically scanned the marquee on full alert. Nothing seemed out of the ordinary, but he didn't relax. 'What's up?'

'Just off the radio with control. The background you wanted me to do on—'

'You get something?'

'Did I ever. You'll never believe it, Sarge.'

'I might. If you tell me what "it" is?'

'Oh, yeah, right. Thing is, Sarge, the doc . . . sorry, the witness, Dr Richard Durkin, has no siblings. None. So how can he have a twin?'

'How can he indeed,' Tom muttered, chewing hard on his toothpick. Records didn't lie. If their background check said Dr Richard Durkin didn't have a brother, then he didn't. But Tom's eyes didn't lie either. The body on the Devil's Teeth and the groom he'd just met were most definitely twins – the man had just admitted as much. So, if the records weren't lying, and his eyes weren't lying, that left only one conclusion: the good doctor was lying through his perfect pearly teeth. Why? And what else wasn't he telling them?

Chapter Seventeen

A gust of wind caught Sean and Tina as they left the lighthouse. 'You were kinda tough on them, don't you think?' Sean said.

'You think that was tough? Trust me, when the Senior Investigative Officer and his cadre of plainclothes get here, they're going to be a hell of lot tougher – as will prison.' Tina kicked at her long skirt, striding firmly back in the direction of the marquee.

'You don't believe it will come to that, do you? Not Ricky and Jenny? No one could believe—'

Tina stopped so abruptly, Sean almost barrelled into her. 'I believe anything is possible, and good people aren't exempt from bad shit happening to them.'

Sean was staring at her, then his gaze flicked over her shoulder, brow wrinkling. 'Is that . . . your dad? What's he doing?'

Tina turned. Her dad's size made him hard to miss. He was standing close to the woods, deep in discussion with a stocky, muscular man, who, if he'd been standing next to anyone other than her father, would have appeared impressive, intimidating even. There was something familiar about the figure. Tina searched her mind, but it was only when the man turned and she saw his face that she recognised him. Pete McAvoy, also known as Pretty Pete – a derogatory name if ever there was one as the unfortunate man had been hit more than once with the ugly stick – a low-life lackey to Innisard's local drug dealer Big Benny. Seeing Pete so soon after her conversation with Jenny about Dermot and his drug use had Tina's senses on full alert. What was her dad doing talking to a man like that? Although 'talking' was the wrong word. The pair appeared to be arguing, Hugh towering over the younger man, face and fists clenched in anger. Something had her usually mild-mannered dad riled up. Did it have anything to do with Dermot?

'Are you OK?'

Tina returned her attention to Sean. One problem at a time. 'Look, I'm not out to get anyone, Sean. I'm just doing my job, and I'm damn good at it.'

'That's what I'm afraid of.'

'What does that mean?'

Sean rested his hands on her arms, not pushing, barely touching, but it was enough to send a delightful ripple of heat over her skin.

'Jenny is your cousin; your loyalty is always going to lie with her.'

'It is.' Tina's blue eyes were steady on his, unflinching. 'You think it's OK her husband kept a secret of that magnitude from her?'

'No. But I know Ricky. He would have told her. Something must have happened. He would never start their married life with a lie.'

His words held a ring of truth. He truly believed what he was saying. 'And yet he did.' Tina slipped free from his hands. 'Maybe you don't know your friend that well after all?' She pushed open the marquee door. A wave of heat, stale beer and noise greeted them.

'Maybe he's not the only person I don't know all that well,' Sean retorted, striding past her into the crowd.

Damn. Tina hadn't meant to offend, but Sean needed to know this was who she was. The law was everything to her. She'd defend it; pursue it with every fibre of her being – no matter who was in its crosshairs. She just knew that this time it wasn't Jenny. She prayed for her cousin's sake that it wasn't Richard either. Plus, she knew anger came from fear. Sean was afraid of something and she was determined to find out exactly what that was. A flicker of adrenaline. It had been a long time since a man had intrigued her this much.

She followed Sean's rigid back to the table where her family sat and her heart sank when she noticed her cousins Dana and Dermot were conspicuously absent. *Damn. Damn and double damn.* Other than Jenny and Richard, the Double Ds were the only other people she knew for sure were at the murder scene – apart from the murderer, that was, and she was really hoping that person was a totally separate entity.

Chapter Eighteen

Jenny and Richard held each other after Tina and Sean left the lighthouse. They didn't talk, just stood, arms wrapped tightly around one another. Eventually, Richard spoke. 'I'm so sorry. This wasn't exactly what I had in mind for our wedding day.'

Jenny's response was half laugh, half sigh. 'You and me both.' She leaned into his embrace, breathing in the familiar citrus tones of his aftershave. The only good thing to come out of this horrendous day was that she was married to this man – this wonderful, clever, darling man.

'I hate that I've spoiled our wedding day.'

'You haven't spoiled anything, Richard. None of this is your fault.'

'It sure feels like it.'

He sounded so despondent that Jenny ached to cheer him up. 'You know what, we don't have to stay here.' Jenny wasn't sure where the words came from, but the idea took shape in an instant. 'Why don't we start our honeymoon early?'

'You think we could do that?' Richard's face immediately lit up.

Jenny was suddenly afraid that she'd raised his hopes unfairly. 'The investigation might get in the way of us leaving . . .'

Richard paused, brow furrowed in thought. 'I don't think they've any grounds to hold us. And leaving early means we'll definitely beat the storm – figure we'll both be happy to miss that.'

'The biggest storm in Ireland's history. No. I'd *so* love to be here to see that.' Jenny nestled closer to him. 'So, are we doing this?'

He shook his wedding band at her. 'I answer only to you, and you to me. I just need to convince Sergeant Carr to let us go.' His handsome face wrinkled with anticipation. 'Thank you for suggesting this. In life, John stole my family from me; I don't want his death to ruin what's meant to be the start of a new one. I love you, woman.' Richard swung her around in his arms. 'Tatty wedding dress, borrowed flip-flops and all.'

His words and his dimple worked their magic, Jenny melting into his embrace. 'I love you, too.'

'Forever and always.'

'Forever and always,' she agreed, excitement beginning to fizzle. 'It's going to be difficult changing our flights at short notice. The storm has had everyone scrambling for weeks; they're probably all booked up.'

'Leave it with me.' He grinned. 'Right. Kiss for luck?' He kissed her like it was the first time, last time, forever.

'Wow, that was some smooch, Mr Durkin – or should I say *Doctor* Durkin?' She raised a brow.

'I know, I know. I was an ass,' Richard said, sounding embarrassed. 'Blame my heightened emotions – along with my elevated position on that damn cliff. I'll apologise to Sergeant Carr before I ask him for our favour.' He winked. 'As for the kiss.' He slipped an arm around her waist. 'I want you to hold on to that until I come back.'

Jenny wanted to hold on to more than his kiss – after all, this *was* their wedding day – but Richard was gone, the solid thud of the lighthouse door closing after him as he left.

Right, if Richard meant what he said and her fears were proved unfounded, then they could be leaving a lot sooner than she'd planned. Which meant she had to pack and say goodbye to her family. Strangely, that was what felt like the sticking point, the one that rooted Jenny's feet to the tiled floor when she knew she had so much to do. Why was this so difficult? She'd left them before; not just left, she'd run, bolted from Innisard without a backwards glance, grateful to escape the accusing, pitying looks, but now . . . She recalled her talk with Aunt Gert at the reception, finally being grown up enough to thank the woman who had taken her in after her parents had died.

Only now, with hindsight, could Jenny see that Gert had been scared, too. Widowed, alone, sole guardian of the fourteen-year-old brat that Jenny remembered herself to be . . . Who wouldn't have been scared? She owed her aunt. She owed her *big* time. But she would repay her. Being back in Innisard these last few days had, contrary to Jenny's expectations, settled her somehow. She wouldn't leave it as long again to visit.

In her mind was a bigger draw. She was married now, looking to the future. Maybe she and Richard would bring their kids up here – there were worse places than Innisard to raise a child. Jenny's stomach tickled with excitement at the thought. But first . . . she needed to see her aunts and cousins, tell them what she and Richard were planning. If they got the go-ahead, it was going to spoil their plans. Scuttlebutt had let slip that they had a big family breakfast scheduled for tomorrow morning.

'Hello,' a voice called from the lighthouse doorway. 'Anyone home?'

'Ita?' Jenny had never been so grateful to see anyone.

'Yeah, Sean told me I should get my ass up here. That guy is totally enamoured by your kick-ass cousin Tina, even in that shit-awful bridesmaid dress.'

'Really?' Jenny was delighted. 'I think they'd make a great couple.'

'Pish.' Ita mimicked sticking her fingers down her throat, gagging.

'You can't fool me; deep down you're a total romantic.'

'Double pish and a pox on you,' Ita said, joining Jenny on the bottom step of the spiral staircase. 'What's up?'

'It's all changed,' Jenny said sadly, 'You, me, Richard . . . Everything is changed.'

''Course it is, you're married now. No more girls' nights out that last two – or more – days. No more ogling sexy guys, debating which one we're taking home – at least for you.' She grinned, then heaved a weighted sigh. 'Damn! You've just decimated my whole social calendar, you know?'

'I know.' Jenny knocked Ita's shoulder, knowing she wasn't really angry, just sad, like she was. Being married was bound to change things, but not as much as Ita feared. Ita didn't know Richard like Jenny did. It would be OK, they'd still be friends, things wouldn't be that different. She tried to reverse their roles – Ita married, her alone, could almost comprehend the desolation. Not a chance that was happening to them. 'Friends forever.'

'No way you're doing that girly shit stuff! You drunk?' Ita asked suspiciously. 'I thought I emptied this stone cone of all its alcoholic beverages last night?'

'You did, and I'm stone-cold sober. So, hear this . . . You and me, Ita. I'm gonna say the words, plug your ears if you want, but I'm going to say it . . . we're *friends*. FOREVER.'

'No, take it back. Take all that arty-farty hearty stuff back,' Ita said in mock horror.

'Arty-farty hearty? Really?' Jenny began to laugh. Ita joined in.

'I told you I'm not good with words,' Ita said when they could finally speak.

'I know, but . . . arty-farty hearty . . .?' Jenny started laughing again, stopping suddenly. 'Oh, God! I shouldn't be laughing. My brother-in-law has just been murdered and I'm—'

'Yeah, no, not doing that.' Ita steered Jenny to the kitchen. 'We can do water, coffee, or . . .' She opened the drinks cupboard, confused to find it empty. She turned, spied the empty whiskey bottle on the counter. 'Bugger. Did that twat Sean finish my emergency stash off?'

'Sean *and* Richard, yup.'

'No worries, I stashed a bottle of vodka in the oven for emergencies – knew there was no way you were cooking this weekend.' She winked. 'Voilà.' Her face fell when she saw the oven was empty. 'What the—?'

'Guess the guys beat you to it.'

'When? I mean, we were here all night, did you have a little tipple this morning – a tiny bit of Dutch courage before your nuptials?'

'Not a chance.'

'So those twats did drink it.' Ita marched from the kitchen.

Jenny knew the guys had finished off a bottle of whiskey, but not vodka. Richard didn't even like vodka. So where had it gone? She was reminded of the missing cups, moved from where she had left them. A chill crept up her spine. Had someone been in the lighthouse? Could it be the stalker?

'Well, I refuse to drink coffee at a wedding – especially your wedding – even if you refuse to drink.' Ita threw herself atop the plump blue and white striped cushions on the couch. 'You want to talk about it?'

About the stalker being in the lighthouse? How did Ita know? Jenny would have laughed if she weren't scared silly as she realised Ita was talking about John. Today was the gift that just kept giving.

'I'm easy either way,' Ita continued. 'As long as you know I got your back, no matter what.'

Jenny knew that, had always known that, from the day she and Ita had first met – her A & E rotation – mad day, multiple pile-up on the motorway, school bus involved with thirty-plus kids. Fun time! Unlike Ita, Jenny had been glad to leave the hectic carnage that was A & E behind. It was too . . . frantic. Too . . . sad. She much preferred midwifery. Yeah, they had their own sad times, but they had many more good ones. However, the bond between her and Ita had been formed in the blood and muck of A & E, and that bond was unbreakable. And she needed that bond now, more than she ever had before.

'Jeeze, Ita, you've got to be the best friend ever.'

'Well . . . duh. So? Spill.'

Jenny wasn't sure how many times she could tell Richard's story, but she knew that she would do it once more for her best friend.

When she was done, Ita looked at her for the longest time. 'Damn, I really wish I had a drink.'

'What? Is that it? No words of support, comfort . . .?'

'First time rendered speechless. Need a moment.' Ita stared into space.

Funnily enough, Jenny wasn't offended. Of all the responses she'd been expecting, this was pretty much nowhere on her hypothetical list, but, as she sat in the quietness of Ita's thoughts, Jenny felt her own mind clear.

For the first time in hours, she was herself again. They couldn't leave. Even if the gardaí gave them the go-ahead, she and Richard couldn't run away on their honeymoon.

If there was one thing Jenny had learned over the last eighteen years, it was that you couldn't run from your problems, your memories, your regrets . . . . Like ghosts, they followed you, haunted you until you found the courage to turn and face them. Jenny was finally ready to face hers, even though the very idea scared the shit out of her. She hoped Richard was ready to do the same, because they needed to stay and find out what had happened to his brother. After the mention of their stalker, Jenny had to wonder if they weren't all still in danger.

Almost as if she'd read her thoughts, Ita said, 'Do you think this John is the person Richard said was watching him and maybe you, too?'

'Maybe.' Jenny thought about the moved cups and missing vodka bottle. John couldn't have moved them; he was dead. 'Or maybe whoever is stalking Richard killed John?' she said slowly, her brain spinning with the thought. 'Oh my God! What if it was really Richard the killer was after, and they killed John by mistake?'

'But why would anyone be after Richard?'

'I don't know. Why would anyone stalk him – us? Could be one of his patients? Could be some random psycho? Who the hell knows. This is serious, Ita. I need to warn Richard.'

'Yeah, totally got the serious vibe. It's not as if the dead body and the gardai questioning us didn't give it away.' Still, she didn't move. 'I really need a drink,' she said at last. 'Let's go back to the tent. Least there they have alcohol . . . Bad music, but alcohol. You coming?'

Seeing as Jenny had been going in that direction in the first place, she nodded. 'Let's go, my little alcoholic buddy.' She opened the lighthouse door, halted. 'What's this . . .?' She stooped to pick up a bunch of wildflowers nestling against the brick-red door. She inhaled their sweet scent. 'How beautiful.'

'Where did they come from?' Ita scanned the area.

'I don't know; they must be from Richard.'

'But if they're from Richard, why didn't he leave them inside, or hand them to you himself?'

'Maybe he wanted to surprise me. He's so thoughtful like that.' But Jenny's voice was no longer sure.

'I don't know, Jenny, this seems a bit odd.'

It *was* odd. It was also all too reminiscent of their stalker back in Dublin, but Jenny didn't want Ita to know how freaked out she was. One of them panicking was more than enough.

'Well, we can stand here and debate the issue, or I can put this gorgeous bouquet in water and then we can go to the marquee – you know, the place serving alcohol . . .' she said brightly.

'You just said the magic words.'

Jenny quickly found a vase and filled it with water, dropping the flowers inside. Then she and Ita made their way back to the marquee and with every step Jenny could feel the heat of unseen eyes on her back.

Chapter Nineteen

She loves the flowers. I knew she would.

Jenny Hislop isn't a fancy bouquet kind of girl, she is fresh and real, just like the wildflowers I've picked for her.

I take a swig from the vodka bottle; a taster, nothing more. I must keep my wits about me.

I wonder if she's missed it yet, knows I've walked among her things; touched them.

My heart races at the image she makes, framed in the lighthouse doorway, those stunning red curls of hers whipping around her face as she bends to breathe in the aroma of my gift.

I take another drink. I wish I was those flowers; that close to her.

Soon, I console myself.

Soon, Jenny and I will be as close as any two lovers can be. And no one will ever take her away from me again.

Chapter Twenty

As Tina and Sean approached the family table in the reception marquee, Tina's aunt Scuttlebutt jumped to her feet. 'What's happening? What have you found out?'

Tina filled them in, saw them all fall silent. Even Scuttlebutt appeared stunned, collapsing back into her chair next to her husband Cap.

'Richard had a brother?' Evil was the first to break the silence. 'And he was the one they found . . .' She waved a hand in the direction of the Devil's Teeth. '. . . Murdered?'

'Is Jenny OK?' Gert asked.

'Jenny is strong; she'll get through this, Aunt Gert.' Tina patted the frail hand.

'Aye, if God wills it.'

'He will.' Tina's blue eyes held firm on the watery green ones, impossibly large behind the thick black frames and filled with worry. 'Our Jenny is on the side of the angels on this one, Aunt Gert. Never doubt it.'

'As is Ricky,' Sean shot in. 'If they can get through having a stalker, then they—'

'Stalker?' Gert asked quickly.

Tina's Heat-O-Meter slipped a notch or two. She glared at Sean before replying, 'Yeah. Not confirmed yet, but it seems Richard and Jenny have had quite a lot on their plate lately.'

'Right,' Gert said firmly. 'What can we do to help?'

'We need to give the plainclothes someone else to focus on, get their attention off Jenny and Richard,' Tina told them. 'The victim is related to Richard, which means Richard is the only one with a direct link to the body – that we know of,' she added quickly. 'He is now most definitely a person of interest. As is Jenny, if only by association.'

'Plainclothes?' Scuttlebutt asked. 'You mean Sergeant Carr and his team?'

'The plainclothes will be outsiders. Probably from Dublin and they will be here any minute.'

'Oh. Do you think they'll consider us suspects?'

Scuttlebutt sounded oddly excited, Tina noted. 'Did you know the deceased, Aunt Sheila?'

'No, but will the outsiders believe that? That we didn't know our new nephew-in-law's brother?'

'Sheila has a point,' Evil said. 'For once.'

'Which is why we need to take Richard out of the equation, prove he had nothing to do with his brother's death,' Tina told them. 'We do that and it's going to make things a lot easier for our bride and groom – and us. Agreed?' She waited for Gert and the others to nod. She caught Sean's dart of surprise. Her intention had never been to abandon Richard; he was her cousin's husband, after all. She would defend him and Jenny with everything she had; and the truth was the best defence possible. 'Good. Then I need alibis.'

'For what kind of time frame?' Her dad appeared and took a seat. Tina eyed him. He looked calm, like his normal self. She wanted to ask him what he had been doing with Pete McAvoy, but figured now wasn't the time.

'Garda will want the last seventy-two hours, or so.' At the bemused looks, Tina added, 'But us Innisarders can whittle that down. High tide was at one a.m. this morning and again at one twenty-five this afternoon, so the body on the Devil's Teeth had to be there between those times or it would have been taken out to sea.'

No one questioned Tina's timing. Living by the sea they were all well-schooled in the high and low tide schedule, because sometimes that could be the difference between life and death, especially in dangerous areas like Smugglers Cove.

'Normally, I'd say a dead body on the Devil's Teeth wouldn't go unnoticed for long, but with Jenny's wedding, and everyone knowing she and Richard had booked Maggie's Point, most people would have been respectful of their privacy, giving the lighthouse a wide berth. So hit me with your twelve-hour window alibis.' Tina gazed around the table. 'Dad?'

'Your mum and I were together all night, obviously,' he said.

'And this morning?'

Hugh crossed his broad arms, tattoos straining. 'I worked the farm, then got ready for the wedding. Drove myself into town,' he said gruffly.

Tina was a true daddy's girl, she loved him, trusted him implicitly, but she was also a trained observer. Her dad was hiding something. Had it anything to do with the argument she'd observed between him and that scumbag Peter McAvoy? 'You didn't stop off anywhere? See anyone—'

'No.'

'Tina is only trying to get at the truth.' Gert placed a hand on her brother's rigid thigh.

'And that's what I'm doing, telling her the truth.'

It was at times like this that Tina realised how little she knew about her dad – as a person. His past was a closed book. He never talked about it, but she'd lived with him, seen the gang tats lining his body. Yes, he'd turned his life around, but it was only too easy to get dragged back into that life. It frightened her to think that it might not only be her cousin Dermot who could be involved in this debacle.

Gert rushed to fill the strained silence. 'Your aunt Sheila drove Evie and I to Maggie's Point this morning. We arrived around ten a.m. to get Jenny ready for her big day. We figured two hours would be plenty. And it was. We left ahead of Jenny, who was waiting on Cap to arrive to chauffeur her to the chapel, and took Jenny's friend Ita with us. Got there about . . . eleven-thirty?' She looked at her sisters, who nodded in agreement. 'Plenty of time before Jenny and Cap arrived, because, as usual, Cap was late.' Gert's smile was without malice, everyone knew Cap was the worst timekeeper in the world.

Cap didn't react, seeming lost in thought.

'So, you were together from ten a.m. until now?' Tina confirmed.

'Yes.'

'I must admit I do feel guilty,' Scuttlebutt said.

'Why's that?' Tina asked quickly.

'We should have let Jenny and Richard stay together last night. I understand where you were coming from,' she told her sisters, 'but if they'd been together, they'd be each other's alibi right now.'

'A bride shouldn't be with her groom before they meet at the altar,' Evil exclaimed with an extra-loud sniff. 'It's not seemly.'

'That horse has well and truly bolted, Evie,' Scuttlebutt said. 'Jenny and Richard live together in Dublin, have done for months.'

'Doesn't really matter,' Tina said before the sisters could come to blows. 'Jenny and Richard being together last night wouldn't have been a good thing. Husbands and wives are inclined to alibi one another. The fact that Ita was with Jenny might be the best alibi she could have. Same with Richard staying with his best man at the B&B. It gives them all an extra level of security.'

'I never thought of that.' Scuttlebutt sounded relieved.

'Did you see anything when you were driving the wedding car this morning?' Tina asked Cap.

'Hmmm?' Cap looked up, shook his head. 'No, I didn't see nothing.'

'You OK, Cap?' Even for a man of few words, Cap was being particularly terse.

'Yeah, I . . . I gotta go.' Without another word, Cap rose from his seat and disappeared into the crowd.

What was that about?

Disappointed, but not to be deterred, Tina forged on, asking Scuttlebutt, 'And you and Cap were together last night?'

'Er . . . yes.' Scuttlebutt avoided Tina's gaze.

'Aunt Sheila, was Cap out last night? On his boat for one of his "midnight fishing expeditions"?' Tina made quotation marks with her fingers. Everyone knew Cap wasn't averse to doing a little smuggling; small stuff, mainly cigarettes and alcohol. Or so she hoped.

'I don't know what you're suggesting, Tina Connors. Don't you forget I changed your nappy when you were little – don't come the big lawyer with me now.'

Tina knew that tone of voice. Scuttlebutt was closed for business. For now. She added a mental question mark over their names before turning to Gert. 'And you?'

'Living alone might have its perks,' Gert said, 'but alibis aren't one of them.'

'I phoned you around three this morning,' Evil said quickly. 'Wanted to make sure the bride and groom were where they were supposed to be. You were a tad abrupt on the phone, as I recall.'

'It was ten past three in the morning, Evie,' Gert retorted, exasperated.

'Yeah, but I'll bet you're glad for it now, seeing as I'm your alibi.' Evil sniffed loudly.

'And Aunt Gert is yours,' Tina said quickly. 'What about Jim? Was he with you?'

'Where else would you expect him to be?' Evil answered. 'Unlike some, who shall remain nameless.' She looked pointedly at Scuttlebutt. 'A man remains abed with his wife at night.'

'That's great,' Tina said, not telling them that until they got a firm time of death, all their alibis could be for shite.

'Maybe you should focus elsewhere?' Evil swung her gaze to Sean.

'Er . . .' Sean shifted uncomfortably. 'I . . . er . . . I was in the B&B with Ricky.'

'And your . . . friend, that girl, Ita?'

'Ita was with your niece at the lighthouse all night,' he said firmly.

'Hmmm. If you say so.' Evil didn't sound convinced. 'I need to check on Dana.' She rose from her seat. 'Your cousin is close to her time, and all this must be most upsetting for her.'

'Before you go,' Tina said, 'will you tell Dana I need to talk to her, and do you know where Dermot is?'

Evil's face tensed in anger. 'Why are you asking about my children specifically?'

'I'm not singling anyone out,' Tina said softly. 'I'll check in with the others when I'm done here. But Dermot and Dana were on the Devil's Teeth when Jenny found the body. They're the ones who phoned the gardaí . . .

it would be kinda odd if I didn't want to talk to them, don't you think?'

Tina's calm voice and rationale didn't make a dint in Evil's demeanour. 'I don't have to listen to this.' She stomped off, dragging her husband with her.

'I'll leave you to it.' Gert pressed a hand to Tina's shoulder as she stood, slim and regal in her new burgundy outfit. 'I have something I need to do, but I will scoop up Dana and Dermot first.'

Tina nodded, wondering what Gert was up to. She gazed around the table at her aunts, uncles, cousins. Her eyes lingering longest on her dad. Her gut clenched. Familiar faces, beloved faces. Not drug dealers, petty thieves or unfaithful spouses. This was her family, and they had no idea how bad this shit was about to get.

Chapter Twenty-One

Sean O'Hare was feeling uncomfortable, and not just because of Tina Connors' close proximity, although that wasn't helping. Something Tina had said a minute ago had his mind in overdrive. A throwaway remark that had set off a tiny bomb in his brain.

'Penny for them?'

Her perfume was as unique as the woman herself. Sean inhaled the musky scent before answering. 'I'm not sure they're worth that.'

'Oh, I beg to differ.' Tina leaned closer – or as close as her dress would allow – blue eyes studying his face. 'Are you OK?'

The memory of their almost kiss lay between them. Sean fought down a surge of lust, saw an answering gleam reflected in her eyes. She licked her lips almost nervously and his groin tightened. 'Feeling a bit . . . of an ass, if I'm honest,' he told her.

Tina pulled back, laughing. 'Not quite what I expected you to say there, but yeah, remind me not to tell you any secrets.'

He liked her laugh, it was light, easy. Not forced. Honest. Like her words. It had been a long time since he'd been with someone who was honest. And yes, the irony of it being in the middle of a murder inquiry – and with a lawyer to boot – didn't escape him.

'Yeah, total foot and mouth back there. But I think it's good everyone knows. Who's to say Ricky and Jenny's stalker doesn't have some bearing on the murder?'

'Agreed. I fear I was more focused on keeping any more bad news from my aunts – Gert in particular – that I may have verged on being overly cautious.'

Sean liked that she readily admitted her failing, which made him more eager than ever to admit his. But he honestly couldn't say what it was that was bugging him about their earlier conversation.

Around them, music played, people dancing, moulded together in a way that made Sean itch to take Tina in his arms.

Tina seemed to read his mind. 'Oh, to be footloose and fancy-free, huh?'

Sean took her hand, but she appeared distracted, looking towards her dad – the man mountain. A tiny wrinkle marred her perfect brow.

'Something wrong?'

'Honestly, I don't know.' The wrinkle spread.

Sean wondered if not knowing was catching and whether the thing she didn't know was the same thing that was bugging him. 'Anything I can help with?'

Her gaze returned to his. 'I wish, but thanks for asking.' She pressed his hand. 'I think this is something I need to deal with myself.'

'OK.' Sean was happy to sit with her; hold her hand in his and let his thoughts still for a moment.

Chapter Twenty-Two

We all have first loves,
  the one we can't forget,
  the one we measure every other love by.
  Jenny wasn't my first love,
  but she is my last,
  my most enduring.
  We are soulmates.
  And soon she will know it, too.

Chapter Twenty-Three

Tom Carr spied the groom making a beeline for him through the throng. *Good. Saves me a trip to the lighthouse.* There was still so much to be done, and not long before the new SIO and his team of soft knuckles appeared from Dublin. In fact, he'd expected them to be here by now. His tongue flicked the toothpick in his mouth, and he winced as it caught on the sharp tip. He wondered what was keeping the plainclothes, but he wasn't about to look a gift horse in the mouth.

'Ah, Sergeant Carr, I would like a word with you.'

'Well now, if we're not perfectly in sync on that score, Doctor *Durkin*.'

Richard faltered at the garda's tone. 'Is something the matter?'

'Why don't you tell me?'

'I would if I knew what it was you want me to tell you.'

'Let's start with the results of our preliminary background check.'

'Background . . . check?' Richard looked shocked. 'On me?'

'Yes, we do one on all people of interest in a case.'

'Oh.'

'Yeah, oh. You care to explain why they show you as being an only child?'

'I . . . eh . . .' Richard tried to laugh it off. 'You got me,

Sergeant. After what happened to my family, I felt I had no choice but to change my name. I was in hiding, after all.'

'I get that. I understand *why* you changed your name. What I don't understand is why you lied to the gardaí about it. To me,' Tom said, face hard, voice unyielding.

'What I did wasn't illegal,' Richard blustered.

'That's debatable, and something we will investigate further. Does your wife know?'

Richard's guilty look said it all.

'So, let me get this straight, you not only lied to your wife about your family history, you also lied about your name?' Tom's voice left Richard in no doubt how he felt about that.

'I was going to tell her, it's just—'

'Of course you were . . . sir. But that's a matter between you and your wife. For the purpose of our investigation, I need to know your brother's full name. That would be your original birth surname,' he added, in case Richard didn't get the dig.

'I swear, Sergeant, I was going to—'

'Name,' Tom barked, taking out his notepad and pen.

'Filmore. I was – am – Richard Filmore.'

'Hmmm.' Tom wrote the name down. 'I need to know if there's anything else you haven't told me? And keep in mind this is a murder investigation.'

'No, nothing,' Richard said sullenly, obviously upset at being caught out.

Tom stared at him a moment longer, taking in the man's pale complexion, the trying-to-be-defiant stare, pearly teeth no longer on view. Their eyes locked. Richard was first to lower his.

'Right. Thank you for your time.' Tom put his notebook away.

'Er, one other thing, Sergeant Carr.'

'Yes?'

'I was . . . that is, my wife and I were wondering if we could leave on our honeymoon this evening. This has all be so stressful, especially for Jenny.' Richard's voice was gaining in confidence as he talked, posture straightening.

Tom hated that he had no clear evidence to hold the man. Lying to the police was a dick move, but it wasn't an arrestable offence – more's the pity. Something he was sure the good doctor was well aware of. 'If you can get a change of flight this late, sure. Go ahead.' He chewed angrily on the toothpick. 'Just make sure you leave details of where we can reach you before you go.'

'Of course, Sergeant.' Richard was all smiles. 'Escaping from all this sounds pretty good right about now.'

Tom watched the groom leave with narrowed eyes, consoling himself with the thought that in this day and age no one escaped for very long – no matter how far they ran.

Chapter Twenty-Four

When Sean O'Hare saw his buddy Ricky in the tent talking to the garda sergeant, he reluctantly excused himself from Tina's side and hurried over to his friend. The garda moved off as he approached.

'You look happy with yourself, mate.' He slapped Ricky on the shoulder.

'You bet I am. I've just had a chat with our fearless Garda chief and he's told me that Jenny and I are free to go on our honeymoon.'

'Seriously?' Sean couldn't hide his surprise. 'That's . . . great news, Ricky. I was worried you'd have to cancel. Bet Saturday afternoon can't come soon enough for you, huh?'

'We're not going tomorrow. We're going tonight, if I can get a flight, that is. I'll need to work the phones, so I'm going to have to love you and leave you, mate.' Richard winked at Sean.

'Tonight?' Sean said, surprised. 'What about . . .' unsure how to say what he was really thinking, he finished with '. . . the storm? People have been panic booking their flights all week; surely, there'll be none left—'

'I want Jenny away from all this.' Richard's voice turned hard. 'And I'll do whatever it takes to make that happen.'

'I suppose I can't blame you,' Sean said, still wondering how Ricky could even contemplate leaving when his brother had just been murdered. 'I guess I'd want to get my lady out of here, too, if the situation was reversed.' He paused, not asking the question he so desperately wanted to ask: why hadn't Ricky told him about his terrible family history? They were best mates, after all. Then he reminded himself that they were guys, and guys didn't do all that touchy-feely shit. Ricky wouldn't even have told him about their stalker if he hadn't noticed Ricky's uncharacteristic behaviour one night when they were out. The guy had been spooked, totally unlike his usual calm self, and when Ricky had finally explained what was going on, Sean could totally understand why.

'Gardaí are still questioning everyone. They asked if I could "account for your whereabouts" last night.'

'That's standard,' Richard told him. 'Especially now – what with John.'

'Yeah, I guess.'

'Something wrong?' Richard asked.

'No. Yeah. I didn't tell them that I woke up and you weren't in the room?'

'Went to the loo, mate. We did drink quite a bit last night.'

'That's what I figured.' Sean hesitated. 'You were a while, though?'

'Well, we did drink rather a lot.' Richard laughed, throwing his arm around Sean's shoulder.

'That we did, as both my head and stomach can attest to. But not you, you lucky git – you look as fresh as a bloody daisy.'

'Don't you mean as lively as Wilfried Gnonto,' Richard said, striking a pose as he named the Leeds United player.

'You wish.' Sean punched his arm. 'Hey, isn't that the guy we were telling Tina and Jenny about? The one who tried to pick a fight with you when we arrived?' He pointed through the crowd to where a tall man stood.

The figure, as if aware of their scrutiny, turned and sauntered off. Soon lost in the crowd.

'Never mind. Think the discovery of that body's just making me paranoid.' Sean pulled his friend in for a quick hug. 'Congratulations again, mate. Now go, make those damned calls, get that early flight.'

'You're the best best man a guy could have.' Richard's voice was full of emotion as he held on to Sean, extending the hug.

'Oh, get out of here.' Sean wriggled free. 'Go, sort that honeymoon of yours. I'll catch you when you get back home.'

When Ricky left, obviously eager to get back to his bride, Sean turned to survey the room. People were dancing and swaying to the music, which, he had to admit, was pretty good. Couples, friends, families . . . you could sense the closeness of the people here.

His brow furrowed. Small towns. He'd stayed away from them, not understanding their lure. Until now. There was something to be said about knowing everyone and being known by them. City life could get lonely sometimes.

His gaze turned to Tina Connors, now sitting with her family, and even in her god-awful yellow dress, she ruled the table, commanded it as easily as a judge did their chambers. The others looked up to her, he could see that. She was needed here. Oh, he saw the ambition in her eyes, knew that hunger. He also knew she'd never sate it, even if she didn't know it herself yet. She would never leave these people; they needed her too much. Why did the thought sadden him? When had Tina Connors become so important? *How* had she become so important in such a short space of time?

Lust had a lot to answer for. But Sean knew he was kidding himself. It was much more than lust he felt for Tina Connors.

Confused, and needing air, Sean pushed his way out of the tent. He moved to the expanse of green lawn behind the marquee, leading to the woods that sat between the lighthouse and the village of Innisard a few kilometres beyond. The wind was picking up, even though the sky was still a cloudless blue. A foreboding sign of the huge storm forecast for Sunday. It seemed unbelievable, in the pristine, sultry perfection of the late September Friday afternoon.

Sean loosened his tie, inhaled deeply, almost tasting the salty air. This was a place to breathe in, to live in. No hustle and bustle like Dublin. No mad clubs and pubs either, he reminded himself. Innisard might have its attractions, but it also had its drawbacks. Sean loved the city vibe; he was not, and never would be, a townie. It wasn't meant to be, him and Tina, and that was that.

His furious steps had taken him closer to the woods than he had realised. He was about to turn and head back to the tent when he saw something that would set in motion a chain of events that would change his life forever.

Chapter Twenty-Five

Everyone was looking for Dermot Gibson, but Dermot was doing a damn fine job of avoiding them, because, if there was one thing Dermot excelled at, it was hiding.

He was in no mood to answer questions. From anyone, but especially not his sister. Yeah, he held his hands up. He was wrong to get her involved, especially when she was preggers, but Dana had a knack of sticking her nose in his business. Not his fault she ended up getting her snout caught.

Dermot loosened his tie and, with the knot still tied, slipped it over his head before shoving the offending article in his suit pocket. Goddamned monkey suit. He wished he were in his normal jeans and T-shirt, comfortable, not here with the whole fucking fam!

Talk about nightmare.

He drained the last of his whiskey and dropped the glass on the grass verge. Drink wasn't doing it for him, he needed something . . . more. Luckily, he had that something with him. His hand checked his trouser pocket, glad now that he'd been interrupted earlier. If not, he'd be having the jitters with nothing to look forward to.

Excitement flared. Dermot could almost taste the high, the relief, the freedom . . . He knew he'd have to make it last. This was the end of the stash from Big Benny. He'd get no more until he paid his debt. In full! Not even Dana could save him now.

Dermot cursed. Bloody Big Benny was getting greedy, hiking up the price for his gear. Not that Dermot needed the drugs, or anything. He wasn't an addict, he just liked a little . . . buzz once in a while, nothing wrong with that. He completely ignored the fact that he was liking that buzz a little more than once in a while lately, needing a fix daily, which was why his bill with Big Benny was mounting.

Fuck him, Dermot thought. And fuck Dana and Pete McAvoy, too. If Pretty wanted a piece of him, Dermot would give it to him. As soon as he fortified himself with a little pick-me-up, that was.

Eager to get the party started, Dermot edged into the trees, unaware of the figure that slipped silently into the woods after him.

Chapter Twenty-Six

Jenny tried not to let on to Ita how desperate she was to find Richard, to warn him that their stalker could be here, in Innisard. And not just watching, but actually *in* Maggie's Point – her tower of solace. Even worse, he could be responsible for the death of his brother John. If she was right, it didn't bear thinking about who he might hurt next. She quickened her step, almost racing down the path to the marquee. She needed to warn her family, all their guests.

'And here's me thinking I was the one eager to get to the bar,' Ita said, trying to keep up with Jenny's furious pace.

'Sorry.' Jenny slowed, but knew Ita wasn't fooled, seeming as spooked as she was.

Maybe Richard had already told the gardaí about their stalker? Maybe, even now, they were grouped; ready and willing to find the bastard. And if it was the same person who had confronted Richard yesterday, they finally had a face to put to the monster who had been stalking them all this time.

Jenny had first noticed someone watching them a few months ago. She had put the uneasy feeling she'd been experiencing down to wedding jitters – she'd had a lot on her plate, trying to finish up before she left the hospital. Most of her ladies were young and healthy, but pregnancies were notorious for being unpredictable and she didn't want any surprises. She spent months with these women, reassuring them, building a relationship with them. Being a midwife wasn't just a job to Jenny; her mothers-to-be became like family to her. She was with them all the way until they delivered safely; called out at all hours, especially as their time grew closer. She was calm in the face of their fear, encouraging when they flagged, easing and soothing them as required. And on the rare occasion when things didn't go to plan, she was with them through their grief, sharing their sorrow.

On one such occasion, an emergency call-out that had, luckily, ended well – mother and baby doing fine – she thought she had sensed someone following her, but every time she had looked back, the path behind was empty. Still, the feeling persisted, and Jenny had been almost running by the time she'd got to her car. She had mentioned it to Richard later that evening, expecting him to laugh it off, but his handsome face had creased in concern.

'Are you sure you didn't see anyone?'

'No. It was more a . . . feeling, than any real threat. Next, I'll be seeing the bogeyman around every corner.' She had tried to make light of it. Then the gifts had started arriving; flowers left on the bonnet of her car, chocolates handed into reception with her name scrawled on a gift card; silent phone calls. With every instance she mentioned, Richard's face grew paler and paler.

He had been the next to notice something. One evening, standing in the kitchen, chatting to her, Richard had suddenly gone still.

'What's wrong?' Jenny had moved to stare out the window. 'Did you see something?'

'I could have sworn I . . .' He'd shaken his head, laughed. 'Is paranoia contagious?'

But Jenny knew, under his joking manner, he was worried. The next day, Richard arranged for a new house alarm with motion sensor lights. Jenny thought it was overkill, but admitted the added security did make her feel better. Things improved after that, although, the day before they came to Innisard, Jenny had found a dead cat in their garden, the body bloodied and stiff, splayed like a sacrifice on the decking at their back door. Richard had reassured her that the cat had probably been hit by a car and wandered into the garden to die. Their gated, locked back garden. But, with the whirlwind of the wedding, the excitement of the preparations, Jenny had managed to put it out of her mind. Now it was back, front and centre.

She couldn't help it; her footsteps gained momentum again. This time, Ita didn't say anything, keeping pace with her.

A man was dead. Dead! Could their stalker really have followed them and murdered John by accident? Guilt coiled in Jenny's gut. Had their silence, their inactivity, killed her brother-in-law?

Chapter Twenty-Seven

When Sean spied Jenny's cousin Dermot sneaking into the woods, he didn't immediately follow him. Yes, Tina Connors and the gardaí needed to talk to the man, but was it his place to order the guy to return? And what a question to be asking himself – at his best mate's wedding, of all places.

Which brought him back to the conversation they'd just had. He didn't for one second believe Ricky's excuse about going to the toilet last night.

He had to wonder if telling Jenny the truth about his family had been the real reason Ricky had slipped out of the B&B. Obviously, for whatever reason – and Sean reckoned hot pre-wedding sex was the culprit. Those aunts of Jenny's were right out of the Dark Ages, expecting a man to sleep separate from his wife-to-be on the eve of their wedding – Ricky had chickened out, leaving Jenny as much in the dark as he was. Or had been.

Tina saw that as a strike against Ricky. Sean could tell she was already working on how to separate Jenny from her husband if the worst came to the worst – whether Jenny wanted that, or not.

Their very different lifestyles might have decreed that they weren't meant to be, but Sean could still admire the woman; her single-mindedness, her passion. Tina Connors was one hell of a woman, but her participation didn't bode especially well for his mate. Dermot disappeared between the trees and was lost from sight. Should he, or shouldn't he? The question was answered when Sean spied another figure following Dermot into the wood. The figure wore a dark coat, hood up covering his – her? – face.

Intrigued by the person's furtive manner and remembering Ricky and Jenny's stalker, without any further thought, Sean followed them both into the dense thicket.

Chapter Twenty-Eight

Meddlers!
  All these aunts, uncles, cousins.
  They are like gnats, buzzing.
  Irritants that need sorting.
  My patience wears thin.
  If Jenny and I are ever to be alone, they need to go.
  I want this done.
  Now.

Chapter Twenty-Nine

Sean O'Hare hated to admit it, but he was lost. Worse than that, he'd also managed to lose Dermot and whoever was following him. 'Some tracker you are,' he muttered, stopping among the trees, hoping to see or hear something – anything – to tell him where he was.

Apart from the light whistle of wind along the treetops, and an odd rustling sound that could have been next to him or a mile away, there was nothing.

'Damn it.'

Sean considered whether to keep following the path he was on in the hope he'd come upon Dermot and whoever was tailing him, or return to the wedding party. Seeing as the path wasn't really a path and he had no clue what he was doing, Sean decided to head back. No one need know of his embarrassing lack of woodsman abilities. He'd return to the delicious Tina and—

A sharp noise, like someone stepping on a twig, had him spinning.

Too late.

The figure was upon him, something heavy smashing into his head.

Oddly, it wasn't his life that flashed before Sean's eyes, it was Tina Connors, in her god-awful bridesmaid dress, looking more beautiful than anyone had a right to.

And then he was falling, and there was only regret and a deep, eternal darkness.

Chapter Thirty

Gert Foley had made a promise – to find Dana and Dermot and bring the siblings back to their cousin Tina. But she'd made another promise. An older one. And that one held an urgency she couldn't ignore. Didn't want to ignore.

Time was her enemy. Gert sensed it slipping away even as the urgency inside her grew, making her heart flutter in the strangest manner. She prayed for guidance and, as always, the Lord didn't disappoint.

In the distance, amid the crush of people, she spied a diamanté-encrusted ice-blue smock. *Dana*. No sign of Dermot, but one sibling would suffice. She'd pass along Tina's request, then Gert would do what she knew had to be done, no matter how painful the chore might be.

God's will *would* be done.

She stopped to catch her breath, hating how age slowed her, especially now when she needed to be on top form. She lost sight of Dana. But she knew where her niece was going, and why. Her old heart clenched with sadness. Dana was hiding from her mother, Evie. And ever since they were little, the cousins had all run to the same place when they were in trouble, or in need of solitude.

Maggie's Point.

Now that the lighthouse was inhabited, Gert figured Dana would go to the next best place, the lighthouse keeper's shed; a tiny building off the main structure, little more than six by six wide. Back in the day, it had stored kerosene for the oil lamps, wicks, ladders, odds and ends of paint, fishing gear; rods, nets and an old wooden currach the old lighthouse keeper had sailed in on his days off.

Like Maggie's Point, it too, had been lovingly restored with crisp whitewash, and a glossy red wooden door. Inside was spick and span, furnished neatly with heavy-duty shelving for storage. That's where she found her niece, sitting against one of the iron shelves, knees pulled tight to her chest — or as tight as they could go with her huge pregnant belly in the way. She had her phone out and was staring at it, almost as if she were afraid of it.

'Dana?'

'Aunt Gert?' Dana startled at her aunt's voice.

'You OK?' Gert asked.

'Not even close.'

'Hmmm.'

'Is that all you can say?'

'What do you want me to say? That everything will be fine? Because it will. The Lord never sends more than you can handle.'

'I think this time he's bitten off more than I can chew.' Dana's laugh strangled in her throat and she stared at her phone again.

'Oh, sweetheart.' Gert dropped to her knees, old bones protesting, stupid feather in her hat-thing flapping, but she didn't care. 'You are one of the strongest people I know.'

'Strong?' Dana hiccupped a sob. 'How can you say that?'

'Because you survived Evie.' Gert smoothed a lock of hair from Dana's sweating face. 'You'll get through this. Not to state the obvious, but you really don't have a choice in the matter.'

Dana smiled. 'That's why I love you, Aunt Gert. You don't pull your punches.'

'A lady never punches.' Gert winked. 'I love you, too, but enough of this sentimental tosh. This is Jenny's wedding day and—'

'Jenny!' Dana's pretty face turned ugly. 'It's always about Jenny, isn't it? Perfect cousin Jenny who always gets what she wants: the perfect man, the perfect wedding—'

'You think this is the perfect wedding? Really?' Gert raised an eyebrow.

'I suppose not.' Dana looked shamefaced. 'It's just . . . she always wins in the end, doesn't she?'

'I don't know what you mean about winning, but you're the one having a baby – no greater blessing than that,' Gert said softly.

Dana brightened. 'That's true. I finally beat Jenny at something.'

'Not exactly how I would have worded it,' Gert chided. 'Now, come on, Tina needs to speak to you and Dermot. Do you know where he is?'

'Last I saw, he was heading into Wishers Woods. Guessing Tina wants alibis from us?' She huffed in annoyance.

'She only wants to keep us all safe, that's all.'

'Hey, I'm not arguing. If anyone wants to know what I was doing, I'm more than happy to tell them. Last night, I was at home, in bed, not sleeping, because who can sleep when you have seven pounds of baby jumping on your bladder every five seconds. Plus, I'm worn out just trying to get my shoes on. Even if I wanted to, I just don't have the energy to kill someone.'

Gert believed her, Dana looked exhausted, not even the sparkle of gems on her ice-blue dress was able to lift the shadows under her eyes. Weren't pregnant women supposed to bloom? She glanced at her niece's hand as Tina's swollen fingers stroked her huge belly. How on earth could skin stretch so tight without splitting?

Dana stood, groaning. 'Don't say it,' she warned. 'I know I look like crap.'

'That wasn't exactly the word I had in mind,' Gert said primly, restraining a groan of her own as she struggled to stand. 'You sure you're all right? You look awfully pale.'

'I'll be fine once I get this blasted baby out of me.'

'Not long now,' Gert consoled, leading Dana out of the shed.

'Fourteen days. Fourteen. Very. Long. Days.'

'Baby will come when it's ready, and not before.'

'Well, I wish it would bloody hurry up,' Dana muttered.

'Go,' Gert shooed her on. 'Find Tina. I'll look for Dermot.'

Dana, too tired to argue, waddled towards the marquee.

The pain in her chest was back. Gert breathed in and out, waiting for it to pass. Doctor Taggart had warned her not to overexert herself, and yet that's all she'd done the last couple of days.

She gazed over at Wishers Woods. What was her nephew up to? She worried about him. He'd got in with a bad crowd and, knowing Dermot, probably owed them money, too. Not a good combination.

A figure slipping out from between the trees caught her eye. And it wasn't Dermot.

Interesting. Someone was most definitely somewhere they shouldn't be. She thought back to Tina telling them about Jenny and Richard's stalker and the cogs in her mind began to whirl.

Gert watched the figure scurry towards the side door of the marquee. What on earth were they up to? She hurried after them – or as much as her aged bones would allow – determined to find out what in the good Lord's name was going on.

Chapter Thirty-One

Ita left Jenny the second they hit the bar area. 'I'm just going to fortify myself before, you know . . .' She gestured vaguely over to Evil and Scuttlebutt.

'Don't blame you.' Jenny wished she could join her.

'Don't worry, I'll have one for you – or maybe two.' Ita winked before thumping the bar to get the barman's attention.

Jenny had thought the wedding guests would have thinned by now, news of a murder sending most scurrying home. No such luck. It looked like the party was just taking off. She smiled and nodded, evading hands, looks and voices, until one in particular stopped her in her tracks.

'Jenny Hislop. So good to see you again.'

'Oh, my God . . . Fintan Callaghan?'

'In the flesh.' Brown eyes twinkled down at her behind wire-rimmed glasses.

'You look . . .'

'Different?' A self-deprecating smile.

'Well . . . yeah.' Jenny laughed with him. Fintan Callaghan had been her first serious boyfriend. They'd dated for about a year when they were thirteen; just before she'd gone off the rails after her parents' deaths. She had felt kinda sorry for him back then. His dad was the headmaster; a stern disciplinarian, and the other kids had given him a hard time. Tall and thin, he wasn't a bad-looking lad, just wound too tight and a bit . . . nerdy. He still looked nerdy, but it was a carefully polished look now; hair artfully tousled à la Hugh Grant, glasses purposefully selected to suit the shape of his face. He'd obviously done well for himself.

A long drip of water with glasses. Sean's description of the man who had 'given Richard grief' when he'd first arrived in Innisard flashed in her mind. Could it be Fintan? He hadn't taken their break-up well, but that had been eighteen years ago, when they were kids. Surely, he still wasn't hung up on it? On her?

'It's so good to see you again, Jenny.' Fintan took her hand, gazing at her intently.

'You, too, Fintan.'

'It's been much too long. Welcome home.'

'Er . . . thanks. I'd love to talk more, but I have to find my husband.' Jenny tried to slide her hand free, but it was held tight in Fintan's sweaty grasp. 'It's important.' She saw Fintan wince, but not for the reason she expected.

His face softened. 'I totally understand. What's happened . . . well, it can't be the easiest of wedding days.' He squeezed her hand a moment longer, before reluctantly letting it go.

'It's not. And thank you for understanding. Hopefully, we can catch up later?'

'I'll hold you to that.' With a solemn nod, Fintan turned and melted into the crowd.

Jenny watched him go. He'd changed. Still intense, but no longer the insecure, lost boy she'd once known. From the side of her eye, she spied her husband at the far door of the marquee, blond hair tousled with sweat. 'Richard,' she shouted when it seemed he hadn't seen her.

'Jenny? What . . .?'

He looked dishevelled and slightly out of breath. 'Are you OK?' she asked.

'Energetic dance with Scuttlebutt,' Richard grimaced. 'That woman can move, talk about disco queen.'

'Scuttlebutt? The day just gets weirder and weirder.'

'Oh yeah, and I totally get the nickname now. That woman can talk for Ireland. But enough of that.' Richard grabbed her, swinging her around. 'I was successful in my mission. Sergeant Carr said we can leave. I need to phone and change our flights, get things sort—' He stopped at the look on her face. 'What? You haven't changed your mind, have you?'

'Richard, I—'

'You have, haven't you?' Richard stepped back from her, looking crushed. 'Why?'

'I can't leave Aunt Gert and the others to face this alone. And I don't think you should leave either. We can't run away from this, Richard.'

'But it was OK for you to run away from your past?'

Jenny flinched at the hardness of his tone, the cruelty of his words. 'No, it wasn't. I was young, stupid. I was trying to outrun my pain, my guilt, not knowing that I would never be able to run fast enough or far enough. I guess that's something we both have in common, don't we?'

'Oh, God.' Richard immediately looked ashamed. 'I'm sorry, I shouldn't have said that.'

Jenny took his hand. 'You need to know what happened to your brother. You'll never forgive yourself if you don't.'

'Oh, I think I could forgive myself OK – on a beach, Mai Tai in hand, my wife by my side . . .'

'I want that, too, Richard. I want that so much, but you know I'm right. We can't leave now.'

Richard muttered something under his breath.

'Didn't hear that, husband.'

'You're right, you're right.' He held up his hands. 'No comparison between Mai Tais and killers.'

She dropped a kiss on his lips. 'And thanks for the flowers, I love them.'

'Flowers?'

'At the lighthouse. You left a bouquet of wildflowers at the door.' Even as she said it, Jenny knew Ita was right. Richard would never have left flowers for her outside; he would have handed them to her. Richard's face only confirmed her suspicions.

'How can he be here?' Richard asked, looking around. 'That's just . . . that's not possible.'

'I don't know, but he is.' She told him about the moved coffee cups, the missing bottle of vodka that Ita had stashed in the oven. 'God knows what else he's done, or touched.' She shuddered. 'Which reminds me, the crazy drunk guy who shouted abuse at you your first day here. Have you seen him?'

'Here?' Richard looked around the marquee. 'No, but Sean thought he saw him earlier. Why?'

Jenny didn't want to mention Fintan's name, get him into trouble without any clear evidence. 'Just let me know if you spot him, will you?'

Richard nodded.

'We need to talk to Sergeant Carr again, about the stalker,' Jenny said. 'I think he might have something to do with John's murder. Don't you see,' she said, grabbing his hand, squeezing it so tight her fingers hurt. 'You and John were twins. What if . . . what if our stalker thought John was you? Killed him by mistake?'

Richard's face creased in concern. 'Jesus, I never thought of that.'

'We need to find Sergeant Carr, tell him. Who knows,' she said, a smile lightening her face. 'This information might help them close the case quickly and we can still slip away to have those Mai Tais on the beach.'

'I'm going to hold you to that, my love. But first, I have something else I need to tell you. It's about my . . . our name.'

Chapter Thirty-Two

Tina Connors had a bad feeling. It presented itself as a fist-like ball in her stomach that expanded and tightened with every passing second. Where on earth was Sean? And why was she so sure something had happened to him? Did it have anything to do with the fear she'd sensed in him, the one hiding beneath his angry outburst earlier? It was absurd to be so focused, so aware of one person – a person she'd only just met – and yet she couldn't help herself.

She also wondered where Gert had got to. Had she found the Double Ds? She wanted to have everyone's alibis locked in place before the plainclothes arrived from Dublin. Forewarned was forearmed. And she liked to be well-armed when she dealt with the Gardaí.

She spied Jenny and Richard and hurried towards them. 'Has either of you seen Sean?' she asked, then stopped, eyeing them closely. 'Sorry, am I interrupting something? And please don't tell me it's a totally obvious newly-wed thing – my Heat-O-Meter is waaaay out of sync today.'

'Oh, it's totally a newly-wed thing,' Jenny said, not looking at Richard. 'Just not an obvious one, but that's a problem for another day.'

'Problem—?'

'Ignore that,' Jenny said, her voice rising with excitement. 'I've figured it out, Tina. The stalker we told you about. He's here and I think he was after Richard and when he saw John, he—'

'—Thought he was Richard?' Tina had reached the same conclusion back at the lighthouse when Jenny had first mentioned the stalker. Not that she was telling her cousin that. 'We can't know for sure he's here, but—'

'But we can,' Jenny said, face flushed. 'He's been inside Maggie's Point and he's left me flowers.'

'Been inside? Flowers?'

Jenny repeated her story about the missing cups and vodka. 'And I found a bunch of wildflowers at the door of Maggie's Point. At first, I thought they were from Richard, but they weren't.'

'It's your wedding day; anyone could have left you flowers—'

'It's him, Tina. Trust me on this. He did the same back in Dublin – flowers, chocolates . . . He's here, he murdered John thinking he was Richard and now he's taunting us.'

'But why would he want to murder Richard?' Tina asked, confused. 'So far he's been . . . what? Playing with you? Mind games. Why would he—?'

'We don't know.' Jenny sounded exasperated. 'Just like we don't know why he started stalking us in the first place.'

Richard took her hand. 'Jenny thinks it could be one of my patients.'

'Could it?' Tina asked.

'I can't discount it,' Richard said wearily. 'But if I thought for one second that I might have brought this down on us. On John . . .' His voice broke.

Tina watched her cousin comfort her husband, her mind slipping and sliding through the ramifications of everything she'd been told, working the optics.

'Whether the stalker angle is true or not,' she mused, 'it's great news, serves to muddy the waters.'

'What do you mean "whether or not it's true"? It has to be true.' Jenny looked crushed. 'What other explanation is there?'

Tina wasn't going there. 'No, no, this is great. Gives the gardaí someone else to focus on — always a good thing in these situations.' She smiled. 'We should tell Sergeant Carr.'

'That's where we were going when you stopped us,' Richard said shortly. 'Which reminds me, why were you looking for Sean?'

'I . . . er . . . wanted to ask him a question about . . .'

'Oh my God.' Jenny laughed, all rancour forgotten. She gave her cousin a sly look. 'I know exactly what you wanted to ask him.'

Richard seemed to catch on at the same time, grinning. 'Damn. I think I saw him step outside.' He gestured to the side door leading to the huge back lawn. 'Jenny and I can talk to Sergeant Carr if you want—?'

'No, no,' Tina shook her dress out of the way. 'Duty first.' She glanced back over her shoulder, muttering under her breath, 'Fun second.'

'Let me get this straight.' Tom chewed furiously on his toothpick. 'At a wedding, with multiple people present, we have two moved cups, a missing bottle of booze and flowers . . . And this all equates to a stalker how?'

'It's not just here,' Richard told him. 'Back in Dublin, we had numerous . . . strange events. Someone was following us, watching us.'

'And you're only bringing it up now?' Tom glanced at Tina, eyebrows raised. 'Sounds a tad . . . contrived to my mind.'

'Are you suggesting my clients made this stalker up?'

'Of course not, and I'm sure they have gardaí reports to back up their . . . *story*?'

'Actually, we don't,' Jenny said, almost apologetically. 'We . . .' She looked at Richard for help.

'We weren't a hundred per cent sure someone was stalking us. It was more a feeling.'

'*A feeling*? I see.' There wasn't a lot Tom could do with a feeling. Emotions weren't exactly part of a garda's remit. However, Tom was that rare investigator who believed that intuition played an equal, if not vital, role in his job. As did suspicion.

While he wouldn't dismiss the couple's concerns out of hand, he would take everything they said with an enormous pinch of salt.

For now they were his only lead.

And best suspects.

'It was enough of a feeling,' Jenny shot in, 'that we invested in a completely new security system. Then there was the cat.'

'Cat?' Tom asked, confused.

'The day before we were due to leave for Innisard, we came home to . . . a dead cat in our back garden. Our locked, totally secure, back garden. The poor thing was battered and slashed.' Jenny closed her eyes. 'I had every intention of going to the gardaí to report it, but we were coming to Innisard the next day – to get married,' she added pointedly, gesturing to her wedding dress. 'So, we had quite a bit on our minds at the time, as you can imagine.'

Tom's face softened for an instant, then immediately hardened. 'I can't work with hearsay. I only deal in facts, evidence.'

'Well, here's a fact. My husband was accosted by someone here in Innisard yesterday.'

Tom immediately straightened, looking at Richard. 'Do you know who it was?'

'No. He was a stranger. Then again, almost everyone here is a stranger to me. He called me a bastard, was quite abrasive. I figured he was a drunk, but now I'm not so sure.'

'Did you report it?'

'No. As I said, I didn't think it was important at the time. My best man Sean was with me, he can confirm everything I've said.'

'Whether you believe us or not,' Jenny said, 'I need you to make sure my family is safe. If we're right' – she clutched Richard's hand – 'someone means us harm, and he doesn't seem to care who he hurts along the way.'

Tom stopped chewing on his toothpick. 'Do you have any reason to think someone else here may be in danger?'

'If you're talking facts, proof . . . then no. I just . . . This isn't over.' Jenny wrapped her arms around her waist as if hugging herself. 'I know there's something more coming. Something bad. Please, you need to believe me. We' – she gestured around the tent – 'are all in danger.'

'OK, Mrs . . .' Tom stopped. 'I have to ask; would you prefer to be addressed as Mrs Durkin or Mrs Filmore?'

'I'm sorry, what?' Tina looked at her cousin. 'What's he talking about, Jenny?'

'Richard changed his name. After the murders. He had no choice. He knew John would never rest until he killed everyone in his family, so he ran. Changed his name. It makes perfect sense, if you think about it.'

'I guess. And you've known this all along? Or was this the totally not-so-obvious newly-wed thing I interrupted earlier?'

'I'm doing the questioning here, Ms Connors. So, if you don't mind . . .?'

'In answer to your question, Sergeant,' Jenny said, 'I prefer to be addressed as Mrs Durkin. It's the legal name on my wedding certificate after all.'

'Noted. To continue . . . I understand you're upset, but no one is in dan—'

'My son is missing. I demand you look for him.' Evie Gibson stormed towards them, her face pinched and tight with worry.

'I'm sorry, but I'm talking to—'

'I know what you're going to say, but something is wrong. I know it. I just know it,' Evie said, raw fear clear in her eyes and her voice.

Jenny reached for her aunt. 'Is Dana missing, too?'

'No, she— No,' Evie said firmly. 'Just Dermot.'

'Settle yourself. We'll find Dermot, won't we, Sergeant Carr?'

'I'm in the middle of a murder investigation, Mrs Durkin, that takes preceden—'

'And what if Dermot disappearing has something to do with your murder investigation and you were told that others may be in danger, too, and you ignored that warning?' Tina stepped in. 'What then, Sergeant Carr?'

Tom had no answer to that. Tina was right. No matter what he believed, Dermot Gibson's disappearance needed to be investigated. 'I will put someone on it.'

'Good,' Tina said, but she sounded distracted.

'Anything else you'd like me to do while we're at it, Ms Connors? Like get a hoist for that super-stunning dress of yours?'

Tina didn't respond, searching the marquee with her eyes. 'No, I . . . It's just . . . No one has seen Sean in quite some time.'

'Sean?'

'My best man,' Richard said. 'Sean O'Hare. I saw him a while ago heading out the side door to the back lawn,' he gestured casually. 'I'm sure he's just taking a breather. Been a long day – for everyone. Nothing to worry about.'

Tom wasn't so sure. He knew Tina Connors, trusted her instincts in the same way he respected her acumen as a lawyer. 'You're worried?' He watched Tina closely.

Tina hesitated, blue eyes shifting uneasily, then she nodded, almost biting the words out, 'Yes. I'm worried.'

'Good enough for me.' Tom spoke into his radio, adding Sean O'Hare's name to the search detail.

'Oh, you're quick to look for a stranger. Not so fast when it comes to my son,' Evie muttered, glaring at them before flouncing away.

'Thanks, Tom.'

At any other time, Tom would have enjoyed Tina Connors owing him a favour, but her uneasiness was rubbing off on him. 'I think it's time you told your guests to disperse,' he told Richard and Jenny. 'We have their names and addresses; we can talk to them later in our house-to-house if we have any further questions. For now' – he motioned to the packed marquee – 'we should clear the area. I'm happy to do it, but I think it might be better coming from you—'

'We'll handle it, Sergeant. I'm guessing you still want us on hand?' Richard asked stiffly.

'Yes, unfortunately for you and your bride, the wedding *will* go on. Unless, that is, you managed to change your flights to this evening?'

'No, we . . . er—'

'Good.' It might have been petty of him, but Tom enjoyed seeing the doc squirm.

'Right,' Tina said into the awkward silence. 'Let's clear this crowd, then we can take a moment to sit down and chat. Plan?'

'Plan,' Jenny agreed. 'Shall we?' She held out her hand to her husband.

Richard linked his fingers with hers. 'Lead on, Mrs Durkin. Let's go and tell our guests the party is over.'

Tom watched them for a minute, then turned on his heel and strode off, barking instructions into his radio.

Chapter Thirty-Three

Tom Carr found Garda Fern at the marquee's main door. 'You finished questioning the family?' he asked.

'Yes, sir— Sarge.' Fern stood to attention.

'And that bugger, Dermot Gibson, you find him yet?'

'No, Sarge. No one's seen him.'

'What about the best man, Sean O'Hare?'

'Didn't know he was missing, Sarge?'

'Not sure he is, but I have a bad feeling.' Tom took the toothpick out of his mouth. 'Right, Maggie's Point has only two modes of entry or egress – the beach and Wishers Woods. Seeing as the beach is cut off by the tide at the moment, that leaves only one place to search.'

'You want me to search the whole of Wishers Woods? By myself?' Fern's voice rose a notch.

'Yeah, because I reckon you and your size thirteens are so legendary. You know, can leap immense areas in one bound.' Tom laughed out loud. 'Don't be daft, lad, I have Devlin, Peckham, Ryan, Tomey, Serrige and anyone else who's free coming from Innisard town direction. Plus, the SIO should be here soon, he'll bring his own men. For now, we'll move in from this side, make a quick sweep. That OK with you?' he asked when Fern didn't move.

'Yes, Sarge, straight away, Sarge.' Fern exited the door, making his way towards the line of trees.

Tom followed. 'The others are coming from the west,

so follow east as far as you can, then move north and I'll do the same and go south. And, Fern,' Tom called as the garda moved away.

'Yes, Sarge.'

'Head on a swivel. Understand?'

Fear covered the excitement on the young garda's face at Tom's serious tone. He swallowed hard, nodded.

Youth was wasted on the young, Tom thought as he watched Fern scurry off. He followed, much slower, unclipping his radio, ready to direct the search.

'Thanks for keeping my scene warm for me, Carr,' a voice boomed behind him. 'Bloody accident on the motorway had traffic snarled for kilometres, bastard of a thing to get through.'

O'Shaughnessy. Of all the—

Tom turned, fixing a smile to his face.

Pat O'Shaughnessy, pressed suit, polished shoes, crisp white shirt and tie, stood with his equally well-dressed crew of plainclothes detectives, his beady brown eyes alight with barely restrained malice. It might be ten years, but the guy would never get over not making the cut for the Emergency Response Unit (ERU) with Tom. As if that was Tom's fault. You either had the goods, or you didn't. And O'Shaughnessy hadn't. He did, however, still cut a trim figure; obviously worked out, watched his carbs. Tom quickly sucked his stomach in. Not quick enough.

'Old-age spread getting to you, pal.' O'Shaughnessy faked a punch at Tom's midriff. 'Time to let the big boys take over.' He winked. 'Don't worry, you're still free to continue the grunt work, there's a good lad.'

Good lad? Tom was ready to punch the sanctimonious git, but common sense prevailed. 'Whatever you say, Pat, you're in charge.'

O'Shaughnessy appeared nonplussed before quickly re-establishing his authority. 'Er . . . right. Before you go, report.'

Tom did, quickly and succinctly filling O'Shaughnessy in on events from when he'd arrived on scene at the Devil's Teeth, to Richard Durkin's recently confessed name change and Jenny Durkin's mention of a stalker, who may, or may not, be the same man who had accosted her husband the day before.

'A misremembered twin and a stalker only too conveniently remembered? Yeah, right.' O'Shaughnessy flicked a glance at his men, who mirrored his look of comic disbelief. 'So, let me get this straight, we're on the hunt for a "stalker".' He made quotes with his fingers. 'A lost best man – who hasn't had one of them at a wedding?' Muted grins. 'Oh, and a drug-addled usher, who is probably our prime suspect? Guess I've had worse to go on.' O'Shaughnessy slapped Tom on the back. 'Look it, I'm only messing with you. Winston filled us in on all the pertinent details. My exhibits officer is already retaining and recording the evidence at the scene. I've put another of your officers at the entrance to this place; one won't cut it. The paparazzi are going to have a field day with this.'

Tom didn't want to say that a hundred gardai wouldn't be enough to police Wishers Woods once the press got wind of the story. He'd leave the guy his illusions. And he disagreed with O'Shaughnessy's assessment of the would-be stalker, was more concerned than he let on by Jenny's assertion that someone had been in Maggie's Point. That was a deviation from the stalker's behaviour in Dublin. There, he'd worked on the outside. Here, he seemed intent on being on the inside, closer to the couple, and that did not bode well – for anyone.

'Right, I'll co-ordinate things from here. Fill your men in, there's a good chap.'

Instead of punching the gobshite as he wanted, Tom replaced the toothpick in his mouth, and chewed – hard – before nodding affably to O'Shaughnessy, wishing more than ever that he still smoked.

The wind caught Tom as he worked his way to the treeline, gusting from the north, fresh and growing in volume, causing the trees ahead to twist and sway. He spoke into his radio, his warning clear with his first words, 'SIO O'Shaughnessy and team on scene. We have two missing people to find. Let's get this done.'

Answering squawks echoed back as the members of his team checked in, acknowledging the new information. Tom chewed harder on his toothpick as he moved deeper into the woods, trying not to think of the havoc O'Shaughnessy and his merry minions might be doing behind him with the unwary residents of Innisard.

His gut was working double time, and his hand wasn't as steady as he would have liked as he checked his utility belt, wishing, not for the first time, that he still carried a gun. He took a deep breath and pushed further into the thicket, hoping, for once, that his instincts would be proved wrong.

Chapter Thirty-Four

Dana knew she should do as her aunt Gert asked, find her cousin Tina, give up her alibi. Only problem was, she had lied to Gert. She didn't have an alibi. And if she told Tina where she was and what she was doing, her cousin would be the first one to shop her to the gardaí. So, the second she entered the marquee, she moved quickly to her right, or as quickly as her protruding body would allow, fighting her way through the crowd.

The marquee had a main door and two side doors. One side door led out to a floored and canopied space that people were using as a smoking area. The other led to muddy grassland and the dark edges of Wishers Woods. Few of the guests wanted to soil their wedding finery so they gave this door a wide berth. Not Dana; the lack of people drew her – well away from the presence of the gardaí in the main area.

She needed to be alone for what she had to do next.

It was a relief to step out into the fresh air, away from the heavy thrum of music. The wind tugged at her dress, but Dana welcomed its coolness. It felt like her skin was burning. She made for the large tree stump near the edge of the woods, relieved to sit down and rest her swollen, aching feet.

Her brother had really dumped her in the shit, putting not only her life in danger, but her baby's, too. The phone call she'd received from Big Benny, before Aunt Gert had found her . . . The man was one mean, dangerous bastard. He meant every word of his threat. Shit had just got real. She could bloody kill Dermot for this. He'd gone too far this time. She was done with him.

As far as Dana was concerned, there was only one way out of this mess. She opened her phone. It was every man for himself – or, in this case, every pregnant woman for herself. But, before she could dial the number, she felt a cramping sensation in her abdomen. She waited for it to pass, not overly concerned. She'd had them before – Braxton Hicks – normal at this point in her pregnancy. But it didn't pass. It grew stronger, the pain radiating across her middle and into her back. No. It was too early. It was—

Another pain struck; harder, stronger. *No. Jesus, no. Not here, not now.*

Not with both of them here!

Dana's will was great, but nature was greater, and she couldn't stop the cry of pain that escaped her lips, the phone slipping from her grasp.

'Help,' she cried, worry for her baby stronger than any reservation she might have had.

But no one came, the heavy beat of the music inside the marquee covering her ever more frantic screams.

Chapter Thirty-Five

Dermot Gibson was running. He didn't know where he was going, blind fear and terror drove him; adrenaline supercharging him better than any drug.

I didn't mean to kill him, it was an accident, but who will believe me, Dermot Gibson, the druggie, the screw-up? No one. Not a chance. They'll lock me up and throw away the key and everyone will cheer — my family included. Self-pity swamped him. How the fuck had it all gone so wrong, so quickly? One minute he'd been ready to party, the next . . .

The man had appeared from nowhere, but the second Dermot saw him, he knew what he was there for.

It had been instinctive. The branch had been right there. He'd lifted it and swung. Bull's eye. The guy's nose had exploded, spewing blood, but he didn't go down. He'd kept coming. When those big hands had wrapped around his neck, thick fingers squeezing, Dermot knew he was going to die. Desperate for air, he'd stumbled backwards, tripped over the fallen branch he'd used earlier and gone down, taking the guy with him. The fall had broken the stranglehold around his neck and Dermot was quick to take advantage, scrambling to his feet, frantic to get away.

He'd barely gone two paces when his assailant had caught him, grabbing the back of his suit jacket. Dermot had twisted, veered to his left, then quickly to his right, trying to break the killer's hold. So focused on getting away, he didn't realise how close he was to the edge above Gilly's Gully. His ankle had twisted and, with a grunt of pain, Dermot had fallen, managing at the last second to avoid the steep drop. His attacker wasn't so lucky. With an angry curse, he had fallen the short distance, tumbling down the slope to land with a stomach-churning thud at the bottom.

Dermot had heard the snap from above. Almost afraid to look, he'd shuffled until he was peering down at the body. The man lay, head twisted at an unnatural angle, eyes staring sightlessly up at him.

Holy shit! He had to get out of here. Dermot had struggled to his feet, wincing as his foot touched the ground, his twisted ankle protesting. His head throbbed painfully, and he reached a hand up to touch it; it came away bloody. He was hurt, and none of this was his fault. The guy had attacked him, but he knew no one would believe him. No one ever believed him.

Dermot sniffed, wiping tears of self-pity away, even as he wondered whether he had time to stop and have a quick fix before he hauled his ass out of here, out of Innisard altogether.

And he was never coming back.

Chapter Thirty-Six

Gert, unable to move quickly enough, had lost sight of the figure she'd spied exiting the woods. She made it back to the main door of the marquee in time to see the local gardaí head off towards the trees, and it didn't take a rocket scientist to understand the two were probably connected. Still no sign of Dermot. Where was the boy? Her eyes followed the disappearing gardaí, wondering if their urgency had anything to do with her errant nephew.

She knew in all likelihood that someone was out there, in the woods; hurt, maybe dead, and her old heart ached because, odds were, it would be someone she knew. Loved. Gert knew she had to say something, tell someone what she saw, what she suspected, but still she hesitated.

She needed to be sure. She *had* to be sure.

Uncertainty was an unknown emotion for Gert. She didn't like it. She had been born blessed with an innate sense of right and wrong, an ability to know what action was required for every occasion and when said action should take place.

Until now.

The problem was she still hadn't put all the pieces together – yet. And while she knew what she *should* do, she didn't want to be the one to do it, to say the words that would destroy another human being – more than one, if her suspicions were correct. So she prevaricated, wrestled with her conscience.

What if I'm wrong, Lord?

She quietened her mind, awaiting a response, even as she knew she didn't need one. She was right and she knew deep in her soul what she had to do.

The Lord never sends more than you can handle.

There was a reason why she was the one to have this knowledge, this burden. This truth.

Heart heavy, Gert made her way through the marquee.

God's will would be done.

Chapter Thirty-Seven

If the situation had been different, Tom would have enjoyed his walk through Wishers Woods: the chattering birds, the sway of the trees, branches dancing in the growing breeze, the clean, sharp scent of pine and fresh air mingled with dirt and sap and, in the distance, the muted roar of waves crashing to shore.

His radio buzzed, breaking the silence.

'Need forensics at the following co-ordinates,' a tinny voice said.

Tom had been half expecting the call, so he wasn't overly surprised to hear the pronouncement. What he didn't expect was a second voice saying: 'Me, too. I got one here, as well.'

'What?' Tom thought he'd misheard. 'Say again, Fern.'

'I've got a body, too, Sarge.' The young garda's voice shook with excitement. 'Possible ID as known drug enforcer.'

'Shut that fecker up,' O'Shaughnessy barked over the radio. 'Carr, that one of yours?' He didn't wait for an answer. 'Fecker needs to be sent home to his mammy. Saying all that shite over the radio. Jesus!'

More expletives sounded, but Tom wasn't listening. Two bodies? Shit!

As he was closest to Fern's location, he turned in that direction, but before he could go more than a few steps, he heard someone, or something, running, and not quietly.

Whoever, or whatever, it was, was speeding through the woods at full tilt. He braced himself, ears and eyes tracking the noise. He swivelled to his left and moved forward, quickening his pace.

Now that he was closer, he could hear ragged panting, the frantic hitch of a sob — a very human sob — followed by a very human curse and then a flurry of sound as the person fell, coupled with more curses.

The trees were too thick to see through, but Tom could clearly hear the feet begin running again; an awkward gait as if the person were hurt or fleeing for their life. Neither option made Tom feel any better. He took out his radio, but before he could speak, a figure barrelled into him, knocking him off his feet. Training had Tom holding on to his assailant, twisting as he fell so he was atop the guy, automatically pulling his hands behind his back and snapping on the handcuffs.

'Get off me, man. Get off. I didn't mean to do it. I didn't.' Sobbing. 'Honest, I didn't.'

Tom turned the figure over. Dermot Gibson, face and hands covered in blood, clothes torn and dirty. 'What didn't you mean to do, Dermot?'

'Nuthin'.' Dermot seemed to realise where he was, and, more importantly, *who* he was with. 'I did nuthin', man, let me up. Get these fucking things off me.' He shook the handcuffs.

'I think I'll keep them on for the moment, Dermot. You don't seem to be quite yourself.' Tom looked pointedly at the blood.

'That's mine, man. I er . . . fell and cut myself.'

Tom studied the pathetic figure, no open wounds that he could see, but Dermot did appear paler than usual — and that was saying something. The guy looked positively skeletal, which was why the marks around his throat stood out so clearly, angry bruises already beginning to form. Someone had tried to strangle Dermot Gibson and while Tom knew the list of would-be doers would be long, he didn't need a degree to know that at least one of them was somewhere behind them in Wishers Woods and, judging by the blood on Dermot, not in full health.

'It's my blood, man. I tell you, it's mine. Get off!'

'Gladly.' Tom stood, dragging Dermot upright. 'Let's get you to the station. And before you start whining, we'll have medical check you over.'

'Oh, man!'

Tom spoke into his radio and O'Shaughnessy was immediately on the other end. 'Marquee end of the woods. I'll be waiting.'

'Received.' Tom would be damned before he'd go cap in hand to O'Shaughnessy with Dermot Gibson, not with Fern out there alone. So, instead of moving towards the marquee, he veered left and, seconds later, just as he surmised, he came across Garda Anne Devlin.

'Sarge, what are you doing here?' Anne Devlin might be small in stature, but she was tough and wiry and packed a powerful punch. Something many an assailant didn't see coming.

'Handing off my prisoner,' Tom told her. 'O'Shaughnessy wants him at the marquee.'

'And you want to be with Fern. Got it, Sarge.' Devlin was not only tough; she was also smart. They both knew O'Shaughnessy would be after Fern's blood after his radio blooper. If the guy messed up the crime scene, his career would be over.

'Let Tomey and Ryan know you're leaving.'

'Understood.'

Tom left Devlin with the prisoner and fast-tracked it back to Fern's position. What did these deaths, if anything, have to do with his body on the Devil's Teeth? Were they connected? Fern had mentioned a drug enforcer. Seeing as there was only one drug dealer in town who had the wherewithal to hire an enforcer, he was betting one of the bodies was Pete McAvoy, or Pretty Pete as he was otherwise known; Big Benny's one and only muscle man. Big Benny, local drug dealer and all-round pain in Tom's ass.

Known druggie Dermot Gibson and druggie enforcer Pete McAvoy . . . that made sense. Dermot obviously owed Big Benny money, Pete came to collect and somehow – and the mind just boggled on the how – the weakling Dermot Gibson had bettered the obscenely muscled Pete McAvoy.

Now, *that* was a story Tom couldn't wait to hear.

But who was the second body?

Tom made his way through the woods, oblivious now to its beauty. His feet slowed as he approached the co-ordinates Fern had given him. He knew this place; a beautiful but dangerous spot. A grassy clearing full of wildflowers and long grass, deceptive because, to the unwary, the only way out of the clearing lay straight ahead, along a pristine path of blanketed grass that led to a sheer drop into what was known locally as Gilly's Gully.

Or at least the path used to be pristine. Tom noted the signs of a struggle in the earth as he moved closer to the gully's edge, clumps of grass disturbed, scuffs in the ground. He moved carefully around these disturbances to tug the abandoned warning sign out of the long grass. He bent, picked up a stone and used it to hammer the sign back into place. Not for the first time – and, he knew, not for the last. Gilly didn't like people near his spot. Tom would have to have words with him – again.

Tom knew for sure Gilly wasn't the victim below. For one, the town drunk was far too wily, and far too familiar with the gully to fall into such a trap. Secondly, Gilly was, at the moment, availing himself of the delights of St Mary Margaret's Hospital – something he did every few weeks after one of his mammoth binges.

'Sarge?' A nervous voice sounded below. 'That you? I'm down here.'

Tom skirted the area of struggle and peeked over the edge. Below stood Garda Fern and splayed beside his enormous boots, head twisted at an angle no normal body could withstand, lay Pete McAvoy – no doubt now – dried blood caking his nose and lips.

Tom gingerly manoeuvred his way, none too gracefully, down the steep slope, again giving the obvious path Pete had fallen a wide berth in an effort to preserve evidence. He arrived almost at full tilt and took a moment to steady himself before saying, 'What we got?'

'Broken neck, looks like.'

'That's a no-brainer, Fern.'

'No, Sarge, er . . . I'm sorry about the radio announcement thing, I—'

Tom figured everyone had at least one screw-up in them. He also figured Fern wouldn't make the same mistake again. Lesson learned. Time to move on. 'What else we got?' He scanned the scene, taking in the pristine ground around the body, the broken and twisted branches on the slope above and the signs of a struggle he'd noted in the clearing. Each told their own story.

'Vic has blood around the nose and mouth, but no other visible signs of trauma.'

'Apart from a broken neck.'

'Yeah, er . . . apart from that, Sarge. Lucky punch, you

think?' Fern indicated the busted nose. 'Threw the guy off balance and . . . whoosh!' He made a sweeping motion with his hand.

Whoosh? That was one word for it.

Tom digested the information the scene provided: bloodied nose – vic obviously alive when the blow landed – dead hearts didn't pump blood – the disturbed undergrowth in the woods above, the scuff marks on the edge and slope detailing a fall – the broken neck. The body lay where it had landed; whatever had happened had occurred above. 'We investigate the who; the how is up to Winston and his postmortem. And remember the most important rule of all: accept nothing as fact. Verify. Verify. Verify.'

At Fern's crushed expression, Tom added, 'But yes, all evidence points to a lucky punch and what was it you called it? A whoosh!'

Fern grimaced, looking at once delighted and embarrassed. 'Poor choice of words, Sarge, won't happen again.'

'See to it that it doesn't,' Tom said. 'Next time, you might not be so lucky that it's just you and me. What if the family had been within earshot?'

'Noted, Sarge.'

Tom wasn't going to belabour the point. 'Stay with the body. Winston is on his way. Your scene is closest, so he should be here soon.'

As if in answer, they heard voices above them.

Fern looked relieved. 'Who do you think the other DB is, Sarge?'

'I'm about to find out.' Tom pulled a toothpick out of his pocket and stuck it in his mouth, wishing it was a cigarette full of delicious, carcinogenic nicotine. He could really do with a hit right now.

Knowing O'Shaughnessy would probably have his ass for it, but determined to find out who was next on Winston's table, Tom made his way back up the slope to the next crime scene. His third of the day.

Chapter Thirty-Eight

Oh, delicious mayhem.
 Little bunnies scurrying
 here and there and getting nowhere.
 It is hard not to laugh.
 Too late, little bunnies.
 Much, much too late.

Chapter Thirty-Nine

'What the hell are you doing here, Carr?' O'Shaughnessy bellowed as Tom appeared at the next crime scene. 'And why didn't you bring Dermot Gibson to me yourself instead of sending an underling?'

It looked like he'd got there at almost the same time as O'Shaughnessy and his men. 'Didn't realise you meant me to. If I had, of course I would have—'

O'Shaughnessy's curses were colourful and extremely loud. 'Then I repeat, what are you doing here now?'

'Heard the call. Came to help.'

O'Shaughnessy glared at Tom, as did the plain-clothed cohorts at his side. 'Guy is beyond help.' O'Shaughnessy looked pointedly at the bloodied body, lying face down in the grass.

Tom had to agree. The body was deathly still, untouched, except for the bloody mass at the back of the head, blood pooling, sticky and thick, in the surrounding grass. Looked like he'd been hit from behind.

The victim had dark hair, Tom noted, and was tall, muscular, wearing a fitted navy suit. A description that could have matched half the wedding guests, including the groom himself.

Someone had clubbed the guy over the head. No great feat of detection needed, seeing as a large stone with dark red congealed blood lay next to the body. Just like the body on the Devil's Teeth. Something flashed in Tom's mind quicker than he could decipher.

'You need to realise, Carr, that you're no longer in charge. I am. I don't care about your big-shot history in ERU. Here is what matters, and here I—'

Tom blanked out the sound of O'Shaughnessy's voice. What was it? What was niggling at him? He moved closer, kneeling next to the corpse.

'Back off, Carr. You're contaminating my crime scene.'

Tom knew O'Shaughnessy was right. He was bang out of order, but there was something off here, something that had him willing to brave O'Shaughnessy's wrath. What was it?

He eyed the scene again. Bloodied body, bloodied stone ... *Oh shit!* The answer hit him in an instant. The blood on the stone was dried; the blood on the grass wasn't.

'Look it, I'll have your job for this, Carr.' O'Shaughnessy grabbed Tom's arm. 'Back off,' he said again.

'No can do, Pat.'

'I swear, Carr, you're going down for this—'

'Blood is still pooling.' Tom inclined his head to the grass, pressing his fingers to the pale neck. 'Got a faint pulse,' he shouted. 'This man is still alive.' He turned the body over, furiously beginning CPR.

'Feck.' At Tom's words, O'Shaughnessy jumped into action, calling for an ambulance over his radio.

'Too far out,' Tom said between pumps.

'Winston,' they both said together. Winston might be a pathologist, but he was the closest medically trained person they had.

O'Shaughnessy sent his order over the radio, then knelt next to Tom. 'Breath or compressions?'

'Compressions. My arms are fecked.' Tom gave over to O'Shaughnessy, and together they worked in tandem – thirty compressions to two breaths.

'Move.' Gone was the carefree pathologist of earlier as Winston dropped to his knees beside them. 'You do know this is like the opposite of my job description,' he said as he checked for a pulse. 'Weak, but detectable. Well, look at you two. See what you can do when you actually work together – you bring the dead back to life. Carville,' he called to a thin, acne-ridden man next to him. 'Take over.'

Gratefully, Tom and O'Shaughnessy rose and stood on the sidelines as Winston and his sidekick Carville worked their magic. An ambulance sounded in the distance.

'Guess it could still be a serial killer if this guy doesn't make it.' O'Shaughnessy sounded almost disappointed.

'The guy has a name.'

'Look it, I'm only fecking yanking your chain, Carr, don't be such a tight-ass. So it is—'

'Yeah,' Tom looked at the figure on the ground, face clearly visible. 'It's the best man, Sean O'Hare.'

The ambulance had left and Winston, who looked like he'd been kicked in the balls, muttered, 'This is why I don't do the living. Dead is dead, no aggro, no drama. None of this' – he gestured at the chaotic scene – 'shite.'

Tom threw his arm around his friend. 'Bloody well done, mate.' Winston had been impressive, working coolly and calmly on Sean until the paramedics arrived. If the best man survived, he'd have a pathologist to thank for his life.

Winston rubbed his bald head as if wishing there were hair he could tug. 'Thanks, but I'm never doing this shite again. OK.' He lifted his case and strode off.

Tom made a mental note to check in with him later.

'So,' O'Shaughnessy said. 'We've got a groom's brother murdered on the day of his wedding. A known drug enforcer for a local drug dealer also dead. But what in the great feckful of hell does a hedge fund manager slash best man have to do with either of them?'

'I have no idea,' Tom said, frustrated. 'But Sean O'Hare has to be the key. He's the anomaly. An out-of-towner, never set foot in Innisard before. According to what we know, there's no link between him and the body on the Devil's Teeth – apart from the body being his best friend's brother, who he claimed to know nothing about. Ditto with Big Benny. No link. No history. I'm guessing he probably got caught up with whatever happened here between Dermot Gibson and Pete McAvoy.'

'Yeah, most likely scenario,' O'Shaughnessy agreed. He seemed to come to a decision. 'Right, I need you at the conference later. Your knowledge of the key players will save us a lot of time,' he said in case Tom got the idea he was actually wanted. 'I want your files on this Big Benny. Also, any other local info you think pertinent.'

Tom could see how much the offer grated and rethought his assessment of the man. Maybe O'Shaughnessy *was* SIO material after all?

'The emergency services have made a right fecking mess of our crime scene,' O'Shaughnessy said glumly. 'But I guess that can't be helped – saving a life takes precedence. I've radioed for more men from neighbouring stations to start a fingertip search of the woods, but I don't like the look of that sky. Let's speed things up,' he told the waiting plainclothes and uniformed gardaí. 'I know it's not ideal, but we could lose everything if it starts to rain. I've a feeling those fecking weathermen have buggered up their timeline. Looks like that storm is going to hit any minute now.'

Tom had to agree. Thick clouds had filled the once blue sky, and a chill danced on the breeze, bringing with it the scent of rain. They would have their work cut out for them, trying to process three scenes. The two murder scenes, would, of course, take priority, but they'd need to be equally thorough with this one in case Sean O'Hare didn't make it, which was looking extremely likely at the moment.

'With me, Carr.' O'Shaughnessy came up beside Tom.

'To where?'

'To inform the bridal party. I want you to be the one to impart the good news – leave out the maybe not dead yet bit for the best man, there's a good lad.'

Tom didn't relish having to lie to Tina Connors, but seeing as Winston had given Sean O'Hare a fifty-fifty chance of survival, he reckoned it was only a small lie. Hopefully, if the man pulled through, she'd be too happy to reproach him. 'You want to watch how they react.'

'Yup. If the killer is part of our wedding group, he's not going to be happy to know one of his victims is still alive. Maybe he'll give himself away.'

'Or maybe he'll try again?'

'See, win-win.' O'Shaughnessy grinned. 'Get one of your men to the hospital to guard Mr O'Hare, there's a good boyo. I want to know the instant he wakes up – *if* he wakes up.'

Boyo? Tom gritted his teeth. Was that a step up from 'Good lad'? He knew where he wanted to shove both, but he anchored his anger and radioed in instructions before following O'Shaughnessy back to the marquee.

Chapter Forty

Jenny surveyed the marquee. It was an empty shell; half-drunk drinks on the tables, chairs pushed back, abandoned. Pristine white tablecloths hanging limply over drink-splattered floorboards; the uncut wedding cake still taking pride of place on the empty stage. She was worried about Sean and Dermot, but she was also tired, worn out. Clearing the marquee of her guests, chatting with old friends and neighbours had taken a lot more time and energy than she expected.

She spied her ex, Fintan Callaghan, in the exiting line of guests. She still couldn't make up her mind about him. Stalker or not? Yes, he was wound a little tight, but he'd never been cruel – to animals or humans – when she knew him. Could he really have changed that much?

Fintan caught her gaze and stared back at her intently, making Jenny recall how he'd held her hand earlier, as if he never wanted to let it go. He'd been like that when they were dating all those years ago – clingy; more invested in the relationship than she was. That was one reason why she'd finished with him. Well, that, and the fact that they were fourteen and nothing lasts forever when you're that age – it just feels like it.

Before she could point him out to Richard, see whether he was, indeed, the man who had confronted him yesterday, Fintan inclined his head towards her, slipping quickly away.

Jenny watched him disappear, knowing she avoided Fintan now because he reminded her of a time in her life that she wanted to forget. If she hadn't finished with him, got in with that older crowd . . . She put a brake on her thoughts. Today, even with everything that was going on – *especially* with everything that was going on – she wanted to bask in good memories and everyone, it seemed, had a story to tell – of her mum and dad, of her – and they weren't at all bad, not like she expected.

Inside, Jenny felt the first curl of hope. No one seemed to hate her, blame her, for what she'd done. None of them had mentioned that awful night, and there was no malice in their words, no guile on their faces, and she had looked – looked hard. She sagged against Richard in relief.

'You OK, my love?' Richard wrapped his arms around her.

Jenny leaned into him, absorbing his strength. 'Yes.' She smiled, before reaching up to cup his face with her hands. 'Most definitely yes.' She kissed him, and his lips tasted of fresh air, and lust, and love, and new beginnings.

'Ahem.'

Jenny and Richard broke apart to find Sergeant Carr and a trim, grey-suited man staring at them.

'How can we help you, Sergeant Carr?' Richard tensed, arm curling around Jenny's waist, holding her close.

'We're sorry to interrupt,' the suited man said, not looking the least bit sorry. 'My name is Pat O'Shaughnessy and I'm the Scene Investigative Officer. We need to speak to you and your wife again.'

'Seriously? We've told you all we can. My wife and I would like to—'

'Have you found Sean? Mr O'Hare,' Tina approached with the others in tow.

Sergeant Carr, his face pale, answered. 'I regret to inform you all that a body has been found in Wishers Woods.'

'What?' Jenny recoiled as if struck, holding a hand to her chest. At her side, Tina stiffened.

'Who?' Richard asked, and Jenny could feel him bracing himself. She did the same, awaiting the garda's response.

'We can't give out that information until—'

'Is it Sean?' Richard shouted. 'Just tell me, for God's sake. Is it Sean?'

'No, the body isn't Mr O'Hare, but,' Sergeant Carr added as everyone sagged with relief, 'we did find Mr O'Hare badly injured in the woods.'

'But he's OK? He's alive?'

'He's alive,' Tom told Tina.

'Oh, thank God!' Richard buried his face in his hands. 'Thank God.'

Jenny held her husband; felt his shoulders shake beneath her hands. She was shaking herself. She pressed her head to his. 'This can't be real? What the hell is happening?'

'Small towns. Told you, they're a breeding ground for serial killers.'

'Not helping, Ita.'

Only immediate family remained inside the tent. The last of the wedding guests could be heard outside, bemoaning the lateness of the bus to ferry them back to Innisard.

'The body you found, is it . . . is it Dermot?'

The voice was so unlike Evil's normal strident tone that it took Jenny a second to realise it was indeed her aunt speaking. Guilt flared. How could she have forgotten her cousin was missing, too. So caught up in celebrating the fact that Sean was OK, none of them had thought to ask who the body was.

They all waited for Sergeant Carr to speak, but it was the other garda, the one in charge, O'Shaughnessy, who said, 'No. I can categorically state that the second body is *not* your son, Mrs . . .' He looked to Tom for the name.

'Gibson,' Tom supplied.

'Oh, thank the good Lord,' Evil said. 'Dermot's OK.'

'That's not quite what I said,' O'Shaughnessy told her firmly. 'Your son is being held on suspicion of murder. Maybe attempted murder, too.'

'He's being what?' Evil gasped.

'Did Dermot hurt Sean?' Tina asked at the same time.

'Undetermined,' Sergeant Carr answered Tina first.

'I need to see Sean. Was he taken to Saint Mary Margaret's?'

'Tina, please.' Evil stopped her niece with a trembling hand. 'We need your help. Dermot needs your help.'

Jenny could see how torn Tina was; how desperately she wanted to see Sean, make sure he was OK. But Sean was in hospital, surrounded by professionals who would take very good care of him. Their cousin Dermot had no one. He needed a professional, too. And Tina was the only one available.

Jenny could tell the second Tina made up her mind, could see it in the tightening of her cousin's face. Even if it turned out that Dermot had hurt Sean, Tina would help him. It was just who she was. Tina believed everyone deserved a defence. But God help Dermot if he was responsible for Sean's injuries. Jenny was sure her cousin would tear him apart with her bare hands. And Tina knew enough about the law to do it *and* get away with it.

There was movement on the path leading to the marquee from the woods, and a group of gardaí appeared. At the same time the clank and thrum of the bus returning to pick up the disgruntled wedding guests sounded.

'That's our cue,' O'Shaughnessy told Tom Carr. 'We have a full-scale search to conduct, and judging by that sky, not much time to do it.'

'Before you go.' Jenny held out her hand. 'Is it possible . . . is our stalker linked to all this? Have you discovered any more about him?'

'Seeing as you failed to file a report, that's kind of hard to do,' O'Shaughnessy said. 'But we are taking it on board for our investigation.'

Which meant he wasn't.

Jenny looked at Sergeant Carr. 'I told you this guy would hurt someone else.'

Tom stared at her, his face closed and hard.

None of them were taking the stalker angle seriously, which meant they were looking at them – her and Richard. God! This was surreal. How had her wedding day gone from the happiest day of her life to this total utter nightmare?

Chapter Forty-One

'Tom, wait up.' Tina hurried after Sergeant Carr, stopping him just outside the marquee, where the wedding guests waited to board the bus to take them back to Innisard.

'I'm in a bit of a hurry,' Tom told her, but slowed his pace, letting O'Shaughnessy and his men move ahead of them. 'What's up?'

'I, er . . . I wanted to—'

'Not like you to be so coy, Ms Connors. That dress is definitely rubbing off on you.' He seemed to take pity on her. 'You want to know more about Sean O'Hare's condition, don't you?'

'That's not actually why . . . Yes,' she said finally. 'How bad is it, Tom?'

'I can't lie, Tina. It's bad.' He placed a hand on her arm. 'But where there's life, there's hope. Now I've got to—'

'It wasn't actually Sean I wanted to talk to you about.'

'Oh?'

'Can you tell me who the dead body is?'

Tom looked at her quizzically. 'You know I can't give out that information, Tina. The family haven't been informed yet.'

'I know. I don't want to get you into trouble, or do anything you're not comfortable with, but what if I say a name, and if I'm wrong, you can tell me so.'

'And if you're not?'

'Then you still won't have said anything?'

'Why's this so important to you?' Tom eyed her quizzically. 'You looking to get a step ahead in your defence of your cousin Dermot?'

'Something like that.' Tina held his gaze, hoping he wouldn't see the lie on her face.

'Carr!' O'Shaughnessy's voice thundered down the path. 'What the blazes is keeping you?'

Tom stared at Tina a moment longer. 'Say your name,' he said at last. 'And do it quickly. I have to go.'

'Pete McAvoy, AKA Pretty Pete.'

Tina had no need for Tom to say anything, the shock on his face was enough.

'You and I need to talk, Ms Connors,' Tom told her. 'And soon.' He glared at her, before turning on his heel and hurrying to catch up with the other gardaí.

'You're not the only one who needs to talk,' Tina muttered as she re-entered the marquee, her eyes searching for her dad's huge frame. 'What have you done, Dad? What the hell have you done?'

Chapter Forty-Two

After Sergeant Carr and the grey-suited O'Shaughnessy left, Jenny barely had a chance to draw breath before her aunt Gert, who had been unusually quiet while the latest drama had unfolded, stood. 'I need to say something.' She cleared her throat, looking ill at ease. 'It's important. I—'

'Oh, Aunt Gert.' Jenny threw her arms around the woman, knocking her fascinator askew. 'This is just so . . . awful.'

'I fear it may be about to get worse.'

'Worse?' Jenny drew back, staring at her aunt. 'The gardaí have just told us that they've found a body in the woods and Richard's best man was attacked; he's seriously injured, may even die, and they've arrested Dermot. I'm not sure for which crime. Maybe both? How can it possibly get worse?'

'Hush, child,' Gert told her. 'The Lord never sends more than you can handle. Speaking of which, I fear it's . . . what is the saying you young ones use? Time to put your big girl pants on?'

If Jenny hadn't been so freaked, she would have smiled at the phrase, especially linked in the same sentence with the Lord.

Ita wasn't so restrained, snorting loudly, 'Yeah, we so use that phrase every day, and I really wanna see those "big girl pants". They like bloomers? Got frills and all?'

'We don't have time for this.' Gert tugged Jenny's arm. 'Can I talk to you? Alone.'

'Alone?' Confused, Jenny gave in to her aunt's demands, moving away from Richard and Ita. 'What's up, Aunt Gert?'

'I honestly don't know how to tell you,' Gert said. 'But I've found out something that I think you should know. About your stalker—'

'Jenny. Jenny! Help!' Evil's voice rang out, shrill and frightened. 'It's Dana. The baby. Something's wrong.'

'Oh, no.' Gert's ashen face paled even further. 'Darn it.' She raised her eyes heavenward in apology at the curse, taking a deep breath. 'The Lord, as always, works in mysterious ways. What I have to tell you can wait,' she told Jenny. 'You need to make sure Dana and that baby are OK. That girl can't take any more heartache. Not now.'

'You sure?' Jenny asked, worried. Gert seemed unusually upset.

Gert hesitated, only for a second. 'Yes. Go. Go. But when you're done, we need to talk. I mean it,' she said, grabbing Jenny's hand. 'The second Dana and the baby are OK, you come find me. Promise me?'

'I promise.' Jenny kissed the papery skin.

'Good. I'll get someone to phone for an ambulance.' Gert hurried off, purple fascinator bobbing.

'Jenny!' Evil's voice rose in volume. 'Hurry!'

Jenny rushed to where the young garda she'd met earlier at the Devil's Teeth was gently lowering her cousin Dana to the floor, his face sweating and red with exertion.

'I found her outside. Think she's been there a while. She's not in a good way.'

The second Jenny saw Dana's pale face and the blood between her legs, her heart sank. 'Ita.' She had no need to say more. With a deft hand and a firm voice, Ita moved everyone back, leaving only Dana's mum, Evil, who refused to leave.

One look at her aunt's resolute face told Jenny arguing would be futile. 'If you're staying, you do what I say when I say it, nothing more.'

'How dare—'

'No time to argue. Agree, or go.' Jenny knelt next to her cousin, automatically checking her pulse. Much too fast.

'Get away from me. I don't want your help.' Dana slapped at Jenny's hands. 'Anyone but you. Don't touch me.'

What on earth? Jenny had no idea what she'd done to her cousin to cause this kind of reaction. She hadn't seen her in years and had barely seen her since the wedding itself. But now wasn't the time to pull that particular thread.

'There's no one else, Dana. It's me, or you're on your own.'

A groan swallowed any answer Dana might have made as another contraction struck.

'I'm here to help.' Jenny kept her voice soft, calming. 'Tell me what's happening.'

Dana's eyes flashed anger, quickly replaced by fear. 'Don't . . . feel so . . . good.'

'How far along are you?'

'Thirty-seven weeks.' The words were ground out. 'So close. Only fourteen days to go.'

'Fourteen days?' That didn't make sense to Jenny. Full term, forty weeks, left three weeks to go, twenty-one days. *Oh, no.* 'Dana, did you have a C-section scheduled?'

Dana nodded.

'You didn't tell me that.' Evil stared at her daughter. 'What's wrong? Why do you have—'

Jenny's gentle hands were already feeling along Dana's abdomen. 'Baby's breech,' she said to Ita.

'Yeah,' Dana panted. 'Doc couldn't turn it . . . need section.'

Jenny's heart sank further. This wasn't good. Dana needed to be in a hospital, but the ambulance was at least twenty minutes away and, judging by Dana's contractions, they didn't have that long.

Chapter Forty-Three

There were perks to being the sergeant in a small station like Innisard. Even better perks to being on the good side of Paula – the civilian station manager – who had given Tom the heads-up that the conference O'Shaughnessy had invited him to was convening now, not in an hour's time as O'Shaughnessy had told him.

He and Pat might have shared a moment in the woods, saving Sean O'Hare's life, but Tom knew O'Shaughnessy would revert to type; holding a grudge over something that had happened – or, in O'Shaughnessy's case, not happened – ten years ago.

Tom went directly to the station. Thanks to a few shortcuts, known only to locals, he got there before the plainclothes. He entered the conference room and plonked himself down on a stool near one of the windows, knowing better than to take a seat at the table, leaving them for the plainclothes. He took out a toothpick and, chewing happily, went over his notes while he waited, which wasn't long.

O'Shaughnessy strolled into the room, followed by his men, notepads out, ready to work.

'Carr.' O'Shaughnessy halted. 'You're here early.'

As are you, you prick.

But all Tom said was, 'Yes, sir. Early bird, and all that.'

'Indeed. Indeed.' Seemingly nonplussed at being outmanoeuvred, O'Shaughnessy slapped the file he was carrying onto the tabletop. 'Right, let's get to work. We have three victims; I think it's about time we got ourselves some suspects. First up, do we have the original murder report on the Filmore family?'

'Getting it, Guv.' Fitzpatrick, a tubby man with ruddy cheeks, gave him the thumbs up.

'OK. Suspects?'

'No one sticks out,' Tom said. 'Although I can't pin down Cap Byrne's alibi. He's an uncle of the bride and a man who lives well beyond his means. Works in a local shop, wife doesn't work at all, yet he owns his house, a nice fishing boat and a vintage car. We suspect him of doing a bit of smuggling, but he's a wily old bugger, and so far, there's nothing solid we can pin on him.'

'A veritable mastermind, huh? And right here in sleepy Innisard. You must have your hands full, Carr.' Titters around the room. When Tom didn't react, O'Shaughnessy continued. 'Gobs of money, no visible income . . . could be a drug connection, which leads to a whole other cesspit of nasty shite. You need to ask Cap Byrne a few more questions – and this time get the answers we need, there's a good lad.'

Tom tried not to bristle at the 'good lad'.

'Right. Moving on,' O'Shaughnessy turned his back on Tom, signalling that he was done with him. 'Means. Motive. And opportunity. That's what we need to nail down. Let's start with the first vic. If John Filmore killed his entire family, as his brother says, then why was he free to come here and get bloody murdered on my patch? Why wasn't the fecker in jail?'

'I'm guessing the fingerprint thing didn't help, Guv,' a slim man with a mop of tight blond curls said.

'Check into it, Curran,' O'Shaughnessy told him. 'I want that murder file on my desk now. If not sooner.'

'On it, Guv.' Curran all but ran out of the room.

'OK, pathologist puts the time of death for our first vic between the hours of two and four a.m. So, victim one and his brother survived a family annihilator when they were seventeen. Only for one brother to be beaten and stabbed' – he checked Winston's postmortem notes – 'twenty-six times – can anyone say overkill? – to death in our fair Emerald Isle seventeen years later. I don't know whether that's symmetry or design, but it's something to think about.'

'Have to agree, Guv.' A man in a suit and tie almost the same colour as O'Shaughnessy's nodded. 'In cases of familicide, the last one standing has gotta be the doer. So, I guess that means our suspect pool has narrowed to one,' he said eagerly.

Jeez, all the poor guy needed was a collar and lead, Tom thought. The man obviously had a bad case of hero worship.

'We follow the evidence, Rooney,' O'Shaughnessy told the fawning man, but Tom could tell he was revelling in the opportunity to instruct. 'Could easily be whoever killed the family is trying to finish the job and the last one standing – Dr Richard Durkin in this case – is merely a victim waiting to happen.'

'Which would feed into the bride and groom's report of a stalker,' Tom offered.

'Except there was no report, Guv.' Rooney shot Tom an aggrieved look.

'I think you'll find they reported an altercation between Richard Durkin and an unknown person. Happened yesterday when he arrived in Innisard.'

'Let's cover all the bases. Malloy?' O'Shaughnessy pointed to a muscular man with a clean-shaven head and tiny grey goatee. 'Check with the gardaí back in Dublin

– see if our newly-weds' neighbours reported anything suspicious over the last few months. And dig deeper into our good doctor. A guy who had the foresight to change his name – and do it without being caught – to build a second life, that's a guy I want to keep my eye on, whether it turns out he's the doer or another potential victim. And let's not forget that the best man was his alibi. With Sean O'Hare out of the picture for the foreseeable – maybe forever – that alibi goes away.'

'Guv.'

'Right, second victim.' O'Shaughnessy looked at Rooney, who quickly supplied the name along with a folder.

'Pete McAvoy, Guv.'

O'Shaughnessy flicked through the file. 'Also goes by the name Pretty Pete, I see.' He held out Pete's mugshot to the group. 'Ugly bastard. They sure have a sense of humour here in Innisard. Any link to John Filmore or Richard Durkin?'

'None that we can find, Guv. Might be a leap, but could he be the unknown person who accosted the groom?'

'Worth checking. Let's get a photo to Richard Durkin, see if he can ID this Pretty Pete.'

'I think the link is more than likely going to come with Dermot Gibson,' Tom offered. 'Dermot's a known drug user. Word on the street is he owes the local drug dealer, Big Benny, a lot of money, and Pete McAvoy is Benny's muscle guy.'

'Aren't you forgetting someone, Carr?' Rooney said. At Tom's querying look, he added, 'The bride's uncle, Hugh Connors, has a link to this Big Benny and, by association, Pete McAvoy.'

'What's this?' O'Shaughnessy asked. 'Hugh Connors . . . related to that blasted lawyer Tina Connors?'

'Her father. But that link dates back to when Hugh was little more than a child,' Tom said. 'Those records are sealed,' he added pointedly. But he shifted uncomfortably in his seat, remembering Tina asking him to name their victim in the woods. She was the one who came up with Pete McAvoy's name. Maybe Hugh's link to Big Benny wasn't as old as they thought.

'Records might be sealed, but those tats of his tell their own story,' Rooney argued.

'Agreed. So what's the story?' O'Shaughnessy asked Tom.

'Typical thing. Rebellious not-quite-teen looking to make easy money, be one of the big guys. And the guy was big, even back then. Benny took him on as a runner. Lasted a few years before Hugh got out and stayed out. He runs a farm now, with his wife. They're good people.'

'Noted, but I still want him checked out,' O'Shaughnessy told his men.

'Something else, Guv,' Rooney said quickly. 'When the information came up about Hugh Connors, I decided to look closer into the bride's family and I found something.'

Tom saw one of the other plainclothes men grimace and wondered just who had 'found' the information that Rooney was taking credit for.

'Dermot Gibson's sister, Dana Gibson-Mayfield, failed accountant, went bankrupt by all accounts. Not that you'd know it the way she spends. She's another family member living well beyond her means.'

'The woman is eight months pregnant,' Tom protested. 'And the money came from her dead husband. Life insurance, I believe.'

'So, she earned it on her back.'

Tom softly hissed in distaste. What was this guy Rooney's problem?

'Funny,' Rooney smiled slyly. 'There's no marriage certificate to support that.'

Damn. Tom couldn't hide his surprise.

'Good work, Rooney. Least someone is on the ball.' O'Shaughnessy couldn't hide his satisfaction. 'No one loves desperate, bankrupt accountants more than shady drug lords. This Dana and her unknown income could be linked to Pete McAvoy and, by default, to Big Benny through her brother and uncle Hugh. And if Carr ever gets a move on, we may also prove that a second uncle, Cap Byrne, could also be involved. Talk about keeping it in the family.'

Tom ignored the laughter. He'd been totally taken in by the fake marriage – not an uncommon practice in rural Ireland, where pregnancy outside wedlock was frowned upon, even in this day and age. The Gibsons had obviously made up a story about a dead husband. However, Rooney was right about one thing: imaginary husbands couldn't leave huge life insurance payouts. So, how had Dana attained the big house, the money she flashed around town?

And did it have anything to do with the real father of her baby?

'Anyone have a drug link to the best man?' O'Shaughnessy asked.

Head shakes all around.

'From what we can gather,' Tom said, 'Sean O'Hare is clean. No drug convictions, no DUIs. Guy's never been interviewed in connection with any crime.'

'So, with vic one we have a link to an old crime and with vic two, Pete McAvoy, we have a link to a new one – drugs in this case. Could drugs have had anything to do with what happened to the Filmores back in' – O'Shaughnessy checked his notes – '2005?'

'Richard Durkin says no, but without the original report, it can't be discounted.'

'Hmmm. Would be great if the dead brother was into drugs? Tie things up nice and neat, that would. OK, anyone who can't be eliminated becomes a person of interest. Speaking of which, how's it going with the house-to-house. Carr?'

'Still working on it.'

O'Shaughnessy stared at him expectantly. If he was waiting for Tom to say Guv, he'd be waiting a long time. Tom and O'Shaughnessy stared at one another, the seconds growing uncomfortable; feet shuffled, someone coughed.

'Tell your men to get their finger out, Carr, there's a good lad, bring in off-duty if needed. It's all hands on deck at this point.'

If he called him good lad one more time . . . 'Will do.' Tom closed his notebook.

'We need to keep a tight lid on this,' O'Shaughnessy told the group. 'The press is already out in force; a bride and groom finding a body on their wedding day – total catnip. The second they get wind the groom and our first victim are related they'll be swooping in like vultures. Throw in a second murder and the attempted murder of the best man – total shit storm. McNamara.' He pointed to a tall man in a well-pressed suit, pristine white shirt and blue tie, with expertly coiffed hair.

The media liaison officer nodded. 'On it, Guv. I'll steer the media where we want them to go. But they'll want you front and centre at some point?'

A curl of reluctance on O'Shaughnessy's face. 'Yes, yes.' He waved his hand. 'Just give me a time and place. Make it short, five minutes tops, and no questions. OK?'

'OK.' McNamara left the room, working his phone.

Tom had to give it to O'Shaughnessy. The man might be a prick, but he was no glory-hound. Unlike his little lapdog Rooney.

He reminded himself that there was no place in an investigation for pettiness. There was a killer in his town. Someone callous enough, cold enough, to murder two men and bash another man's head in. Their job was to stop him and they needed to work together to do that.

And they needed to do it quickly, before anyone else was hurt.

Chapter Forty-Four

Sean O'Hare is still alive!

Failure grates, stings. This should have ended in the woods, all my problems solved.

I should have made sure the best man was dead, but the gardaí had been closing in and I'd been too quick to deal the killing blow.

Careless.

However, Sean is in a coma. It will have to do. If, on the very slim chance he wakes up, I can always pay him a visit in the hospital. He'll be too weak to fight back.

No need to panic.

Not yet.

And yet, a tremor of anxiety ignites. I may have another problem. Someone is on to me, although I'm not sure how. Did I say or do something to make them suspicious? Could they have seen me leaving the woods?

I am juggling too many balls; one is bound to drop at some point. But I haven't come this far to fail. No way a bunch of village idiots are going to take me down. I have beaten better than them before, and I will again.

However, in order to do that, I need to play the long game; confuse and misdirect. A little nudge here, a whispered word there.

Maybe even another death – or two.

I can do this. I just need to stick to the plan.

No one else will be allowed to interfere. If they do . . .

I have no problem adding them to my body count.

Chapter Forty-Five

Gert watched Jenny and Ita as they tended to a clearly distressed Dana.

Dana! Gert closed her eyes in prayer that her niece would deliver her baby safely. Judging by the look on Jenny and her friend Ita's face, things weren't exactly textbook, but she had faith in them. In the Lord.

The young garda with the big feet had been helpful, radioing for an ambulance, saying it would be quicker than her phoning. She only hoped he was right and that it would be in time.

To have been so close to telling Jenny . . .

'Lord, I'm not one to doubt your methods, but I really do have to question your timing,' Gert muttered as she made her way to the side door of the marquee. She needed air, a moment to herself. Her brother Hugh would keep things under control – or as much as anyone could where Evie was concerned.

Gert pushed the door open and stepped out into the wind and rain, breathing deeply, surprised to find she was trembling.

'Seems your big unmasking will have to wait,' a voice said.

The person she'd seen slipping from Wishers Woods was waiting for her outside. There was no longer any doubt in her mind. This was Jenny's stalker. No joy in knowing she was right. Gert could have kicked herself for leaving the security of the marquee, but she couldn't bear to be in Evie's company a second longer. Dana was the one in labour, fighting for her and her baby's lives, but Evie was doing all the complaining as usual, her constant wailing and recriminations tiring, in what had already been a desperately tiring day.

'Oh, will it?' Gert nudged her glasses up her nose, facing the figure, unafraid. 'I can just step inside and—'

'I don't think so.'

Gert's arm was taken in a steely grip. She tried to pull free, but the hand held firm, fingers cruelly tight around her thin forearm. Pain radiated into her shoulder, across her chest. 'Let me go.' She hated how weak her voice sounded.

'I don't think so,' the voice said again, tugging her away from the safety of the marquee; the smell of drink and sweat, and Evie's shrill voice fading away.

Rain splattered Gert's glasses, blinding her; the wind catching her stupid feather in her hat-thing, ripping it free, chilling her extremities, even as her insides froze as she realised the precarious predicament she was in.

Gert had never known true fear before, but she did now. She tried to hide it. 'I demand you let me go,' she squirmed. 'Let. Me. Go.'

A quick movement ahead and to her left caught her eye; police tape flapping in the wind atop the entry to the Devil's Teeth. Surely the gardaí would have left someone to protect the scene. Gert knew it was her only hope. She opened her mouth to scream, but the stalker, as if reading her mind, placed his hand roughly over mouth.

'I can't let you do that,' he said, dragging her towards Maggie's Point, veering off the path as they grew closer, taking her towards the lighthouse keeper's hut, where Gert had found Dana such a short time ago.

Gert had given up resisting. Her arm was throbbing where the figure held it, her heart racing as she panted, trying to keep up with the furious pace. The face in front of her held no mercy; hard, cruel and devoid of emotion.

'What was it that gave me away? Tell me.' He shook Gert, voice harshening. 'I need to know. What was it?'

He didn't know how he'd slipped up. Gert would have smiled, if she'd had the energy. Her niece was clever. Gert had to believe Jenny would discover the same thing she had, unmask the killer.

'Tell me, damn it. Tell me.'

Gert didn't fear death – and she knew it was near – the Lord would be there to lead her. But she had a promise to keep.

A promise she needed to . . .

Pain, like she'd never experienced before caused Gert to fall to her knees. *No, Lord, not yet. I'm not ready yet, I need to . . .*

I need . . .

To—

The pain was all-consuming now; stealing her breath, her hope.

Forgive me, child of my heart. Oh, Jenny. I wish I could be there to help you, save you.

Silence was Gert's only weapon; the last gift she could give her beloved niece, and so she relaxed, let the pain take her, sweep her towards her reckoning with her beloved Lord.

Chapter Forty-Six

Jenny had gone from bride, to niece, to seemingly hated cousin and midwife in a blink of an eye. As Dana's situation worsened, she ordered Evil away, uncaring of her aunt's spew of angry invectives about Jenny's youth and how she'd killed her parents and how she wasn't about to let her – the devil's spawn – kill her daughter and unborn grandchild, too. Ita raised an eyebrow at Evil's performance, but didn't ask any questions. Questions, Jenny knew, would come later. Fortunately, her uncle Hugh stepped in, shepherding his sister away. Jenny was oblivious as she and Ita stared at one other over Dana's head.

'Damn.'

Jenny wanted to curse, too. 'We need to try another ECV,' she told Ita.

Jenny knew Dana's doctor had probably already tried an external cephalic version to turn the baby, but with the ambulance miles away, there was no choice but to try again. Breech babies usually turned themselves in the womb before birth. On the odd occasion when they didn't, a C-section was scheduled to make sure mother and baby were OK. No such luxury here.

'This is going to be uncomfortable,' Jenny told Dana.

'More than labour?'

Jenny grimaced. 'Not going to lie, they're both gonna hurt. You ready, Cuz?'

'Just get on with it,' Dana snapped. 'Do what you have to do.'

Jenny took no offence at Dana's tone. Childbirth brought a person down to their basest level, erasing polite civility. Not that Dana had much civility to begin with – especially, for some reason, where Jenny was concerned.

She couldn't help but recall Gert's worry about Dana's pregnancy. The old girl had been right – as always – which made her wonder what Gert had wanted to talk to her about. She'd looked so upset, so . . . old. Gert had always seemed invincible, but for the first time, Jenny realised Gert was only human, and an incredibly fragile human at that. The thought was lost as another contraction struck and Dana screamed.

Time to act. 'I'm sorry,' Jenny said, placing her hand on her cousin's abdomen. 'I may hurt you, but I really need to do this.'

'Then do it,' Dana panted. 'Don't just talk about it.'

Jenny shut off her emotions, her training taking over. Even though she knew she would be causing her cousin pain, Jenny pressed harder, focused on trying to manipulate the baby back into position even as it struggled to be born. 'Almost . . . there,' she told Dana, 'Just a . . . few more . . .'

'I need to push,' Dana screamed.

'Don't,' Jenny ordered. 'Don't push. Breathe. Just breathe. I'm almost . . .' Jenny firmly cupped and pressed Dana's stomach, twisting and turning the baby, desperate to manoeuvre it into position. This should be done in a hospital, under supervision, with back-up. She was out of her depth. And then she felt the baby move. 'Hold it. Hold it.' Finally, Jenny had the baby where she thought it needed to be – or as close as she figured she was going to get. 'Push now,' she told Dana.

'Oh, my God!' Dana pushed, strained. 'No one said it would be this hard.'

'Anything worth waiting for is usually hard. But I'm here, with you.' Jenny patted Dana's thigh. They were in an area next to the stage, blocked off by a hastily arranged circle of chairs, draped with tablecloths, coats and whatever came to hand, to preserve Dana's modesty. Ita had placed black bin bags under Dana, and procured plastic gloves from somewhere, before positioning herself behind Dana, supporting her back. 'You're not alone,' Jenny told her cousin. 'I'm here. Ita is here; we won't leave you.'

'But I *am* alone. My partner . . .'

Jenny levered herself up slightly from her stooped position until she could look Dana in the eye. 'I should have said earlier . . . I'm so sorry about your husband. It must be so difficult for you. This should be the happiest time of your life—'

'Like today should be yours?' Dana gasped as another wave of pain hit her. 'Guess we were both misled, huh?'

Jenny wasn't sure what Dana meant. Yes, Richard had misled her about his brother – and his surname – but Dana's husband was dead. Maybe it was a poetic kind of misleading . . . he had promised to love her forever, be with her forever? 'Dana, I—'

'Shit!' Dana screamed as her abdomen contracted again. 'Don't you get it, *Cuz*, there is no saintly rich dead husband, that was all Mum's idea. I mean, how could she let her friends and family know that her daughter was having a child out of wedlock? Christ!' The epitaph was the result of another contraction. 'This bloody hurts.'

'I know,' Jenny soothed, 'but you're doing great.' Her worried fingers checked the position of the baby. It looked like it was finally head down and everything was progressing nicely. Ita had arranged towels and a basin of hot water from the bar area, along with a pair of scissors and a shoelace she'd sterilised with alcohol to cut and tie the umbilical cord.

'I loved him, you know,' Dana gasped. 'I'm not some floozy homewrecker. I really loved the guy; thought he was the one.' The plump features twisted with sorrow and something close to hatred. 'He said he loved me, but he lied.' Her breath was now coming in shallow pants. 'He. Loved. Someone. Else. More.'

'Sounds like you're well rid of him. What a tosser.'

Dana laughed, looked like she wanted to say more, but seemed to think better of it, saying instead, 'I . . . loved him. So much. I was. So stupid,' she gasped, crying harder now with pain and grief. 'So stupid. Women are so stupid.'

'No, you're bloody not.' Jenny squeezed her cousin's knee. 'Don't you ever apologise for falling in love. Don't you dare,' she said, wondering where the anger came from. But she knew. She'd seen too many girls, too many women, shamed into denying their love, sometimes even their babies. 'You loved him, and you will love this child, and you will both be loved by all of us. You hear me, Dana? You just hang on and we'll get through this, and you know the first two things I'm going to do?'

'What?' Dana gasped, sweat dripping down her brow.

'First, I'm bloody going to strangle Evil, and then I'm going to get DJ Joe to announce to the whole of Innisard that my cousin Dana GIBSON – no double barrel – has just given birth to the most gorgeous baby EVER. You hear me, Dana?'

'I hear you. I hope you still feel the same way when you tell them who the father is—' The last was lost as another contraction peaked and Dana moaned.

'Don't talk, Dana. Save your strength.'

'Christ's sake, Jenny, are you totally stupid? It's Richard. Richard is the father.'

'What?' Jenny froze, sure she'd misheard. 'My Richard?'

'Yes. Owwww.' Another scream. 'Why do you think I . . . fainted at the chapel this morning? When I saw him there, I couldn't—'

Ita looked at Jenny in disbelief, but Jenny was grappling with her own emotions. Richard, her Richard, the father of Dana's baby? No way. No fecking way!

Her gaze shot to the crowd, found her husband. He looked concerned, worried, but no more than anyone else. Definitely not expectant father worried.

But why would Dana lie about something so important?

'Are you OK?' Ita mouthed, softly from her position behind Dana.

Jenny nodded. Whatever game Dana was playing, she couldn't let it affect her focus. Dana was her patient. She – and her baby – were the only consideration here. So Jenny put a lid on her questions, her emotions, concentrating on her cousin as another scream rent the air.

'OK, Dana. With the next contraction, I need you to push.'

'Is that . . . all . . . you . . . can . . . say?' Dana panted.

'The only thing that matters right now is your baby. Agreed?'

Dana, after a second, nodded.

'Then I need you to push. That's it. Push.'

Ita joined in. 'You're doing great, Dana. You're almost there. Just one more push. Take a deep breath, that's it. Push. *Push* with all your might.'

'I can't do it . . . it's too hard.' Dana was tiring. They could hear it in her voice.

'You can do this,' Jenny told her cousin, back in full midwife mode. 'You've come this far. You're not a quitter, not Dana Gibson. And neither is your baby. This little tyke refused to turn until he knew his momma needed him to. You're not going to give up on him now.'

'Him? It's a boy?'

'Sorry, just a turn of phrase. I'm a superhero midwife, but I don't have X-ray vision. Boy. Girl. This baby wants to be born and it's coming whether you want it to or not.'

'Bloody right it's coming. Jesus, that hurt. Please tell me you have some drugs hidden in your wedding gown?' When Jenny shook her head, Dana groaned. 'The one time my brother could actually be helpful and the bastard's not here. Too busy getting himself arrested.'

'Sorry, Cuz, like it or not, you're doing this au naturel, but you're almost there. I just need one more big push.'

'I can't. I—'

'You totally can.' Ita reached forward to grab Dana's hand and helped her ride the next contraction. 'We're with you. Every woman here' – Ita gestured to where Dana's mother and aunts stood – 'is with you. Now PUSH.'

And Dana, as if galvanised by Ita's words, gritted her teeth and bore down, pushing as hard as she could.

'That's it. That's it.' I can see the head. 'You're almost there, Dana. You're doing great. A few more pushes, that's all I need.'

'You promise? A few more and I'm done?'

Jenny was quite happy to agree. The baby was almost there, she just needed to— 'Stop! Don't push, Dana.'

'What?' Dana, already mid-push, froze. 'But . . . I can't. I need to . . . I have to—'

'Breathe,' Ita said calmly behind her. 'Focus on your breathing. Huh. Huh.' She made a huffing noise, motioning to Dana to follow suit. 'That's it. You're doing great. Jenny?'

'Nuchal cord.' The words were clipped as Jenny worked to free the umbilical cord, which was wrapped around the baby's neck, strangling it.

'What does that mean?' Dana screamed, trying to look to where Jenny was working. 'Is my baby OK? What's happening? Don't hurt my baby, Jenny, it's not its fault that your husband is a lying, cheating bastard.'

'Jenny is just helping your baby into the world,' Ita said calmly.

'But I need to push. Oh, God! I need to push.' Dana groaned as another contraction hit. 'Please—'

Jenny didn't answer. Ita was more than capable of calming and comforting Dana; her focus was the baby now, and only the baby. They'd been lucky with the ECV, the baby turning in time to be delivered, but unfortunately the umbilical cord had caught around the baby's neck, cutting off its oxygen. The baby was strangling and she needed to free it.

Now!

Gently, carefully, Jenny eased her fingers under the slippery umbilical cord, loosening it until she could finally slip it over the baby's head, knowing every second meant extra agony for her cousin. Finally, she had the cord looped free. 'Push, Dana. One more push, that should do it.'

Dana groaned from deep in her belly, straining, and her baby was finally free. 'What is it?' she asked eagerly. 'Is it a boy? A girl?'

Jenny didn't answer, couldn't, frantically working on the infant.

The silence grew.

'Where's my baby? I want my baby,' Dana wailed. 'What's happening?'

'It's OK,' Ita consoled Dana. 'Your baby just needs a little help to breathe.'

'Jenny?' Dana tried to rise. 'Is my baby OK?' she began to cry. 'Tell me my baby's OK?'

The newborn was turning blue, but Jenny didn't panic. Calmly, she checked the baby's mouth and nose, clearing them of any mucus left from the birth canal. *Come on. Come on*, she chanted. *Breathe, little one. Breathe.*

But the baby remained still and quiet.

Jenny bent her head, mouth covering the child's mouth and nose. Mindful of the baby's tiny lungs, she breathed lightly. Once. Twice. *Come on. Come on.*

And just like that, the baby cried. The most welcome sound in the whole entire world.

'My baby. Give me my baby.' Dana was crying.

Jenny deftly tied off and cut the umbilical cord, before wrapping the infant in a towel. 'Say hello to your new son.' She laid the baby on her cousin's chest, trying not to look at the baby, to see if it had her husband's eyes, his dimple . . .

'You *do* have X-ray eyes.' Ita's grin was half-hearted. Dana's utterance heavy in the air between them. 'Never gets old, though, does it?' she said, watching mother and baby bond.

Jenny shook her head. 'It really never does,' she said, her eyes searching for Richard in the crowd.

Chapter Forty-Seven

Jenny and Ita stood outside and watched the ambulance leave with Dana and her new baby. They were alone for the moment, the rest of the family still inside the marquee, giving the new mother and baby space. As much as Jenny longed to see Richard, confront him about Dana's allegation, it felt the right moment to wrap up one of the bombshells that had been thrown at her this evening.

'Evil was right,' she told Ita, not looking at her. 'I killed my parents.'

'Jenny, you don't have to—'

'I know I don't. I want to.' It was true. Being back in Innisard, confronting old memories, old friends . . . it finally felt like the right time to face the past. To be honest. 'It's time, Ita, and I want to be the person I tell.'

'Then I would be honoured to listen.'

Ita wasn't her best friend for nothing; the acceptance in her voice was almost Jenny's undoing. She cleared her throat, unsure where to start, then figured where better than the beginning.

'I screwed up, pure and simple. I was a nightmare teen – no one more strong-willed or cruel than a pissed-off fourteen-year-old, huh?'

'Having been one myself, I can totally concur,' Ita said calmly.

'Yeah, well, I had no idea where all the anger came from, but the second I hit puberty . . . Pow! Getting wasted helped, until it didn't. Which is why my parents grounded me – I was grounded a lot back then,' Jenny said ruefully. 'This one night, I snuck out to go to a party.' For the first time, Jenny realised how similar her and Richard's backstories were . . . both sneaking out to a party with devastating consequences. 'Getting drunk was my way of getting back at them. Friday the thirteenth – God, can you believe the irony.'

Ita remained quiet, knowing it wasn't really a question.

'Well, the party got out of hand – as parties often do – and the gardaí were called. When they saw the state of us – most of us underage – they contacted our parents to come and collect us.'

Mum and Dad must have been so upset. Jenny could only imagine how they'd felt leaving the house in the early hours after discovering she'd snuck out.

She could only imagine it, because they'd never made it to pick her up.

'The roads were icy and the other car was going too fast.' The fact that the drunken teenager in the other car had escaped with only minor injuries felt like an insult. Her parents hadn't been so fortunate.

'Dad died instantly, Mum a few hours later.'

'Oh, Jenny.' Ita threw her arms around her. 'That must have been so awful.'

'It was.' How to explain the desolation of her loss, the grief. The guilt. She had shut down, going through the motions for the next four years until she could escape to college; escape what she thought were accusing stares and baleful whispers. 'I thought . . . I thought everyone blamed me,' she whispered into Ita's neck. 'Aunt Gert told me it wasn't my fault, that no one thought that way, but how could they not? My parents would never have been driving along that road if I hadn't—'

'Gert's right.' Ita pulled away from her to stare Jenny full in the eyes, so there would be no doubt about what she was saying. 'You were a child. It was an accident. Gert. Was. Right,' she said again, enunciating every word.

'She usually is,' Jenny said with a wry smile.

The need to talk to Gert, all her mother's siblings – Evil, Scuttlebutt, Hugh – was overwhelming; to finally ask for the forgiveness she needed so desperately from the people she'd wronged the most.

'Stop,' the voice in her head said. 'You already know you have it.'

Jenny slumped in Ita's arms as she recalled the welcome she had received the second she stepped foot back in Innisard, the wedding her aunts and cousins had arranged for her. And she finally understood that the problem wasn't getting her aunts and uncle to forgive her. It was that guilt and unresolved grief were stopping her from forgiving herself. The realisation came and went in an instant. Eighteen years of running, of guilt, distilled into seconds. Jenny clutched her stomach as if her internal pain had manifested itself into a physical one. In a way it had.

'You OK?' Ita asked, concerned.

'You know what, Ita. Evil's spiteful words and all the other crazy stuff notwithstanding, I think, for the first time in a very long time, I very well might be.'

'Evil is a nasty aul biddy,' Ita said, as if that was an end to it. And in her mind, it probably was.

'As for the other thing, what Dana said about Richard—'

'That's between you and your husband.' Ita held up her hands. 'But you know I'm here for you, if you need me?'

'I know.' The two friends hugged again before walking back into the marquee.

'You sure you're all right?'

'I'm fine,' Jenny told Ita, and it was true. Inside, she felt . . . immensely light, like she'd let go of a huge weight.

One down, two to go.

Ita scanned Jenny's face, seeming relieved by what she found. 'Right then, I'm in need of a very large glass of wine.'

'And I need to talk to Richard. I also need to find Gert. You see her anywhere?' Jenny looked around the sadly depleted marquee.

'Nope. But I promise if I see her at the bar, I'll send her right over.' A mischievous grin accompanied the words.

Jenny laughed at the thought of her pioneer aunt holding up the bar, then sobered as she recalled her aunt's insistent tone and grave expression earlier, knowing instinctively that she wasn't going to like whatever it was Gert wanted to tell her. How did she even know about the stalker? Then again, Gert was a canny old bird, Jenny thought as she sat and rubbed her tired feet. From her crumpled wedding dress to her borrowed slippers, she was bone-tired.

Big girl pants. Jenny figured she'd take a leaf out of her aunt's book and pull hers on, face whatever was to come head-on. First, though, she needed to find Richard.

As if conjured from her thoughts, her husband appeared. 'Have I told you lately how amazing you are?' Richard knelt by her side, taking her foot in his hand, massaging it gently.

Jenny couldn't help herself; she flinched. She might tell herself that she trusted her husband, knew he would never betray her, but there was still that little kernel of doubt in her mind. After all, he'd lied to her about his family, his real surname. She pulled her foot away.

'What's wrong?' Richard rose to his feet.

'I have to ask you something and I need you to answer me honestly, no lies.'

'OK.' Richard looked concerned at the seriousness of her voice.

'Have you ever been to Innisard before we came here to get married?'

'No. First time was with you yesterday. Why?'

'Have you ever met any of my relatives before today? My cousins?'

'Again, no.' Richard looked at her, confused. 'What's going on, Jenny?'

'Last question: did you leave Dublin at any point during the month of December last year?' Jenny had done the maths. Dana had to have got pregnant then. And while she didn't remember Richard leaving the city for any length of time, his clientele did span the whole of Southern Ireland and it wasn't unknown for him to travel to see a patient, if needed.

Richard, as if realising how important this was to her, considered carefully before answering. 'No. Hold on, yes. The first weekend in December. Galway. With you. Our engagement,' he said when she didn't answer.

'Apart from that.'

'I was kinda caught up in that Dempsey case. Spent most of November and December in court. You said you were going to be the first bride to divorce her husband before they even got married if I didn't make time for you. Remember?'

How could she have forgotten? It had been a harrowing case for Richard, a young boy and his sister caught up in a sex-trafficking ring. He hadn't left their flat for weeks on end, working on his report, determined to bring the guilty parties to justice. And he had. There was no way he could have been in Innisard at the same time.

Jenny released a breath she didn't realise she'd been holding, before telling him of Dana's accusations.

'What?' Richard reeled back. 'Jesus, Jenny, that's . . .' He stopped, lost for words. 'You didn't believe her, did you?' Before she could answer he dropped his head into his hands, groaning. 'I haven't really given you much cause to trust me, have I? But I swear to you, Jenny, I didn't tell you about my family because I wanted to protect you, that was the only reason.'

'I know.'

'I am not lying about this. I would *never* cheat on you.' Total sincerity in his voice. 'I love you. I—'

Jenny stopped him with a kiss. 'I know. I love you, too.'

'Oh, thank God.' Richard pulled her in for a hug. 'I don't know what I would have done if you hadn't believed me. Why would your cousin Dana tell such an awful lie?' he asked, bewildered.

'The thing is . . . I don't think Dana *is* lying.' Jenny put up a hand to forestall Richard's protest. 'She really believes you're her baby's daddy, which can only mean—'

'John!' Richard's shoulders slumped. 'That bastard impersonated me and impregnated your cousin. Jesus! That poor woman. What she must be going through.'

'Yeah, she actually fainted when she saw you at the chapel this morning and has been so traumatised that she's been avoiding us all day. She totally missed the news that you have— had a twin. Now I've got to tell my cousin that the man who fathered her child is dead. Oh, and that he was a psychopath.'

'Maybe we should leave out the psychopath thing? Dana has enough to deal with as it is, don't you think?'

'Agreed. Bright side: you have a new nephew. *We* have a new nephew and he's pretty darn cute.'

Richard kissed her hard, deeply. 'Not what I was expecting on my wedding day, but not the worst news.'

He smiled at her. 'We need to go to the hospital, talk to your cousin; explain a few things. And I'd really like to see how my best man is doing.'

'Of course. I just need to find Gert first.'

'Gert? Why?'

'She wanted to tell me something, before Dana went into labour. Made me promise to come find her the second I was done.'

'Then lead on, m'lady.' Richard swept an arm out in a flamboyant gesture. 'Maybe she can also tell me why she wanted to talk to me. Are we both in for a lecture, do you think?'

Jenny smiled, linking arms with him. 'Quite possible.'

Together they moved through the almost empty marquee.

'You seen Gert?' Jenny asked the first person she spied, her aunt Scuttlebutt.

'She was here a minute ago.' Scuttlebutt looked around. 'You know, I don't know who's worse – Gert or Hugh. Tina was here looking for her dad, but he's gone AWOL, too. She looked pretty annoyed, let me tell you.'

Jenny's shoulders drooped. She was exhausted. All she wanted to do was go back to Maggie's Point and spend some time alone with her new husband, but first she had to talk to Gert, face whatever it was she had to say, and then get to the hospital, talk to Dana and check on Sean.

'Maybe she's gone to the hospital,' Scuttlebutt mused. 'Although, I'm not sure how she'd get there?' Her face creased in bafflement, then cleared. 'Cap could have taken her. He did say he'd be available to take you and Richard there, if you wanted. So he's got to be around here, somewhere.' Her eyes searched the marquee for her husband.

'OK, thanks.' Jenny went to walk away.

But Scuttlebutt wasn't finished. 'You hear any more about the other body the gardaí found in the woods?' she asked eagerly. 'Who it was?'

'I've been kinda busy, Aunt Sheila.'

'Oh, yes, of course you were. Don't worry, I'll find out and let you know.' She winked.

'Er . . . thanks?'

'She could have also gone to check on the best man. Gert,' Scuttlebutt said at Jenny's puzzled expression. 'You know my sister, she'd hate to think of the man lying there, in a strange place, all alone.'

'That's true.' But then why had Gert made her promise to come and find her the second Dana and the baby were OK? Maybe she meant Jenny to find her at the hospital? All the signs pointed there, and Gert most definitely wasn't here.

'To the hospital?' Richard asked hopefully.

'To the hospital,' Jenny agreed. 'Oh, what about Ita?'

'Don't worry about me.' Ita sauntered over, glass in hand. She looked between Jenny and Richard, seemed satisfied by what she saw. 'The bus will be here soon to take the rest of us back to Innisard.'

Even as she said the words, they heard the asthmatic rumble of Innisard's only bus as it trundled back up the worn path to the marquee for its last trip of the day.

'And my car awaits the bride and groom.' Cap appeared from nowhere, red-faced and wheezing heavily.

'Where on earth have you been?' Scuttlebutt bustled towards him. 'I've been looking everywhere for you.'

'I . . . er . . . went for a . . . walk.'

'In this weather? Daft eejit.' She poked him. 'I'll see you back at the Lucky Leprechaun.'

'Yeah . . . see you—' But Scuttlebutt was gone. Cap stared after her, a look on his face that Jenny couldn't decipher, before he turned to them, saying, 'I'm ready for my final duty as chauffeur.'

Jenny heard the relief in his voice and bent to hug him. 'Thanks for everything, Cap. You've been an absolute star.'

Cap blushed, muttering something under his breath as he headed out of the marquee to get his car.

'That's our cue,' Jenny said, taking Richard's hand and waving a quick goodbye to Ita and her remaining family. Maybe the answers to what was going on at her wedding would be found at the hospital. At this point, Jenny didn't know what else to do. Her husband needed to see his best friend, and Jenny, worried about what they would find there, needed to be with him.

Chapter Forty-Eight

Well, I've added to my body count a lot sooner than expected.

Jenny's blasted aunt, Gert Foley.

The damn woman wouldn't tell me what had given me away, but I bet I know what it was.

She'd seen me leaving the woods.

Another misstep.

I couldn't afford any more.

Nosy bitch was everywhere, watching everything, asking questions.

I knew she'd put it together, sooner or later.

I wasn't about to wait, not now, not when I was so close to my goal.

If I was to have Jenny all to myself, Gert had to go.

Chapter Forty-Nine

At the hospital, the conversation between Jenny and her cousin Dana hadn't been an easy one. Richard had been there for the initial chat – to explain his and John's history – but had bowed out gratefully in order to let them talk. Jenny wished she could have gone with him. Unable to forget the desolation in her cousin's eyes when she told her John was dead.

'In some ways that's good news,' Dana said, cradling her newborn son. 'He didn't leave me for you.' She swallowed hard. 'I feel terrible. I thought John had lied about his name; that he was really Richard. I hated you for nothing. I'm so sorry, Jenny.'

Jenny took the hand resting against the baby's warm body. 'No apology needed; Richard and John are at fault here. They should have been honest with us.'

'What? John should have told me he murdered his family?' Dana shrugged Jenny's hand off. 'I can do without that kind of honesty, thanks very much.'

'Just hold on to the fact that he didn't leave you willingly. He was murdered, that has to mean something.'

'Oh, Cuz, you always were so naïve. The bastard disappeared the second I told him I was pregnant. Him being killed just made his disappearance permanent.'

There was little Jenny could say to that and, knowing Dana didn't want her there, she rejoined Richard, both of them hurrying to Sean's bedside.

Tina, now dressed in more lawyerly garb, jumped to her feet as they entered. 'There was nothing more I could do for Dermot this evening, so I . . . I know I shouldn't be here, not being next of kin, or family, but—'

'Relax, Tina.' Jenny hugged her cousin. 'You're exactly where you're supposed to be. I've been in touch with Sean's parents. They're on a cruise in Hawaii, and his sister Siobhan lives in Dubai. They're on their way home, but it will take some time. It's good that Sean isn't alone.' She felt Tina sag against her. Love, it seemed, had struck her cousin hard and fast.

To outsiders, Tina and Sean were strangers. After all, they'd only met a few hours before. But for anyone who believed in, or who had experienced, love at first sight, it was plain these two were meant to be together. Even if the pair didn't seem to realise it themselves. Or, as far as her cousin was concerned, was actively fighting the attraction. Tina was a brilliant lawyer, but she hadn't a clue about affairs of the heart. As far as Jenny was concerned, Tina had as much right to be here as she and Richard did – maybe even more.

'Has Gert been in?' Jenny asked.

'Not since I've been here.'

'Do you know if she's visited Dana and the baby?'

'Don't think so.'

No artifice in Tina's gaze. She obviously didn't know John was the father. Jenny wasn't about to enlighten her. Tina had enough on her plate. So had she. Tina would find out soon enough.

'Must admit I'm surprised I haven't heard from her. You know Gert. There's a big, fluffy, mothering hen wrapped somewhere deep – very, *very* deep – beneath that frighteningly rigid exterior.'

Jenny didn't smile, feeling a sense of disquiet. 'When was the last time you talked to her?'

'When she headed off to scoop up the Double Ds, around three, half three. Although, she did say she had something to do after she did that.'

'Did she say what?' Jenny pressed.

'No. You know Gert. She plays her cards close to her chest.'

'And that's the last time you saw her?'

'Hold on, no. I saw her when the gardaí came to tell us about Sean and Dermot. I was a bit upset,' Tina admitted. 'So I wasn't as focused as I should be. Why?'

That would have been around the time Gert had told Jenny she had something to tell her, which was hours ago. 'And you haven't seen, or heard from her, since?'

'No.' Tina came to attention. 'What's going on, Jenny? Is something wrong?'

Jenny had no need of Richard's gentle hand squeeze to know Tina didn't need any more stress right now. 'No,' she said quickly. 'Everything's fine. She's probably at home, asleep. It's been a long day. I'm sure she'll check in on you soon.'

When Tina relaxed, not asking the questions she usually would, Jenny knew her cousin was beyond smitten. *Good for her.* Tina needed a bit of . . . *life* in her life. And it seemed like she was finally getting it.

Jenny's gaze turned to Sean, still and silent on the bed, and her heart sank. 'What's happening with Dermot?' she asked.

'The daft fool won't talk, even to me.' Tina shook her head in disbelief. 'And the gardaí aren't saying much. They're waiting on blood evidence coming back. You didn't hear it from me, but they think Dermot is responsible for killing a guy called Pete McAvoy?'

'What? Who on earth is Pete McAvoy?'

'He's muscle for the local drug guy.'

'Innisard has a local drug guy?' The hits kept coming.

'Yes. More than one, actually, but Pete works for the biggest and worst of them.'

'Jesus! Is it really that bad?'

'Yes.'

Tina's voice was tight, hard and there was something in it that Jenny didn't understand. 'And Dermot, he knows this Pete McAvoy?'

'Yes. It seems our cousin owes Pete's boss, Big Benny, a lot of money, so Big Benny sent Pete to collect what was owed.'

'I'm sorry, Big Benny?' Jenny tried not to laugh.

Tina didn't smile. 'I know. It's not very gangster. Or maybe it is?' She shrugged.

'Sorry, not really a laughing matter. Do they know what happened? How—?'

'As I said, Dermot's not talking, but he was found in the vicinity of the body – of both bodies, or assaults, to be exact.'

'Surely the gardaí don't think—'

'No. They appear open to there being a second attacker in Sean's case.'

'But they're not sure.'

'No, not yet. As I said, evidence is still being collected.'

Tina was being cagey, lawyerly. Jenny understood that.

'But they're seriously considering Dermot? *Dermot!* I mean, I've seen heavier dishcloths.'

'I know. It's farcical. But maybe Dermot – being the lucky git he is – was able to land a sucker punch?'

'One, maybe. But two?' Jenny said incredulously. 'If the gardaí are wrong, and the same guy is responsible for both attacks, then he has to have more skill than luck. And most definitely more muscles than Dermot.'

'The gardaí seem content that they have the right man.' Tina's voice was sharp.

'For Pete. What about Sean?'

'Dermot swears he had nothing to do with what happened to Sean. It's about the only thing he *did* say.'

'And you believe him?'

'I have to.' Tina's face took on a hardness Jenny had never seen before. 'But, given the evidence, I'm inclined to. If I'm wrong, no one will ever find his body.'

Jenny didn't think her cousin was joking and could only pray Dermot was as innocent as he professed. Anything else would lead to very awkward family gatherings.

The hours passed slowly, filled with strained conversation, followed by long silences and terrible coffee. Eventually, Richard stood. 'Enough, my gorgeous bride. Your patients are all safely abed for the moment and so should we be. We need to be up early to get to the airport for our flights.'

'Up early? But—' Jenny thought she'd misheard. Surely, they'd talked about this and decided they couldn't leave Innisard, not with everything that had happened.

'Listen to your husband,' Tina told Jenny. 'Get some sleep. It's been a hell of a day. You look worn out.'

Jenny knew she did. She was beyond tired, knew Richard had to be the same, probably why he'd forgotten they were delaying their honeymoon. Grief and terror, even relief, did something to a body – the adrenaline high always followed by a low, and the low was hitting, and hitting hard. They would talk when they were back at Maggie's Point.

'Things will look brighter in the morning,' Richard said, cradling her hand in his larger one.

Jenny wanted to believe him, but she'd seen Sean's charts. The next few hours were critical. But she didn't tell him, or Tina, that. She'd leave them with hope. Everyone deserved a little of that, especially when she was about to burst his bubble about jetting off tomorrow on their honeymoon.

Daylight was straining to lift itself over the rooftops, pushing against the corpulent dark clouds, the wind huffing and whistling around their feet as they left the hospital. Jenny pulled the coat Tina had loaned her tighter around her body, as rain slammed into them. Huddled into Richard's side, they looked around the almost empty car park.

'Damnit!'

Cap had taken them to the hospital, just as he'd taken them to the church, but Cap was long gone, probably sound asleep next to Scuttlebutt, or, more likely, bartering some deal or other with one of his shady cronies.

'Taxi?' Richard said.

'In Innisard, at this time?' Jenny laughed. 'Not a chance.'

'Damnit,' he said again.

'Need a lift?'

Jenny had never been so happy to see anyone in her life. 'Ita. How?'

'Kinda borrowed . . . OK, stole, your cousin Liam's car, but I'm sure he won't mind; he was passed out at the time.'

'You're an absolute star,' Richard told Ita as he and Jenny clambered into the back of the car.

'All part of a best friend's duty,' she retorted, saluting. 'The second I get you back to Maggie's Point, I shall consider myself off-duty and you two can fend for yourselves. Deal?'

'Deal,' Jenny and Richard said together.

Dana watched her cousin and her new husband get in the car from the window of her hospital room. Talk about jammy. Anyone else would have been stranded, but oh no, not perfect, wonderful Jenny, who had someone appear out of thin air and pick her up, even at this ungodly hour. The girl definitely had the luck of the Irish, that was for sure. Not Dana. 'If I didn't have bad luck, I'd have no luck at all,' she muttered.

Then, as if to give lie to her words, her son mewled, twisting in his crib, before settling back to sleep. Dana watched him, overwhelmed with a surge of love so strong it took her breath away. She hadn't expected that. To feel this way about someone she'd just met. She thought when John dumped her that she'd never love again, but this little man had punched through all her defences.

And that was the problem.

The birth had been traumatic, emotional. That was the only reason she could think of for her loss of control, telling Jenny who the father was. Well, that and a modicum of spite, she admitted. In that moment, alone, scared, she couldn't help but spew out the truth – or what she thought was the truth at the time.

'You've a lot to answer for, little one,' she told the baby.

Because now she had a problem – bigger than Big Benny's threats. Once word got round that John – dead, *murdered* John – was the father of her baby, the gardaí would want to talk to her. The dumped, pregnant ex. Talk about motive. Plus, she had no alibi for the time John was murdered, least not one she could give the gardaí without them arresting her on the spot. She cursed her careless tongue, her jealousy.

Her child had only one parent now. He was relying on her. 'I will be Mum *and* Dad to you,' she whispered fiercely to the sleeping baby. 'No one – *no one* – will take you away from me. No matter what I have to do.'

Dana turned back to the window, to where she'd last seen Jenny, and took her phone from her pocket.

She was out of options.

And out of time.

Chapter Fifty

It wasn't long before Ita pulled up outside the lighthouse. The gardaí were still busy at work at the clifftop and in Wishers Woods. Jenny could see the faint flash of torchlight through the trees, as they searched and gathered evidence.

Ita looked forlornly at her car, still sitting where she'd parked it when she arrived on Thursday. 'You think Liam would be pissed if I left his car here and took mine? I've got my keys here somewhere . . .' She tapped her pockets.

'I think one car is plenty for anyone, Ita.'

'Word.' Ita nodded sadly.

'Have you seen Gert this evening?' Jenny asked as she opened the car door.

'I like booze, your aunt doesn't, so . . . that would be a hard no. Well, not since the reception. Why?'

'Nothing, really. She wanted to talk to me, but I guess it can wait.'

'It's two a.m.,' Richard told Jenny. 'You bet your ass it's going to have to wait. It's time to go inside and get some sleep – it's our wedding night . . . er, day . . .'

'Technically,' Jenny said, taking his hand as she stepped out of the car, 'It's our honeymoon.'

'Then go moon.' Ita threw back her head and howled. Roaring with laughter, she sped off, spraying water and gravel.

'That girl definitely has a screw loose.'

'Is that your professional diagnosis, Doctor Durkin?'

'Totally,' Richard said, steering Jenny inside and out of the rain.

With the thick door closed, it was uncannily quiet inside the lighthouse. Jenny could see the rain slamming against the windows, but the sound was oddly muted. The first thing she saw was the vase of bright wildflowers on the hall table where she'd placed them earlier. Richard followed her gaze.

'I'll sort them.' He lifted the vase and took it to the kitchen, returning empty-handed. 'Time for bed, Mrs Durkin.'

Jenny felt suddenly shy. 'It's been quite a day.'

'That it has.' Richard took her hand. 'What say we head upstairs, fall into that sumptuous bed and . . . sleep for the next six hours?'

Jenny sagged against him. That was exactly what she wanted, too tired for anything else. 'I love you.'

'Love you, too.'

Hand in hand, they made their way up the spiral staircase to the bedroom – Richard, for once, seemingly oblivious to his acrophobia.

'God! I'm tired.' He took off his jacket, folded it over the back of a plumply padded chair, before emptying his pockets into the delicate glass dish on the long dressing table that encircled the huge window.

Jenny smiled at the sound of the coins clinking. It was all so . . . normal; undressing, going to bed, they'd done it a million times before, except they hadn't . . . not like this. This time, they were married. Their first night as a married couple. Tired as she was, the thought was electrifying. For a second, she could almost forget the horrors of the day, but they soon came crashing back.

Jenny stripped off her wedding dress. It felt tainted now, dirtied in a way no stain remover could clean. The same with the lighthouse. She felt another presence here, an unwelcome one. Had their stalker been up here, touching their private things? A shiver of distaste and, yes, fear, then Jenny straightened. This was her tower of solace, her safe space, and no one – *no one* – was going to take that from her. For the first time in this whole horrible day, Jenny felt like she was finally in charge.

She went to the en suite and returned wearing a green silk negligee that emphasised her eyes, and brought out the fiery red of her hair.

'Well . . . just, well . . . Wow!' Richard levered himself up in bed as Jenny re-entered the bedroom.

'You like?' Jenny twirled.

'Oh, I like.'

Jenny laughed at the passion in her husband's voice, slipping into bed.

'Come here.' Richard folded her in his arms.

'I thought you were tired.'

'I was, until I saw you in this tiny little bit of lace and stuff.' A phone buzzed. 'Damnit. Who would be messaging at this time?'

'Sounds like your phone,' Jenny said, snuggling deeper into the bed, muscles aching. 'You'd better check it. It could be important.'

Richard grabbed his phone from the bedside table. 'Damnit,' he said again.

'What?'

'That was the airline, our flights have been cancelled.'

'Oh?' Jenny tried not to show her relief. She hadn't relished having that conversation with him – again! The darling man probably wanted her out of harm's way, but surely he understood there was no way they could leave Innisard until they found out what had happened to John, and whether Richard, himself, was still in danger?

'Yeah, seems the storm has come in quicker than expected. All flights are cancelled until further notice. We're stuck here.'

As is the killer, and our maybe stalker. The thought was there before Jenny could stop it.

Chapter Fifty-One

Tom made sure he was the first one to the conference room the next morning. O'Shaughnessy had said to meet at seven a.m.; Tom was there at five-thirty. He yawned as he took a stool next to the window and pulled out his notebook. He and the other gardaí had gone house to house, questioning everyone in Innisard until after midnight. No one had seen anything – or at least nothing they were admitting to.

By six a.m., the room was full, everyone eager to get things moving.

'Report,' O'Shaughnessy said, as he took his seat. 'Did the house-to-house shake anything loose, Carr?'

Tom shook his head. 'Nothing.'

'Damn and blast. And Cap Byrne's alibi?'

When did O'Shaughnessy think he'd find the time to question Cap? Yes, Innisard was small, but the house-to-house had taken up all his time and manpower yesterday. However, Tom kept his voice mild as he said, 'Catching up with him today.'

'Make sure you do. Oh, which reminds me, that blasted waste of space, Garda Fern. Keep him on duty at the Devil's Teeth, but move him to the beach entrance. Now that the tide's out, the crime guys will be there, searching for the murder weapon.'

Tom clenched his jaw at O'Shaughnessy's pettiness, but didn't respond. Fern had screwed up on the radio yesterday, although he had redeemed himself by finding Dana Gibson and getting help for her and her baby. Which reminded him that they hadn't discovered who the baby's father was. He'd need to check up on that. Fern had also been on guard duty at the top of the Devil's Teeth all night in pretty miserable weather. Tom figured the young garda had learned his lesson; any more was overkill. He decided to have Paula, the station manager, backtrack medical leave, or something equally important, for the lad. Hopefully, O'Shaughnessy would have something else to focus on by the time Fern returned.

'Anyone got any good news?' O'Shaughnessy asked. 'Or news at all?'

Head shakes all around.

'Damn. Where's Curran?' O'Shaughnessy looked around the room. 'Did he get the Filmore murder file? I need that bloody file.' He slapped the desk. 'What's taking so fecking long?'

Rooney shot to his feet. 'I'll find out, Guv.' He was dressed similar to O'Shaughnessy again; same suit and tie. Only difference was O'Shaughnessy wore a pale green shirt and Rooney's was dark green.

'Good man. We need to know if any of the Filmores were into drugs. A question to ask Doctor Durkin.' O'Shaughnessy looked pointedly at Tom. 'The man has lied more than once, so be on the alert this time.'

Tom bit his tongue. 'Noted.'

Rooney bounded back into the room holding a file aloft. 'Got it, Guv.'

Curran trailed behind Rooney, clearly having done all the work but unable to say anything without coming across as petty.

Tom shot Curran a commiseratory look, which the other

man returned with a shrug of weary acceptance. Obviously not the first time it had happened to him.

'Good job, Rooney. What we got?' O'Shaughnessy held his hand out for the file.

'You're gonna love this, Guv, the English police had Richard Filmore down as a person of interest in the original murders.'

'What? Richard, not John?' O'Shaughnessy flicked through the file. 'Goddamn.' He read for a few minutes before looking up at the assembled group. 'Says here John Filmore was found at the scene, sobbing over the bodies of his slain family, and testified that his brother, Richard, was responsible for the murders.'

Tom blew out a breath. 'Shit!'

'I'll see your shit and raise you a feck!' O'Shaughnessy slapped the file on the desk.

'But this is good, Guv.' Rooney looked between O'Shaughnessy and Carr. 'This guy, Richard, has been fingered in his family's murder and he's here, front and centre, in at least two more.'

'You want to tell him?' Tom asked O'Shaughnessy.

'What we have here, Rooney, is a case of he said/he said. Crime scenes where both men were present so DNA and fingerprints wouldn't exclude either one. Not that they would in this case – neither brother has fingerprints – and while there may be tiny deviations in their DNA, they either lived in the murder site, or admit to being there. Which means we have nothing. Goddamn it.'

'We have the English police report,' Tom said. 'Richard is noted as a person of interest and the investigation is still open. It's enough to bring him in.'

'You bet your ass it is. Let's get this fecker in here and get some blasted answers.'

Chapter Fifty-Two

Jenny woke to a grey, overcast sky; thick black clouds marching together as if preparing for the battle to come. Rain slammed off the toughened glass that circled their bedroom, chilling the air inside. Cradled in the hollow of Richard's back, she breathed in the scent of his skin, the muted tone of his aftershave. It may be dismal outside, but inside, next to her new husband, she felt totally at peace.

God! He was gorgeous.

She trailed her fingers over the taut contours of his body, from his neck down to the scar nestled in the curve of his back. Richard was usually supersensitive whenever she went near it, and now she understood why. It was a reminder of that terrible night when his family were murdered. But with him fast asleep, she enjoyed the sensation of having time to enjoy it, tracing the ragged, circular scar before trailing her fingers lower, to his hip, lower still . . . She felt him stir, mutter something as he drew the covers closer and burrowed deeper into the bed. Let him sleep or bring him to delicious wakefulness?

Her stomach growled, reminding her she hadn't eaten since breakfast yesterday. Food first, she decided, sex later.

Jenny pulled on the green silk dressing gown that matched the sheer negligee she wore and slipped down the spiral stairs.

In the kitchen, she switched on the coffee maker and grabbed her phone, settling into one of the comfy window seats, staring out at the stormy sea below.

She called the hospital first, hoping for an update on Sean. Seeing as she wasn't immediate family, she was given the standard reply: 'As comfortable as expected . . .' Jenny consoled herself with the fact that at least it meant he was still alive. He'd weathered the first, critical hours, which was the best they could hope for.

Her next enquiry went better: Dana and her new son were doing well. Evil had been positively chipper, freakishly so. Unnerved, Jenny quickly finished the call.

Next, she called Gert, wanting to catch up, but there was no answer. Damn the woman and her hatred of technology. Gert only had a landline phone; an ancient dial contraption, which sat in her hall, so if she was upstairs, or outside, she wouldn't hear it. 'Bugger!' Jenny tapped a finger on the thick stone wall of the windowsill, hating to move out of her 'love vibe', but she couldn't help thinking of Gert's words and expression yesterday; the promise she'd extracted from Jenny to come and find her. There had been something . . . Damnit.

She called Scuttlebutt.

'Have you spoken to Gert today?' she asked when her aunt answered.

'No. Is something wrong?'

'She wanted to talk to me; it sounded important. I was just wondering whether you knew—'

'Gert thinks everything is important. What *is* important is this is your honeymoon. Focus on your new husband. That auld bag of bones Gert will pop up to annoy us sooner or later. Enjoy the peace and quiet while you can. I know I will.'

Scuttlebutt sounded unperturbed, but Jenny couldn't let it lie. She tried calling her uncle Hugh next, but it went straight to voicemail. Was he with Gert? What was going on? What did Gert want to tell her so desperately yesterday? Worry gnawed.

Pragmatic as ever, Jenny knew there was nothing more she could do right this minute, so she pushed her worry down as far as it would go, concentrating on what she *could* do.

Scuttlebutt was right. Time to focus on her husband.

The scent of fresh-brewed coffee filled the room, and Jenny quickly prepared a breakfast of toast and croissants, plating the food on a large tray. Two cups and the carafe of delicious coffee, and she was ready. However, the second she reached for the cups Jenny had a flashback to the missing vodka and moved items in the kitchen.

Stop! She refused to dwell on that. On anything other than her honeymoon. This was *her* place, *her* time, and she would not let the stalker intrude any further on it.

To the ever-growing sound of wind and rain hurling against the windows – not even the thick walls of Maggie's Point able to contain the fury of the escalating storm – Jenny carefully inched her way up the winding staircase to the bedroom.

'Wakey, wakey, husband.'

But Richard was already sitting up in the bed, looking almost as hungry as she was. 'I don't know which I want to devour first: you or this amazing spread?' He sprang from the bed, taking the tray from her.

'I vote we eat first. We need all the energy we can get,' she added, dropping a kiss on his lips.

'If I didn't have this tray in my hands . . .' Richard growled.

'Eat first, play later.'

'I can do that.'

They both sat cross-legged on the bed, working their way through the food she'd prepared.

'Man, that was good,' Richard said when he was done, patting his firm stomach. 'So good.'

Jenny snuggled closer to him, content now her tummy was full, but any thoughts of sleep faded as Richard slipped the thin straps of her negligee off her shoulders, his lean fingers trailing down her arms.

'Happy first day of marriage, Mrs Durkin.'

'Happy first day to you, too, Mr Durkin,' Jenny retorted, trying not to let on what his fingers on her skin were doing to her.

'You know,' Richard's hands stilled. 'I don't think we can consider ourselves well and truly married until we consummate our union.'

'Consummate our union?' Jenny giggled. 'Well, if that's what it takes, I vote you remove that tray from the bed and let's do some . . . consummating.'

Richard almost dropped the tray in his eagerness and Jenny giggled again as he grabbed her, lifting her atop him.

Jenny sat astride him. 'I wonder if married sex is better than engaged sex.'

'Let's find out.' Richard's voice had deepened with passion.

'Oooh, let's.' Jenny's laugh cut off, ears pricking at a faint banging sound. 'What was that?'

'Don't you even think of getting out of the married sex thing, wife.'

'Wouldn't dream of it, husband, but . . . There. Do you hear that?'

Now they were quiet, the sound was clear. Over the sound of the wind and rain, someone was hammering on the lighthouse door and whoever it was, it didn't sound like they were going away.

'Goddamn and blast!' Richard pulled on a pair of sweatpants and T-shirt. 'I'm going to kill whoever that is.'

Jenny would gladly join him.

She heard Richard clatter down the stairs and open the front door. Deep voices; hard, stilted. Formal. She sat up. That sounded like . . . She was already out of bed, getting dressed. What on earth did the gardaí want with them now?

Chapter Fifty-Three

Richard Durkin is a fool.
How can he jeopardise what he has with Jenny –
what he thinks *he has with Jenny.*
I watch the gardaí place him in the back of their car, drive away.
My gaze returns to the door where my love stands.
She looks sad now, but that won't last.
Now Richard is out of the way, I can make myself known.
She and I can finally be together.

Chapter Fifty-Four

Jenny stood, shivering, in the door of the lighthouse, as she watched Sergeant Carr put her husband in the back of the Garda car. She didn't think it was possible for things to get worse, but judging by the look on the garda's face, they were about to.

As the car sped off down the gravelled drive towards Wishers Woods, Jenny pulled the collar of her light blouse she had changed into, tightening it around herself. She had the strongest sensation that she was being watched, which was weird, seeing as she was alone.

Wasn't she?

Jenny scanned the path around the lighthouse, the grass leading to the forest, the track to the Devil's Teeth, where a lone garda stood, surrounded by flapping tape. The garda was hunched over, staring out to sea, not looking at her, but the feeling of being watched persisted. Could it be a newspaper reporter? She'd heard they were in town, following the story and annoying the residents. Another thing to feel guilty about. But surely someone from the press would want to talk to her; an interview better than a long-range photo? Plus, it wasn't a benign vibe she was getting from whoever was out there. Remembering their stalker, she quickly stepped back inside the lighthouse, shutting the door firmly behind her. Then she ran to where she'd left her phone.

'Tina?'

'Yeah,' her cousin answered sounding half-asleep.

Only then did Jenny realise it was only 7.25 a.m. on a Saturday morning. 'Sorry, did I wake you?'

'No, just . . . I didn't get home from the hospital till a few hours ago. What's up?'

At the mention of the hospital, Jenny instantly felt guilty. 'How's Sean? Any more news? The hospital wouldn't say much when I phoned earlier.'

'No change,' Tina said curtly. 'But that's not why you called, is it?'

'No, but that's not to say I'm not concerned.'

'I know.' Tina's voice softened. 'Don't mind me, I'm a teeny bit sleep deprived. What's going on?'

Jenny filled her in and Tina immediately became alert. 'Did they arrest him?'

'I don't think so. They said they were taking him in for questioning, but they didn't say why.'

'Don't worry, I'll find out.'

Jenny heard sounds of Tina dressing. 'Thank you, Tina. I really owe you for—'

'I told you before, we're family,' Tina said as if that was an end to it. 'I've got to go. I want to be at the station when they bring Richard in.'

Jenny stood for a moment after Tina rang off. The last thing Richard had said to her was that she needed to rearrange their flights. She knew he was frightened for her, wanted her away from harm, but he should know her better than that. She was stronger than she looked. They needed to face this. Together. No running away. That's not to say she didn't want a honeymoon at some point, but, honestly, all she really wanted right now was to talk to her best friend. She dialled Ita's number.

'What's wrong?' Ita answered on the first ring. No pleasantries, straight to the point.

Jenny should have known her friend would guess something was up, but she prevaricated anyway. 'Does something have to be wrong to call my best friend?'

'At seven-thirty in the morning, the day after your wedding, and after your cousin named your husband as her baby daddy . . . you bet your sweet ass there's something wrong. Now, spill.'

'The baby daddy thing is sorted. As for the rest, I'd rather talk in person.'

'You want me to come over? Or you could take my car and meet me here, at the B&B? Damn. No, you can't. 'Cause I got the keys here.'

'I'll come to you. I fancy a walk anyway.'

'A walk? Have you looked out the window?' Ita asked.

Jenny didn't care. She wanted fresh air, needed to clear her head. She could only hope the stalker had given up, the bad weather sending them scurrying indoors. As the steps to the shore were still cordoned off, the only way to the village was through Wishers Woods. 'I'll be about an hour.'

She rang off before Ita could ask any more.

Jenny ran upstairs to grab a jumper and looked forlornly at her silk negligee lying crumpled on the floor where she'd dropped it. Not exactly the start she'd been anticipating for the first day of married life.

She dialled Gert's number again and put her phone on loudspeaker as she slipped her feet into waterproof boots and rummaged for a coat. This time the phone went to answer machine.

'Where are you, Aunt Gert? I'm heading to Innisard. Hopefully catch up with you there.'

Jenny found their travel agent information and programmed the number into her phone. She'd call them while she walked.

Hood up, head ducked low to her chest, Jenny stepped into the storm. For the first time in her life, she was oblivious to the beauty of Maggie's Point and the lush gorgeousness of Wishers Woods as she moved between the trees. She still felt uneasy, watched, but she was also angry, fed up of being scared.

'If you're out there, show yourself,' she screamed into the wind and rain.

No answer.

'What? You're only brave when it's a defenceless cat you're facing? Show yourself.'

Buffeted by wind and rain, she waited. Again, there was no answer, but then, what had she expected? The stalker – and she was sure it was the stalker and not a reporter – was a coward. He craved the shadows; too afraid to step into the light and face her.

'Coward!' she shouted.

Head down against the ever-growing storm, and burrowed beneath the hood of her coat, Jenny called the travel agent to ask them to rearrange their cancelled flights and inform the hotel they were going to be delayed. When the agent asked when she should rebook their flights, Jenny froze. How long did it take to catch a killer? She didn't even know how long the gardaí would hold Richard. Was it twenty-four hours? Forty-eight? Longer?

'Everyone's rebooking after all the storm cancellations,' the travel agent urged. 'You need to be quick if—'

'I'll be in touch,' Jenny said, shutting off the phone. She had no idea how any of this was going to end. When, or if, they'd ever be allowed to leave Innisard.

Chapter Fifty-Five

Jenny wants me to show myself, but even though I want to — so badly — now isn't the time.

But what did she mean by 'a defenceless cat'?

I hold a picture in my mind of her screaming out to me in the woods; so angry, and yet so scared.

It doesn't make sense, but she is right to call me a coward.

I bear her no ill will for her harsh words. I am a coward.

Nerves got the better of me.

Next time.

Next time I will show myself, and I can't wait to see her face when she sees me in the flesh, so to speak.

Chapter Fifty-Six

Tina had to fight her way through a throng of reporters to get to the Innisard Garda Station. But she was there and waiting when Tom Carr arrived with a haggard-looking Richard, who appeared relieved to see her.

Tom Carr, on the other hand, didn't look quite so happy. 'How . . .?' He answered his own question. 'Jenny phoned you.'

'And they say you're not a detective.' Tina winked.

Tom Carr didn't share her humour. 'We need to talk.'

From the second she'd voiced Peter McAvoy's name and had Tom confirm he was the murder victim, Tina knew he would be back, demanding answers from her. It was an acceptable trade – at the time. But she still didn't have any answers. In fact, she only had more questions. Her dad was avoiding her, and doing a bang-up job of it. She hadn't managed to pin him down to ask why he was arguing with Pete McAvoy yesterday – arguing with him yards from where he was later found murdered. She knew deep in her soul that her dad wouldn't kill anyone, that he would have a perfectly reasonable explanation for what she'd seen. She just needed him to tell her. *Where the hell are you, Daddy?*

'Now might not be the time,' she told Tom pointedly, staring over his shoulder.

Tom muttered something under his breath; a mutter that turned into a full-blown curse as Pat O'Shaughnessy appeared.

'I see you've brought company, Carr. Great work. Sure, isn't there a few of those paparazzi out there that you'd like to invite in, make it a party? Jaysus!' A dirty look. 'Come this way, Ms Connors. Not you, Carr. You've things to be getting on with, don't you? An alibi to firm up, if I'm not mistaken?'

Tina watched Tom bite down on his toothpick and she threw him a sympathetic, if somewhat relieved, look.

O'Shaughnessy tapped in a code and opened a door to a long corridor painted an obnoxious shade of beige, with an equally obnoxious and anonymous brown carpeted floor tile. He stopped halfway down and opened a windowless door that led to a tiny grey room, also windowless: grey walls, grey floor, steel grey desk with four grey chairs – two on each side – and nothing else. It smelt of damp and desperation. 'In here. We'll just be a minute.' He waited for Tina and Richard to enter, then shut the door behind them.

'What on earth is going on?' Richard asked. He paced, seeming shell-shocked to find himself in an interrogation room.

'I was going to ask you the same thing.' Tina pulled out a chair. 'Did the gardaí give you any indication as to why they want to question you again?' She sat, opened her briefcase and took out a notebook and pen, set them on the worn and scraped tabletop.

'No, just that they had more questions for me.' Richard ran a hand through his hair. 'This is a nightmare. How are you so calm?'

'It's kinda my job,' Tina told him. 'Put me in front of one of your patients and I'd be a gibbering wreck. I suggest you take a seat. We're going to be here a while.'

She was right. It was almost thirty minutes later before O'Shaughnessy and another plainclothes detective appeared.

'My client has a right to know why you've brought him in for questioning,' Tina said before O'Shaughnessy and his partner could sit.

'And Garda Rooney and myself are about to tell you, Ms Connors.' O'Shaughnessy and the other garda settled themselves into chairs opposite her and Richard. 'As for why we're here . . .' O'Shaughnessy laid a folder on the desk. 'It seems Doctor Durkin – or should I say, Richard Filmore – is a person of interest to the London Constabulary, who have been looking for him for seventeen years. Your brother named you as your family's killer,' he told Richard.

'No,' Richard said, aghast. 'That's not—'

Tina held her hand over his. 'And you have evidence to back that up?'

'Look it, we have witness statements, testimony taken at the time.'

'But nothing actionable?' When O'Shaughnessy remained quiet, she said, 'As I thought, you've nothing.'

O'Shaughnessy glared at Tina before speaking directly to Richard. 'Try to see it from our point of view. John told the police that you killed your family. You ran, changed your name – that's not exactly the actions of an innocent man, now, is it?'

'I did that because I was in fear of my life. John would have killed me, too.'

'That may be. However, John stayed, gave eyewitness testimony to you murdering your family; he was understandably upset, but he was also clear and coherent.'

'I swear I wasn't there. I was on a date. When I got home John was . . . John was . . . Jesus!' Richard covered his eyes. 'I can't relive this again, it's too painful.'

O'Shaughnessy's voice softened for an instant. 'Breathe,

just breathe. *Tóg go bog é* – take it slow. Talk to me, we can work it out.'

Richard gulped in air, then seemed to steady himself. 'I swear to you; I was on a date with Sharon Sumner. She can confirm—'

'Let me stop you there.' Rooney held up a hand. 'The UK police questioned Ms Sumner. She agreed she was on a date with you. She also stated that you both had quite a bit to drink.'

'Well, we had a few drinks, yes, but—'

O'Shaughnessy flicked through his notes. 'You finished a bottle of vodka between you. I'd say that's rather more than a few drinks.'

'It was a party, and we were teens – stupid teenagers.' Richard threw up his hands. 'We drank more than was probably good for us, but that doesn't mean—'

'The UK cops beg to differ. That amount of alcohol calls into question the veracity of any witness statement. And your brother John swears it was him on the date, not you, that you were the one in the house. That the pair of you swapped places – something you'd done on many occasions.'

'No, that's not—' Richard flopped back in his seat, face ashen. 'Well, yes, we did swap places sometimes, silly pranks, but I swear that's not what happened this time. I went on that date with Sharon. We went to Oliver Stanton's party, had a few drinks – OK, more than a few – but we weren't insensible, far from it. We went outside . . . Jesus! I can tell you everything that happened, but now, when I say I fell off a fence, you're going to put it down to me being drunk, to us being drunk, but it wasn't like that. We were playing around, we fell.' He rubbed his lower back as if in memory. '*I* fell off a fence. *I* did all that.

Not John!' He stopped, growing animated. 'Drinking! I was the one drinking that night, not John. If the police breathalysed John, then—'

'They did breathalyse him. At the scene. He blew positive.'

'No!' Richard sank back into his seat. 'Please, I beg you, get in touch with Sharon, verify what I'm saying. I told John most of the details of our date that night, before I knew what he'd done, but not everything. Sharon will back me up. I promise you; she'll back me up.'

'Why should we go to all that bother? You're the one that ran,' Rooney said. 'John stayed. Guilty people don't run. Seems pretty open and shut to me.'

'Enough,' Tina said firmly. 'We get it.' She looked directly at O'Shaughnessy. 'Richard answers your questions about these Innisard murders fully and truthfully and you make the call to exonerate him from his family murder.'

'Why, Ms Connors, I do believe we've come to an understanding.'

'Right.' Tina glared at O'Shaughnessy before turning to Richard. 'I think this is our best move,' she told him. 'If, as you say, you've nothing to do with John's death, then—'

'I haven't, I promise I haven't.'

'Then let's give them what they want.'

'And in return they'll find Sharon, validate my alibi for my family's murder?' When Tina said nothing, Richard sat back and folded his arms. 'I'm saying nothing more until I know they're going to do everything in their power to clear my name. My family deserves to rest in peace.' He glared at the two gardaí.

'The ball's in your court,' Tina told O'Shaughnessy.

'Look it, your client answers all my questions truthfully and fully, then I agree to find Sharon Sumner and have her answer some questions.'

'I want you to put someone on to finding Sharon now,' Richard said. 'If I'm reading the room, I'm going to be here for a while. Least you can do is put your minions to work while I'm unpacking my soul.'

O'Shaughnessy drummed his fingers on the table, huffed, then signalled to someone in the mirror behind him, saying, 'Check it out.' He turned back to Richard. 'Right. Time to answer some questions, Doctor Durkin.'

Chapter Fifty-Seven

Sergeant Tom Carr was both preoccupied and fuming as he left the garda station. Tina Connors was hiding something. It wouldn't be the first time, of course. Being the local lawyer, Tina hid a lot from him – as he did from her. This, though, felt different. Personal. And that wasn't Tina Connors at all. Tina was a by-the-book lawyer. When she'd asked him back at the reception to reveal the name of a victim before family notification, that was totally out of character. Asking for a favour . . . that was personal. Tina already knew about her cousin Dermot, so it had to be something more personal than that. Did it have anything to do with her dad's history with Big Benny? Did she even know about Hugh's criminal past?

Mostly, though, Tom was fuming. Did O'Shaughnessy really have to dismiss him so arrogantly in front of Tina and a bloody suspect? It wasn't his fault the news had got out about the groom being taken in for questioning. The station had more holes in it than the dartboard at the Lucky Leprechaun. He chewed harder on his toothpick as he elbowed through the pushy reporters, the look on his face causing them to back off.

It was a two-minute drive to Cap Byrne's house from the station and he used the time to call Paula, who had, of course, already heard the trouble their newest garda was in and was well ahead of him.

'Sergeant Carr, I know the SIO wants Garda Fern to do duty at the beach end of the Devil's Teeth, but I'm afraid he's booked off – medical leave – nothing I can do about it.'

Obviously, someone was hovering within earshot. Tom played along. 'Damnit. I'd forgotten about that. SIO O'Shaughnessy said to call in all off-duty, and gather people from the closest stations. Maybe you can have one of them cover that?'

'On it.'

'Thanks, Paula. I owe you one.'

'Oh, honey, you owe me so much more than that.'

Her sultry laugh made Tom smile – a bright sound in an otherwise shitty day.

Right, time to question Cap Byrne about where he was the night John Filmore was murdered.

Cap Byrne and his wife Sheila, or Scuttlebutt as she was better known, lived in a stunning detached house overlooking the sea, with large landscaped gardens to the front and back. *Nice work, if you can get it*. Tom examined the premises, the courtyard filled with top-of-the-range cars.

Scuttlebutt opened the door before Tom could knock, almost as if she had been expecting him. 'Come in, Sergeant Carr.' She walked before him down a long hallway filled with family portraits, mainly of their twin daughters in every awkward, painful, pimply stage of development, and into a long kitchen-cum-dining room, tastefully, and expensively, kitted out in marble and chrome. 'Can I get you something?'

'I'm actually looking for Cap. Is he about?'

'Er, I'm not sure—'

'Because if he's not, then I shall have to apply for an arrest warrant, seeing as I believe he could be a material witness to a crime.' Which was all true, if not exactly legal. No way he'd get an arrest warrant with little to no evidence.

'Now, now, no need for that, Sergeant Carr.' Cap's enormous stomach entered the kitchen long seconds before the rest of him did. 'Howya doing? Miserable day out there, isn't it?' The florid face was all bonhomie, but the dark eyes were tight, watchful. 'Sheila, make the man a hot cuppa, take the chill from his bones.'

'I wouldn't say no to a brew, thanks.' Tom settled himself on one of the high chrome and leather chairs next to the granite kitchen island where Scuttlebutt was busy fixing cups and saucers. He was obviously getting the 'good china', which, in Irish speak, classed him as an uninvited visitor, there on business. Normally, it would have been a chipped mug and a plate of Rich Tea biscuits. Although – Tom glanced quickly around the immaculate kitchen – he doubted there was a chipped anything in this room. Or any room of this palatial house.

'So, what can I do for you, Sergeant Carr?' Cap asked, once they were settled with their cups of tea and a plate of dainty traybakes.

'As you know, we're investigating two murders – one on the Devil's Teeth in the early hours of Friday morning, the other in Wishers Woods around three/three-thirty Friday afternoon. There was also an attempted murder in the same location, around the same time.'

'Heard you brought in Sheila's nephew Dermot for that. The boy has always been into bad stuff, owes people, I hear.'

'You hear a lot, Cap.' Tom took a sip of his tea; too weak for his taste, but he drank it as if it were the finest nectar. 'Anything else you've . . . heard?'

It was Scuttlebutt who answered. 'It's probably this stalker of Jenny's who followed them from Dublin. An outsider. You should be looking for him, not good, honest people like us.'

'We're investigating every avenue.'

'You think he's like a spurned lover, or something?' Scuttlebutt asked eagerly. 'This stalker? I've read about them. You say something nice to them once, and poof – they think they're in love. Touched in the head, they are.'

'You know any spurned lovers of either Jenny or Richard Durkin?'

'Well, not Richard, obviously,' Scuttlebutt said with a fake laugh, 'We hardly know him, but Jenny had her share of beaus when she lived here. Fintan Callaghan in particular.'

'Oh?' Tom asked, not especially interested, but eager to keep her talking. Gossips were a boon of information.

'She fair broke that boy's heart, running off with nary a word. First he knew, he was at her door, flowers in hand, and she was gone. You know about the accident?' Scuttlebutt asked. 'My sister and her husband?'

Tom nodded. He'd read the incident report on Jenny's parents. Tragic. It seemed death had followed Jenny Durkin all her life.

'Jenny escaped Innisard the second she could. Fintan never got over her leaving so abruptly. He moped around for months. He hasn't settled with any other girl. I think he still holds a candle for Jenny,' Scuttlebutt told Tom. 'Probably why he hassled Richard when he did.'

'He hassled Richard?' Tom asked, immediately interested.

'Yeah, the day he arrived in Innisard. Silly stuff; saying Richard wasn't good enough for Jenny. And, at the wedding today, he did nothing but talk about her. Totally obsessed, he was.'

Obsessed? The word caught Tom's attention. Stalkers were notorious for being obsessed; it was one of their biggest traits. And Scuttlebutt's mention of flowers caused alarm bells to ring. The stalker had left flowers in Dublin and here in Innisard. He made a mental note to have someone check into Fintan Callaghan, his whereabouts especially, and whether he had any occasion to travel to Dublin this last year. But well aware Scuttlebutt was attempting to throw him off his real reason for being there, he didn't ask any more, simply thanking her for the information, before turning back to Cap.

'We're trying to firm up alibis for Thursday night into the early hours of Friday morning. According to my notes, you don't have one.'

'That Tina Connors.' Scuttlebutt stood, furious. 'No loyalty between family now, I see. And to think I changed that girl's nappy when she was a wee'un, wiped her nose.' She shook her head in disgust.

'It's OK, Sheila, pet. Calm yourself.' Cap waved his wife back to her seat. 'I have nothing to hide.'

'That's good to know, Cap. So, you were where . . .?' Tom pressed.

'At Seamus Blaney's house, playing cards; drinking too much whiskey and losing far too much money.'

Scuttlebutt looked confused. 'But—'

Cap glared at her. 'Wife doesn't agree with the auld gambling thing, do you, pet? She's still a tad miffed at me. Isn't that right, pet?'

Scuttlebutt nodded, but wouldn't look at Tom.

'You can check with Seamus; he'll confirm all I've said.'

Tom had no doubt that Seamus Blaney would. He and Cap were tight; friends from school. This interview was a waste of time. Cap had his fake alibi all neatly sorted. And it *was* fake, Tom would bet his badge on it. He also knew there was no way he would be able to shake it, but he had to try.

'Two men are dead, another badly injured, and your wife's nephew is a prime suspect. Anything you share would be appreciated.'

'Dermot Gibson brought his troubles on himself,' Cap said firmly. 'He's a blasted waste of space. As for the two dead guys . . . I'm sorry they're dead, but I had nothing to do with either of their deaths. Now,' he stood, 'if there's nothing else.'

'One more thing. I need your alibi, Sheila.'

'What? I . . .' Scuttlebutt shot an anxious look at Cap. 'I was here, with the girls. All night.'

'I'll need to confirm that with them.'

'Of course. I'll have them phone you.'

Tom finished his tea, placed the cup and saucer gently on the breakfast counter. 'Thanks for the cuppa, Sheila, much appreciated.'

'I'll show you out.' Cap moved as quickly as his huge belly would allow, escorting Tom down the long corridor and out the door.

'If you think of anything else—?'

'I won't.'

But a guilty conscience didn't sit easy, even with a man as practised a liar as Cap, and the genial smile slipped as he said goodbye.

Tom got into his car, waited, hoping Cap would do the right thing. When he didn't, Tom put his car in gear and reversed out the drive. It was up to O'Shaughnessy now. Hopefully, he'd prise some answers loose from Richard Durkin. If not, they were clear out of leads.

Scuttlebutt came up behind her husband, stood with him in the doorway as Sergeant Carr left. 'You should have told him.'

'Man's business is his own business.'
'This is serious, Cap. We're talking family here.'
'Exactly. Family. Loyalty. They're everything.'
But he looked worried.
And so was Sheila – and not just for her husband.

Chapter Fifty-Eight

Tina Connors glanced surreptitiously at her watch. Eight thirty-five. O'Shaughnessy was shuffling papers, pretending to look for something; an obvious play to make her client, Richard, think he had information on him. Otherwise the room was quiet, muted sounds from the garda station trickling faintly through the grey door.

She wondered how Sean was doing in the hospital, knowing no news was good news, but the absence of news was playing havoc with her concentration. Something that had never happened to her before. When she was on a case, she was laser focused – on the client, nothing else. Not this time. Her thoughts kept shifting to Sean, their almost kiss. His smile. The fear she thought she'd seen in him. What was that about? But he'd been right to be afraid. Someone had hurt him, tried to kill him. Why? And did it have anything to do with what was happening to Jenny and Richard?

Tina wished she could ask Sean, talk to him. Was he in pain? Or worse – had he 'succumbed to his injuries', as the newspapers would announce in their desperate effort for clickbait. Dread was an anchor in her stomach, and the urge to get out of the room so she could phone the hospital and check on him was overwhelming, but she fought against it. She had a job to do. She needed to get her cousin's new husband back to her. That was what was important. That was what she could control; *all* she could control for the moment.

Tina focused her eyes, and her mind, back to the windowless grey room with its four grey chairs and scraped metal table. 'Ask your questions, O'Shaughnessy. Time's a'wasting.'

'Your wish is my command, Ms Connors.' O'Shaughnessy pulled a file towards him, opened it. 'I asked my men to look into you, Doctor Durkin. Interesting reading.' He flicked through the pages slowly.

'Again, any time you're ready,' Tina said, wise to his posturing, hoping Richard would know the tactic for what it was. He seemed composed and she let out a sigh of relief. Always good when the client was halfway intelligent.

'Where were you exactly when you brother John died?' O'Shaughnessy began.

'What time did he die?'

'Coroner puts it between two and four yesterday morning.'

'I was at the B&B, asleep.'

'You didn't slip out, you know, like you did the night your family were killed?'

Richard rubbed a tired hand through his hair. 'Dear Lord, if you only knew how I wish I'd stayed home that night, been there with my family when John—'

'But you arrived home too late.' Sympathetic.

'Yes. I thought everyone was asleep, but John was there, in the kitchen when I slipped in the back door.'

'Why don't we leave any further questions on the Filmore murders until you fulfil your part of the bargain and get in touch with Sharon Sumner?' Tina smiled tightly.

'Right.' O'Shaughnessy flicked through his file again. 'So, back to yesterday morning. You were asleep in your B&B between the hours of two and four a.m.?'

'Yes.'

'And you have someone who can corroborate that?'

'You know I can't,' Richard said angrily. 'But I will when Sean wakes up—'

'And if Mr O'Hare doesn't wake up? What then?'

Tina jumped in. 'That's a tad harsh, don't you think?'

'A question for later, then. Here's an easier one: do you know of anyone who would want to hurt your brother?'

'Apart from me, you mean?' Richard asked harshly. 'You might find this strange, but I got over my anger at my brother a long time ago. He's more to be pitied than anything. John was ill. His illness was so far beyond our comprehension back then that it may as well have been a black hole in our universe. We understand so much more now. My brother has . . . had extreme ASPD – Antisocial Personality Disorder.'

'And what is that?'

'It's characterised by impulsive, irresponsible behaviour. A person with ASPD can appear quite charming, but they're extremely manipulative and deceitful. They lack empathy, have no real understanding of other people's feelings and find it hard to form attachments.'

'So he was a sociopath?'

'I'd say John was more a psychopath,' Richard said sadly. 'If he had the help that's available now back then, who knows, my family might still be alive. My brother might be alive, too.' He stopped, obviously fighting his emotions. 'Sorry, that was unprofessional of me.'

'You're not here in a professional capacity, Richard,' Tina soothed. 'John was your brother. This is your family we're talking about; a huge bereavement. You have every right to your emotions, and he also has a right to not relive them for your titillation,' she told O'Shaughnessy.

'Just to be clear, you're saying you don't know anyone who would want to hurt your brother?'

'As my wife and I have already told you, we believe our stalker murdered John thinking he was me. And I have to say I'm baffled that no one seems to be taking us seriously. This person seems to be fixated on me. And, by extension, those around me.' Richard turned to Tina. 'Which includes Jenny. She's out there alone. What if this madman . . .' His voice hitched. 'What if he goes after her next – with more than flowers – and I'm not there?'

'Look it, we're aware of your assertion that someone has been stalking you, but without bonafide gardaí reports, our hands are somewhat tied.'

'The report has been made now,' Tina said, scribbling in her notebook. 'I would say that unties your hands a little, doesn't it?'

O'Shaughnessy coughed. 'Moving on. Do you know a Pete McAvoy?' he asked Richard, but his eyes were fixed on Tina.

'No.' Richard seemed confused by the shift in conversation.

O'Shaughnessy slid a photograph across the table. 'Are you sure you don't know this man?'

Richard checked the picture. 'No. Never seen him before.'

'Why are you asking about Pete McAvoy?' Tina asked. She figured the gardaí had settled on Dermot as Pete's killer. To their minds, it was an open-and-shut case, surely? Unless . . . O'Shaughnessy's stare now seemed ominous. Did the garda know something? Something about her dad and Pete McAvoy? A reason for them to have been arguing? *Damnit!* Why was her dad avoiding her? This could be settled with one conversation. *Where the hell are you, Dad?*

'He's one of the murder victims, Ms Connors. We're just exploring every avenue.'

'Explore carefully. Land mine carefully,' Tina warned, keeping her expression neutral, hoping none of her inner turmoil showed.

'Noted. Which leads me to my next question. Is it possible your brother was into drugs, or linked to the drug scene in some way?'

Richard looked at Tina, who nodded to say he could answer. 'Anything is possible. I haven't seen John in almost eighteen years. Back then, John was into a lot of stuff. You have to understand; my brother was ill, and he knew it, even if our parents refused to admit it. John was looking for a cure. He knew there was something wrong with him. It's not like he just snapped one day. He tried so hard to get help. No one wanted to know, or maybe they just didn't know how to help,' he finished sadly, 'but John tried, he really tried.'

'So, who do you think is stalking you?'

The change of direction seemed to confuse Richard for a second, then he said, 'I have no idea.' There was a ring of truth in his voice that was obvious. 'I honestly thought it was—'

'Your brother John?' O'Shaughnessy's voice was soft.

'Yes. Much as I hate to admit it, I did. Until . . . until he was . . . murdered.' Richard's face crumpled and his hands rose to cover his face. He stayed that way for a second or two and then, with a deep sigh, he lowered his hands. 'I was so wrong.'

'Did you hurt Sean O'Hare?'

'What?' The question coming from left field seemed to shock Richard, just as O'Shaughnessy intended. 'Of course I didn't. I would never hurt Sean.' Outrage in his voice. 'He's my best friend. I love the guy. What happened to him . . . it's unconscionable.' Richard struggled to compose himself. 'Jesus! What a question. Do I have to stay here and answer this shit?' he asked Tina.

'Does he?' Tina lifted a ginger brow, knowing exactly what O'Shaughnessy was going to say.

'No, that's it for now. But I would ask that you don't leave Innisard without notifying us.' O'Shaughnessy stood, before banging his way out of the room.

'What happens now?' Richard asked Tina.

'Unfortunately, now you don't get to go on your honeymoon.'

'But the garda didn't say anything about not going?'

'If you have any sense, Richard, you will stay and see this through. The only strike against you in your family's murder is that you ran away – don't do the same thing here.'

'I know you're right.' Richard ran a hand through his hair. 'But Jenny is going to be pissed. I'm pissed.'

'I know you are.' Tina placed a hand on his arm. 'It's not fair, but then life isn't fair, as you know only too well.'

Richard gave her a wry smile as he stood. 'After you.' He opened the door.

'I'm going to stay. I want to keep pushing them to find Sharon Sumner and nail down your alibi.'

'Then I should stay, too.' Richard closed the door.

'No. Jenny needs you. You might not be able to go away on your honeymoon, but the pair of you both deserve a honeymoon of some kind. Go, be with your wife. Your wedding breakfast starts in . . .' She looked at her watch. 'Thirty-five minutes.'

'Damn. I'd forgotten all about it.'

'But the aunts won't. Go. The second I know anything, I'll let you know.'

But Richard didn't move. 'A few minutes ago you said I should stay and see this through. That the only strike against me in my family's murder was that I ran away. Well, this feels like running away. And even though I'm worried about Jenny, she's with family who will keep her safe. I think I should stay a bit longer.'

'Getting a video link set up for Sharon Sumner could take hours. Days,' Tina warned him.

'I'll take my chances.'

Tina studied him for a moment, knew by his face that he wouldn't budge. 'OK. I'll go and set a rocket under the gardaí, see if I can speed the process up. And I'll get one of them to pop in with a cuppa or something for you.'

'Thanks, Tina.' Richard hugged her. 'Sean is one lucky guy. And he'll tell you that himself soon.'

'From your lips to God's ears,' Tina whispered, wishing she had time to phone the hospital. The sooner she was done here, the sooner she could check on Sean.

With renewed fervour, she exited the room and made her way down the disgustingly dank corridor, heels clicking, until she spied her prey.

'O'Shaughnessy. My client and I have things to do, people to meet, as I'm sure you do, too.' She barrelled past him into what she knew was their conference room, smiling inwardly as he followed like a little lapdog. 'So, let's get this done.'

Chapter Fifty-Nine

In the end, Jenny reached the B&B where Ita was staying in a lot less than an hour. Ita, obviously having more sense than Jenny, had ordered a taxi, which picked Jenny up a few kilometres from the lighthouse. Spooked by the episode in the woods, and soaked to the skin, Jenny was grateful for the lift.

'Look at the state of you,' Ita greeted her, pulling Jenny inside her room. 'Strip off immediately and go and take a hot shower. I'll have the B&B owner Mrs Mooney throw your clothes in the dryer.'

Jenny didn't have the energy to argue. Shivering, she took off her clothes and handed them to Ita.

'In you go.' Ita pushed her into the steaming shower. 'I'll be back in a tick.'

After Ita left, Jenny rested her head against the tiled wall and, without warning, began to sob. She wasn't sure what she was crying for: herself and Richard and their disaster of a wedding? Sean fighting for his life in the hospital? Dermot sitting in a jail cell awaiting an uncertain future? Dana and her lost lover? All of the above?

'Big girl pants,' she reminded herself. The thought of Gert brought a smile to her face. The smile faded as worry kicked in. Where was Gert? Why hadn't she been in touch? Jenny knuckled away more tears. Slowly, she regained her equilibrium, the task of washing her hair and soaping her body relaxing her until she felt almost human again.

'You decent?'

'Never,' Jenny replied.

'Good.' Ita opened the door, a thick towelling dressing gown over her arm. 'Mrs Mooney said for you to wear this while your things dry.'

'Thanks.' Jenny finished drying herself, before slipping the dressing gown on, tying it snugly around her waist and returning to the bedroom.

'Better?' Ita asked.

Jenny knew Ita had clocked her puffy face, knew full well she'd been crying. 'Actually . . . yeah, I feel a lot better. I'm ready to face the world.'

'The world, no, your family . . . yeah. In about . . .' Ita looked at her watch, 'thirty minutes. The breakfast your aunts and uncle have arranged in the Lucky Leprechaun,' she reminded Jenny. 'Fab pub, great vibe.'

'And you know this how?' Jenny asked suspiciously.

Ita grinned. 'Because after I dropped you off at Maggie's Point this morning, I went back there and your cousin Liam and his partner DJ Joe were gracious enough to let me re-avail myself of their services. Those two really know how to part-eeee.'

Jenny could imagine. Liam and his boyfriend worked hard – running the pub, plus Joe DJ'ing – and they partied even harder.

'I'm glad you had a good time,' she said, and meant it.

'Hey, wasn't like I expected to spend your wedding night with you guys.' Ita laughed, full-bodied and contagious. 'Or should I say wedding morning, seeing as you didn't get home till the early hours.'

'The gardaí took Richard in for questioning this morning.'

'What?' The laughter died on Ita's face. 'Why?'

'I have no idea.' Tears were close again. Jenny willed them away. 'They just said they wanted to ask him more questions.'

'Anything to do with his brother being Dana's baby daddy?'

'You figured it out?'

'Wasn't hard. Richard is no cheater; the guy loves you to distraction. Could only have been that absolute bollocks John.'

Jenny loved her for her certainty. Glad someone else knew Richard as well as she did.

'So, are they questioning Richard about his brother, or his best man and the other guy who was murdered?' Ita asked.

'I honestly don't know. I feel sick to my stomach about what's happening.' As if the thought sparked the action, Jenny felt bile rushing into her throat. She raced to the bathroom. The sound of her throwing up seemed loud in the quietness of the room. Jenny took her time, washed her face, rinsed her mouth, before returning to the room.

Ita was still sitting on the bed where she'd left her. She looked Jenny over with a practised eye. 'And now you not drinking the night before your wedding makes sense. You're pregnant, aren't you?'

'Yes.' Jenny sat on the bed next to her friend. 'But I wanted Richard to be the first to know.'

'Richard doesn't know?' Ita's voice was almost a squeal. 'Whyever not? Oh.' Her voice quietened. 'Doesn't he want kids? Not surprised with a nutter for a brother. Could be hereditary.'

'Great. Another thing I didn't know I had to worry about.' Jenny wondered if Ita had actually hit on the truth. Had Richard's reluctance to get pregnant stemmed from the secret he'd been keeping; the fear that his brother's illness might resurface if they had children? He hadn't been particularly pleased to find out he had a nephew either, probably for the same reason.

'Sorry. Not sorry. It's something you both need to consider.'

'I guess, but initially it wasn't like that. We both wanted to wait until after the wedding; have a little "us" time before we tried for a baby.'

'Methinks you both tried just a little too hard,' Ita snorted. 'Sorry.'

'We have this little . . . joke,' Jenny admitted. 'What we'd do whenever we actually got pregnant; like, what we'd say. I had it all planned. I was going to get all nice and cosy and romantic and then I'd say, "I've brought my work home with me." And then we'd . . . we'd . . .'

'Ah, you didn't get any cosy and romantic time this weekend, did ya?'

'No.' Jenny knuckled back tears. 'I don't know why I'm so upset. I mean, two men are dead, Sean's in hospital—'

'Hormones, get used to it.' But for all the harshness of her words, Ita's voice was tender and she hugged Jenny close. 'The right time will come, and when it does, it will be perfect, whether it's this weekend, next week or next month.'

'Sounds a bit like our honeymoon.'

'Huh?'

'Don't ask. It's been on, off, cancelled – by us, and then everyone else.' Jenny's laugh was hollow. 'It's like the universe is trying to tell me something.'

'It is. It's telling you that everything happens in its own good time.' Ita took Jenny's face in her hands. 'This is not a surprise, is it?'

'No.'

'And it's not always a bad thing?'

'No.'

'So, we're stressing, why?'

'Because I'm neurotic,' Jenny admitted, cupping her hands around Ita's. 'It's just . . . Richard is so fixated on getting me away from here.'

'He's looking after you, like any good husband.'

'I know.'

'He loves you.'

'I know.'

'And now we're back to: so, why are you stressing?' Ita raised a brow and the two friends smiled at each other.

'Thanks, Ita,' Jenny said at last.

'You're welcome.'

The two sat in companionable silence until Mrs Mooney knocked on the door to say Jenny's clothes were ready.

'Liam and DJ Joe's wedding breakfast is going to be a little odd without a groom,' Ita said when Jenny was dressed.

'Liam and Joe's . . .? Damn, what time do we have to be at the Lucky Leprechaun again?'

'Now,' Ita said, checking her watch. 'I can make excuses for you if—'

'No. I'm not running. Not this time. And I really need to talk to Aunt Gert.'

'Then let's go, my little hormonal buddy.'

Chapter Sixty

Tina sat with SIO O'Shaughnessy, not in the windowless room where she'd left Richard, but at the head of a long conference room, their two chairs pulled up tight to a sturdy wooden table where a laptop sat. The decor here was brighter, but not by much. Still the same shitty brown carpet tiles and beige walls from the entrance hallway, the same smell of sweat and pizza.

The other plainclothes had cleared out shortly after she'd stormed in, hopefully off doing their various jobs. A lone man remained; overweight with the reddened complexion of either a drinker or a man with serious high blood pressure – or both – who worked quietly at the end of the room, seemingly oblivious to their presence.

The dial tone of the video meeting began. Funny how quickly O'Shaughnessy admitted to finding Sharon Sumner when faced with a very irate lawyer. A face appeared on the screen.

Sharon Sumner – or Armstrong, as she was now called – had aged well. A natural blonde, her pale complexion remained unlined. Her hair was cut in a simple bob that swung elegantly as she talked and gestured. And she gestured a lot, effusively moving her hands to make a point.

'My parents weren't happy with me, sneaking out to Stanton's party that night,' she said now in her crisp English accent. 'I got in so much trouble.' She grimaced at the memory, then seemed to realise where she was. 'Jesus . . .' She waved her hands. 'Nothing like what Richard had to face. I mean . . . his whole family . . .' Her face twisted with remembered grief. 'Sarah was just the sweetest girl and Mr and Mrs Filmore . . . Awful. So awful.' Her voice trailed into silence, and her hands stilled.

'So, Richard was your date that night?' O'Shaughnessy asked.

'Yes.'

'You're sure?'

'Of course I'm sure. Why are you asking me this after all this time? I told the cops then, and I'm telling you now, I was with Richard Filmore that night. Not John.'

'The thing is, Ms Sumner . . . sorry, Mrs Armstrong, the police report we have states that John Filmore said he was the one with you that night and that it was his brother Richard who committed the murders.'

'No way! As I told you, one of the cops did ask me at the time whether I was sure. I was sure. Trust me. John was a total psycho. You just had to look at him. There was nothing behind his eyes. Oh, he had a good act, most people fell for it. Not me.' She shivered. 'He was one scary dude. I wasn't surprised when I heard that he'd murdered his family. But now you're saying it wasn't him, but Richard? No way.' She shook her head, bobbed hair dancing, hands waving. 'Not a chance.'

O'Shaughnessy checked his file. 'Says here there was drink involved . . .'

'Oh right,' she threw up her hands. 'The drink thing. Jesus, I'm never going to live that one down. The cops wrote me off as a drunken teen. As if I didn't know my own mind. Bastards. Let me tell you again, just to be clear. Yes, I had a bit to drink, but no, I wasn't so out of it that I didn't know who I was with.' She glared down the screen. 'We were teenagers. There was *always* drink involved. You ever been one of them?' she asked O'Shaughnessy, not hiding her irritation.

Tina smothered a laugh. She liked this woman. O'Shaughnessy had requested she stay quiet during this meeting, so for that reason she said now, 'I believe you, Sharon.'

'Well, thank fuck for someone with sense.'

'But we need something more from you, something that will clear Richard.'

'Is he OK?' Sharon asked, sitting closer to the camera. 'I've often wondered about him.' She gave a half-smile. 'He was the guy that got away, you know what I mean?'

'I do. I have one of those myself,' Tina admitted. 'And yes, he's OK. He just got married to a lovely girl.'

'Oh, that's good. Tell him I say hi, and that I'm sorry.'

'Sorry for what?' Tina asked.

'Oh,' Sharon giggled. 'It's silly really, I was a klutz and he was my knight in shining armour. Stupid schoolgirl stuff.'

'So, there's nothing more you can add to your initial statement?' O'Shaughnessy shot in.

'Um, not that I can think of. I really want to help,' Sharon said, her face earnest. 'I just don't know what else to tell you, except I was definitely with Richard that night, not John. John was a creep.' She shuddered. 'Trust me, they might have looked identical, but they were two very different people.'

'OK, thank you for your time, Mrs Armstrong.' O'Shaughnessy slapped his file closed.

'One more thing,' Tina shot in, desperate to keep the woman on the line. 'You said Richard was your knight in shining armour – can you expand on that?'

'Can I?' Sharon swiped a hand through the air. 'Still gives me goosebumps to this day. Happened that night,' she said, as if just remembering.

'The night of the murders?' O'Shaughnessy was now paying attention.

'Yes. Richard and I slipped away from Olly Stanton's party, went out the back. There was a fence there, next to a large field – the guy next door had horses, or a farm, or something. It wasn't a large fence, but Richard . . . he had this thing, a phobia, I guess you could call it. He was petrified of heights.' Her voice lowered with shame. 'I didn't understand back then. All I cared about was that it was dark, secluded.' Her face flushed attractively. 'We went there to neck, except, yes, we'd had a little too much to drink and we . . . sorta toppled off the fence. Richard was such a gent; he took the brunt of the fall. But we didn't know there was a huge jagged boulder in the field and he landed on it. He said he was OK, but there was so much blood. That stone was razor-sharp, and it cut deep, right to the bone. Right here . . .' She pointed to the bottom of her spine. 'It had to hurt, but all he was worried about was me. He was such a gent,' she said again, her voice soft with memory.

'Could the fall have left a scar?' Tina asked quickly, before O'Shaughnessy could finish the call.

'A scar? I don't know. I never saw Richard again after that night so I have no idea.'

O'Shaughnessy's finger hovered over the 'End' button. 'Well, thank you—'

'But I have to say,' Sharon continued. 'With the amount of blood I saw and how deep the wound was, I'd be surprised if there wasn't a scar of some sort.' She stared into the camera, not at them, more into the past. 'I'm glad

Richard was able to get away. He was a really nice guy. Tell him . . . tell him I said hello, will you?'

'Not a word,' O'Shaughnessy told Tina as he shut down the computer. 'This doesn't mean your client is innocent.'

'Then let's go and find out. He's just down the hall.' Tina raised an elegantly plucked auburn brow. 'Well?'

'Fitzpatrick,' O'Shaughnessy shouted to the red-faced man still working away at the other desk. 'Any word of an old scar, lower back, on our first victim?'

Fitzpatrick didn't even need to check his notes. 'You mean among the twenty-six stab wounds, bruises and other contusions? Nothing else noted. You need me to check?'

'Yeah, get on to the pathologist.'

'Will do.'

'And while we wait . . .' Tina made a sweeping gesture out the door, towards the room where Richard still sat.

'At last.' Richard jumped to his feet when Tina and O'Shaughnessy entered the room. 'I've been here for—'

'Lift your shirt,' O'Shaughnessy ordered.

'What? You can't just—'

'Trust me, Richard,' Tina said, holding out her hand. 'We need to check something. It's important.'

For a second, it looked like Richard wouldn't comply, then, with a muttered curse, he stood, pulling his T-shirt from his tracksuit trousers, lifting it up. 'Satisfied?'

'Turn around,' O'Shaughnessy barked.

'I don't—'

'Please, Richard, just do as he asks – for now,' Tina told him. 'I promise you I'll step in if I think it's against your best interests.'

Richard huffed a sigh, but did as Tina asked, turning and lifting his shirt higher. 'How far would you like me to go? You want me to remove my trousers next?'

Tina and O'Shaughnessy moved closer, staring at the lower part of Richard's smooth back. There, nestled in the groove of his spine, just above his waist was a ragged-edged scar, thick and white with age.

O'Shaughnessy went to the door, called to someone in the hallway. A muted conversation ensued and minutes later a young female garda entered holding a camera.

'What's going on?' Richard asked.

'We're hopefully getting you out of here,' Tina told him. 'Do you mind if I take a picture, too?' She took out her phone.

'Why not? Looks like everyone wants a bit of me.' When they were done, Richard tucked his T-shirt back into his tracksuit bottoms and sat down. 'Now, are you going to tell me what's happening? I'm guessing you talked to Sharon? She's the only one other than Jenny who knows about my scar.'

'Before we answer that, can you tell us exactly how you received the scar you have on your back?' O'Shaughnessy asked.

Richard looked at Tina, who nodded that it was OK to tell him. 'I told you before, it happened the night my family was murdered, which is why I don't talk about it.'

'Look it. I understand, Doctor, but we really need to know the details, if you wouldn't mind?'

So, Richard told them the story of that fateful night; the party at Oliver Stanton's house, the fall off the fence . . . When he was done, there was a minute's silence.

'I reckon we're done here,' Tina said. 'The scar proves conclusively that my client was the person with Sharon

Sumner the night the Filmores were murdered. John Filmore lied and the English cops fell for it. Now, is my client free to go?'

O'Shaughnessy nodded curtly. 'You're free to go. For now,' he added.

'Come on, Richard, let's go and find your wife.'

Richard rose eagerly.

'Look it. I . . . em, didn't want to say anything while we were . . . em, conducting our interview,' O'Shaughnessy said. 'But I have something I need to tell you both.'

Tina didn't like O'Shaughnessy's tone. If she didn't know better, she'd think he was feeling sorry for them. 'What's wrong?'

'Garda Turley just told me there, when she brought in the camera, that your aunt, Mrs Gert Foley, is missing.'

'Gert?' Tina froze. 'What do you mean she's missing? Since when?'

'Consensus is yesterday evening. That's the last confirmed sighting of her.'

'Yesterday—?' Tina looked at Richard, who appeared equally horrified.

'Jenny must be out of her mind with worry.' He pushed past O'Shaughnessy. 'I don't believe you people. We told you something like this would happen. Someone is stalking us, been in our home, killed my brother. What more evidence do you want?' He shook his head in disgust. 'Let's go, Tina. I need to be with my wife.'

Chapter Sixty-One

Jenny could feel the walls of the Lucky Leprechaun, like the censure of the crowd, closing in on her. Some wedding breakfast this was turning out to be. Gert was missing; hadn't been seen since late yesterday, at the wedding. Word had also gone round that the gardaí had picked up Richard for questioning and, like Chinese whispers, the news had spread through the crowd quicker than you could say free drinks. Small-town gossip being what it was had linked the two events, and not in her or Richard's favour.

It was strange; Jenny had returned to Innisard expecting to be treated as an outsider, but had been welcomed with open arms. Now . . . now she felt like the stranger she always knew she was. But Jenny didn't give a shit about the gossipers, the maligners.

Gert was missing!

Fear for her aunt slid like molten lava in her stomach. Jenny's knees began to shake, tremble so violently she wasn't sure they'd hold her up. She felt hot and cold at the same time and the world began to tilt.

'Sit here.' Ita lowered her to a chair. 'I'll get you some water. Won't be a tick.'

Jenny barely heard her; the heat and smell of so many bodies overpowering; voices rising and falling making her dizzy.

'Here, drink this.' A glass was pressed into her hand.

Jenny looked up, surprised to find not Ita but Fintan Callaghan and his perfect Hugh Grant hair standing over her. 'Thanks, but I want to keep a clear head—'

'It's water. You look like you need it.'

Jenny didn't realise how much she did until she took a long gulp of the cold, refreshing liquid, relishing its icy trail down her throat. Her mind instantly cleared, stomach settling.

'Told you.' Fintan smiled, glasses glinting in the overhead light as he cupped her shoulder with his hand, pressing firmly.

'Thank you.' Jenny went to stand, but Fintan's hand remained heavy on her shoulder.

'Don't rush yourself. You've been under a lot of pressure. You need to look after yourself, Jenny.' Dark brown eyes stared at her intently. 'Do you want something to eat? Or do you want to get out of here? I'll happily take you somewhere quieter. This must be so—'

Over the roar of voices in the pub, one stood out, moving closer, 'Jenny? Jenny?'

'Thank you for the water, Fintan, but my husband is here now.'

This time when Jenny went to stand, Fintan let her.

'Richard.' Jenny threw herself into her husband's arms.

Richard settled his arm around Jenny's shoulder, glaring at Fintan. 'I know you. You're the guy who accosted me my first day in Innisard.'

'What?' Jenny looked at Fintan, aghast.

Fintan hung his head, shamefaced. 'I'm really sorry about that. You see, I knew about Dana's baby, the father, and I thought . . .'

'That I was a two-timing bastard?'

'Yeah, something like that.'

'Anything else you've done?' Richard snarled. 'Like attack my best man?'

Fintan stepped back, holding up his hands. 'No. I didn't hurt anyone. I was only looking out for Jen—'

'That's *my* job.' Richard's voice was firm, implacable.

'Noted,' Fintan said stiffly. 'I'll . . . er . . . go.'

'Yes, you do that.'

With a last soulful look at Jenny, Fintan scurried off.

'Are you OK?' Richard asked.

'I'm more concerned about you,' Jenny said, relieved to see him. 'What happened with the gardaí?'

'I'll tell you later. What's this about Gert being missing?'

'Oh, Richard, I'm so worried about her.'

Richard tilted her chin with his thumb and forefinger. 'You look awfully pale.'

'I'm . . . fine.' Now wasn't the time for her good news. 'I just had a bit of a . . . scare back at the lighthouse.'

'What happened? Are you sure you're all right?' Richard stepped back to examine her face.

'Probably my imagination, but I convinced myself that someone was watching me after the gardaí took you away, and again in Wishers Woods on the way here.'

'The stalker?' Richard glared to where Fintan had disappeared.

'That's what I thought, but it could just as easily have been a reporter.' Jenny tried to downplay how scared she'd been.

Obviously her acting skills needed improving, because Richard wasn't buying it. 'Oh, my love.' He pulled her into his arms. 'You must have been so frightened. Makes me more determined than ever to get you away from here. Were you able to rebook our flights?'

'I— Can we chat about that later? I'm more interested in what the gardaí wanted with you.'

Richard let her change the subject, filling her in on what had occurred at the station.

Jenny gasped. 'John told the police that you killed your family? Oh my God! How awful. And they got in touch with Sharon. The one who got away,' she mocked gently. 'I'm so grateful to her. She *saw* you then and she sees you now; saved you.'

'Yes, she did.'

'Are you OK?'

'I am now that I'm with you,' Richard said, squeezing her waist. 'Tina was great. I don't know what I would have done without her.'

'Speaking of which, I'd better go and thank her.' Jenny dropped a kiss on Richard's lips, hurrying over to Tina, who was just closing her phone.

'Sean?' she asked.

'Yeah. No change.'

'I'm sorry.'

'You and me both. Have you seen my dad?'

'Uncle Hugh? He was here a minute ago.' Jenny turned, but the immense figure of her uncle was no longer visible. 'That's odd.'

'Not really.' Tina's voice heaved with frustration. 'He's making a bloody sport of disappearing. But that's a problem for later. I have to say, Cuz, an awful lot of bad shit has happened since your husband arrived in Innisard.'

'Don't you mean my husband and me? After all, we arrived here together.' This conversation wasn't going the way Jenny intended.

'Maybe.' Tina didn't back down. 'I will ask you this once, and only once: are you one hundred per cent sure your husband has nothing to do with what's going on here?'

Tina had every right to ask the question, but her cousin didn't know Richard. He was a good man and, even given the revelations of the last few days, an honest man.

'I can tell you, hand on heart, that my Richard has never willingly hurt another human being; never would, never will. Come on, you've just cleared him of murder, that's gotta mean something?'

'The fact that I had to do that isn't a great defence, Jenny.'

'True. But I am confident that Richard would never be part of what's happening here. Someone else is involved, Tina. You have to believe me. We have a stalker. He's followed us from Dublin; he's been in Maggie's Point. He's messing with us . . . me.' Jenny told Tina about feeling watched that morning. 'We think it might be Fintan Callaghan,' she whispered.

'What? Why? Richard didn't say anything back at the station.'

'He didn't know then. He only recognised Fintan, just now, as the man who accosted him the day we got here.'

'My God. Why would Fintan do something like that?'

Jenny explained how Fintan had thought Richard was two-timing her with Dana.

'Dear Lord, the day just gets weirder.' Tina's face turned haggard. 'Be it your stalker, Fintan or some random psycho, someone *is* responsible. Sean is in hospital, could be dying right at this very minute. Dermot, our reprobate, pain-in-the-ass cousin, is being held on suspicion of murder – the gardaí are trying to link him to John's death. No great surprise, I'll grant you. And I don't want this to get out yet, but there's word that Dana might be involved, too.'

'Dana? No. That can't be right.'

'Trust me, that's only a fraction of what's going on. But when you tack on Aunt Gert going missing . . .' Tina's voice faltered, composure cracking. 'Aunt Gert, Jenny. She would *never* disappear without a word, let us worry like this. Never.'

Jenny agreed. 'No, she wouldn't.'

'This isn't good, Jenny.' All the fire died out of Tina's voice and her body sagged.

Jenny hugged her cousin. 'No. This is really, really not good.'

Finally, Tina stepped away, roughly swiping at her eyes. 'I'm sorry I intimated that Richard was involved.'

'We're all involved – one way or another.'

'True.'

''Xcept me.' Ita joined them, quickly followed by Richard. 'I'm just here for the food and drink – oh, and the quiet, relaxing couple of days Jenny promised me.'

'Yeah, sorry about that.'

'Long as the drinks keep coming, I'm good.' Ita grinned, tipping her glass in salute.

'Lush,' Jenny's cousin Liam said good-naturedly, as he dropped a platter of food on the table next to them. 'Hi, Sis.' He hugged Tina before turning to Jenny. 'You bearing up, Cuz?'

'Ask me later.'

Soft hazel eyes studied her. 'I most definitely will. As for you, lush,' he nodded to Ita, 'I thought you'd be on the road by now?'

'And leave you and DJ Joe to all the fun? I don't think so.'

Liam laughed. 'Your friend here,' he told Jenny, 'has almost drunk us dry. She may say she's Nepalese, but I definitely think she's part Irish.'

'*Póg mo thóin*,' Ita said slowly, carefully enunciating the words.

Jenny looked at her friend in surprise, but Ita appeared oblivious. She obviously didn't know what she'd just said. 'OK, how drunk did you all get last night?' she asked Liam, who was trying hard not to laugh.

'It means let's be friends,' Ita said. 'Doesn't it?' she asked, the penny finally dropping.

'Only if you really want to *kiss my ass*.'

'Oh, my God! You outfoxed me.' Ita flapped a good-natured slap at Liam.

The humour was welcome. For a second, the knot in Jenny's stomach unravelled. It tightened again as Evil and Scuttlebutt approached.

'The gardaí have been notified and are arranging a search party for Gert. Cap has taken his boat out,' Scuttlebutt told them. 'He'll search the shoreline for as long as he can, but the sea is really rough out there.'

Jenny and Tina looked at each other. They both knew Cap wasn't searching the beach; he was searching the water for a body. Jenny was glad to feel Richard's arm around her. It helped chase away the chill at the thought of Gert out in the icy sea in the gathering storm. She wasn't stupid. Tina had called it: Aunt Gert would never worry them this way, not if there was a breath left in her body.

Chapter Sixty-Two

She dismisses me so easily,
  like I mean nothing to her.
How dare she!
Can't she see what I've done for her?
What I'm willing to do for her?
I love her so much.
How can she turn her back on me?
She is the love of my life,
but she needs to understand.
She HAS to understand –
Or I won't be responsible for my actions.

Chapter Sixty-Three

Tina spied her dad ducking out of the Lucky Leprechaun, shoulders hunched, trying to make himself as small as possible, as normal as possible. It was never going to work.

'You're not built to hide, Dad.' She stopped him in the narrow hallway, as he went to push open the door. Outside, the wind howled like a strangled cat, making the front door next to them shudder.

'Tina.' Slowly, her dad turned. 'I wasn't hiding. I—'

'Spare me, Dad. I know when someone's trying to avoid me. It's kind of a prerequisite of my job. But now it's time to talk. Past time,' she told him.

Hugh's face folded in on itself. 'I know.' He hung his head. 'Yes, I was avoiding you. I knew you'd seen me with Pretty at Wishers Woods. Damnit! I knew how that would look. The position it would put you in, especially when Evie asked you to represent Dermot. Dermot needed you, I would just . . .' His sigh rose from deep within his chest. 'I would just have complicated things.'

'Then uncomplicate them, Dad.' But it hadn't escaped her notice that her dad had called Pete McAvoy 'Pretty', like he knew him well; friends even. She recalled O'Shaughnessy's intense look in the garda station. What was she missing?

'Does it have something to do with those?' She pointed to his tattoos.

Hugh's fingers trailed over the lines of thick ink on his arm. 'I keep them as a reminder; a warning to never go back.'

'Back where?'

'To the person I was when I got them.'

'You said you were very young?' It was about the only thing he *had* said about them.

'Eleven,' her dad said now. 'I was eleven. Thought I knew everything; a tough guy. I knew nothing.' He didn't look at Tina as he continued, seeming to shrink smaller and smaller with every word. 'I got in with a bad crowd. A *very* bad crowd. Started with small things, but those small things led to bigger things. Before I knew it, I was doing messages for Big Benny.'

'Big Benny? Oh, no, Dad. Drugs?'

'Yes.' Hugh looked her straight in the eye, shame clear on his face. 'I was stupid. A complete and utter fool.'

'And Gran and Granddad, couldn't they—'

'It was shortly after Granddad died, love. I went off the rails a bit. OK, more than a bit.'

The same way her cousin Jenny had after her parents died. Now Tina knew why her dad had been so patient with her cousin. He'd been through the same thing.

'I have a past, I admit it. But I overcame it. I changed. I'm *not* that person anymore.'

'You think I don't know that, Dad?' Tina was angry now. 'You think I can't separate the child you were when you got those . . .' She swiped her hand angrily at the tattoos she could see, and the one she knew lay beneath his clothes. '. . . To the person you are now? You think that little of me?'

'No, I—'

'We can discuss that failing later, Dad. There's no time now. Gert is missing, and I need to know if it has anything to do with your argument with Pete McAvoy.'

'No. God! No.' Hugh threw up his hands. 'Damnit.' He took a deep breath, huge chest straining with emotion. 'I knew Dermot was in heavy with Big Benny. I tried to pull him out, talk to him, help him. But he was beyond help. He owed that bastard money. So much money, Tina. And I knew Dermot wouldn't be the only one to pay. I was keeping an eye on my sister – Evil is a pain, but she's family. As is Dana, and I knew she would become their main focus – an accountant, pregnant *and* loyal to her brother. The perfect trifecta. She'd do anything for Dermot and being pregnant made her vulnerable. These people are animals. I knew they'd work on her, hurt her, if need be. So, when I saw Pete skulking around Wishers Woods, I warned him off, that's all it was. A warning.'

Tina didn't tell him that his warning had come too late. Dana was in this up to her beautiful no-longer-pregnant neck. 'But why avoid me?'

'Oh, darling. When Dermot was arrested and Evie asked you to represent him, I knew that if I told you what I knew that would have been so bad for Dermot. I'm sorry, honey.' Hugh's face creased with sorrow. 'I had to hide from you, at least until the gardaí found out the truth.'

'And what if they hadn't?' Tina slapped her dad's chest. It was like slapping a slab of concrete.

'Then you would have,' Hugh said simply, because he believed it. Believed in her.

Damn. The man was gonna make her cry. And nothing pissed Tina off more than having her anger spiked – just when it was about to go nuclear.

'You need to tell the gardaí everything you've told me.'

'I will. Do you . . . do you think Gert's OK?' her dad asked, sounding nothing like his usual confident self.

'No.' Tina couldn't lie to him.
'Me neither.'
Damn.

Chapter Sixty-Four

Tom stood outside the Lucky Leprechaun amazed at the size of the gathered crowd. It looked like the whole town had come out in wretched weather to help search for Gert Foley – the whole town, plus a clatter of reporters trying to blend in. The Innisarders weren't falling for it, giving the interlopers a wide berth. Tom knew Gert was well respected in Innisard, but he hadn't quite appreciated *just* how respected.

He spied Fintan Callaghan among the throng, doing his best to edge closer to Jenny while also attempting to stay out of sight – and doing it badly. Callaghan had been on his radar ever since Scuttlebutt had fingered him as the man who had tackled Richard, and everything he had learned since had his antennae pinging. The man was a loner, and made no bones about his infatuation for Jenny. Definitely someone who bore watching.

A decision that was almost immediately validated when Tina Connors had confirmed the assault mere minutes ago. The lawyer had also relayed the kicker that Richard's brother, John, was the father of Dana's baby. *That* was a whole other soap opera. Tom had informed the station, determined to keep an eye on Fintan Callaghan.

Someone else who bore watching was Cap Byrne, who had taken his boat out, ostensibly to search for Gert, but who knew with the man? Cap could just as easily be disposing of a body, or doing a smuggling run, although the encroaching storm would surely put paid to that.

Tom's third person of interest – Big Benny – was conspicuously absent. No surprise there. Big Benny wasn't exactly known for his altruistic personality, or for getting personally involved in a gardaí investigation. In fact, the opposite was usually true. So, with only one of his persons of interest available, Tom kept his steely gaze focused on Fintan Callaghan.

He gathered the crowd together, standing atop a park bench in the pouring rain so he could be seen *and* heard over the icy wind whipping in from the sea. His team of gardaí, plus every garda they could gather from outlying towns – both north and south of the border – stood next to him, ready to help co-ordinate the search. Coats billowed and snapped, heads inched deeper into necks, but everyone was silent, waiting.

'Right, the house-to-house has found nothing, so we're going to work our way from here to Wishers Woods. Our counterparts from plainclothes, with the help of gardaí seconded from other stations, will begin at Maggie's Point and work their way back to us. We're going to take it slowly,' he shouted over the howling wind, trying to keep his balance on the bench. 'I know it's miserable out, but the tiniest thing could help, so be alert. We move together, no one leaves the formation.' He caught the eye of each and every reporter. 'Agreed?'

Resounding shouts, and sullen nods from the newspaper reporters.

'Then let's do this.' Tom took the lead.

They were over thirty wide as they left the town. A number that multiplied quickly when they hit the perimeter of Wishers Woods until over five hundred people stood ready to search for Gert.

'Fan out,' Tom told the gardaí. 'Intersperse yourselves between the villagers, and keep a bloody eye on the vultures.'

The officers nodded.

'Make a line,' Tom shouted to the crowd, almost screaming to be heard over the wind. 'Start walking in slow, measured steps. And remember,' he told them. 'No detail is too small.'

Tom waited to make sure everyone followed his instructions. The line of hunched figures snaked as far as the eye could see as the inhabitants of Innisard stepped into the thicket of trees.

It was hard-going; already, the forest floor was a quagmire. Tom hitched the collar of his waterproof coat, glad of its fleece lining, but the rain was insidious, sliding into every available gap. Any evidence not collected from the Devil's Teeth and Pete McAvoy's murder scene, never mind Sean O'Hare's attempted murder scene, would be washed away by now, Tom thought as he ploughed on. He didn't want to dwell on what might have happened to Gert and, if the worst had happened, to her crime scene. He tried not to look at Gert's nearest and dearest next to him, not wanting to see the hope on their faces, knowing he'd be the one to crush it.

'Scuttlebutt told me Gert was visiting Doctor Taggart,' Jenny said at his side. 'Something to do with her heart. Do you think she could have had some kind of cardiac episode, be lying out here?'

'It's possible.'

'I mean, it's only September, the nights aren't that cold. She could survive one night, couldn't she?'

'She could.'

Jenny wasn't stupid. 'But you don't think we're going to find her alive, do you?'

Tom let the other villagers move ahead, standing with Jenny and her family. 'I respect you all too much to lie to you. You all know Gert. *I* know Gert. She doesn't mess about. Something is keeping her from getting in touch with you. Best case, she's in distress, as you said, and needs our help. Worst case . . .' He kept his gaze steady. 'Either way, the sooner we get to her, the better.'

They were a pathetic-looking group, rain dripping into eyes, off noses, and into necks and boots, but, as one, the rounded shoulders straightened. 'Then let's get to her,' Jenny said, holding her hand out to her husband on one side and her cousin Tina on the other. They both did the same to the person next to them. And it didn't stop at the relatives, continuing until everyone in the line was holding hands, forging through the forest with renewed purpose.

Tom Carr had never felt prouder in his life to call a place home, and these people his friends.

Chapter Sixty-Five

They hadn't been in Wishers Woods more than twenty minutes — twenty very long, very wet and very mucky minutes — when Jenny saw Sergeant Carr stop. He moved behind them, speaking softly into his radio. When he returned to their side, Jenny didn't need him to say the words. She knew. She'd known the second his radio had squawked and he had angled his body away from hers, his voice dropping. How many times had she done the same thing when she had news she would have done anything not to impart to an expectant parent; to change their world — and not in a good way?

Her hand moved unconsciously to her belly. Life and death. They walked hand in hand, and both were with her now.

'Where?' she asked.

To his credit, Sergeant Carr didn't attempt to misunderstand. 'The old lighthouse keeper's shed.'

So close! Had Aunt Gert been there all night? While she slept? While she laughed and ate today, was Gert lying there all alone?

'When?'

'Winston thinks early yesterday evening. Not confirmed,' he hurried to add. 'Just a best guess.'

The other family members had stopped, moved until they were huddled next to one another. The rest of the line, as the news filtered through, stayed away, giving them privacy.

'How?' Tina asked. 'Was it foul play or—'

'Again, best guess, there appears to be no outward signs of trauma.'

Jenny released a breath she didn't know she was holding. Please God it would be natural causes, but that still begged the question: why had Gert gone to Maggie's Point, to the lighthouse keeper's shed?

'Any idea why she—'

'Why?' Evil wailed. 'Why our Gert?' She bent at the waist, sobbing.

Scuttlebutt – after a war of eyes with her brother Hugh, who reacted like a deer in the headlights and refused to move – hurried to comfort her sister.

Sergeant Carr and his officers formed a barrier around them, fending off the reporters with steely looks. As the trees shook beneath the growing might of the wind, and the rain grew in volume, the rest of the search party stood in solidarity with Gert's family, then, one by one, they came, pressing a hand, offering a soft grimace or a whispered 'sorry', before slipping into the trees and back to Innisard.

Fintan Callaghan knew better than to approach her and Richard. Brown eyes creased with sadness, he nodded curtly before moving on.

'Bastard,' Richard muttered after him.

'Leave it. It doesn't matter.' Nothing mattered. Not now. Not without Gert. But she noted Sergeant Carr's eyes following Fintan as he left. He wouldn't escape so easily. The gardaí were on to him now.

Jenny stood with her new husband, her aunts and uncles, her cousins and a handful of gardaí and wished Gert could have seen, could have known, the esteem in which she was held. She knuckled back tears as she heard Gert's voice in her head.

As God wills it. So will it be.

None of them had really cared about the wind and rain as they'd started out – too focused on their search – but as they were led back to the village by the gardaí, Jenny knew each and every one of them was feeling the chill now; the chill of death's icy breath.

The Lucky Leprechaun hadn't changed when they returned to the warmth of the bar, but they had.

Gert was more than a sister, and aunt, she was the backbone of their family, and they were broken, lost without her.

Chapter Sixty-Six

Losing Gert will hurt her.
 I hold up my hands.
 I know I'm responsible for hurting my beautiful Jenny.
 And that causes pain like you wouldn't believe.
 But Gert isn't my fault – I couldn't let her spoil my plans.
 Jenny will come to see that.
 When we are finally together, she will understand everything.

Chapter Sixty-Seven

Jenny and her family gathered in the Lucky Leprechaun, a bedraggled, desolate bunch.

Liam barred the door. No one but family allowed. Then the stories came; anecdotes about Gert that were both funny and beautiful. And so, so painful.

Liam and DJ Joe bustled about, offering food, tea, coffee, alcohol, but no one was in the mood. Not even Ita; for once passing up the offer of free drink. She rose reluctantly at 6.30 p.m. 'I don't want to go, but my taxi's booked to take me back to the lighthouse to pick up my car. I'm on early shift tomorrow and I already pulled in favours to get off for your wedding . . .'

'I know. It's OK.' Jenny pulled her in tight for a hug.

'How are you feeling?' Ita whispered. 'The baby? You've had an awful shock.'

'I'm fine, I promise,' Jenny told her. But the truth was, that while physically she was fine, emotionally she was a mess.

'Just doesn't seem right.'

'I'm more than capable of looking after my wife,' Richard came to stand next to Jenny. His voice was playful, but his face was hard.

'Keep your knickers on,' Ita told him. 'I know you'll look after her. But are you sure you don't want to share the taxi with me to the lighthouse?'

'Our car's at the B&B,' Richard told her. 'We'll take that.'

'OK. Call me,' Ita told Jenny before letting go. 'I want to know the second Sean wakes up. And you' – she dragged Richard in for a hug – 'guard that woman with your life.'

'*Jawohl, mein Führer.*'

'*Póg mo thóin.*' Ita grinned. 'I think that's my favourite phrase now.' She slapped Richard on the back. 'Look after yourself, too. Jenny, fool that she is, needs you.'

'And I need her,' Richard answered seriously. 'She'll come to no harm with me.'

'Word.' With a last wave, Ita left to begin her long journey back to Dublin.

'Alone at last,' Richard said facetiously.

And suddenly that was all Jenny wanted. To be alone with Richard in her tower of solace as she tried to come to terms with her loss. But it took another thirty minutes before they could extricate themselves from her family.

'C'mon.' Liam was at her side. 'My car's outside. Let's get you out of here.'

'We've imposed enough,' Richard told him. 'We'll take my car. It's still at the B&B. I haven't had a chance to pick it up yet.'

'Sorry, mate.' Liam shook his head. 'One of the punters told me some little scrotes noticed your car sitting unattended for a few days and the little buggers thought it would be great craic to let your tyres down. I can help you pump them up, but I thought, in this weather, you'd rather—'

'Few days? Jesus. It's only been a day and a half. What kind of town is this?'

'I know. But they didn't know all this shit was going to kick off. Don't worry' – Liam's genial face hardened – 'I have their names and they will rectify the damage once the storm has cleared. For now, better to get your lady home, don't you think?'

'Of course, you're right. Sorry, Liam. And thanks, for everything.' Richard shook Liam's hand.

'What about the pub?' Jenny asked. 'DJ Joe . . .?'

'He's fine, aren't you, love?' Liam waved to his partner working the pumps behind the bar.

DJ Joe waved back and blew Jenny a kiss, shouting, 'Go. I can handle this; you need to go home.'

Home, Jenny thought as she slipped into the back seat of Liam's car, letting Richard take the front. She bent her head as cameras flashed and voices yelled. Where was home now? Now that Gert was gone.

She fought back tears. It was so unfair. They'd only just reconnected. She'd been hoping . . . *to come home*. The thought was there, stark and clear in her mind. And it was true. Finding out she was pregnant, being back here . . . This is where she wanted to raise her child, with her family. But a big part of that dream was Gert. A girl needed her mother at a time like this and she'd just lost her second one. And it hurt so damn much.

'We're here.' Richard opened the car door, holding tight as the wind threatened to pull it out of his hand.

'Oh.' Lost in thought, Jenny hadn't noticed time passing. 'Thanks for the lift, Liam.'

'You're more than welcome.' His smile was sad, devastated. 'Try to get some sleep. You look like crap.'

She gave a wan grin at his attempt at humour and clambered from the car, hit by a blast of wind that almost knocked her off her feet.

'Let's get inside,' Richard shouted, slamming the car door, waving goodbye to Liam.

Jenny tried not to look at the lighthouse keeper's shed, yellow garda tape flapping angrily, as they ran for the postbox-red door. Tina had argued that, as the shed wasn't connected to Maggie's Point, the lighthouse couldn't be considered a crime scene, therefore the gardaí couldn't refuse Richard and Jenny entry to their legally rented abode. While Jenny was grateful to have a roof over her head, the lighthouse seemed much too close to where Gert had breathed her last.

Richard unlocked the lighthouse door. Shivering, they stepped inside into a welcome blast of heat. 'My God, it's like winter out there,' he said, taking off his coat, shaking the rain from his hair. 'You must be frozen.' He took Jenny's hands, rubbing them between his own. 'You're like ice, love. Here, let me.' He removed her handbag and took off her coat. She leaned on his shoulder as he slipped her boots off her feet. 'Your socks are wet, too. Let's get them off.'

Jenny stood, like a statue, as Richard rubbed his hands up and down her arms, trying to warm her.

'Why don't you go upstairs and have a shower. I'll make us a hot cuppa. Go on,' he said when she didn't move. 'You'll catch a chill if you don't get those wet things off you. Last thing you want right now is to be sick.'

'Sick?' His words finally penetrated. *The baby.* She had to think of the baby. 'Thanks, love.' Jenny kissed Richard and made her way wearily up the twisting lighthouse staircase.

For once, the glorious panorama window in the bedroom didn't elicit a second glance as she made her way to the bathroom. *Warm.* She needed to get warm. Jenny felt cold to the bone, beyond the bone. She was chilled to her very soul.

The shower heated her body, but did nothing to alleviate the chill in her heart. Weary beyond belief, Jenny didn't have the energy to soap herself, she just stood beneath the hot spray until Richard knocked the door.

'You OK in there?'

'Yeah. Be out now.' Jenny reluctantly switched off the shower and began to towel herself dry. No sexy negligee for her tonight. She pulled on a pair of workout leggings and a long-sleeved T-shirt, wrapping her damp hair in a towel.

'There you are.' Richard's worried eyes followed her progress as he emptied his pockets into the glass dish, before picking up the tray next to him. 'Get into bed and drink this. No argument,' he said. 'When you're done, I'll dry your hair. There's a plug next to your side of the bed. And then,' he said firmly, 'we sleep.'

Jenny was too tired to protest. She drank the tea Richard had prepared and sat quietly as he dried her hair with the hairdryer he found in the dressing-table drawer.

Then Richard switched off the light and got into bed, wrapping his arms around her. 'Now,' he breathed into her hair. 'We're finally alone.'

Jenny tried to make light. 'Yeah, if you discount the gardaí, crime tape and fingerprint residue.' *And your dead brother and my dead aunt.* But some pain was too deep to be verbalised.

And they both knew it.

Chapter Sixty-Eight

Sean O'Hare was in the battle of his life. The darkness was everywhere and had been for a long time. How long, Sean didn't know, but it seemed like forever. Oh, sometimes he heard things; soft, muted things that had him straining into the inky blackness. Were the sounds friend or foe? He didn't know.

He couldn't move his hands to test what was in front or behind him. He couldn't move anything. It was just pain. And blackness. And fear.

He knew he slept. Sleep was safe. He wanted to stay in the warm cocoon of slumber, but something told him he couldn't. Shouldn't. Sometimes he pictured a flash of yellow, a face. The face was strange to him and yet at the same time familiar. He wanted to see that face again, and that's why he fought to rise beyond the pain and the darkness.

There was something else he had to do; another reason to wake. He had to tell them – whoever *they* were – who had hurt him. Because he was hurt. His head ached so badly that he wanted to escape the pain, and sometimes the darkness was the escape he needed.

The people he loved were in danger and Sean knew he had to use the pain, not avoid it.

But the pain was too much. He couldn't fight it.

Slowly, he sank beneath the darkness again.

Chapter Sixty-Nine

Sunday morning screamed into existence with blasting gusts of wind and torrential rain. It seemed the *Oíche na Gaoithe Móire* the old folk talked about wasn't an overexaggeration. In fact, unbelievable as it sounded, it looked like it was about to be usurped, Tom decided when he finally reached the garda station for the morning conference. At least the older storm had only lasted one night. This one looked set to last a hell of a lot longer.

The phone lines had gone down around 3 a.m. and he knew it wouldn't be long before the electric went the same way. Luckily, the station had a generator, but the same couldn't be said for the rest of Innisard.

The whole country was in chaos; all transport grounded. Fortunately, the gardaí who'd come to help in the search for Gert Foley had managed to get away before the roads were closed. Otherwise, they would have been stuck in Innisard for the duration. Even luckier, the paparazzi had decamped back to whatever hole they'd slithered out of. One less thing to worry about.

O'Shaughnessy called the conference together. 'Postmortem results are in for Gert Foley. Cardiac event is the recorded cause of death – heart attack in layman terms. But Winston noted bruises on her arms consistent with someone grabbing her roughly. There were also marks on her face, as if someone had placed a hand over her mouth, and held it there with force. Both injuries occurred on, or around, time of death. Suspicious, but not proof of a crime. We'll hopefully find that at the scene. Unfortunately, we've had to suspend garda duty at the lighthouse – it's just too dangerous in this weather. We'll reconvene the second it's clear. Weatherman says late Monday, but they also said the fecking storm wouldn't hit us until this evening. So, not holding our breath here, are we, lads?' A smattering of laughter.

Tom didn't fault O'Shaughnessy and his men their humour – most garda used it as a shield, but he didn't join in. This time, it was too close to home. Gert Foley had been murdered. The marks Winston noted meant someone had manhandled the old woman. Her heart might have given out due to exertion and shock, but, ultimately, the person who had accosted a defenceless old woman was responsible for Gert's death. And that made Tom Carr angry. Coldly, furiously angry.

'Let's use the time to firm up what we have,' O'Shaughnessy said. 'Fitzpatrick,' he asked the ruddy-faced man. 'Did you get on to the pathologist to see if our first victim had a scar on his back?'

'I did, Guv. He can't say with any certainty, there was too much damage to that area, but he said he can dig deeper, if you wanted.'

'Tell him yes. Let's tick all our boxes, and I want that information the second you get it.'

'Yes, Guv.'

'Rooney, what did you find out about our bride and groom and their neighbours in Dublin? Any mention of a stalker?'

Rooney stood, again wearing a suit and tie similar to O'Shaughnessy's. 'Not as far as I can tell, Guv. Neighbours say they're a nice couple; friendly, polite. No drama, although one – a Mr O'Bannon – who lives next door, did mention a distraught Jenny Hislop asking him if he'd seen anyone near their garden, telling him about the dead cat they'd found. He's an elderly gentleman, and was most upset.'

'Did he see the cat?'

'Yes, from a distance.'

'Anything else?' O'Shaughnessy asked.

'No. Friends, neighbours, work colleagues, all say they're good, honest people.'

'Hmmm.' O'Shaughnessy tapped a finger on the desk. 'Then we need to rethink. Much as it fecking pains me, Carr, you might be right; we may need to give more credence to this stalker angle.'

Rooney jumped to his feet. 'I got on to the doc's office, trying to get the lowdown on any patients with a grudge. No joy. Secretary was a total shark. Gonna need a warrant for that. But I'm guessing Doc Durkin's clientele will throw up a stalker – or two, if we're lucky.'

'Great. Good job.' But O'Shaughnessy sounded distracted. 'Carr?'

'As I informed you earlier, we have a confirmed verbal assault on Richard Durkin here in Innisard,' Tom said. 'Fintan Callaghan is an ex-boyfriend of the bride, who, according to witnesses, is still besotted with her. With that in mind, I asked for a check to be made on Callaghan's whereabouts during the Durkins' stalker episodes in Dublin.'

'And? We get anything?'

Fitzpatrick checked. 'Callaghan is a lecturer at Trinity College Dublin, and was working there in and around the dates we were given. So, conceivably would have been in the vicinity at the times of the stalking incidents.'

'A few people have seen him hanging around the lighthouse,' the shaven-headed Malloy offered, checking his notes.

'Still could be a patient, or ex-patient,' Rooney said quickly. 'I can—'

O'Shaughnessy ignored him, turning back to Tom. 'This Callaghan guy deserves a second look. According to our bride and groom, the stalker started off with flowers and presents, aimed mainly at Jenny Hislop, then came the cat . . . Then what? Here, in Innisard, they left flowers at the lighthouse door – didn't even go inside.'

'Not that time,' Tom said. 'But they did earlier, when they moved things—'

'Yeah, yeah, cups and whatnot.' O'Shaughnessy waved his hand. 'The whole thing doesn't make sense. How do you go from eviscerating a cat to flowers and fecking teacups?'

The same thing was bothering Tom. The stalker had conformed to type, starting small – simple things, flowers, gifts, silent phone calls. Then, when they hadn't got the attention they craved, they'd escalated; mutilating the cat. Yet, here in Innisard they'd de-escalated. Although entering the couple's abode was a worrying step, there seemed to be a more mischievous element to the crime than any real malice. So, why the de-escalation? Was the stalker in the midst of some kind of psychotic episode? A question to ask the good doctor Durkin – if only he wasn't a suspect.

'Moving away from stalkers for now. Let's tie up our loose strands – Cap Byrne. Alibi. Go.'

Tom shook his head. 'He gave me one. I don't believe it, but can't disprove it.'

'Feck. And Dana Gibson. Have we discovered the source of her sudden wealth? And has it anything to do with her baby's daddy being our first victim, John Filmore? Talk about twisted families, huh?'

This time, no one laughed, the stress getting to them. They wanted to solve this, preferably before someone else was killed.

'Two points to consider,' O'Shaughnessy continued. 'One. Maybe the good doctor's stalker had nothing to do with John Filmore's death. Maybe John Filmore had everything to do with his own death? What else did he get up to when he was sneaking around Innisard, apart from impregnating his new sister-in-law's cousin? Something to check into. Which leads me to my second point: Dana Gibson. A woman scorned. We've had worse motives than a spurned lover.'

'Agreed, Guv.' Rooney's eagerness was almost painful. 'I've pencilled in an interview with her later at the hospital. Giving birth may have loosened her tongue. But we still have her brother bang to rights for Pete McAvoy. Admittedly, that's looking more like self-defence, but it does put Dermot Gibson in the vicinity when the best man was attacked, so we can't rule him out. He's also still in the frame for John Filmore's death. The fact that his sister was in a relationship with the man only makes the connection stronger. He has no alibi so far. So, that's three of our crimes we can link him to.'

'But not Gert Foley,' Tom reminded him. He ignored Rooney's glare, saying, 'Dermot was in custody when his aunt died.'

'No, feck it, not to her,' O'Shaughnessy agreed. 'But Gert Foley might still be an accidental death.'

No one really believed that – not even O'Shaughnessy.

'Maybe the cause of death could be the link, Guv?' Rooney offered.

'Seriously?' Tom didn't try to hide his scepticism. 'A stabbing, a broken neck, blunt-force trauma and a heart attack? Please, show me the link?'

'Only throwing it out there,' Rooney said defensively. 'That's what these conferences are for, after all.'

O'Shaughnessy slammed a fist on the table. 'We need something. Because at the moment we have feck all.'

Failure wafted in the air like a bad smell. And, unfortunately for him, Garda Fern chose that moment to knock the door. All eyes swung in his direction.

Face beetroot red, earnest gaze searching the room, Fern gave a watery grin as he spotted Tom. 'Sarge,' he whispered. 'You're wanted at the front desk.'

'Well, if it isn't the Big Foot eejit himself,' O'Shaughnessy boomed. 'To what do we owe the honour? Another secret you want to let loose? A crime scene you want to trample?'

As laughter ran round the room, Tom restrained the urge to leap to Fern's rescue, knowing the young garda needed to learn to stand up for himself.

'Sorry to interrupt, Guv.' Fern's voice trembled into the crowd. 'Sergeant Carr is wanted at reception; a witness has come forward.'

'Witness? To what exactly?' O'Shaughnessy asked.

Fern looked at Tom, then back at the SIO. 'Not sure, Guv. It's the alibi the Sarge was checking earlier, Cap Byrne. His wife is here; says she wants to amend his statement.'

'Interesting.' O'Shaughnessy levered himself from his chair. 'I shall accompany you, Carr. This might just be the break we need, and we've nothing here.' A dirty look at the grouped men and women. 'Get me something to work on by the time I get back,' he said, marching from the room, slamming the door behind him.

Chapter Seventy

Jenny hadn't slept. She couldn't. Every time she closed her eyes, she saw Gert. She saw her in pain, struggling to breathe. Alone. Always alone. Her strong, fearless aunt. Alone and scared.

And so close. That's what hurt most. Gert dead in the lighthouse keeper's shed, yards from where she lay right now.

She should have been there. Jenny clenched her fists. She should have been with Gert. Someone should have been with her. To die alone . . . it was the worst thing imaginable, although Jenny knew Gert would have said different.

'You're never alone when you're one with the Lord.'

She knew Gert had her faith, envied her that absolute certainty that there was something more, something she, Gert, was a part of.

Was she part of that something? Jenny wondered. Her baby?

Her thoughts circled, grew deeper, darker, just like the storm outside. And for the first time, she wondered if the aunts weren't right and this storm would rival *Oíche na Gaoithe Móire*. Her world was being torn apart internally, why not externally, too?

Finally, worn out, Jenny nestled deeper in to the heat of Richard's body, burrowing into the fresh sheets, sleep raising a bony hand to claim her. Then the bony hand became part of the body on the steps. John. Her husband's brother rose in a disjointed tangle of limbs, bloodied, beaten; the face at once familiar and grotesque as he moved closer to her, mouth opening as if to kiss her. Closer. Closer. Then the mouth moved, trying to speak, and now it was no longer John, it was Gert; the wizened face mottled moth-white, lips blue-tinged.

Aunt Gert! Jenny shot up in bed. As she did, the realisation hit her anew. *Gert was dead.* The woman who had raised her; the woman she'd fought with most of her life, hated, then loved, then . . . lost.

Grief struck with all the force of an ocean wave, its current dragging a squeal of anguish from Jenny before she could call it back.

'Jenny?' Richard reached for her. 'Darling, are you OK?'

'Sorry.' Jenny held her hands to her mouth as if she could hold back the tide of her grief. 'Sorry. I'm so—'

'Oh, darling.' Richard took her hands in his, brought them to his mouth, kissed them. 'Don't ever feel like you need to hide how you're feeling from me. I'm here for you, no matter what.'

Knowing that he had experienced more grief in his life than most people his age, Jenny felt comfortable saying, 'I just . . . miss her so much. Miss what we could have had. We talked, the day of our wedding, the pair of us finally talked. And it was good,' she told her husband. 'It was honest and true and grown-up. I owed her so much.' The tears were back and she couldn't stop them.

Richard held her as she cried, but she couldn't help but wonder if her tears, her grief, were for Gert or herself and, even worse, if they were hurting the baby, but she couldn't stop.

Eventually, she was cried out. Spent, weak, she lay, nestled in the crook of Richard's arm.

And then she finally slept.

And for a few hours, her mind and body were at peace.

Chapter Seventy-One

Tom could almost feel O'Shaughnessy's breath on his neck as they strode down the brown-carpeted hallway. They needed a break on this case, and he knew they were both hoping this might be it. Could Scuttlebutt have the answers they needed? Stranger things had happened.

'So, that tosser Fern is back from his . . . medical leave,' O'Shaughnessy said. 'Convenient that.'

'What?' Tom asked, playing dumb.

Before O'Shaughnessy could answer, the garda on duty jumped to his feet as they appeared and flicked the switch to open the door to the front entrance hall. A well-dressed, yet slightly rumpled Scuttlebutt stopped pacing as they entered. 'I didn't ask for you,' she told O'Shaughnessy, giving him the once-over and obviously finding him wanting.

'I'm SIO on this case, Mrs Byrne. That's to say, I'm the senior investigating officer—'

'I'll only speak to him.' Scuttlebutt pointed to Tom, lips settling together mutinously.

'Of course.' O'Shaughnessy stepped back, gesturing Tom to go ahead.

'How can we help you, Sheila?'

Scuttlebutt glared at O'Shaughnessy before moving closer to Tom. 'I couldn't rest easy after your visit yesterday.' She swallowed, double chin wobbling. 'I want you to promise me he won't get into any trouble.'

'Who?'

'I need you to promise.'

'I can't promise you that, Sheila, but,' he said as she made to protest, 'what I will promise is that we will listen to everything you say with an open mind and do our very best to help you. No matter what.' He took her hand. 'No matter what, Sheila. OK?'

Scuttlebutt, after a second or two, nodded. 'Cap lied to you. He wasn't playing cards with Seamus Blaney, he was out in his boat, Thursday night, into the early hours of Friday morning.'

'Doing what?'

'Sailing. Just . . . sailing. A bit of fishing. You know . . .'

Tom did. Scuttlebutt might be willing to dob her husband in, but she wasn't ready to throw him under the bus altogether. Excitement flared. The fact that she was here, telling him this, meant that Cap had seen something. Please, Jesus, let it be something that would help their investigation.

'On his return to the harbour, he'd have to sail past Maggie's Point and the Devil's Teeth, yes?' Tom waited, not exactly holding his breath, but close.

'Yes.'

'Did he see something, Sheila? Something that would help with our enquiries?'

'I'm going to let him tell you himself.' Scuttlebutt nodded over her shoulder. 'He's outside, in the car. He refuses to come in, but I've told him, he tells you everything or he can pack his bags.'

Tom knew better than to smile. 'Thank you, Sheila.'

'Do you think . . . if Cap had spoken up sooner, would Gert . . . would she still be alive?' she asked in a rush.

How to answer. Tom could tell Scuttlebutt was hurting, grieving; a grief compounded by the thought that her husband's secrets, her own collusion in keeping those secrets, may have factored in her sister's death.

'I have no idea.' He saw her face fall. 'But I do know that Gert would be so very proud of you right now.'

Scuttlebutt's plump face crumpled and she stifled a whimper of despair. Then, with a shake, she straightened her shoulders and marched outside. 'With me,' she told Tom.

The station door was almost torn from their hands by the wind as they exited.

'Dear Lord,' O'Shaughnessy muttered as they struggled outside.

The car park was almost empty, the storm keeping all but the keenest in their homes; and the keenest were all gardaí, except for the man in the high-spec Saab.

Cap sat in his fancy car, looking at once belligerent and strangely cowed. The belligerence was ingrained, a by-product of being a smuggler; always on the other side of the law. The cowed was pure husband-in-deep-trouble-with-his-Mrs. Tom had worn the same look more than once himself.

The trio fought their way through the wind and rain to the Saab. Scuttlebutt clambered into the front passenger seat, while Tom and O'Shaughnessy settled in the back. 'You tell them the truth, Cap,' she began, wiping moisture from her face, trying to tame her hair. 'Or, by God, I'll make you suffer.'

'I'm not sure you can—'

'Shut it,' Scuttlebutt told the SIO. 'Who invited you here, anyway?'

Tom hid a smile. Scuttlebutt had just hit his cool list. Yes. The day really was *that* strange.

'All we want to know is what you saw, Cap. We don't care what you were doing.' Tom didn't look at

O'Shaughnessy. Murder trumped smuggling any day of the week in his book. O'Shaughnessy obviously agreed because he remained quiet.

'I'm no tout,' Cap muttered sullenly.

'You can be a tout or you can be divorced,' Scuttlebutt snapped. 'And then I'm going to tell them anyway.' She sat, arms akimbo, magnificently, furiously angry. Even Tom was impressed.

'Aw, pet. Feck it.' Cap turned in his seat to face Tom and O'Shaughnessy. 'I was out that night – sailing, just chillin' – enjoying the open water, you know.'

Tom nodded. 'We know, Cap. Just get to it.'

'OK, I was rounding the bend by Maggie's Point, edging past Smugglers Cove when I saw them.'

'Them?' The loud drone of the wind made it hard to hear.

'Yes, two guys. I can't swear to what I saw, the boat was moving fast on the tide, it was only an instant . . .'

'And?' both Tom and O'Shaughnessy said together.

'I'm almost sure one of the guys had a knife and stabbed the other one.'

'And you said nothing? Until now?' Tom asked.

'It was dark, and it happened so quickly I wasn't sure what I saw.'

'But when a body was found, surely you must have realised what you'd seen?'

'Well . . . yeah. It wasn't that simple.'

To Tom's mind, it really was that simple. You see someone being stabbed, you phone the gardaí. Simples.

And then it wasn't.

When Cap told him what he saw – *who* he saw – it changed everything, and nothing about this case was ever going to be simple.

Chapter Seventy-Two

Jenny woke, stretched happily, listening as wind and rain battered against the windowpane. She snuggled closer to Richard, revelling in the bliss of having a roof over her head, and the shelter of her husband's arms around her, as the storm raged outside.

Husband! The events of the last few days hit and Jenny sat upright in the bed. Dear Lord, how could she have forgotten. John. Gert . . . Grief welled, but she fought it back. It wasn't good for the baby.

The baby! Her hands cradled her stomach and she looked at Richard sound asleep at her side, unshaven and gorgeous. Some good news to impart. They would both have so much sadness to deal with in the next few days, they surely deserved a moment of joy?

As soon as Richard woke, she was going to tell him about the baby. With that decided, Jenny slipped out of bed. She'd been a wreck last night. When she gave Richard the good news, she wanted to look . . . not exactly sexy, more really hot momma.

Jenny went to the bathroom, grimaced at the sight of herself in the mirror. 'Girl, hot momma is so far out of your league at the moment.' Figuring she'd have to settle for clean, fresh momma, Jenny pulled a shower cap over her red curls and stepped into the shower. There, she soaped herself all over with the expensive shower gel Ita had bought her, trying not to think of the risqué quip that had accompanied the gift. Ita wasn't one for subtlety.

Refreshed, Jenny stepped from the shower and dried herself off. She looked at her leggings and T-shirt. 'I can do better than that.' She found her bag and lifted out a silk vest top and matching shorts in passion red. They guaranteed a hot honeymoon, the salesgirl had told her.

Well, she wasn't looking for passion this morning, but she did want her new husband to think she was hot. OK, yes, maybe she could be hot momma after all. She bundled up the leggings and T-shirt, smiling, as she re-entered the bedroom and slipped into bed next to Richard.

'Hmmm.' Richard turned. 'You smell good.' His arms wrapped around her.

'Thank you.'

'Feel good, too,' he said, hands slipping up and down her body.

'Well, thank you again, kind sir.'

'If you really want a way to thank me, I know how you can do it,' Richard said, levering himself upright.

'Maybe later, stud. For now, would you mind if we just lie here?'

'Of course.' Richard took a moment to settle himself, taking Jenny in his arms, resting her head on his chest.

Jenny could feel excitement and worry gnawing in her chest. Yes, her being pregnant was sooner than they'd planned, but they both wanted children. She was ready, but she knew Richard had wanted them to have a few years to themselves before they started their family. She tried not to remember Ita's words about Richard maybe being nervous about a hereditary link to John's mental illness. Dana's baby was here now, as hers would soon be. She guessed they'd all find out together. No going back.

'You OK?' Richard asked.

'Yes.' Jenny took a deep breath. 'But I'm afraid I've taken my work home with me.'

She waited.

'I blame Ita. Did she tell you about one of your patients? You can't seriously need to go to them now? I mean,' he said, lowering his voice, 'not after everything that's happened.'

'No, it's not one of my patients. I—'

'Well, thank God for that,' Richard said, springing out of bed. 'Sorry, need the loo.' He strode off in the direction of the bathroom.

Jenny lay in the bed feeling like a fool. OK, maybe only she remembered their little joke about taking her work home with her? She was hurt and a little disappointed, but determined not to let it spoil her news. Another tactic was needed. One that didn't involve bed, she decided, throwing back the covers. She'd make Richard breakfast, then she'd tell him in front of the huge window overlooking the elements – although, not so close that it set his acrophobia off.

This storm was scary, exhilarating, as was news of their child. Her heart thudded in excitement. They would weather both – together.

On the plus side, no way the stalker would be watching them.

Outside.

In this weather.

They were completely safe for once.

Weren't they?

Chapter Seventy-Three

Sean O'Hare woke in darkness. Nothing new there. It felt like he'd been in the dark for a long time. It covered everything with its heavy, sable cloak. There was no centre, no edges, just pure, unremitting blackness. And as he awoke, so did the pain. His head throbbed. He tried to reach up to hold his aching temples, but his hands refused to move. He groaned but knew he made no sound – the darkness swallowed everything. But not him. Not yet.

He had to wake. He had to see the girl in the yellow dress, tell her who hurt him, save his friends. When the pain came again, he fought the urge to escape it. The memory of the girl in the yellow dress giving him strength. He didn't know her name, could barely remember her face, but he knew he wanted to see her again, talk to her. So, he battled against the lure of sleep, to fall into the darkness and let the pain fall with him.

He had fought and lost so many times, but refused to give up.

Eventually, after more times than he could recall, he finally saw something; a flicker on the edge of the dark, a shimmer that was there and, just as quickly, gone again.

What was it? Sean peered into the gloom. Was there something there, or was he just deluding himself—

The shimmer came again, this time ringing the dark; the most beautiful corona.

Yes!

Sean wanted to scream at the pain in his head as he tried to open his eyes, but his eyelids seemed weighted down.

You can do this.

He *needed* to do this if he ever wanted to see the girl in the yellow dress again, tell her what had happened to him; to save his friends.

'Just going to give you a wash, Sean; freshen you up a bit.'

The voice sounded young, not one he knew.

Sean struggled to say something, but his lips refused to move.

'That's it. You'll feel so much better now,' the voice continued, gentle hands roaming over his body, soothing, cooling.

I'd feel better if you'd notice that I'm awake.

'I'm awake,' he screamed, but the words stayed trapped in his mind.

He tried to move his hand, felt something. *Yes.* His little finger twitched.

'Look at my finger,' he shouted. 'Just look at my finger.' He tried to make it twitch again.

'Just going to dry you off . . . Oh, sorry, did I hurt you—' The voice stopped.

Yes. That was me. Look. Sean focused his mind on making his finger move again. This time, all five fingers moved.

'Oh my God! Sean?' The voice moved closer. 'Mr O'Hare. You're in hospital. You're OK, you're safe.'

I'm safe, but the others aren't.

Sean could feel his body coming alive, the darkness receding – but not the pain, which was ever present. He wriggled his fingers, his toes. It felt so damn good.

'Let me get someone.'

'Don't leave me,' Sean wanted to say, but the words wouldn't come.

The voice seemed to understand. 'I'm not leaving. I just need to press this button. OK?'

Only then did Sean realise he was holding her hand. He squeezed it, felt an answering pressure. And nothing had ever felt so good.

'Just take it easy, Mr O'Hare, there's no hurry. You're going to be fine.'

She was wrong. He did need to hurry.

As the full weight of what he knew enveloped Sean, he almost wished for the darkness back.

'Gardaí,' he managed to get his lips to move enough to push out the words. 'Need . . . the gardaí.'

Chapter Seventy-Four

Tom and O'Shaughnessy battled their way back to the garda station, trying to absorb Cap's bombshell.

'We need more than the word of a smuggler,' O'Shaughnessy said.

'Suspected smuggler,' Tom reminded him.

'Suspected just means he's never been caught. And clever doesn't mean honest. It's usually the opposite.'

'Agreed. But I believe the guy. You've met his wife; he has every reason to tell the truth and absolutely none to lie.'

'Except that's exactly what he does for a living.'

Tom's frustration grew. They were going round in circles. 'So, you're discounting Cap's story?'

'Not a chance,' O'Shaughnessy said, surprising Tom. 'I'm just saying I'd like a little more corroboration.'

As if in answer to his plea, the station phone rang, heralding another, even bigger bombshell. The best man, Sean O'Hare, was awake.

They immediately braved the elements again, racing for Tom's car. With the storm alert out, the roads were more or less clear – of traffic at least; debris from shrubs and trees swirling and gathering – and they arrived at St Mary Margaret's not ten minutes later.

Sean O'Hare lay in the hospital bed, head bandaged, his face matching both the bandage and the pristine white of the pillowcases.

'Fecker looks more dead than alive,' O'Shaughnessy said out of the side of his mouth.

'I have to ask that you make this quick,' a doctor entered on their heels. 'Mr O'Hare is still in critical condition and isn't up for a lot of questions. I didn't want to allow this visit, but Mr O'Hare was most insistent.'

'We won't be long,' Tom said quickly as he saw O'Shaughnessy's face redden. The man didn't like being told what to do.

'Make sure that you're not,' the doctor retorted before stepping out of the room.

'Pompous git,' O'Shaughnessy muttered. 'Let's see what it is Mr O'Hare wants to tell us, before that fecker comes back and turfs us out.'

They pulled two chairs next to the bed. Sean was asleep – or dead, it was hard to tell.

'I've seen better-looking corpses,' O'Shaughnessy whispered. Not low enough.

'Not dead yet, mate.' Sean O'Hare opened his eyes, wincing in the harsh overhead light. His voice was weak, but clear. 'Thank you for coming.'

'You know who did this to you, Sean?' Tom asked.

'Oh yes, I know,' Sean answered. 'I'm hazy on quite a few things, but that isn't one of them.'

Just then the door opened, but it wasn't the doctor back to make them leave, it was Tina Connors.

'The girl in the yellow dress,' Sean breathed.

'Sorry, what's that?' O'Shaughnessy asked.

When Sean remained silent, staring at Tina, O'Shaughnessy swivelled in his seat and glared at her.

'Give us a moment, Ms Connors. We need a few words with Mr O'Hare here, if you don't mind.' It wasn't a question.

Tina ignored him, sitting on the bed next to Sean, taking his hand. 'Ask your questions. I'm not going anywhere.'

'Harrumph.' O'Shaughnessy could tell there was no way he was moving her. He glared at her once more before turning to Sean. 'You were saying, Mr O'Hare, that you know who it was that assaulted you?'

The three waited with bated breath for him to answer, but even after Cap's testimony, which only Tom and O'Shaughnessy were aware of, none of them were prepared for what Sean O'Hare said next.

Chapter Seventy-Five

Once Jenny had breakfast cooking nicely, she raced back up the stairs. Richard was in the shower and she hurried to the dressing table, wanting to look her best for him. She checked her image in the mirror. God! She was such a mess; face flushed from the heat of the kitchen, her long curly red hair exploding madly with the humidity.

Jenny hunted through the dressing-table drawers. It was going to take more than a brush and hairdryer to tame her unruly mane, but she did the best she could, adding a bit of make-up. Not much, just enough to erase the lines of grief and more than one sleepless night. As she was putting away her make-up bag, she glanced at the delicate, ornate bowl in the centre of the dressing table where Richard had emptied his pockets the night before.

A coin caught her eye and she picked it up. It was old, silver and worn almost smooth in places. It wasn't in circulation now, but it was familiar somehow. She turned the coin over between her fingertips. One side held the faint words *Eire* and *1969* etched on it, with a harp in the middle. The other contained what looked like a fish and the number ten.

A ten pence? Memory sparked. Where had she heard that before, and lately? And just like that, the scene was with her; Uncle Hugh at the reception explaining to her and Ita the history of the Arras coin. Jenny heard her own voice in her head. '*I vaguely recall Mum and Dad saying something about a coin at their wedding. Something silly like a five or ten pence piece? Can that be right?*'

And Hugh answering.

'*It was ten pence. Your dad said he couldn't afford gold, so he gave your mum silver and promised that she would have all the silver he had to give for the rest of his life.*'

But this couldn't be the same coin, could it? Jenny clenched the ten pence in her hand so hard it hurt. Ireland had been using euros since 1999. Jenny barely remembered the Irish punt or coinage, except for the memory of beautifully drawn notes; each one a work of art, as were the coins.

Why would Richard have an old Irish coin? The same one that her uncle Hugh said her dad gave to her mum on their wedding day? Jenny didn't like the way things were stacking up in her mind, because now she remembered Gert wanting to talk to Richard after the wedding, and then, later, wanting to talk to her. Was it about the Arras coin?

The puzzle pieces began to shift, click into place. This was the Arras coin. It had to be. Jenny looked at the innocuous silver coin in her hand. This was the coin her dad had given to her mum as a token of his love and devotion. The coin Gert had given to Richard to surprise her on her wedding day. Which meant either Richard had totally disregarded the huge honour Gert had bestowed on him, or he had no knowledge of being given the coin in the first place.

Jenny clutched hold of the dressing table, staring at her face in the mirror; eyes wide and fearful, mind spinning. Reflected behind her lay the rumpled bed; the one she'd left, disappointed but resolute, not fifteen minutes ago. She hadn't been wrong about her little joke about taking her work home with her. Richard knew that was their secret in-house joke for when they got pregnant, and yet he'd acted oblivious earlier.

Jenny gripped harder on the edge of the dressing table until the whites of her knuckles showed, the thought sliding like a blade into her brain: *What if he wasn't acting?*

'Oh, sweet Jesus.' She stared out of the huge expanse of windows. It was like Armageddon out there: black sky, black water, waves higher than she'd ever seen them before. It was the end of the world. It was the end of her world as the realisation crashed over her: if Richard didn't remember Gert giving him the Arras coin, or their secret joke, then it could only mean one thing . . .

Richard isn't Richard.

And if Richard wasn't Richard, that meant . . .

Jenny bent almost double, putting her hand over her mouth to strangle her wail of anguish.

Richard was dead.

It was the only thing that made sense. The body she'd blithely stood next to on the Devil's Teeth, discussing ever so rationally how they should proceed, was the man she loved; the light of her life. Her soulmate. *Richard!*

A scream bubbled in her throat. The man in the bathroom wasn't her husband. He was a stranger. Worse than that. He was a murderer.

Bile rose in her throat. Jenny fought it back. She couldn't let him know. That was her first thought. The second: if he wasn't Richard, then he had to be . . . John.

The father of Dana's baby.

The brother who killed his family.

Killed his twin.

Killed Gert?

Jenny could no longer hold back the bile, vomiting into the bin she hastily grabbed from beneath the dressing table.

John had killed her beloved Richard and taken his place. What kind of wife, lover, was she not to notice? *Dear Lord*. Dead bodies, missing aunts, pregnancy, dealing with emotions dragged up from her past . . . none of that was enough to excuse her. How could she not have known, been so blind?

Jenny fell to her knees, cradling her stomach, wailing silently into her hands. 'Richard. Oh, my love. My love.' Grief took her breath away; disgust left her nauseous. And then she remembered the baby – her and Richard's baby.

John had taken everything else from her, the bastard wasn't taking any more. She looked for her phone. Damnit. She'd been so tired last night that she'd left her stuff downstairs. She needed to get her phone, call the gardaí. But, most importantly, she needed to get out of Maggie's Point and find safety.

Feeling exposed in her sexy nightwear, Jenny stripped, grabbing her workout leggings and long-sleeved T-shirt from where she'd dropped them, pulling them on. She lifted the Arras coin. She didn't know why, except it was part of her parents. She didn't want to leave it behind.

'Where you going in such a rush?'

The bathroom door had opened and Richard stood in a billow of steam.

Jenny froze. No, not Richard. The man who had killed him.

Chapter Seventy-Six

O'Shaughnessy and Tom said little as Tom drove them back to the garda station. Tom parked as close as he could to the front door, but they were still battered and soaked to the skin by the time they entered the foyer.

'By God, that's some wild weather,' O'Shaughnessy said, taking off his coat, shaking it out. 'Gather everyone in the conference room,' he told Tom as he headed to the office he'd been allocated – Tom's office – to dry himself off.

Tom made do with the communal shower room, towelling his hair dry and grabbing a fresh polo shirt from his locker, leaving his old one to steam on the radiator. He felt better when he was dry and warm – outside. Inside, he felt very different.

He gathered his six-person crew still on duty on his way to the conference room, where the other plainclothes waited. With not enough chairs, Tom and his people were forced to stand at the back.

O'Shaughnessy entered minutes later. 'Right, we now have confirmation of Mr O'Hare's attacker, from Mr O'Hare himself. It seems his best friend isn't really his best friend, as Mr O'Hare has fingered Doctor Richard Durkin as his assailant, which further confirms what Cap Byrne told us earlier.'

Tom could remember the disbelief in Sean O'Hare's voice as he told them what had happened. 'I only saw him for an instant, but it was definitely Ricky. My friend. My friend,' he'd said again, his voice weak and disbelieving. 'I can only think he had a nervous breakdown, or something.'

Tom had said nothing, but he figured things were much worse than Sean O'Hare feared. There was only one reason for Richard to try to kill his best friend, and that was to stop him from telling them he had no alibi for the murder on the Devil's Teeth. And why would a mild-mannered psychiatrist, who, to all accounts, wouldn't hurt a fly, want to do that?

The only thing that made sense was if he'd murdered his brother. Maybe in revenge for John killing their family? But that didn't work in Tom's mind. Richard Durkin had spent most of his adult life caring for people with mental illness, trying to make up for what he probably perceived as his lack of empathy for his brother. That wasn't a man who snapped on the eve of his wedding and killed his brother.

That was a victim.

Some cases hit home more than others, and this was one of them. It was like the perfect storm: identical twins born with a genetic defect that meant they had no finger prints . . . Who was to say which twin lay in Winston's morgue, and which twin was, even now, alone with Jenny at Maggie's Point? Perfect storm. Perfect crime.

O'Shaughnessy's mind had obviously travelled the same path. 'Which bugger do you think we should make the arrest warrant out for? Richard Durkin or John Filmore?'

Tom knew, and it sat like acid in his stomach. 'I vote we haul John Filmore's ass in here and ask the man himself.'

'That we will do. Tomorrow.'

'Tomorrow?' Tom thought he'd misheard. 'Surely, we'll grab the bugger today—'

'Guv said tomorrow, Guv means tomorrow,' Rooney, O'Shaughnessy's little lapdog, said. 'Ain't that right, Guv?'

'That's right. No one's going anywhere today, not in this weather – it's too dangerous.'

'But we can't leave Jenny alone with a killer,' Tom protested. The only reason he had come back to the station, instead of heading straight to Maggie's Point, was to get reinforcements. 'He's already tried to kill Sean O'Hare and probably had a hand in hastening Gert Foley into a heart attack.'

'Man's innocent until proven guilty,' O'Shaughnessy reminded Tom.

'That's a load of twat and you know it.'

'Look it, I feel the same as you.' O'Shaughnessy sounded like he meant it. 'And if the situation were different, I'd be at that lighthouse right this second. But it would be a suicide mission. There are reports of trees down, we've electricity here with our generator, but out there . . . power's about to go out, there's no phones, no chance of back-up. I won't endanger any of my officers. I can't.'

Tom knew he was right, but it stuck in his craw that Jenny was up there, defenceless.

'As long as Jenny Durkin is oblivious to what the guy has done, she'll be safe enough,' O'Shaughnessy said.

Tom wasn't so sure Jenny Hislop – he refused to call her Durkin or Filmore, because to his mind she was neither – would remain oblivious. She had been in love with Richard; events this weekend had overtaken the couple, but the more time Jenny spent with her new 'husband', the sooner she'd realise he wasn't who he said he was. Tom knew they couldn't wait, no matter what O'Shaughnessy said.

O'Shaughnessy's hands might be tied. His weren't. But he wouldn't put anyone else's life in danger. So Tom said nothing as he left the garda station and made his way to his car, where he found his team waiting for him in the blistering wind and rain.

'What are you lot doing here?'

'You didn't think we'd let you go alone, Sarge?' Anne Devlin said, shouting to be heard over the wind.

'I can't ask you to—'

'You're not,' Fern shouted back. 'We're offering.'

The others all nodded.

Much as he hated to admit it, Tom was glad of their presence. 'We'll need two cars.'

'Sorted, Sarge,' Devlin shook a set of car keys.

'Let's go then.'

The seven gardaí clambered into the two cars and set off, lights blazing, in the direction of Wishers Woods.

Chapter Seventy-Seven

Jenny couldn't move.

'Cat got your tongue, darling?' The man pretending to be Richard posed, the pristine white towel around his waist in danger of slipping. 'Or are you just rendered speechless by the sight of my half-naked body?'

'I . . .' Jenny had lost the power of speech. He looked so like . . . *Richard. Oh, Richard!*

'What's that you have?' John, the Richard wannabe, strode forward, plucking the coin from her hand.

I can't let him know I know. That was the only thing Jenny was sure of. If he knew, there was no telling what he'd do and she had the baby to think of. *The baby!*

Jenny found the strength from somewhere to say casually, 'No idea. I found it in your change.' She prayed the tremble in her voice wasn't noticeable.

'Odd.' Wannabe Richard turned the ten pence piece over in his hand. 'Strange-looking coin, I must have picked it up on my travels.'

It was true Richard travelled a lot for work. He was good at his job, much in demand. But he wouldn't need to travel far for this one. Anyone who lived in Ireland, even after the changeover to euro, would recognise it. Which begged the question why didn't this Richard?

For the same reason he didn't know their code for becoming pregnant.

Jenny couldn't control the shot of fear that raced through her body, the instinctive urge to run. She turned, ready for flight.

'Where are you going, babe?' An arm snaked around her waist, pulling her close.

Babe?

'To . . . er . . . check on breakfast.' Jenny forced a smile, forced herself to remain pliant in his arms. 'Don't want it to burn, do you?'

For a second, she thought he wouldn't answer, staring at her, those glorious blue eyes boring into hers. And she had no idea what she'd do if he didn't let her go. Her skin crawled at his touch, her heart racing with fear and repulsion.

'You sure know the way to a man's heart, wife.'

Wife? The word and the sight of his dimple – Richard's dimple – were double knife blows to her chest, but she fought hard not to show it, to show how much she hated this man. Feared him. 'I'll only be a tic. Why don't you . . . go back to bed and I'll bring it up to you.'

'You seem a little tense. Everything all right?' Lean fingers kneaded her shoulders.

Jenny wanted to scream. Wanted his hands off her. His murdering hands. 'Just . . . you know . . . Gert . . . everything that's happened.'

'Of course. Totally understandable.' The hands stilled, dropped away. 'Don't be long, though. I'm not just hungry for food. It's time we finally consummated this marriage of ours, don't you think?'

Jenny wanted to throw up again, but pasted what she hoped was a sexy smile to her face. 'Food first, sex second, big guy.'

A guffaw of laughter, followed by a slap on her rear. 'Feed the belly, then feed the soul. I like it. Let the feeding begin.'

Jenny didn't wait to be told twice, racing down the spiral staircase.

Where was her phone?

She checked the entrance hall, no sign of it. She looked in the living room and there on the long table lay her mobile. Hands trembling, Jenny lifted it and tapped in 112. Nothing. She looked at the display; no bars, no signal. The storm had obviously knocked out the telephone masts. Jenny's frightened eyes looked out the window. No escape by sea, which meant no escape down the Devil's Teeth. She cursed the fact that their car was still in Innisard, waiting to have its tyres reinflated. Those kids would never know the consequences of their prank; the danger they had put her in.

The only way out was through Wishers Woods. Twenty minutes by car to the village. At least an hour on foot. Jenny wanted to cry at the thought of facing the long trek through the woods in this weather, but then she thought of the alternative, and her baby, and what Gert had told her just before she disappeared. *'The Lord never sends more than you can handle.'*

Time was spinning too fast, and just when she thought things couldn't get any worse, the lights went out. She heard Richard call out, moving around the bedroom upstairs. *Not Richard*, she reminded herself. *John. Oh, God! Not Richard.* Because Richard was dead. A scream rose from the very core of her being, wanting to be free, but she didn't dare let it loose, let John hear.

She was out of time.

Jenny ran to the coat rack and pulled on her jacket, slipping her feet into her boots that were still damp from last night's search. Jenny didn't care, wanting only to get away. She pulled open the door, hesitated, then ran back to the kitchen, rummaging in the drawer next to the microwave, where she'd seen a torch earlier. Luckily, it was still there and she grabbed it.

Then she raced out the door and into the full, terrible fury of the storm.

Chapter Seventy-Eight

Last night was the happiest night of my life. And now it's over. I can hardly bear it. We could have been so happy, if Jenny had only given us a chance. But she had run from me. Run from my love. And I can't have that.

I know people will say I'm sick, insane. But I'm not. I'm clever. Clever enough to cover my tracks and get Richard blamed for my crime. And twice as clever in copying that damn scar of his; the one he got that night. Oh, he'd tried to hide it – as if he could conceal anything from me!

I also knew he had been drinking. With Sharon. *My* Sharon. I smelt it on his breath, smelt her. Dad's whiskey sorted that. I was thirsty after all that physical labour; needed a drink. The alcohol gave me quite the high. It also gave me my alibi – drinking with Sharon at Olly Stanton's party.

The execution – pardon the pun – of my plan was . . . seamless. And, for a while, I was content. It was my time to shine; the brave, stalwart survivor of a terrible family tragedy. And I played the role to perfection. But, as always, the novelty quickly wore off and I ached for more.

Needed . . . more.

As the years passed, that need festered, grew.

Richard never should have run. It was supposed to have ended that night. Just knowing he was out there . . . I couldn't settle, couldn't be myself. And I needed to be myself, but every time I looked in a mirror, there was

Richard, staring back. He had to go. Once he was dead, I would be the only one.

An original.

And so I began to search, scouring the country for my brother. More years slid by until it looked like Richard had, for the first time in his life, outsmarted me. Then I had an epiphany; an inkling where I might find him. We had grown up on stories of our Irish roots. Richard could have gone to Ireland, following a romantic notion of finding kinship there. It felt right.

But Ireland, for such a small island, was still pretty large when you were looking for only one person. I had to break it down further. North or south? Our roots, our history, lay in Southern Ireland, so I figured that's where he would go, which was a pity, because Northern Ireland was so much smaller.

Undeterred, I searched on. Thankfully, money was no obstacle. Being my family's sole survivor had upped my inheritance from a third of the folks' estate to all of it. Richard, being a suspect, couldn't profit from his crime. So I could bide my time, which was a bloody good job, because it took another five years. And with every year that passed, my anger and hatred of my brother grew.

Slowly, painstakingly, I narrowed my search parameters. Richard would need a job and, not to sound conceited, I knew I was the most important thing to my brother. The soft git has always wanted to understand me, fix me. As if he – anyone – can ever comprehend my genius. And I don't need fixing. But it gave me a place to focus. I trawled endless lists of therapists, doctors, faith healers . . . anyone remotely connected to the field of mental health, and that's when I struck gold.

A name. Richard Durkin.

Clever Richard, keeping his real first name – less chance of being caught out – coupling it with our great-grandmother's maiden name. *Ding!*

A job. Psychiatrist – with a sketchy background. *Double ding!*

High up in his field, but doing more than his fair share of pro bono work. Can you say *triple ding!*

Everything connected. Everything came back to me.

Richard becoming a psychiatrist was no surprise, and the life I found him living in Dublin was no surprise either – except for Jenny.

When I finally located my brother a year ago, I watched him and Jenny, studied them in great detail; even going so far as travelling to Innisard to see where Jenny grew up. That's where I met Dana; a distraction only. A pale image of her cousin that had resulted in more than I'd bargained for. Anger at the thought of the child. Another usurper I would have to deal with.

Truth is, I probably ended up knowing Richard and Jenny better than they did themselves. And that became my downfall. Because the more I watched Jenny, discovered her tragic past, the more connected I felt to her. Was it so strange that identical twins would fall for the same woman?

Again?

Like Sharon, I knew Jenny would have fallen for me had I met her first.

So I solved that particular problem.

I'll admit to feeling slightly nervous, thinking I'd never get Richard on his own. When he left the B&B the evening before his wedding, I followed him, calling to him when he reached the Devil's Teeth. That look of confusion and fear in his eyes when he saw me . . . delicious. The mighty Doctor Durkin left wrong-footed. Even more so when my first words were an apology, a cry for help. Such a sap. He believed it – or wanted to.

Immaterial.

The instant he hesitated, I struck; hitting him on the temple with the rock I'd concealed behind my back. For a millisecond, his eyes displayed surprise, then betrayal. Laughable, really. I mean, I'd murdered his parents and sister and he believed I was prepared to talk, to beg for forgiveness. Some psychiatrist he was.

Once he was unconscious, I dragged him down the steps, closer to the waterline, swapping clothes with him before proceeding to obliterate the scar on his back.

Honestly, I'd only meant to stab him a couple of times, but I found it oddly cathartic, enjoyable even: the scrape of blade on bone, the blood . . . Every cut was so bloody satisfying. But not as much as stepping into his life. I was overcome with a sense of elation; daring to believe that my story would have a happy ending. I would have Richard's charmed life and, more importantly, I would have Jenny.

And it had worked. I'd married the girl of my dreams and no one had suspected a thing, least of all my beautiful Jenny. Until that buffed and over-tanned dickhead Sean O'Hare had clicked that I wasn't Richard.

OK, he might not have 'clicked' that I wasn't Richard, but he was moving in that direction. All that talk about how long I'd been at the loo. Pervert. But he'd been on the right track, and I couldn't have that.

Talk about a total eye-opener. The guy had seemed so far up his own ass that it was a surprise he could see daylight, never mind what was right in front of him. Yet the man had been about to figure out I wasn't my sainted brother in just a few hours. Go figure. Just went to show that you shouldn't judge a brain-dead body builder by the size of his muscles, or the number of times he might wake up to go for a piss after a feed of drink.

Asshole. He should never have followed Dermot Gibson and his would-be murderer into the woods. Gave me the perfect opportunity. Bastard got what he deserved.

As for Gert Foley . . . She kept sticking her nose in where it wasn't wanted. Who would have guessed that the old bitch would have struck gold. She'd been about to tell Jenny something that undoubtedly would have spoiled my plans when I stopped her. Stubborn cow wouldn't tell me what it was, probably hoping someone would figure it out.

Well, they had.

Jenny had.

And if I could have killed Gert all over again, I would have done. Only this time I would have made her suffer a hell of a lot more.

Killing Richard should have been the end. Now I realise it is Jenny who will be the real end. Pain at the thought. I loved her so much. But she is like all the others who have claimed to love me. Unfaithful. Traitorous.

Maybe once she and my bastard son are gone, I'll be able to move on.

There will finally be nothing left of Richard to haunt me.

It will be as if Richard never existed.

I smile.

That's all I ever wanted.

Really.

Chapter Seventy-Nine

Jenny wished she could go back, return to Maggie's Point, her tower of solace. But it was no longer that. Not while *he* was there. John. The man who had murdered her husband.

Realisation crashed. *Oh, God!* John was her husband. She'd married him thinking he was Richard. Was the marriage even legal? She hoped not. Oh, God, she hoped not. Married to a murderer. Jenny could barely comprehend the horror of it.

She hadn't gone more than five steps from the lighthouse before she was soaked, chilled and in danger of being blown off her feet. She'd never experienced a storm like it. She was incapable of standing upright, bending into the wind tunnel that funnelled up from the sea. When an opposing gust hit, she was sent reeling. At one point, Jenny was petrified she would be blown onto the Devil's Teeth, and over the cliff to the angry waters below.

Somehow, and she had no idea how, she made it to the edge of Wishers Woods and clambered over the fence. For an instant, she was relieved to be sheltered beneath the huge trees, but then they began to dip and sway, the gentle *shush, shush* they usually made growing in volume until it was like a voice from beyond yelling at her to run. But to where? Behind her lay the lighthouse and the Devil's Teeth, ahead, Wishers Woods with its menacing, angry trees.

John lay behind, safety ahead. No choice.

Jenny flicked on her torch and plunged into the trees.

Chapter Eighty

The normal speed limit in this area was thirty km/h, but today, even in the terrible weather conditions, Tom kicked his speed up to fifty. Something inside him telling him he needed to get to Maggie's Point as quickly as possible. Anne Devlin, following in the car behind, did the same.

The two Garda cars sped through Innisard and up the long, winding road towards Wishers Woods. They didn't get far, maybe two or three kilometres up the track to the lighthouse, before skidding to a halt; the road ahead blocked by a huge tree, uprooted in the storm.

'Thought we were being too lucky,' Tom muttered, stopping his car and switching off the engine.

The car behind did the same, and in the silence, the full fury of the storm now could be heard.

'It's only a couple of kilometres to Maggie's Point. We can do this.'

The other gardaí remained silent. Tom didn't blame them. He was talking out his ass and they all knew it.

With nothing for it, the gardaí checked their gear, making sure they were well wrapped up, and then, torches in hand, they got out of their vehicles and edged their way around the fallen tree.

On the other side, Tom and the others could only stare in disbelief at the debris-strewn road – large branches, twigs and leaves carpeted the path until it was hard to tell where the path ended and the woods began. It might be nine in the morning, but the sky was so dark that it could have been much later; visibility badly compromised by the elements.

The noise of the storm was deafening; a cacophony of shrieks and wails. It was a struggle to stay on their feet.

'Let's stick to the treeline,' Tom yelled, pointing to the edge of the wood with his toothpick. 'It might give us some protection from the worst of the wind.'

None of them looked convinced. Neither was Tom, but there was no other choice; the road ahead was too debris-laden, the forest too dangerous with falling trees. The only option was to skirt the treeline and hope for the best.

If this storm doesn't kill me, my wife definitely will. Risking his life like this . . . disobeying orders . . . he had to be out of his mind. But Tom trusted his instincts. He knew, with a deep certainty, that Jenny Hislop needed their help. And she needed it now.

'Stay together,' he shouted. 'We don't want anyone getting lost. We make our way to Maggie's Point, make sure Jenny Hislop is OK and arrest Richard Durkin – or whatever the hell his name is. Let's go.'

As they set off, Tom tried not to think of the last time he'd been here, yesterday, looking for Gert Foley.

He hoped this search would have a happier ending.

Chapter Eighty-One

The wind screamed through the trees like a banshee, reminding Jenny of the old ghost folk tales she'd been told growing up. How hearing the voice of the vengeful banshee meant death for a loved one. But to see the banshee, to face her in her full evil, beautiful glory, spelt death for the beholder. The sound was frightening enough.

Jenny longed to close her eyes, afraid to see what was ahead of her, but she didn't dare. It was too dangerous. The wind whipped the trees, causing them to bend and twist in the most alarming manner. The sheer power of the thunderous wind and rain was terrifying. Jenny couldn't breathe; twisting her head, burying it in her arms to try to get a breath. Rain so thick it blinded her. Broken twigs ripped past her face.

She was so lost.

Jenny had no idea how far she'd come from the lighthouse, how far she needed to go. She brushed a long strand of hair out of her eyes, straining to see between the rain and gloom. It felt like she'd been running forever. She knew John would be looking for her; could almost sense him behind her, gaining with every second that passed. Which way to go?

Jenny gazed around her. All she could see were trees, trees and more trees. A sudden crack made her look up. The giant oaks shivered, moved. The cracking noise repeated, followed by a deep groan that shuddered through the soles of her feet and could be heard even over the elements. A tree was about to fall. Which one?

Jenny's frantic eyes scanned the woods. She was surrounded by trees. An animal kind of instinct had her throwing herself forward as the tree right behind her fell; slamming to the ground, causing an eruption of leaves and earth.

'Oh my . . . God!' Jenny, soaked, frozen, felt a chill deeper than the rain and cold. The tree had missed her by inches. She needed to get out of the woods, find some shelter. There was no way she could reach Innisard in this storm.

Her heart sank as she realised her only hope was to return to Maggie's Point. As much as it pained her, she knew the only safe place to hide was the lighthouse keeper's shed where Gert had died. She could only pray John wouldn't think to look for her there. Jenny figured if the lighthouse was to her north, then she'd run west into the trees, so, if she moved right, she'd be heading north again?

Jenny had no idea what she was doing, but her baby was relying on her and she wasn't about to let it down. She turned and ran, stumbling through the trees and muck.

She didn't know how long she ran, but she was out of breath and she was still in Wishers Woods. Even worse, she could hear someone behind her. Over the shrieking wind and battering rain, she heard the slap of running feet.

John had found her.

Jenny pressed her hand to her stomach and ran faster, faster; tripping, falling, picking herself up, moving onwards, moving to what she hoped was safety.

She finally broke out of the trees, and found herself atop the cliff face next to the Devil's Teeth. It was a dangerous spot, mere inches of ground that tipped over the cliff edge. Running so fast, Jenny had no time to stop, she teetered on the edge of the cliff, the ground slipping away beneath her.

'Jenny!'

A hand grabbed the back of her coat, pulling her to safety. But there was no relief for Jenny. Because the person who had saved her was the monster she was running from. The man who had murdered Richard.

'Get away from me.' Jenny flung herself sideways to where the track of land was wider, closer to the safety of the grass atop the Devil's Teeth.

'I mean you no harm.' John held up his hands.

'Stay away.' Jenny shifted as far as she could, past the Devil's Teeth and onto the path back to Maggie's Point. Her long hair was plastered against her face and down her back, rain beating into her eyes, blinding her.

John followed her.

'Why aren't you . . .?' She pointed to the cliff.

'What? Scared of heights?' John, equally waterlogged, darted forward, peering over the edge of the Devil's Teeth, grinning manically. 'Surprise.' He wiggled his hands like a magician. 'I'm cured.' He laughed at her confusion. 'Honestly, Jenny, think about it.' His accent changed, moving from Richard's soft Irish lilt to a clipped plummy English. 'I'm *not* Richard. I never was. He was a bit of a bore, I'm more fun. Admit it, you like me best, don't you?'

When she didn't answer, he continued.

'If you'd only let me explain.'

The sound of the waves, pounding against the cliff below, was horrendous, the noise drowning out even the banshee wind. And then Jenny was the banshee. 'Explain what?' she screamed, not only to be heard, but because the grief was that big. That angry. That loud.

'I love you. I watched you. I watched you for so long that I . . . I . . . fell in love with you.'

'Love? What about Dana? Your baby?'

'Dana was a mistake. It's you I love. Only you. As for the child . . .' John's face twisted. 'I shall dispose of him later.'

'Dispose of—?' Jenny thought she couldn't be any more shocked, but the lack of emotion in John's voice, in his eyes, rocked her to her very core. 'You are a monster. You have no conception of the meaning of love. If you did, you'd never have taken Richard from me.' She dropped to her knees, warding John off as he went to comfort her. 'Don't!' The icy wetness of the grass and granite beneath her fingertips stung. Jenny welcomed the pain. 'Why? How? When?' she screamed.

He knew the last question was the most important to her so he answered that first. 'Before the wedding.'

'*No.*' Jenny's scream was carried over the cliff by the wind.

'As for how . . . Easy. I know my brother, knew there was no way he'd marry you without telling you the truth.'

'So, you murdered him for wanting to tell the truth?' Jenny couldn't believe they were having this conversation. Here. In this place. In the middle of a storm.

'He wouldn't listen.'

'To what? Your lies? How you stalked us?'

'I didn't stalk you; I watched over you.'

'Yeah, the cat was you watching over us?'

'The cat was a message – and I killed it before I cut it open.'

He said it like that was a good thing, like he'd done something benevolent, kind. The urge to vomit was overwhelming.

'You led me straight to Richard's body. How could you? How could you let me stand over him and not know? Not—',

'*You* led us there,' John reminded her. 'You just had to take the beach way back to the reception. You wouldn't listen to me. His body was supposed to have been washed out to sea. No one would have known. It was the perfect crime and you spoiled it.'

'I spoiled . . .?' The man was insane. How could she not have seen it before. But Jenny knew she needed to keep him talking. She needed to find a way to escape. 'Why did you kill him? There has to be a reason – a real one.'

John didn't even hesitate. 'He didn't deserve you.'

'But I deserved him,' Jenny screamed; rage and grief swelling her words until not even the wind could hide them. 'He was my heart, my soul.'

'Don't say that.' John was close enough now to take her hands hauling her to her feet. 'We're the same. Look.' He gestured to his face, his body. 'We're the same person. You'll come to love me in time. I will make you love me.'

Jenny wrenched her hands free. 'Never.' Wind and rain blasted her, slathering her hair to her face. She brushed it angrily out of her way. 'You are nothing like Richard. *Nothing*,' she spat.

'That's not what you said last night, and the night before. You said you'd love me forever. Forever and always.'

His smirk was almost her undoing. He was right. She hadn't noticed a stranger in her arms, in her bed.

Oh, Richard, forgive me. Please, please forgive me.

But her guilt was a nightmare to visit later. Now, she needed to escape this maniac, save her baby, make him pay.

'Why Gert?' she asked, needing to know. 'Why did you have to take her, too?'

'I thought it was because she saw me leaving Wishers Woods after I tried to kill Sean. Turns out she was on to me long before that. That bloody Arras coin. The second I saw it in your hand, I knew. You Irish have the stupidest traditions. Plus, we'd never have had a life with Gert in it; she was too interfering, too blasted nosy. It never would have worked.'

How could she have been so blind? The blue eyes might be the same colour and shape as Richard's, but they held no light, no depth; they were dull. Dead inside.

The person before her might look so much like the man she loved that it caused Jenny actual pain to look at him, but inside he was diseased. A shrivelled husk of a man.

Chapter Eighty-Two

I know the second I've lost her. It is there, in her eyes; disgust written plainly across her face.

Jenny will never love me.

I have a strange feeling in my chest. What is it? Can it be . . . hurt?

It is a novel thought. I'm not sure I've ever experienced the emotion before. If this is what it is, then I will be happy to never experience it again.

My beautiful Jenny will never love me, and I cannot have her loving anyone else.

'What are you doing?' Jenny recoils as I grab her. 'No.' She screams, struggles as I inch her closer to the top of the Devil's Teeth, to the cliff edge.

One good push and it will all be over. The wind will take her, carry her out to sea.

'No, please no. You can't do this to us.'

'Us?'

Only then do I see her cradling her stomach.

A baby? I am stunned. What is it with these Innisard women? Are they particularly fecund?

Jenny takes full advantage of my momentary distraction, wrenching free from my grasp. But I recover quickly, grabbing her before she gets too far.

I know for sure the baby isn't mine. Not that I haven't tried, but we haven't had a chance to consummate our marriage. The slut is carrying another man's baby. And not just any man's – Richard's.

Hate fills me. I am beyond thinking, beyond even attempting to control the rage. In fact, I welcome it.

My twin will not win again. Once she is gone, there will be nothing left of Richard.

I drag her back to the cliff edge, and now her screams have absolutely no effect on me.

Chapter Eighty-Three

Tom had never been so grateful to see anything as he was when he spied the tall shape of the lighthouse ahead of them.

'We made it,' Fern said, relief clear in his voice.

'Told you we would.' Tom slapped the young garda on the back, but he hadn't been as sure as he'd maintained. For a while there, he actually feared for their lives.

Out in the open, away from the trees, the full force of the wind could be felt as it screamed over the top of the cliff. They bent into it, heads down, and charged towards Maggie's Point.

Anne Devlin was first to point out the obvious. 'No lights, Sarge.'

'Power's out everywhere,' one of the other garda shouted.

No one said anything. If the couple was inside and everything was fine, then why hadn't they lit candles, or one of the huge oil lanterns kept in reserve for times like this? No, the lighthouse being in darkness wasn't a good sign. Neither was the open door, banging in the wind as they approached. No, not a good sign at all.

'Eyes peeled,' Tom warned, readying to enter the lighthouse. But before they could move, they heard a scream over the wind.

Pete Serrige spun, looking around. 'Was that . . . human?'

Tom wasn't sure. The wind was shrieking and howling, but the last noise had definitely sounded like a woman in trouble.

Another scream sounded, and this time there was no mistaking it.

'It's coming from over there,' Devlin pointed towards the cliff next to the Devil's Teeth.

'Tomey, Fern, Peckham, check out the lighthouse,' Tom ordered. 'Devlin, Serrige, Ryan, with me.'

Tom and the others set off, running towards the cliff top. As they got closer, they saw two figures grappling dangerously close to the top of the Devil's Teeth. A man and woman, Tom guessed. It was hard to tell for sure through the driving rain, but in his heart, he knew it was Jenny and the murderous John Filmore.

John was dragging a struggling Jenny closer to the edge, his intention plain. He was going to throw her over the cliff!

Tom had no idea where he found the extra spurt of energy, but he did. He raced over the grass, arms pumping, breath racing like he was twenty and a non-smoker again. But as fast as he ran, as desperately as he wanted to get there, he knew he wasn't going to make it in time.

Chapter Eighty-Four

Jenny knew she was going to die.

The look in John's eyes, the fury on his face was unmistakable. There was no softness within this man. But for the sake of her baby, she had to try.

'Please, John. Please, don't do this.' Jenny fought to gain purchase on the slippery cliff edge. It was no good. The ground was too wet, her boots had no traction. There was nothing to hold on to except the man who was hellbent on throwing her over the edge.

And then, suddenly, she was the one who was angry. This . . . *thing* – she wouldn't call him a man, there was no humanity in him – had taken the lives of two people she loved dearly and wanted to take the life of her unborn child.

This was Richard's baby, living inside her, the result of their love, their faith, their hope for the future. She wouldn't let John destroy that. She couldn't let him destroy that. Like he'd destroyed everything else.

No way. No freaking way!

Jenny's anger grew; so hot, so intense that she no longer felt the wind and rain battering her aching and frozen body. She drew on that anger, mixed it with the pain she felt inside, screaming and pummelling at the monster who held her.

But even that wasn't enough. John was too strong.

The top of the cliff was there, right under her feet. The sound of the waves pounding below so loud, so frightening that Jenny was momentarily paralysed. She was going to die! The thought was surreal and yet all too real.

Oh, Richard, I've let you down. Let our baby down. Forgive me.

She closed her eyes, waited to be hurled into the abyss.

'Noooooo.' A figure exploded from the woods next to them.

'Fintan?' Jenny thought she was seeing things.

'Leave her alone.' Fintan Callaghan's handsome face was ugly with anger. Gone was the polished, bespectacled man she'd met at her reception with the artfully tousled Hugh Grant hair. He was like a man possessed.

Jenny found herself released as Fintan tackled John with such ferocity that the two men tumbled, dropping onto the first step of the Devil's Teeth, teetering dangerously over the chasm below.

The steps were too narrow and jagged for two people. John realised that immediately, planting his feet firmly, elbowing Fintan even further off balance and closer to the edge.

'Oh my God!' Jenny couldn't bear to watch as John, with his superior height and strength, inched Fintan closer to his death. 'Fight, Fintan,' Jenny screamed. 'Fight back.'

Her words seemed to galvanise him because Fintan, bereft now of his glasses, pushed back against John, fighting with everything he had; slipping, scrabbling to find a foothold, something, anything, to stop himself from being hurled into the void beneath him.

Jenny could only look on in horror as the two men grappled on the tiny step. The howling wind and punishing rain not helping. One of them was going to lose.

From that point, everything seemed to happen in slow motion. Jenny didn't believe it was possible, but, even as she watched the drama unfold, the storm increased in intensity; wind screaming in from the sea, barrelling up Smugglers Cove, funnelling up the cliff face like a whirling dervish. Richard and Fintan, already off balance, were no match for its ferocity.

Jenny was close enough to see the fear on both men's faces as they were swept from their precarious perch, towards the thundering sea below. Close enough to reach out and take one of those desperate, flailing hands.

'You saved me.'

Jenny stood, rigid with shock, atop the cliff. She had acted on instinct, grabbing the first hand she saw; watching in fascinated horror as the other man fell, plummeting and shrieking out of sight. To his death.

To his death. 'Oh my God!' Jenny moaned. 'I can't breathe. I can't—'

'You saved me.' Fintan grabbed Jenny tight in a hug, staring at her myopically.

She could feel his body shaking, but that could easily have been her own. She still couldn't believe Fintan was there. Everything had taken on a surreal quality. 'I think you're the one who saved me.'

'I did, didn't I?' Fintan shouted, grinning. He looked around him. 'Can you see my glasses? I can't see a blasted thing without them.'

'Mrs— Jenny?' Sergeant Carr appeared next to them, followed by two other gardaí. 'Are you OK?'

'Yes.' The answer was instinctive, but was she? Oh, physically, apart from being frozen and wet, she was OK, but . . . Jenny tried to peer over the cliff, down the Devil's

Teeth, held back by Sergeant Carr. 'Is he . . . is he dead? Is it over?'

Sergeant Carr took his jacket off, placing it around Jenny's shoulders, steering her back towards Maggie's Point. 'Yes, it's over.'

But she wasn't the only one who looked back, and wondered.

Epilogue

The chapel was filled to capacity the day they buried Gert Foley. Richard's funeral would happen later in the week, but Jenny tried not to think about that as she stood with her family, her aunts Evil and Scuttlebutt and her uncle Hugh as they mourned their sibling. Her cousins crowded in beside her with their children, including Dana with her new baby, who slept right through the ceremony. Jenny envied her newest nephew his contentment, even if there was an unsettled feeling in her stomach when she looked at him.

Dana looked equally content. And why not? She'd brokered a deal with An Garda Síochána that meant she would skate on all charges. Tina's dad, Hugh, had been right, Big Benny *had* roped Dana into his drug business, using her brother's huge debt as leverage. The pay might have been good – fantastic, in fact – but Dana had realised that safety for her and her son was beyond price. Big Benny had used her accountancy brilliance for his own ends. Dana was about to show him just how brilliant she was. She had the goods on not only Big Benny and his operation, but on most of his competitors, which was why her brother Dermot was out on bail, in rehab, getting help for his addiction, and not stuck in a prison cell. Seemed she hadn't totally given up on him, after all.

'Hey,' Tina whispered at Jenny's side. 'You OK?'

Jenny wished people would stop asking her that, but she knew Tina's question was genuine, unlike some, looking for all the gory details, not only for themselves but for the newspapers, who were offering a lot of money for the 'inside story' of the killer twin. No one in Innisard was going to do that, but the vultures kept circling.

Even though Tina was grieving, Jenny detected a glimmer of happiness in her cousin's eyes. Sean O'Hare still had a way to go, but he was making progress. It was early days for the couple and, as much as Jenny was hurting, she was happy for them, hoped they'd make a go of it.

She'd been to see Sean. He was the only other person, apart from Ita, who understood how she felt at being duped. Not recognising a loved one . . . it was almost too incredible to be believed, and yet John had played his part so well. Too well.

The fact that Sean had suspected something first . . . that stung. Jenny knew Richard best. She should have—

She cut the thought off. Tina was still waiting for an answer. 'The incense is making me nauseous.'

'Yet one more reason I never attend mass.' Tina grinned.

'Bet that goes down well with Evil,' Jenny whispered, nodding to their aunt, worrying her rosary beads, eyes closed, mouthing prayers.

'I like to see her head explode every so often when I tell her I'm not partaking of the Eucharist. If you're staying, you'll get to see it, too. I'm taking it that you're more lapsed catholic than—?'

Jenny didn't ask how Tina knew she was thinking of staying in Innisard, of finally using her parents' life insurance money to buy Maggie's Point. A place that, even with everything that had happened, she still considered her tower of solace. A decision still to be made.

'Lapsed,' she said firmly. 'Totally and utterly lapsed.'

'I can attest to the lapsed,' Ita said from the seat behind them, funeral decorum dictating only family sat in the first few pews. 'And now I totally understand why. I mean . . .' She gestured around the chapel. 'What the frick? It's like the Stepford Wives met religion.'

Jenny and Tina giggled.

'What's so funny?' Liam asked.

'Shush,' DJ Joe warned, tipping his head to where Evil had stopped praying and was glaring at them. 'Evil is giving you the . . . evil eye.'

More giggles.

'You can tell Evil to *Póg mo thóin*,' Ita said.

The cousins smothered their laughter, trying to appear respectful.

A moment of lightness in the darkest of times.

Interminable minutes later, Jenny watched as Liam and DJ Joe, along with her uncle Hugh and Evil and Scuttlebutt's husbands, lifted Gert's coffin on their shoulders and began Gert's final walk out of the chapel to the awaiting hearse.

There were fewer people at the graveyard, but not by many. Jenny shivered beneath her wool coat as an icy wind blew in from the sea.

'Least the rain stayed off.' Liam draped an arm around her shoulder, winking at Ita. 'Hey, lush. Have you been beefing up the Lucky Leprechaun to your Dublin buddies?'

'I've no idea what you mean.' Ita tried to look innocent.

'I'm not sure whether to thank you or spank you.'

'I vote spank any day of the week.'

'We've had a rush of stag and hen dos from Dublin,' Liam told Jenny. 'I'm thinking of asking Mum to do astral readings and Dad to invest in yurts, or something equally naff – what do you think?'

Jenny couldn't help it; she laughed out loud at the thought. Not because it seemed far-fetched, but because she could almost see it happening.

'Good to see you smile, Cuz.' Liam brushed her cheek. 'You holding up?'

'Same as you all, I guess.'

'Not really the same, though, is it?' Unspoken was the acknowledgement that it wasn't just Gert's loss Jenny was dealing with. 'You and Gert were closer than any of us,' Liam said gently. 'She loved you like a mother.'

Involuntarily, Jenny's eyes moved to the grave next to Gert's, where her parents lay.

'You do what you need to do,' Liam told her softly. 'Joe and I will look after Ita.'

He knew her so well. How? They'd been teenagers when she'd left. Then again, coming out as gay in a small community like Innisard wasn't without some deep thinking and a lot of soul searching.

'Not a parcel to be passed around,' Ita muttered.

'We have drink,' Liam and DJ Joe said together.

'OK, I'm going with them,' Ita told Jenny.

'Thanks for being here.' Jenny hugged her.

'Where else would I be?' Ita held Jenny in the hug. 'I'll see you later, whenever you're ready.'

Secure that Ita was being looked after, Jenny allowed her thoughts to wander. So lost in the labyrinth of her mind that she didn't realise the priest was finished. The crowd hushed as the pallbearers each took a rope and slowly lowered Gert's coffin; strain clear in their faces and arms. When they were done, Evil was first to the graveside, dropping a rose into the dark void. Scuttlebutt was next, followed by Jenny and her cousins. Then they had the unending meet-and-greet of mourners paying their respects as the crowd lined up to shake hands with the family, and offer their condolences.

Sergeant Carr appeared with a very pregnant woman at his side, who he introduced as his wife Magda. Tina's book club friend, Jenny recalled, running an expert eye over the woman. She looked almost full term and, thankfully, healthy.

'I'm so sorry for your loss,' Magda said softly. 'Gert was a wonderful woman. She spoke her truth without malice and had no back doors, which I liked. A lot.' Her brown eyes sparkled, then immediately saddened. 'She will be deeply missed.'

Jenny instantly liked the woman; there was just something . . . real about her, honest. She also like Sergeant Carr. Oh, she could have cheerfully strangled him at one point after the unending hours of questioning he and the plain-clothed gardaí from Dublin had subjected her to after that awful, terrible, stormy night atop the cliff at the Devil's Teeth. But it had helped clear things up.

It turned out that Jenny and Richard had two stalkers – or rather, a stalker and a watcher. John, Richard's mad twin, had been stalking them for months back in Dublin. Her old school friend, Fintan Callaghan, had been watching over her, as he called it, when she'd arrived in Innisard. Alerted after seeing John and Dana together, Fintan had attempted to warn Richard off, not knowing he had the wrong man. He was the one who had left the flowers at the lighthouse – wanting to cheer Jenny up, he claimed.

When faced with multiple eyewitness accounts of him hanging around the lighthouse, watching Jenny, Fintan told the gardaí that he'd become concerned for Jenny after the first murder, a concern that had escalated when the body had turned out to be her husband's twin.

He had been 'watching over her' when she'd fled the lighthouse and had seen John chasing her and catch her at the cliff top.

Jenny figured Fintan had been watching over her a lot longer than that, especially when she recalled the presence she'd sensed in Wishers Woods after Richard had been taken in by the gardaí. As for that horrendous morning when John died, being out in that kind of weather went above and beyond to her mind – even for a concerned friend.

She guessed Sergeant Carr wasn't buying it either, because he'd pushed Fintan – hard. But Fintan had stuck to his story. He cared for Jenny; having her back in Innisard had brought up a lot of old feelings, feelings that had made him act out of character. But he categorically denied he'd entered Maggie's Point, moved things and, with no evidence, and everyone hailing him a hero, Sergeant Carr was forced to let Fintan go.

Jenny wasn't entirely comfortable with that, but she had other, more pressing matters to deal with. A second postmortem on Richard's body had shown, beneath the multiple stab wounds, a much older scar. The one the devious John had copied. It was hard for Jenny to comprehend the depths John had sunk to try to take over Richard's life, take over her. She still cringed inside at how long it had taken her to discover the truth. People telling her it was the upset of finding a body on her wedding day, the storm, which, indeed, had out-stormed the mighty *Oíche na Gaoithe Móire* of 1839, didn't help.

She should have known!

John's body still hadn't been found. With the violence of the storm, it could be anywhere, might never be found.

Jenny wasn't sure how she felt about that. John had been a monster. He'd killed his entire family, murdered them without a shred of remorse. Talked about killing his son without a modicum of emotion. And yet, she remembered the man she'd held, the one who had cried in her arms. Had he been acting the whole time?

Jenny knew if she were to remain sane, she needed to let go of those questions. Her hand lowered to her stomach. No matter how hard that might be, she had the best reason ever to stay sane.

She hadn't told anyone about the baby. John had guessed that awful day, but the only other person there – Fintan – was too far away to have heard anything, especially over the wind and rain. For now, it was her (and her best friend Ita's) secret. The one thing that kept her going.

But, if she stayed, her child and Dana's child would grow up together, first cousins. Family. Something to think about. But was it enough to keep her here, or make her run away?

'You want a lift back to the Lucky Leprechaun?'

Scuttlebutt and Cap were at her side. Jenny couldn't remember talking to anyone other than Sergeant Carr and his wife and yet the long line of mourners was gone, as were most of the family, including Ita, who she knew was safe in the boozy arms of Liam and DJ Joe. Tina, she guessed, was on her way to St Mary Margaret's Hospital to check on Sean; something Jenny would do later.

'My car awaits your pleasure.' Cap gestured grandly to his gleaming Saab.

Jenny noted the change between Cap and her aunt; a confidence in Scuttlebutt's behaviour and a strange lack of interest in other people's affairs. The two were spending more time together these days. She'd heard the story of Scuttlebutt bringing Cap to the garda station, but instead of tearing them apart, it seemed to have brought them closer together. Cap had stopped 'all that smuggling nonsense' – or so he claimed. Whatever, they seemed happy and Scuttlebutt looked more content than ever.

'Thanks, Cap, but I think I'm going to walk, clear my head.'

'You sure?' Scuttlebutt asked, concerned.

'I'm sure.' Jenny moved to her parents' grave, bowing her head, knowing they wouldn't interrupt her prayers. She had no intention of going to Liam's bar. At least, not yet.

She waited until the last car left the graveyard car park before making her way towards the beach, retracing the path she and the impostor John had taken the day they were married – one more thing she would need to deal with further down the line. This time, she kept her shoes on and her coat buttoned tightly around her, and was oblivious to the beauty of the shoreline.

She had a decision to make. More than one. She was going to be a mother; a *single* mother, and she needed somewhere to raise her child. Yes, she had her flat in Dublin – *their* flat in Dublin. That was the problem. The flat was *theirs*, hers and Richard's. It was where they'd lived and loved; made their plans for the wedding, for the life they were going to have. Where they'd conceived their baby. Jenny wasn't sure she could live in it again without Richard by her side. That's what Tina had sensed. She was a woman in love herself, and had come close to losing Sean. She knew that fear. And that was only in a few days. Jenny and Richard had been together a lot longer; built a past, planned a future. A future that would never happen now.

Could she bear to live next to where Richard was murdered? Where she'd watched John fall to his death? The irony of both men, twins, dying in the exact same spot hadn't escaped her.

'What do I do?' she asked the baby, knowing she was being ridiculous, but there was no one else to ask.

Slowly, she rounded the corner to Smugglers Cove, the pristine beach calm and beautiful, the craggy cliffs towering on either side.

It took every ounce of strength Jenny possessed to climb the first step of the Devil's Teeth, then the second, and around the corner to where they'd discovered Richard's body that fateful day. There was nothing there, no blood, no indication that anything awful had happened, that the love of her life had been brutally taken from her; that this was the place where her dreams had died.

She stood for the longest time at the spot, staring down at it, the ache of grief, of loss, so intense it took her breath away and carved her insides bare. A scrap of crime scene tape fluttered in the bracken on the cliff, a gull screeched overhead, and the tide ebbed and flowed in its steady rhythm below. Life went on and it seemed obscene that it did without Richard being there. Didn't the world know he was gone? That she was grieving? That there was no beauty to be found here, or anywhere? The colour had gone from her life, from the world.

Rage filled Jenny. John had taken that from her. From Richard. From his family. He'd denied them the life they were supposed to have; the one they'd planned to share. Anger grew, built so high, so hot that she needed to release it. So she ran, arms pumping. Up the steps – all 105 of them. Sweat covered her body, dripping into her eyes, down her back. Her muscles ached, screamed at her to stop, especially her calf muscles.

Jenny wasn't an athlete. She was more a couch and pizza person. Her heart thudded loudly in her ears and black spots filled her vision, but she couldn't stop. She needed action, something – *anything* – to stop the pain, the anguish building inside her.

She was wheezing and panting like a ninety-year-old by the time she reached the top of the Devil's Teeth. To her left stood Maggie's Point and, even with what had happened, her heart soared at the sight of the lighthouse. This was her home, where she was meant to be.

Spent, Jenny collapsed on the top step and stared out to sea. And then she mourned, truly mourned. She mourned her aunt Gert, felt guilt that she had, inadvertently, brought her aunt's killer to Innisard. She also knew what Gert would say to that, what she said to everything, what they would inscribe on her grave as she'd once joked: *'God's will be done.'*

Mostly, she mourned the man she'd lost. Richard. The love of her life. The person who had taught her to trust again, who had told her love wasn't only pain. And he was right. Because, even as much as she was hurting now, she remembered the laughter, the joy of being loved by him. Her beloved, darling Richard.

That was what she would hold on to, she decided. That, and the child she carried inside her.

The wind buffeted her, but she didn't falter. Like Maggie's Point, her tower of solace, she knew she would withstand whatever life threw at her.

Jenny placed a hand on her stomach.

They both would.

A note from Cathy Cole

Thanks for reading *The Wedding*.

If you've enjoyed this book, I'd appreciate it if you would leave a review. Word of mouth is the best way – sometimes the *only* way – for a writer to 'get their work out there'.

Go raibh míle maith agat. (Thanks a million.)

Acknowledgements

I owe thanks to so many people for their help and support in getting *The Wedding* to publication. First and foremost, I must mention the Owned Voices Award, which started me off on this fantastic journey and led me to my amazing agent, Katie Fulford, and my even more amazing publisher/editor, Leodora Darlington. Thank you both for taking a chance on me, believing in me, even when I didn't believe in myself. Your insight and friendship have made such a difference to me as a writer, and a person. Thanks are also due to all those working behind the scenes in Orion Fiction. I hope one day to get to meet you all.

Research is a huge part of any novel. And with that in mind, I have to thank Garda John O'Brien (Retired). A man full of great stories, who took time out of his busy schedule to answer my many, many questions. During one of our chats, John mentioned a book by another retired garda, Garda Det. Pat Marry, called *The Making of a Detective*, which was also invaluable in my research. It's a fascinating insight into the mind of an Irish detective, and well worth a read if you're interested in finding out more about the inner workings of An Garda Síochána.

While the idea for *The Wedding* came to me in one line – the line which begins the novel – and I saw the story incredibly clearly in my mind, I couldn't for the life of me work out the antagonist's motivation for the things they did. Enter the fabulous Marion Clarke and Carmel Meehan and an evening of writerly conversation, and yes, that included copious amounts of alcohol. Between the three of us (four, if you count the alcohol), the antagonist didn't stand a chance, giving up their secrets with barely a whimper.

Thanks also go to Mary Ann Michelletti, another writer friend who helped so much with research into pregnancy, and all the things that can go wrong, because . . . well, who wants to read about a perfectly safe and drama-free birth? Thank you all for giving so generously of your time.

Any mistakes in the book have nothing to do with me. I totally blame the alcohol.

Writing can be a lonely pastime. No one understands that more than other writers, which is why they're always there, giving support and advice. To that end, I'd like to thank Linda Gibson, AKA 'Aussie'. And the members of the Mourne Writers' Group – Marion Clarke, Bernadette McAllister, Kate Carville, Anne Mullan, Margaret O'Hare, Sue Morgan and Terry Donoghue. Thanks for being there, guys.

Credits

Orion Fiction would like to thank everyone at Orion who worked on the publication of *The Wedding*.

Editor
Leodora Darlington
Clara Sokhn

Copy-editor
Jade Craddock

Proofreader
Jenny Page

Editorial Management
Jane Hughes
Charlie Panayiotou
Lucy Bilton
Patrice Nelson

Audio
Paul Stark
Louise Richardson
Georgina Cutler-Ross

Contracts
Rachel Monte
Ellie Bowker
Tabitha Gresty

Design
Charlotte Abrams-Simpson
Nick Shah
Deborah Francois
Helen Ewing

Finance
Nick Gibson
Jasdip Nandra
Sue Baker
Tom Costello

Inventory
Jo Jacobs
Dan Stevens

Production
Ruth Sharvell
Katie Horrocks

Communications
Alisha Javaid
Corinne Jean-Jacques

Sales
Dave Murphy
Victoria Laws
Esther Waters
Group Sales teams across Digital, Field, International and Non-Trade

Operations
Group Sales Operations team

Rights
Rebecca Folland
Tara Hiatt
Ben Fowler
Maddie Stephens
Ruth Blakemore
Marie Henckel

RAISING READERS
Books Build Bright Futures

Dear Reader,

We'd love your attention for one more page to tell you about the crisis in children's reading, and what we can all do.

Studies have shown that reading for fun is the **single biggest predictor of a child's future life chances** – more than family circumstance, parents' educational background or income. It improves academic results, mental health, wealth, communication skills, ambition and happiness.[1]

The number of children reading for fun is in rapid decline. Young people have a lot of competition for their time. In 2024, 1 in 10 children and young people in the UK aged 5 to 18 did not own a single book at home.[2]

Hachette works extensively with schools, libraries and literacy charities, but here are some ways we can all raise more readers:

- Reading to children for just 10 minutes a day makes a difference
- Don't give up if children aren't regular readers – there will be books for them!
- Visit bookshops and libraries to get recommendations
- Encourage them to listen to audiobooks
- Support school libraries
- Give books as gifts

There's a lot more information about how to encourage children to read on our website: **www.RaisingReaders.co.uk**

Thank you for reading.

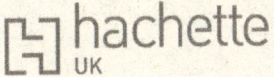

---

[1] OECD, '21st-Century Readers: Developing Literacy Skills in a Digital World', 2021, https://www.oecd.org/en/publications/21st-century-readers_a83d84cb-en.html

[2] National Literacy Trust, 'Book Ownership in 2024', November 2024, https://literacytrust.org.uk/research-services/research-reports/book-ownership-in-2024